# MARTIAN
# KNIGHTLIFE

# MARTIAN
# KNIGHTLIFE

## JAMES P. HOGAN

MARTIAN KNIGHTLIFE

A Baen Books Original

Baen Publishing Enterprises
P.O. Box 1403
Riverdale, NY 10471
www.baen.com

ISBN: 0-671-31844-6

Cover art by Clyde Caldwell

First printing, October 2001

Library of Congress Cataloging-in-Publication Data

Hogan, James P.
  Martian knightlife / by James P. Hogan.
    p. cm.
  "A Baen Books original"—T.p. verso.
  ISBN 0-671-31844-6
  1. Mars (Planet)—Fiction. I. Title.

PR6058.O348   M3   2001
823'.914—dc21                                            2001035799

Distributed by Simon & Schuster
1230 Avenue of the Americas
New York, NY 10020

Production by Windhaven Press, Auburn, NH
Printed in the United States of America

10   9   8   7   6   5   4   3   2   1

# Contents

# Dedication

To Jim, Toni, Marla, Hank, Nancy, Morgan, and the rest of the team at Baen Books. It's about time that they, too, got some credit in the final product.

# HIS OWN WORST ENEMY

## ≋ 1 ≋

Consciousness reintegrated slowly out of fragments, like the threads of a frayed rope coming together. Sarda felt dizzy and disoriented in the darkness—the nauseous sensation of spinning in a void with no reference point. It passed quickly. Thoughts meshed raggedly and began running again. Physically, he seemed to be intact and functioning. He registered the thumping of his heartbeats, chest panting, skin wet and clammy. His body was ridding itself of excess heat, not working to build up heat from cold. So the crucial experiment had worked perfectly. . . .

*Except that he was the wrong one!*

His mind recoiled in protest as images returned of the resigned look on Elaine's face when he last saw her, and Balmer reassuring them that everything would be fine.

*They were going to rob him, sell out his work—and that would be fine?*

Rage and panic overcame him. He tried to struggle, but it was useless against the restraints protecting the equipment inside the reconstitution chamber. Light came on, revealing the planes of densely packed condenser arrays and indexing heads positioned all around and above him like slabs of venetian blind woven with multicolored wires and tubing. The panels in front retracted back from their operating positions to clear the access door, the inside of which carried its own growth of wires and mechanisms, along with a number of technical labels and warning signs. Included among them was a curiously vivid graphic design in the form of a purple disk inside a silver outer ring, containing a spiral pattern of red, yellow, and aquamarine. It seemed to grow in Sarda's vision, drawing his attention like field lines to a charge.

3

In seconds his agitation subsided. He forgot all of his outrages. Latches released in a series of *clacks*, and the door opened.

Stewart Perrel, chief physician on the TX Project, leaned into the chamber, his face anxious. A light shone into Sarda's eyes, while a hand lifted his chin, and fingers felt for a pulse at his neck. "It's okay, Stew. You don't need to bother," Sarda said. "I feel fine."

"He's okay!" Perrel threw over his shoulder to others behind. "It worked fine! Leo's okay!"

Whoops of relief and delight greeted the words. Perrel unfastened the restraints and then draped a surgical gown over Sarda's head, helping him work it down to cover his body in the cramped space of the chamber. The mixed company of project crew and technicians waiting outside crowded forward to press him with backslaps and handshakes as Sarda emerged into the clutter of the R-Lab. After the sweltering confines of the machine, he felt as if he were coming out of a sauna into clean, snowy air.

The expressions of the two men watching from farther back with the small group of specially invited visitors were more restrained, but their eyes had a jubilant look. Their loose, dark jackets, worn tieless with polo-neck shirts, were the closest to business dress likely to be found on Mars, even in Lowell City, generally considered to be the main metropolis. The broad, balding form of Herbert Morch, Quantonix's managing director and technical head of the TX Project, moved forward to grip Sarda by both shoulders as he approached, his fleshy face breaking into a smile. "Leo, today we've made history!" he exulted. "No, *you've* made history! You took the risk. It succeeded. . . ." He shook his head, momentarily unable to find further words.

Beside him, his brother Max, lean and gaunt-faced, cofounder and financial vice president, reached out to add his own bony handshake to those Sarda had already collected. "You'd better get used to the idea of being a celebrity before much longer, Leo," he said. "Quantonix is going to change the world."

"The world?" Herbert turned his head quizzically, looking at him with mild reproach. "Think big, Max, think big. That's what this has been all about, hasn't it? We're going to reshape the Solar System!"

# 2

The last time Kieran Thane was on Mars, he had come posing as a green arrival from Earth, interested in land parcels in the Elysium region that an aggressive marketing company was pushing to young immigrants flush with hard-earned savings. Some suspicious relatives had engaged him to look into the claims of mineral rights potential that would pay back the investment many times over in years to come. The values had turned out to be artificially inflated, based on fraudulent reports by a geological consultant who was in on the deal. Kieran had contrived to salt some of the company's more recent drilling samples with platinum, hence bringing things to the satisfying conclusion of watching the marketeers pursue their customers in order to buy back the tracts at several times what had been paid.

That had been a little over half a year ago (mean standard year, equal to one Terran year). The surface had sprouted visible changes, even since then. Kieran studied them in the view being presented on the cabin display screen of the shuttle descending from Phobos, the inner of Mars's two moons—itself transformed from the cratered knob of rock that astronomers had once described as a "diseased potato" into a gleaming composition of domes, berthing structures, and metallic geometry as the main transfer port for long-range vessels from Earth, the various Belt habitats, the Jovian system, and beyond. The area creeping onto the screen as the planetary outline expanded off the edges was the Tharsis end of the vast system of gorges and canyons flanking the three-thousand-mile equatorial rift of Valles Marineris—three hundred miles wide in places and up to four miles deep. Domes had appeared over more of the craters, enclosing circular cities or orchard farms, with their tiers of housing climbing inner walls reminiscent of steep Mediterranean shorelines; more vehicles dotted the highway west to the mine workings below 50,000-foot-high Arsia Mons; and what looked like a new rail link, already flanked by new excavations and greenhouse constructions, extended southeastward in the direction of Syria Planum and Solis Planum. In the canyon complex itself, a frost of silver and white beads was spreading between the roofed-over parts of the shadowy depths and across the ramparts of crumbling orange rock separating them.

In a seat opposite, Ibrahim, one of the Iranian couple that Kieran had met in the transfer port on Phobos, squeezed his young wife's hand as they gazed down at the scene. They had just arrived from Earth, he a plant geneticist, she a teacher. Kieran shifted his eyes from the screen and grinned across at them. "I suppose all the sand down there could make it feel something like home. A bit short on beaches, though, I'm afraid."

"Give us time, Mr. Thane. Give us time," Ibrahim answered.

"And in any case, this is home now," Khalia said.

Such were the kind of spirits that Mars was drawing away from Earth. That was what new worlds and new visions were built from, Kieran told himself.

The shuttle came out of its aerobraking trajectory to enter the final, vertical phase of its descent, and the view stabilized on the jumble of interconnecting domes, roofs, and terraces that formed Lowell, filling the intersection of two canyons and resurfacing on the overlooking heights as clusters of buildings and roadways that looked from altitude like lichen mottling the pink-orange landscape. As these surroundings in turn expanded beyond the edges of the screen, the view centered on the spaceport of Cherbourg, perched on the open plateau north of the main valley. The scene gradually resolved into domes, service gantries, and turrets bristling with antenna arrays, and then closed on the landing bay, its covering doors open. There was a glimpse of metal-railed access levels bright with lights, umbilical booms and hoses swung back to admit the shuttle, and then the rest was blotted out by braking exhaust. The ship bounced mildly as the landing-leg shock absorbers disposed of the remaining momentum, and the engines cut. They were on Mars.

Life returned to the cabin with an outbreak of murmuring and a few strained laughs to relieve the tension that had taken hold. After several minutes' wait, an announcement cleared the occupants to disembark. Kieran collected the jacket, briefcase, and carry-on bag that he had stowed, and moved nearer to a burly, red-bearded figure in a dark parka who was closing a duffel bag resting on one of the seat arms. He was a construction foreman who had just arrived from Earth on the same transporter as the Iranians.

"Good luck, Serge. Who knows, I might bump into you again out there one day. Let's hope your plans work out." Wages on Mars were up to ten times the rate back home for comparable skills, which with bonuses could enable a man to retire after a reasonably short stint, or alternatively make enough to bring a whole extended family out.

"You too, Knight," Serge grunted.

"Will you guys be staying together from here?" Kieran nodded past Serge to indicate the three others traveling with him.

"Yep. We're all on the same contract."

Kieran moved a pace closer to press something into Serge's hand. His voice dropped. "Let them have this back when you get a chance."

Serge glanced down to find himself holding a folded wad of several hundred-dollar bills in U.S. currency. "What's this?" he muttered. "You don't owe anything back." It was the winnings that Kieran had relieved the four of them of in a poker game during the eight-hour wait on Phobos.

"Sure I do." Kieran kept his voice low. "*Nobody* has that kind of luck. I was robbing you under your noses. Learn to look out for yourselves here. There are a lot of people around who'll take your shirt if you let them."

"Are you telling me you're a card sharp too?"

"Let's just say I have a lot of hobbies and amusements."

"Thanks. I appreciate it. They will too." Serge punched Kieran softly on the shoulder by way of acknowledgment. They moved to follow the other passengers, shuffling slowly toward the exit.

The port too had grown and gained more facilities, Kieran noted as he sauntered down the stairs from Arrivals, ignoring the escalator and elevators—the thirty-eight percent normal gravity and enclosed living meant that people generally took all the exercise they could get. The signs and animated maps indicated that three more launch bays had been added to the complex, one of them still to become operational. A wide, white-tiled corridor that hadn't been there before led from the mid-level concourse to an equally new hotel called the Oasis—apt enough in a heavy-footed kind of way that went with marketing mindsets, Kieran supposed. And, this being Mars, of course there were storefronts and stalls, robot hucksters, and ad displays placed to catch new arrivals straight off the ship, offering currency exchange, accommodation and real estate, vehicles and surface gear, drugs and narcotics, and all manner of human services ranging from legal representation and insurance to sex partners and tour guides. They also bought electronics, optronics, holovids, and other technologies in high demand from Earth or the lunar concessions. For those used to the effects of controls and regulations back home the rates looked unbeatable, and everyone parted happy.

Kieran stopped to scan over the shelves of a candy kiosk and bought a pack of beef jerky before continuing on down to the Freight and Baggage level. He found the office of Two Moons Shuttle Lines ("And Anywhere in Orbit")—enlarged and moved from its former cubbyhole to a new, more prominent position facing out across the floor—and arranged for his checked bags from Phobos to be forwarded c/o Ms. June Holland, No. 357 Park View Apartments, Nineveh. That taken care of, a clerk directed him to the counter where animals, wheelchairs, bicycles, dune hoppers, and anything else in need of special handling were claimed.

Guinness was waiting patiently in one of the company-provided shipping cages, enjoying the attentions of an admiring female Asian counter agent and one of the baggage handlers from behind the scenes. The dog sprang to alertness as his radar picked up Kieran's approach, tongue lolling from a strong mouth, tail thumping against the cage's wire sides. He was mostly black, with tan flashes at the chest and chin, and had a long, broody face with floppy ears.

"Is he yours?" the girl asked Kieran, as if there could have been any doubt.

"That's some intelligent dog," the baggage handler complimented. "I swear he understands everything we say."

"Actually, he's really not that smart," Kieran said. "Languages confuse him. He does it by telepathy." Guinness's brow knitted. He blinked and turned his eyes toward the spaceport workers as if in silent appeal.

"What is he?" the girl asked as Kieran presented the claim document and a card to verify receipt.

"Part doberman, part labrador. The doberman came out in the coloring. The face and the temperament are all lab." Kieran took the leash from a pouch in his bag and stooped to unlatch the cage door. Guinness bounded out and treated him to a slurp of affection across the nose before Kieran diverted him with a strip of beef jerky from his jacket pocket.

"Guinness," the handler read from the transaction details that appeared on the screen, while the girl ruffled the dog's ears. "Are you Irish?"

"Oh, there's some lurking back in the ancestry somewhere, sure enough. But with a color scheme like that, what else could you call him in any case?"

"The trip doesn't seem to have bothered him the way it can some animals," the girl said. "Did you come in on the Earth ship?"

"No. From Urbek Station, near side of the Belt. Before that, places around Jupiter. But he's used to all that." Kieran scratched the center of Guinness's forehead. "Aren't you, boy, eh?"

The girl studied Kieran: tall, broad and powerfully built, with lean, tanned features, wavy brown hair, clear blue eyes, and a smile that came easily. His clothes were casual for traveling, but good quality. "Do you two travel around a lot, then?" she asked.

Guinness looked at Kieran expectantly. The jerky was gone. Kieran tossed another piece, which the dog caught expertly. "We get around, sure. There's a lot out there to see. I've always been insatiably curious."

"So where's home?"

"Oh, a place here, a place there. Maybe I'll check out some possibilities on Mars while I'm here. It's getting more interesting. I suppose you could say the Solar System is home now."

Two levels farther down, a maglev car riding the field trough between two induction rails carried them from the subterranean part of the spaceport, out from beneath the plateau and into Gorky Avenue, one of the three main canyon-bottom arms of Lowell City. The surroundings resembled a curious mixture of multilevel mall, residential units, and recreation spots spread through a confusion of interconnecting spaces separated by normally-open pressure locks. From a grotto of rocks and palm fronds forming a ledge below several rows of office windows, a man-made waterfall cascaded between a restaurant terrace and a children's play area to an artificial beach washed by breakers from a mechanical wave maker. Farther on, the track ran above a sinuous lake with leafy banks and reedy shallows, winding its way around sandbars where wading birds preened beneath steel piers supporting the upper structure. Guinness stood with his front paws up on the window ledge, missing nothing. Everywhere was busy, colorful and vibrant with people—an expression of the thrusting, restless culture that had taken root in and was now rising from the red sands. Yes, Kieran told himself. The time was about right here for a little real-estate investment to tie up some surplus funds.

On the far side of Gorky, the track entered another tunnel to pass through concrete galleries excavated under the mesa, filled with plant and machinery, before exiting into Nineveh, beyond—the other arm of the branching *Y* of canyons containing Lowell. Nineveh was greener and more suburban than the metropolitan setting they had left in Gorky. Algae cultivated in the aquatic radiation shield between the outer layers of the domes and roofing gave its sky a peculiar pale-lime color. Prospect Park lay out toward the end of the roofed-over section, ending at the access lock out to the surface. It contained flower and plant nurseries as well as irrigated slopes of grass with a few trees, and was also a zoo. Near its center was a crescent-shaped lake with an island in the widest part. Opposite the island on the outer curve of the lake, a complex of apartment units rising in terraces overlooked a bathing area next to a parking strip for regular road vehicles. Here, the maglev car halted by an automated cafeteria and shop.

Kieran got out and stood for a moment to take in the view, while Guinness sampled and registered the world of new odors, sights, and sensations. Then they walked up two levels of the terraces to Number 357 Park View, which formed the central section of the complex. June had redone her front door in orange and added a trellis with red and white roses to one side. Kieran nodded approvingly. "The feminine touch," he remarked to Guinness, who pricked his ears up in response but remained unenlightened. Kieran produced a magnetic card bearing the code that June had forwarded and inserted it in the door. The lock disengaged. Kieran led Guinness in and put his carryon and briefcase down in the hallway.

There was a nice, feminine touch to the interior too, as Kieran would have expected—but with the professional, pragmatic feel about it that befitted somebody like June: not too much satins and pink; not too frilly and lacey. The living area had acquired a comfortable-looking couch of eggshell blue that complemented the pale lilac wall at that end, along with a few other knickknacks that Kieran didn't remember seeing before. June had added to her collection of designs, prints and paintings: space views and Mars-scapes; architectural studies; some interesting abstracts; and of course, cats.

No sooner had the observation registered, when a fit of spits and hisses erupted from the passage leading to the back rooms. Teddy was arched to twice her height, fur standing out like the rays of a symbolic all-black sun, yellow-green saucers of eyes fixed on Guinness. The dog looked back amiably, tongue lolling, and sat on its haunches as if to dispel alarm. "Hello, Teddy," Kieran sighed. "Oh, we haven't got to go through all this again, have we? We're long-lost friends back again, you silly animal." He closed the door and ambled across to the kitchen area, with Guinness getting up to follow. At the dog's movement, Teddy shot back to the far end of the passage in an inelegant display of rear end framed in fur, and about-turned to glare defiance from the bolt-hole of the half-open bedroom door. Kieran punched an order for a coffee into the autochef and filled a dish from one of the closets below the sink with water for Guinness. While the dog lapped appreciatively, Kieran unclipped the leash, took his comset pad from an inside jacket pocket, and slid out the handpiece to call June. She answered a few seconds later.

"Hi there. So you made it okay? How was the trip?"

"Smooth and uneventful. About the greatest excitement was fleecing four riggers in a poker game at the layover on Phobos. But I was a good boy and gave it back before we got off the shuttle. You know I only cheat cheaters."

"Of course—you've always had that soft spot."

"Just keeping my hand in. Anyhow, what kind of a welcome is this, when a man comes a hundred million miles and no one shows up to meet him? Things like that play havoc with this delicate complex that I have."

"Sure. Right," June said with just the right note of mock sarcasm. "Kieran, you know we had something big going on here yesterday. You just timed your arrival a couple of days too late. There was no way I could get away." That was evidently as much as she was prepared to be overheard saying in her working environment. Kieran interpreted it as meaning that a crucial experiment he knew Quantonix had been working up to over the past few months had gone ahead.

"How'd it go?" he asked, dropping the flippancy.

She paused just long enough to convey prudence. "Just fine."

"Okay, then I guess I'll have to wait to know more. It's too bad I couldn't have made it in earlier. You know, sometimes I think that Triplanetary plans their schedule just to frustrate me." Triplanetary Spacelines was the carrier that had brought him from the Belt to Phobos.

"And sometimes I think that God runs the rest of the universe just to suit you. . . . Anyhow, I take it that Guinness is well?"

"Of course. In fact, right now, slurping and drooling over your kitchen floor."

"What about the princess who owns the place?"

"Throwing a fit and hurling death threats, preparing to defend the last bastion of her realm at the bedroom door."

"Oh dear. Well, she'll get over it. . . ." There was a pause as June seemed to take an interruption from elsewhere. "Look, Kieran, I have to go. Maybe you could use some time resting up. I should get away, I'd say, between six and six-thirty. Maybe we could meet for dinner out somewhere?"

"How about the restaurant of that new hotel that they've added to the spaceport—the Oasis? Have you tried it yet?"

"No, I haven't. It's only recently opened. Sounds good."

"How about seven?"

"Seven, it is. I've got some quick meals and a few snacks in the apartment if you need them. Or there's some salad, cheese, and a bit of leftover pasta that's not bad. Help yourself. I got some dog food in too—under the counter left of the sink."

"Fine. So I'll see you later."

Kieran put the phone back in its slot, the comset back in his jacket pocket, and looked down to find Guinness watching attentively. "Yes, that was Aunt June. You know she was talking about you, don't you?" Guinness wagged his tail, then looked toward the closet below the counter. "You're right. I could use a bite too. Come on, then. Let's see what she's got for us."

# ⇟ 3 ⇞

The Oasis restaurant turned out to be pleasantly relaxing, with niches opening off a central area and imaginative use of floral partitions among the tables providing a secluded atmosphere conducive to talk. Kieran and June both settled for the seafood buffet—an odd-sounding offering to be encountered on Mars, which was actually fresh, not frozen imported. "Fish-farm-food buffet would be terminologically more exact," Kieran remarked as they collected their plates and sampled the offerings.

June had long, midnight-black hair that fell in a sweep to her shoulders, where it broke in an upturned wave, and a finely formed, angular face with a straight nose and full mouth, which in its natural state hovered just short of an impish pout. Her dark, alive eyes had always given Kieran the feeling that anything short of outright candor with her would be pointless, since they could read his thoughts as they formed in his mind. At the same time, whatever went on in her own remained impenetrable unless she chose otherwise. The dark blue, sleeveless dress she was wearing, along with her black hair, accentuated the paler hue of her face and arms in the subdued lighting above the booth they had found.

She and Kieran were kindred free spirits thriving in the environment of diversity and opportunity being created in the expansion outward from Earth, following orbits that recrossed periodically like those of other errant and adventurous bodies inhabiting the Solar System. June worked for herself as a scientific news explorer and information broker, which she sometimes combined with special commissions as a publicist.

After they had devoted aperitifs and the appetizer course to

13

the required preliminaries of updating each other on old friends and reliving choice snippets of past adventures, Kieran finally came around to the point. "So everything went okay yesterday at Quantonix?" June had said as much over the phone earlier, but it broached the subject.

"Perfectly," she replied.

Kieran looked at her expectantly, but she tantalized him by taking more from her plate and glancing at him challengingly every few seconds while she carried on chewing. "Is it what I think it is?" Kieran asked finally.

June stopped playing with him and nodded. "They did it with a human: Sarda himself—from a lab in the basement to another upstairs. It was practically his technology. He wouldn't let the first subject be anyone else."

"And everything went okay? He's walking around and talking normally? Knows everything that the original did?"

"Absolutely, so far," June said. "And if there were anything amiss, I think it would have shown by now. They've been running him through every kind of test imaginable all day. He registers the same scores on everything: physical, mental, motor; language, numeric, spatial; long-term memory, short-term memory. . . ." She shook her head. "It was astounding. I had trouble believing what I was seeing."

"So how does he feel about it? Did you get a chance to talk to him?"

June nodded. "Pretty ecstatic. 'Relief,' I guess, would be the main impression that came through. But that's hardly surprising. How would you feel?"

Kieran nodded. "Pretty relieved, I'd say," he agreed.

Earth's scientific establishment had largely rigidified into associations of priesthoods preserving their dead religions. Most original thinking and innovation these days happened in environments like Mars, the Belt habitations, and various surface and orbiting constructions on and around the moons of the gas giants, as well as other places in between. Among the various forms of entrepreneurial ventures to turn new knowledge into wealth that had come into existence beyond Earth's effective regulatory reach, Quantonix was of the kind known as "sunsiders"—an allusion to the limited time available to get anything useful done on the daylight hemispheres of rotating bodies. Essentially, sunsiders were small, high-pressure research organizations delving into fringe areas of science that had been laughed off or were deemed to be of no practicable value by institutionalized academia—which meant little chance of finding support from conservative Terran investors. Funding therefore came mainly from more nervy, higher-risk, higher-gain sources found in niches through the off-Earth economy, and the hope was to make some significant breakthrough that could be sold to one of the major interplanetary commercial concerns before it ran out. The failure rate of sunsider companies was appalling, but the return for those that succeeded could be fabulous. Life in them was invariably frantic, often acrimonious, but never dull.

With humanity's numbers climbing rapidly through the high tens of billions and its radius of activity reaching to the outer planets, transporting them and their property around was among the fastest growing and most remunerative industries. But immense though the demand and the future potential were, the means for accomplishing it still took the form of people in cans of some kind being fired off to destinations by engines producing thrust of some kind. Even though the engines might use nuclear fission or fusion, accelerated ions, or in some research that was going on, experimental antimatter, the technologies were all variants on a theme that in essence hadn't changed for centuries. The time was surely ripe for a breakthrough into something totally different.

Major innovations seldom come as a total surprise, confined to one place. When the state of knowledge is such that the right time is approaching, specialists talk among themselves, journals and news media pick up the topic, and public anticipation is usually solidly established before anything actually happens. The general familiarity in concept of aircraft, space travel, and nuclear energy long before they became realities were cases in point. Advances in quantum physics and high-power computation had led to much popular speculation that a longstanding, but hitherto seldom seriously entertained, favorite of fiction might soon become fact: teleportation—the dematerialization of an object from one place, and its reappearance, after transmitting the information to reconstitute it, somewhere else.

The bonanza payoff waiting to be made was by the trans-Solar System communications-carrier giants, who already had most of the essential equipment in place and stood to put the regular spacelines virtually out of business. Hence, with the kind of financial resources and influence that they commanded, it was not really a coincidence that for a long time the ground for general public acceptance had been prepared by spectacles of teleporting heroes becoming virtually a standard prop in futuristic movies, regular coverage in books and documentaries, and a procession of generously rewarded experts giving readers and audiences scientific reasons why the information pattern defined a personality, and reassuring them that its transference from one host configuration of matter to another would pose no break in identity.

A lot of sunsiders were in the race to come up with the first demonstration technology, which would immediately be worth billions. The snag they were consistently running into, however, was the gigantic amount of computation involved in scanning an object at anywhere near the resolution necessary to be believably capable of reconstructing the original—encoding a human to the atomic level, for instance, was estimated as requiring somewhere in the order of ten to the thirty-second–power bits, which would take millions of centuries to transmit. Various shortcuts were being investigated, which attempted to exploit the Uncertainty Principle and other effects which implied that averaging procedures could be used which make the precise derivation of quantum detail unnecessary, but the short answer was that the problem remained mind-boggling.

Quantonix Researchers Reg., however, were following an approach that was different, and as far as Kieran knew, unique. Using a package of results purchased from an earlier outfit that had gone defunct, their process took advantage of the information implicit in an organism's DNA as a shortcut to directing most of its structural assembly. Hence, in a way that seemed paradoxical to some, they could reconstitute a biological object, but because there were no convenient instruction sets that implicitly defined how it should go together, they couldn't apply the process (yet?) to an inanimate one. Over the preceding months, Quantonix had announced successful trials with a progression of unicells, mosses, plant parts, invertebrates, insects, duplicated rats that could still run mazes that the originals had learned, and a chimp that retained its repertoire of acquired skills. The obvious next step was to do it with a human, and the buzz going around the circles of those who kept close to the subject was not about "if" but "when" it would happen. From what June was saying the experiment had been conducted successfully using Dr. Leo Sarda, whom Kieran knew to be the principal scientist on the TX Project and effectively the developer of the technology.

As was often the case with sunsiders, Quantonix hadn't attempted to keep its work a close secret. The idea, after all, was to attract potential buyers who possessed the resources to develop a marketable product, and having a number of competing prospects in the know as to what was going on both shortened the timescale and raised the likely price of an eventual deal. At the same time, the object was not to become a feature of the general mass-media circus, which reveled in sensationalizing the wild and preposterous and usually represented a fast way to getting a far-out but genuine claim discounted by association. The usual course, therefore, was to spread the word quietly, through channels known to be reliable to specialized interest markets, selected influential individuals, and relevant departments of the serious scientific journals.

That was where people like June came in. A huge amount of space existed out there—the toroidal volume of the Belt alone was a trillion times that of the sphere bounded by the Moon's orbit around Earth, with ten billion asteroids over a hundred miles in diameter—and nobody could keep abreast of everything that was going on. But she had particular areas that she followed and a healthy list of clients who benefitted from the leads, referrals, and inside information that she was able to provide. As is so true with many facets of life, buying knowledge was a lot cheaper than paying—one way or another—for ignorance.

Seeing that Kieran was still absorbing the news, June commented, "He'd been working along similar lines on Earth, but it was all too tied up by restrictions and regulations. You know what it's like there: everyone meddling and lobbying to prevent just about anyone else from doing anything."

"Hm. I take it that when this gets out, our friend Leo can expect to be a wealthy man," Kieran said finally. "Instant celebrity, in addition to whatever's in it for him from his deal with Quantonix." He sipped his wine. "I assume they've already got a principal lined up?" He meant a potential buyer who had been waiting for a conclusive demonstration.

June nodded. "They had technical and financial people all over the place yesterday. That's why it was so hectic."

"Who is it?" Kieran asked curiously.

"Three Cs. They should have the deal tied up in the next day or two." It was one of the names that Kieran had expected. Three Cs was the popular term for Consolidated Communications Corporation, one of the major trans-system carriers. It wasn't something that June would have disclosed to anyone, but she and Kieran had known each other too long for melodramatics.

"Well, I suppose they'd want to be sure of all those test results before they sign any big checks." Kieran drank and thought some more. His face creased into a parody of a smile as a macabre thought struck him. "It would be a bit unfortunate if Leo gurgled and fell over now, though, wouldn't it? So what happens when they've got their people-transmitters up and running, do you think? Will they want payment strictly in advance, just in case?"

"I don't think there'd be much risk once it's offered commercially—no more than you accept with the spacelines, anyway. And since this is the first experiment of its kind ever, they're taking insurance," June said. "The original is being kept in a state they call stasis suspension in a vault in the basement until the tests are complete. I gather he could still be resuscitated if the copy failed to work."

Kieran stopped, his fork poised in midair, just as he had been about to bite into a piece of flounder. "What? . . . Wait a minute. Run that by me again," he invited.

"They're keeping the original in a suspended state until everyone's satisfied that the experiment has succeeded."

Kieran's brow creased. "But that isn't the way it's supposed to work. In everything you see everywhere, the original dematerializes as fast as the sent version is being assembled. There *isn't* any original left to have any choice about. Its gone—*poof!*—from here to there."

"Yes, and that's how it'll be once it's proved and working. But right now, with this being the first time ever—"

"Whoa, whoa! Slow down a minute." Kieran shook his head. "What you've just told me makes a big difference. Never mind how it's usually depicted to the world. What you're saying is that dematerializing the original isn't necessary—it's not an inherent part of the process. Speeding things up with some sleight of hand doesn't change it. It means there's an overlap, when both of them coexist."

"That's not the way they see it," June replied. "According to the official description, the other one isn't a functioning person any longer. All the processes that define a person have been extracted and reside in the re-creation. It has *become* Sarda."

"But you just told me it can be resuscitated," Kieran pointed out. "If that's so, then nothing was extracted. It was duplicated. You've got two of them. What do they do with the other one?"

"Well . . . I suppose that once they're satisfied they have a fully functioning copy, indistinguishable in any way . . ."

"There. You just said it," Kieran threw in. "*Copy.*"

June looked mildly perplexed, ". . . they just don't reactivate it."

"You mean they pull the plug?" Kieran looked at her in a way that invited her to think it through again. "I picked the wrong Sarda when I asked how he felt, earlier," he commented. "I should have asked what the other one thinks about it—the one in the basement."

"I guess the whole point is that he won't be thinking anything anymore," June said. Kieran's face remained skeptical. "Anyway, *Sarda* accepts it totally. If it's good enough for him . . ."

"Yes, the one you're talking to now," Kieran reminded her dryly. "But he's come through it okay."

"All the same, he must have known before he went in."

"It's his baby. A true believer can buy anything once he gets a bug in his head—look at those crazies who used to jump off things like the Eiffel Tower, flapping feathers and thought they'd fly." Kieran toyed with his glass while he eyed June across the table. "Is *he* crazy, do you think?"

"That's not for me to say. But he can be pretty intense when it comes to his work, sure." June waved a hand to lay the subject to rest, just for the moment. "Sarda could probably explain it all better," she said. "Why don't we let him do that himself tomorrow?"

"Tomorrow?"

"Yes. A little surprise for you, Kieran. I knew that with your curiosity about everything, you'd have liked to be there yesterday—but I don't think Herbert and Max would have been keen on having an outsider present then, even if Triplanetary's schedule had been different. So I did the next best thing and arranged for you to come there tomorrow—I told them I had this very special friend visiting, that I'd worked with for years. They agreed it would be okay. So you can see the TX Project, meet Sarda, and ask him all your awkward questions yourself. And that's all I'm going to allow said about it for the rest of the evening, Kieran. I'd hoped that our first dinner together for a long time would at least have a chance of getting romantic."

"You're right," Kieran said, leaning forward to refill her glass. "Not another word, so . . ."

# 4

The office and laboratory facility of Quantonix Researchers Reg. was located in a multilevel jumble of industrial and commercial premises that had grown in and under a complex of domes called Wuhan, forming the outer end of Gorky Avenue. The firm's appearance was modest and utilitarian, with an unpretentious sign beside a plain entrance to proclaim its existence, and inside, a counter separating two clerks from the vestibule. Nobody had any delusions of lasting grandeur or of erecting monuments for the benefit of posterity in this business.

It was more crowded and busy than felt normal for a place of its size when Kieran and June arrived—which was hardly surprising in view of what had happened there two days before. A half-dozen or so people, fidgety and impatient, were waiting in the narrow entry space, and there was a constant bustle of others coming and going, phone beeps and call tones, on the far side of the counter and in the partitioned spaces beyond. "Did I ever tell you that story about the after-dinner speaker?" Kieran asked as they waited while the receptionist June had spoken to endeavored to locate one of the Morches.

"Which one?" June queried.

"Well, this fella is introduced as 'John Jones, who made three-hundred-sixty million dollars in two weeks on uranium, and who's going to share some of his insights with us.'"

"Uh-uh," June said, looking mystified as to where this was leading.

"So Jones stands up and says, 'Thank you very much. First, I'd just like to correct a couple of small details. It wasn't uranium; it was uranium oxide.'" Kieran shrugged with the sheepish smile of a toastmaster conceding, *yes, well, who couldn't have got that wrong?* "'It wasn't three-hundred-sixty million dollars; it was three-hundred-sixty-two million. It wasn't two weeks; it was fifteen days. . . . And I didn't make it; I lost it.'" Kieran showed a palm. "You see—my point: a little detail, but it makes a big difference."

They were directed up to the office of Herbert Morch, managing director and TX Project chief, on the floor above the labs. His brother Max, the financial vice president, joined them shortly after. After June performed the introductions, Herbert ushered her and Kieran into two visitors' chairs and then retreated back to the far side of his desk. It was molded, simulated-wood grain with a scratched top, bearing an unruly litter of papers, and a couple of comscreens at one end. The fleshy features beneath his balding dome were smiling, but the eyes gave away nothing. Max perched his sparse frame on the edge of a seat by the wall to one side, outwardly composed but unconsciously tapping a tattoo on the floor with a foot. Kieran took them as typical, stressed-out sunsider management, totally preoccupied with holding the act together until the gamble either died or paid off big. Getting a working, salable technology out there before the others was the only consideration. If Sarda could give it to them, and Kieran had no qualms about the details of what went on, they weren't going to argue. At the same time, he detected them as having something of a fondness for June, which doubtless had a lot to do with their agreeing to accommodate him at such a busy time. He would have been more surprised if he hadn't had long experience of her ways with people before.

She described Kieran as an old professional friend and "planetary privateer." In answer to the four raised eyebrows that greeted the remark, she explained, "Frontiers always create adventurers. He's one of the new kind."

"So . . . what kind of adventures do you find, Mr. Thane?" Herbert asked.

"Anything that helps pay the rent," Kieran replied, crossing a foot over the other knee and smiling easily. "Preferably unusual and interesting. All the better if it helps spare unworthies the temptation of spending ill-gotten gains. It must be a moral calling."

"It sounds as if you make a point of delivering comeuppances to criminal elements," Max commented. And then, half jokingly, "I hope you're not expecting anything in that direction here."

Kieran grinned. "A market of this kind of potential is bound to attract interests of every color, stripe, and persuasion," he said. "Let's just say that with possible future involvements in mind, I'd like to learn as much about it at an early a stage as I can."

Leo Sarda joined them a few minutes later. Maybe in his early forties, with a mane of streaky yellow hair skirting his collar, a droopy mustache to match, and the ruddy appearance that resulted from the absence of UV-screening ozone in the Martian atmosphere, he had the kind of shaggy, weathered look that put Kieran in mind of a fishing-boat skipper or the "doc" from an old-time Western movie.

"Leo, I hope things have calmed down a bit," Herbert opened as Kieran stood to shake hands. "This is June's friend, Kieran Thane, that I told you about—the one who's interested in everything. He just arrived on Mars yesterday, and because of the splendid job June's been doing for us, we agreed to let him see the system. Would you do the honors and give him the tour?"

Sarda nodded. "Okay, let's go," he said briskly, looking at June in an unspoken invitation for her to join them if she was going, too.

"Thanks for setting it up," Kieran said to Herbert as June stood up. "Will I see you again before I go?"

"No need to come back here. June will take care of you. But we'll probably see you again sometime. Enjoy your stay."

"Is it your first time on Mars, Mr. Thane?" Sarda asked as they followed a corridor on the floor below Herbert Morch's office, past walls of windows behind which people were working among computer screens and laboratory equipment.

"No," Kieran answered. "I was here about six months ago—some immigrants were being taken in by crooked land deals."

"What brings you here this time?"

"Mostly taking a break. Although, I thought I might look into getting myself a place while I'm here—as an investment as well as a convenience. The market feels about right. And I figure I've got the experience now not to get burned."

"Got any particular area in mind?"

"Not really . . . Probably somewhere here, around Lowell."

"It isn't bad. I've been here about a year."

"Kieran appears from time to time," June said. "And it isn't usually very long before interesting, adventurous, and usually profitable things start to happen."

Sarda raised his eyebrows. "I'm not sure we can promise anything like that here."

"Don't worry. From what I've heard, I'd say that this project of yours is interesting enough," Kieran told him. "As for the rest, oh . . . give it time."

Sarda's stride was springy and exuberant, as if he were bombproof and the worst that life had to offer was rain—possibly the aftereffects of having come through the process unscathed, Kieran reflected. Although he had made a point of not staring earlier, he couldn't resist glancing at Sarda surreptitiously as they came to a flight of metal-railed stairs and descended. Even after listening to June the previous evening, it seemed incredible that this person walking beside him could have been a formless aggregate of nonliving molecules just two days before. Every hair, every pore— even nongenetic, environmental effects such as the sunburn and evident wear and toughening of the hands and fingers—were exactly reproduced. Kieran was unable to find a flaw. It was uncanny.

They came to a concrete-walled room filled with consoles and equipment racks, items of unidentifiable apparatus, tangles of wires and piping, several desks partly hidden amid it all, and a workbench along one wall. But the centerpiece was a padded, recliner-like piece of furniture surrounded by more gadgetry, obviously built to take a human body. A sturdy white metal door was set in the wall nearby. Sarda ran over the basics of the process, keeping things short in view of the limited time that he could give them. Kieran could probably have helped a little by airing some of what he had learned from June, but it seemed wiser to just shut up and listen.

"You could think of a factory, along with all the machines and people in it, as a computer that translates design information and raw materials into products—an automobile, or a space plane, say. In the same kind of way, the protein transcription machinery in a cell is a chemical computer that translates DNA information and raw material into . . ." Sarda glanced at June for a suggestion.

"A cat," she supplied promptly.

"Right." Sarda looked at Kieran questioningly. Kieran nodded that the concepts were familiar. Sarda continued, "But it's unimaginably more complicated. The DNA tells you not only how to make a cat, but a *self-assembling* cat. You don't have an equipped factory and a bunch of engineers standing by already there, waiting to just read the blueprints and make a plane. The whole works has to make *itself* as well as make the plane. Can you imagine writing any kind of computer program to do something like that?"

Kieran did find himself staring this time, but it was from fascination, not impertinent curiosity. Although he had been aware of as much before, the implication had never struck him so forcefully.

Sarda waved a hand. "And that's not all. Everything the cat inherits that tells it how to behave is coded in there too: the variability for adapting to different conditions; its immune reactions, repair mechanisms for wear and tear, cuts and burns, broken bones. . . . It's all in there somewhere, implicitly. You just need the right computer to express it."

"Like a mathematical system," Kieran remarked. "Everything it says is contained in a few premises. But it takes thousands of theorems to make it explicit."

"You've got a good grasp of principles," Sarda said, showing some surprise. "Do I hear a scientific background talking?"

"Nothing formal that I could wave degrees in your face about. I just like keeping abreast of what interests me."

Sarda turned toward the recliner and its surrounding equipment. "What we've done, in essence, is use a different kind of computer to extract that information rapidly and speed up the assembly of what normally takes years. It's still a lot of computing, but we end up ahead of the game. You could think of our way as generating an image by taking a photograph to capture the scene all at once, compared to scanning it as a bit stream. All those guys who are trying to scan at the atomic level . . ." Sarda shook his head. "They're not going anywhere. All the computers in the world couldn't hack that amount of data, even if they ran till the end of the universe. But the way we do it, you don't *need* that amount of raw data because implicitly the DNA can tell you how to generate almost all of it—*if* you know how to read the DNA."

"The way Leo described it to me compared it to sending a

code to specify a phrase from a code book," June put in. "Most of the information is already there, at the receiving end. The code just triggers which part to use. It's the same with what DNA specifies. Most of it's general and can be supplied in advance at the receiving end to begin with, so you don't have to send it."

Kieran nodded. Natural language worked in a similar way. Most of the meaning derived from a sentence was in the listener's head already from a human's knowledge of the world, and not contained in the words. That was why predictions of translation machines within five years, heard from the AI community in the 1960s, had turned out to be wildly optimistic. He looked around the room, unable to decide whether it felt more like something surgical or a macabre, sophisticated form of torture chamber. His eyes came to rest on the sturdy white door. Suddenly, he suspected that he knew its significance.

"*Almost* all the data," Sarda repeated. "Environmental modifications, we have to derive from the original. I came out of the process with my hair cut like I wear it, my nails clipped, and a few other things that obviously didn't come from DNA." Which took care of the first question that Kieran had been forming to ask. "Likewise, the acquired memory patterns in the brain have to be derived and implanted. But again nature gives us a break. There are ways of getting enough out of the wave functions such that you don't have to go down to quantum levels of detail."

"So this is where you get the information from the original," Kieran summarized, indicating the recliner with a nod.

"Right," Sarda confirmed.

"And the reconstituted version comes together . . . where?" Kieran looked inquiringly in the direction of the door, even though he knew that to be incorrect—June had told him Sarda was "sent" somewhere upstairs.

Sarda shook his head. "In the R-Lab, upstairs. This is the T-Lab. 'Transmit' and 'Receive.'"

"What order of time are we talking about?" Kieran asked. "Between the process commencing down here and you walking out at the other end up there."

"Right now, about three hours. In the future that should come down a lot." Sarda's mouth twitched beneath the shaggy yellow mustache. "I can't say it will ever be as instantaneous as they like to show it in the movies . . . but we'll see where it goes."

Kieran decided to play dumb a little longer. "So how does it work? . . . For three hours do you have the original you coming apart, being unraveled layer by layer like a ball of string or something, as the other one upstairs is being constructed? . . . But that would be a hell of a risk to take, wouldn't it? Suppose the system seized up halfway through? What kind of protection do you have against something like that?"

Sarda frowned, as if unsure whether he wanted to go into it. Kieran got the feeling it was a subject he had learned to give a wide berth to if possible. Finally Sarda said, somewhat reluctantly, "It's not quite the way you assume, Mr. Thane. The original has to be reduced to a suspended state for the process to work—totally inert. But the decomposition phase can be deferred—which was the choice that was exercised in this instance." He made a quick dismissive motion with a hand. "Of course, once you've raised the confidence level sufficiently, you can make the two phases virtually simultaneous. But in the present case, the option to reactivate is still available. So that risk was covered."

Kieran went through the motions of absorbing this information for the first time, then nodded at a vista of light slowly dawning. "Oh, I see! . . . You're saying that the original is still intact. So where . . . ?" He turned his head toward the white door, letting his eyes widen in an expression of sudden revelation.

"Yes," Sarda confirmed. "It's being kept in there until all the tests are satisfied . . . just in case."

"So when will they . . . deactivate it?" June asked.

"Midnight tomorrow—unless anything negative shows up in the meantime. But that's looking less likely." Sarda obviously had no qualms—at least, this one didn't. Crazy or whatever, or not, Kieran wondered if the one behind the door had felt equally dispassionate all the way through to the final moments.

Sarda followed their gazes, and then seemed to feel uncomfortable about the whole thing, suddenly. "Let's go back upstairs," he said. "I'll show you the reconstitution chamber in the R-Lab—where the other half happens."

But Kieran wasn't prepared to let the matter go so easily. "But doesn't that change everything that we've gotten so used to hearing?" he persisted as they went back up the stairs. "You're saying there are two of you. If I were due to go through that today, I don't see how I could feel any sense of . . . *continuity* with a replica that was going to walk out of a chamber upstairs—or maybe out at Jupiter one day, from what we're told. It might look, talk, and think like me, and satisfy everyone else . . . but I wouldn't find that very convincing. As far as *I'm* concerned, everything that's me becomes history."

"Would you feel better if we sent your own atoms through as well as the information, and rebuilt you from them?" Sarda asked. "But that would be pointless. All atoms of a kind are identical. I feel just fine. Never better. I've no doubt that I'm the same person I was. You can check all the test results for yourself."

"I'm sure *you* do. But you're through it. What would that other character that we just left downstairs say if we asked him?"

Sarda answered without hesitation. "That form behind the door we've just left is just a mass of biological material now. It doesn't have any of the attributes that define a live personality anymore. They're all transferred here." He spread his arms and indicated himself with a gesture of his hands as they walked. "Think of it another way, Mr. Thane. A few years from now, your body won't contain any of the atoms that it's made from today. Every one will have been replaced as new material is taken in and old tissue lost. So all we're really doing is speeding up a little what happens naturally, anyway. Why should you feel any less a sense of continuity with the natural analog of yourself that will be walking around then, than you would for an artificial one created more rapidly? The personality that you insist is you will have moved from the molecular configuration that it resides in now into a different one no less in one case than in the other. Essentially, they're both the same thing."

Before Kieran could take it further, they came to the open door of another laboratory, this time with sounds of voices and people visible inside. The R-Lab seemed to have attracted more visitors than the one downstairs. "Here he is!" someone called out. Then, "Leo, we need you to verify something here."

Sarda observed the exchange of dubious looks between Kieran and June. "Don't worry," he told them confidently as they entered. "Fifty years from now it will be accepted as routinely as organ transplants. Nobody will think twice about it."

"And it was just getting interesting," June said. Sarda spread his hands and indicated his situation with a helpless nod. "Maybe we could grab you for lunch tomorrow, Leo," June said on impulse. "How are you fixed?"

"Nothing scheduled, I think . . ."

"You have to try the new restaurant at the Oasis, out at the spaceport. Kieran and I were there last night. Come on. You need to get away from this insanity for an hour." She was doing it again. The dancing dark eyes, challenging him to rise above the mundanity of a planned routine, were irresistible.

Sarda raised his palms in capitulation. "Okay, you've got it." He grabbed the arm of a frizzy-haired man wearing a gray lab smock. "Stewart, can you show Mr. Thane the reconstitution chamber quickly before he leaves?" He turned back to Kieran and June as the horde closed around him. "Say, twelve-thirty—if I don't have to cancel between now and then, I'll meet you there."

Afterward, they went down through the regular offices to the cubbyhole with a cluttered desk and multiscreen c-com layout that June used for work space, and met some of the other people that she knew. During one of the lulls, Kieran asked her, "Did you ever hear that old puzzle about the ship? I think it came from the Greeks."

"Which one was that?"

"If you replace a rotting piece of timber on a ship, is it still the same ship?"

"Sure, I guess."

"How about if you replace two pieces?"

"Okay." June saw where he was going. "Then three, then four . . . So if you end up replacing all of them . . ."

"Is it still the same ship?"

June had to think about it. "There's nowhere to draw the line," she said finally. "So I'd have to say, yes it's the same ship."

"And by his logic, so would Leo," Kieran agreed. "But now suppose you'd saved all the pieces of the original, and you put them together again. You've got two ships. How could they both be the same one?" He made an inviting gesture. "It's a good question to liven things up in a bar if things start getting dull. You see, even after a couple of thousand years, most people can't agree on that one. How are they ever going to figure out an answer to what we're talking about?"

# ⋛ 5 ⋚

Kieran had just completed a long, wearying trip. June had been embroiled in several days of frenetic activity at Quantonix. The next day, they agreed, should be devoted to some serious relaxation.

They spent part of the morning at a pool near the inner end of Nineveh, where diving took on a slow-motion, soaring quality, and the water splashed twice as high as normal. Then June introduced Kieran to the dynamics of Martian tennis, which was something he hadn't tried before but mastered quickly. Afterward, they lay on a couple of recliners, sipping iced lemonades and basking under an artificial sun. "You should try zero-g football," Kieran said. "I got into some of the crew's games in the transport out to Urbek."

"I'm not sure it would be my style."

"It's wild. Three-D—literally bouncing off the walls."

June turned her head to glance at him. He was sprawled back at ease, lean, supple, firmly muscular. A few yards away, Guinness was being idolized by two female admirers clad in bikinis that were more suggestion than actuality. "So what took you to Urbek Station anyway?" she asked. "What kind of place is it?"

"Oh, another of these experiments in communal living—joy, love, peace to all. A religious sect who say that everything passed off as Christianity since Constantine has been a counterfeit created by Roman imperialism. They put their savings into recreating the world in a hollowed-out asteroid as a place to get it right." Kieran flicked away a fly that had settled on his arm. The variety of life-forms from Earth that had appeared on Mars somehow without being introduced deliberately was amazing. "But they were being targeted by Belt pirates who saw some easy slave labor that the market could use. When I did some checking, they turned out to be the same ones who hijacked the *Far Ranger* about a year ago—remember?—and wiped out all those people."

"Ugh!" June made a face at the recollection.

Kieran raised his eyebrows and shrugged in a way that said nothing could change it now.

"So what were you able to do about it?" June asked.

Kieran's expression was a masterful study in innocence. "Me? Nothing. But there wasn't any need, anyway. It seems the unlovely had an accident with some fuel that must have been unstable. Or somebody was very careless. But they won't be doing any more wiping out—or peddling cheap pickings around the exchanges."

"How tragic."

"Extraordinary, really. Can't understand how it could have happened."

"I trust that the sect was suitably appreciative," June said.

"Yes. The elders were happy to make a small donation to the KT retirement fund. But they really do need protection out there. I've put them in touch with some suitable people." Kieran looked away as Guinness came padding back with his latest conquests. "There's the biggest bandit in the Belt," he muttered.

"He's just *wonderful!*" one of the girls exulted. "What's his name?"

"You mean he didn't tell you?" Kieran looked at the dog reprovingly. "Stop acting dumb and giving the ladies a hard time." Guinness blinked and looked pained.

"He's Guinness," June supplied.

"Oh, you mean like the Irish beer," the other girl said.

"Stout," Kieran corrected.

"Who?"

"Heavy, black Irish beer. It's called stout."

"Oh, really?"

Kieran gave them his standard line about Guinness being part doberman and part labrador, the doberman coming out in the coloring, the face and the temperament being all lab. The girls' names were Patti and Grace. Patti, it turned out, worked at the Oasis.

"What do you do there?" Kieran asked her.

"It's kind of a training program. You get moved around to do a bit of everything. Right now I'm working the bar."

"I might just stop by and say hello sometime," Kieran mused. "I'm never averse to checking out a new bar."

"We had dinner there last night," June put in. "The seafood bar there is good."

"Yes, everyone seems to like it."

"In fact, we're meeting somebody for lunch there later today," Kieran said. "Maybe we'll see you?"

Patti shook her head. "Sorry. I'm off until tomorrow." She glanced at Grace, who was pointing at her watch and mouthing something. "Oh, too bad. I guess we have to go now."

"See you there sometime, then," Kieran said.

"Sure . . ." Patti looked back as the two girls walked away. "Make sure to bring Guinness."

Guinness stretched out in the strip of shade along one side of Kieran's recliner and settled down contentedly, chin on paws, to watch the world going about its business. Kieran sank back into the cushions, abandoning himself to the feeling of warm rays soaking into his skin. It certainly felt like the real thing, anyway.

"So what's your verdict?" June's voice asked through the euphoria. "Do you think Leo's crazy?"

"Well, knowing what I know now, *I'd* never be seen dead going into a machine like that." Kieran laughed at the irony. "There— that just about says it all, doesn't it? . . . But I suppose, yes, he has to have a streak of something that would be judged crazy according to the standards that most of the world goes by. Maybe that defines it about as well as anything does."

There was a short silence. Then June asked, "So do you think people like Consolidated Communications and the other big carriers really believe they're going to be able to get people to accept something like that? I mean, with all their market review committees, hard-nosed accounting scrutinizers . . . ?"

"That's what I've been wondering too," Kieran said. "You'd think not, but then look at some of the crazy things that supposedly rational investors have thrown money away on in the past when a frenzy sets in." He opened his eyes and looked across at her. "Besides, people are being conditioned not to think about it. Do you really think all the popular stuff we're saturated with is coincidence? I'd never really thought about it myself until I got to talking to you the other night." He tossed out a hand. "Sure, with the size of the market they've got waiting out there, the boardroom won't find it too difficult to immunize itself from wanting to know how the sausages and politics are made. And if it's what enough people want to believe, they might well pull it off. I mean, if people are willing to accept unquestionable termination of their tangible existence here for unverifiable teleportation to some promised hereafter . . ." He shrugged and left it at that. As to the others who were directly involved, he could see the technical crew falling into the role of just being paid to do a job and not think too much about it—as had been pretty much the case with June herself. He wondered, though, who exactly was supposed to press the destruct button, or whatever was equivalent. Surely that would take some rationalizing away. And then, on the other hand, if whoever it was accepted, like Sarda, that what was left was just biological matter with all the attributes of personality extinguished, then maybe not.

"I talked to someone this morning who knows you, Mr. Thane," Sarda said across the lunch table in the restaurant at the Oasis. His manner was less brusque now that they were away from the workplace—more colorful, with a touch of flamboyance. Kieran sensed an impulsive personality that could alternate between extremes. "His name's Jason Moody," Sarda went on. "He makes documentaries about interesting people he digs up all around the Solar System. You know him?"

Kieran thought, then shook his head. "I don't think so."

"Well, he seems to know you—knows of you, at any rate. Maybe you're on his list and you don't know it." Sarda broke open a roll and scooped butter onto one of the pieces. "They call you the Knight, yes? I guess from the initials. You get into some strange things. June never told me half of it when she talked about you."

"Kieran's so sensitive and introverted," June explained. "I try not to make him feel too conspicuous."

"I like to get some variety out of life," Kieran agreed, ignoring her.

Whatever Sarda had been told by Moody evidently intrigued him. "So how is the dragons-and-damsels business?" he asked.

"The dragons take on all kinds of weird and wonderful forms

these days." Kieran shot an affectionate look at June. "But the damsels are much the same as ever."

"Is there an Arthur and a Camelot somewhere?" Sarda asked. "Are you part of some kind of organization?"

"I don't really fit in with organizations. Let's just say I have a lot of friends."

"Interesting friends," June put in. "If you ever need a strange job done, or an expert on something weird, Kieran probably knows just the right person."

"I'll bear it in mind."

Kieran had been observing a gray-haired man in a blue windcheater, who was hovering a short distance away, inside the entrance from the bar. He had been walking past in the direction of the lobby, seen them, and changed direction to enter. Now he was making tilting movements with his head, as if trying to draw attention without intruding. "Is that a friend of yours?" Kieran asked Sarda, inclining his head.

Sarda looked across. "No," he said simply. But the gray-haired man apparently took Sarda's look as an invitation and came over.

"Leo! Good to see you again. Hope I'm not interrupting anything. I was just leaving, saw you in here, and wanted to say hi."

Sarda frowned. "I'm sorry. Do I know you . . . ?"

"Well, sure . . ." The man looked puzzled. "Walter . . . Walter Trevany—the geologist. We met here a week or two back. I'm staying at the hotel."

Sarda shook his head. "You must be mistaken."

Trevany forced an uneasy smile, as if offering an out if Sarda was joking. "We were through there in the bar. You were with a woman, Elaine: tall, slim, curly black hair. . . ."

Again, Sarda shook his head. "I'm sorry. I don't know anyone of that name."

"You're not exactly an easy person to get confused over. . . ." Trevany's words trailed away as he saw that Sarda was uncompromising. He looked appealingly at the other two. Kieran sympathized, but there was nothing he could do to help. "Well, excuse me. I didn't mean to crash in." Trevany turned and walked back toward the lobby entrance, pausing halfway to turn for a moment in the manner of someone who *knew* he wasn't mistaken. Then he disappeared. Sarda looked back at his two companions and shrugged.

And Kieran knew that he was being absolutely honest also. Yet at the same time, he had caught a flicker of uncertainty in Sarda's eyes. June raised her eyebrows expertly in a way that could have meant anything and attended to her meal. Kieran sat back in his chair to muse on the situation. It was very odd. At the same time, he had no doubt that it was immensely significant. Just at that moment, however, he had no idea what to make of it.

He continued musing on the incident through the rest of the afternoon. If it was a first hint surfacing of some problem with the experiment, should the "deactivation" scheduled for midnight be postponed? But he wasn't going to put it to Sarda, who would hardly be thrilled at the idea. So should they go and talk to the Morches? On the other hand, Sarda might have had reason for covering up something personal, in which case interfering could result in no end of trouble.

"I say we simply go along with them," June opined after they had talked it through for the umpteenth time. "If all their tests and experts say things are fine, and those are the standards they accepted to go by, who are we to argue? How much of the rest of the world's problems can you be expected to take on?"

Kieran agreed, finally. They left it at that.

# ⟫ **6** ⟪

Kieran finished his coffee and looked across the kitchen area. It was the following morning, back at the apartment. "I really hope Leo doesn't go and have an accident or something now," he said to June, who was putting on her coat, filling Teddy's food dispenser, and trying to unglue Teddy from her feet, all at the same time. "I mean, with his bridge burned, so to speak, it would be a bit unfortunate, wouldn't it?" Sarda had rushed back to Quantonix after lunch the previous day, since things there were apparently still hectic. Kieran and June had continued with their day of relaxation. As far as they knew, the "deactivation" of the original had proceeded at midnight as scheduled.

"Trust you to find a grotesque angle . . . *Wait*, you stupid animal!"

"So what happens when they make a travel machine?" Kieran went on, intrigued by the line of thought. "Do they have it de-ex the original as soon as they press the button, and hope for the best? Or would it wait for a signal back from the receiving end first, confirming that everything there had gone okay? Otherwise, it would be just too bad for the trusting traveler, wouldn't it?" He paused while a new ramification formed in his mind. "You know, I think I've just realized why the spacelines try to get you to buy the round trip up front."

"I thought it was just so they'd have your money in the bank for the duration. Anyway, I've got to go."

"I'll ride in with you," Kieran said. "I thought I might start looking at what the real-estate business has to offer—maybe check out a couple of the offices around the Trapezium." That was the central area of Lowell, where the two canyon arms of Gorky

36

Avenue from the northeast and Nineveh from roughly east, came together—named after the shape of the original structure from which it had grown. The western side of the Trapezium contained the administrative and civic district.

"Sure," June said. "But we need to leave now. I've got a meeting."

Kieran collected his coat along with Guinness's leash and whistled through his teeth. Guinness sprang to alertness and came through from the living room to the front door, where he waited, wagging his tail with uncomprehending trust. "Maybe a stroll around town sounds like a good idea for both of us," Kieran told him.

The real-estate agent's name was Yinge. He had a rounded, pinkish face with babylike features, and a manner that was candid yet genial, inspiring confidence by its suggestion that even if the profession could be guilty of a little overeagerness at times, he had already read this prospective buyer as too astute to be influenced by it. Kieran hadn't made his mind up yet if it was genuine or an art perfected over years.

"Is it a permanent residence or somewhere occasional that you're looking for, Mr. Thorn?" Yinge asked, standing a pace back as Kieran surveyed the living and dining areas. On principle, Kieran didn't like his correct name to be put in computers everywhere to be registered, tagged, sorted, and listed. The place was a little cramped, and the view from the veranda outside the sliding glass doors was of indoor pedestrian galleries and a shopping precinct with a maglev line; but the location was conveniently central, with all amenities close at hand. A possibility, Kieran decided.

"I travel around a lot, so it would be somewhere to use from time to time. Also as an investment."

"I understand. You do have the advantage of better security here in the city, as opposed to somewhere remote. And the value here is solid. It can only go up."

"But that's going to be true of just about everywhere for a long time."

"Yes, of course."

Kieran sauntered through to the main bedroom, and then back to the spare room again. They had false windows with variable graphics. Right now, one was showing a scene of forested mountains with a waterfall, the other, a vista of Antarctica. Plenty of closet space, and the bathrooms were sensibly located. A pity that the kitchen on the far side of the wall tapered at such an awkward angle—a result that derived from the external shape of the structure. Kieran thought for a moment, then pointed at the wall and dragged it in a few feet, at the same time pivoting it about the far corner. It meant that the room they were in was no longer rectangular, but the change squared up the kitchen on the far side and created extra space there. Walking through the wall, he studied the kitchen again and repositioned the sink and its adjacent work tops, autochef unit and breakfast bar into the new layout. "What do you think?" he asked Yinge, who had followed him.

"Much better. You'd be happy with the angle in the bedroom?"

"Oh, I think so. I'd probably only use it for storage anyway."

"That's fine." Yinge gazed around in a way that said that should settle everything. "Does any other party need to see it or get involved?"

"No. Just me and my dog."

"So, is there any reason why we shouldn't start an application?"

Kieran smiled at the choice of term. It was through habit. Kieran had already said he'd be paying cash. He changed the colors of the walls and carpeting to orange and maroon to see the effect. "Not just yet. I'd like to see a couple of places farther out, just to compare them."

"Of course."

The apartment vanished. Kieran took off the VR goggles to find himself back in the office of J.J. Hamblin Properties, standing in one of the showerstall-like cubicles with roller-pebble floors, where wall sensors registered suggestions of body movements more faithfully than the old body suits had—and without the hassle of getting into them. He emerged to find Yinge removing his own goggles and Guinness evidently relieved to see his master acting normally again. Kieran and Yinge sat down to coffees while they selected several more offerings and then reentered the simulations to "visit" a new development on the outer fringes of Lowell—better appreciation prospects but a bit far out; a more spacious unit intended for family occupation in Osaka, on the north side toward Tharsis—

not bad, but set in surroundings too uniform and regimented for Kieran's taste; and a not-yet-complete complex at a fast-growing city called Zerolon on the far side of the planet above Hellas, where the proposed synchronous sky elevator would be built if the project went ahead—surprisingly comfortable and well situated. Kieran said he'd like copies of the files available for review later.

"Just for the record, what kind of timescale do you see yourself on with regard to firming something up?" Yinge inquired as he keyed in the appropriate codes.

"It's elastic at the moment. In any case, I'd need to go there physically before concluding anything—among other things, to let Guinness check it out."

"Guinness?"

"The dog."

"Oh yes, of course."

"You'd be amazed at some of the things he can turn up."

Yinge looked taken aback, if not mildly offended. "Surely you're not suggesting there might be anything not aboveboard," he protested. "I assure you, Mr. Thorn, our virtuals are completely as-is, untouched and unedited from the original scans."

"Yes, of course," Kieran agreed, smiling disarmingly.

Kieran had just emerged and was standing, considering which direction to head next, when his phone sounded its call tone. He drew the unit out and raised it to his face. The caller was Leo Sarda.

"Mr. Thane, how are you fixed? I need to talk to you right now." Sarda sounded strangely agitated after the self-assuredness that Kieran had observed yesterday at lunch and in the labs the day before.

"I'm free," Kieran said. "What's happened?"

"I can't go into it now. Let's meet somewhere away from here. Where are you right now?"

"In the Trapezium area. I'm looking at realtors."

"Fine. Look, there's a small pub and eatery kind of joint up on one of the levels over the main square. It's called the Mars Bar. Can I meet you there in, say, half an hour?"

"I'll be there."

"Fine," Sarda said again, and hung up.

# ⟩ **7** ⟨

Kieran found the Mars Bar without difficulty. It was on a balcony looking down over the main commercial precinct. Not having eaten yet, he ordered pâté and salad with a glass of chablis for himself (from home-grown grapes—a bit on the dry side but not bad), and a couple of thick burgers, a biscuit, and a dish of cold tea for Guinness. There was plenty of time, and he ate at a leisurely pace, taking in the scene. A band was playing in the court below, where figures on roller blades and skateboards maneuvered expertly among the shoppers and strollers. On a level above, members of some kind of sect wearing hooded green robes formed part of an audience listening to a speaker delivering a harangue about something. Farther on, a group of elderly people who had stopped to sit on some benches by a fountain were talking loudly and laughing among themselves. Kieran wondered what would possess a person to uproot and come all this way at such a stage in life. To stay with families who were moving out, he supposed. The changes and necessary adjustments would be all the more difficult for them. He hoped the laughter and the joviality were not too forced.

The compact scale of the architecture increased the density of color and movement, making everything seem more intense and teeming, more *alive*—like some of the Asian cities he had been to. Or was he registering subliminally the restless new breed of humanity that seemed to go about everything it did with such urgency and purpose? There was serious talk already of launching the first missions out to the stars to follow the unmanned probes.

Many said that the human race was perking up again. As with just about every other form of human endeavor contained in the

40

turmoil bursting outward from the home world, science was no longer an establishment-administered conformity as had decreed Truth on Earth, but a rugged diversity of competing, frequently squabbling, beliefs. A vigorous school of growing currency held that the line taught for generations, of humankind evolving sedately over hundreds of thousands of years through progressively higher stages of development from primitive, ape-related ancestors, was wrong. The past had been much more convoluted and complex. An advanced civilization of a still-disputed nature, possessing amazing knowledge of geography, astronomy, mathematics, and other skills which in many ways were still a mystery, had existed long before the previously-supposed cradles of civilization in Egypt and Sumer. Referred to nonspecifically as the "Technolithic" culture on account of the huge stone structures erected in various parts of the world—now generally accepted as the work of the same, or closely related, builders—they had been wiped out in a planet-wide cataclysm that had devastated the Earth some time around 10,000 B.C. According to the proponents, current human civilization was not the result of a steady improvement from barbarism; it was *recovering* toward a grandeur that had once existed, and which in some ways might even have surpassed anything seen since. As he looked around, Kieran could feel himself as being a part of it. After millennia of confusion and strife, the human race was coming alive again and getting its potential back after something had come close to destroying it.

He saw Sarda's shaggy yellow mane appear up a stairwell from a lower level. Sarda saw him, came over, and sat down. A waitress came across from the counter to take Sarda's order. Yet again, Kieran was awed that the person he was looking at—talking, gesturing, acting normally in every way—could have been just a collection of recipe-book ingredients four days previously. But the sun-scorched face behind the straggly mustache was looking grave this time; the eyes beneath the bushy brows, troubled. Kieran's thought again was that some delayed problem with the experiment might have surfaced. But if so, why would Sarda bring it to him?

"Kieran . . . Is that okay?" Sarda began.

"Sure."

Sarda hesitated, making a vague gesture, as if not quite knowing how to begin. "At lunch yesterday, June said that one of the things you do is investigate strange and mysterious things. What did she mean? To me, that sounded like someone who looks into paranormal things—ghosts and psychics, stuff like that . . . Is that what she meant?"

Kieran made a so-so face. "Not really—although sometimes the difference can get debatable. All kinds of things are going on these days that a lot of people might consider strange. They often involve extravagant claims that others are tempted to put a lot of money into—your own work at Quantonix is a case in point. Some claims are genuine; some are frauds, or maybe cases of sincere but deluded people fooling themselves. The would-be investors would very much like to know which are which. And sometimes, yes, they pay me to find out for them."

"I hope that isn't what brought you to Quantonix," Sarda said, looking alarmed. "I promise you that *we're* genuine."

Kieran held up a hand. "No, if that were why I'm here, I'd hardly have told you what I just did. But if you want my opinion anyway, I think TX is genuine." He sipped from his wineglass and raised his icy blue eyes back to Sarda to treat him to a look that was both candid and challenging. "But now that you've brought it up, out of curiosity, if I *were* of a suspicious nature, and say I was considering putting a big wad of money into it, how could I be certain that the you who walked out of the chamber in the R-Lab wasn't the same unprocessed you who was supposed to have been put into suspension downstairs? I mean, it wouldn't be the first time we've seen something like that, would it? Conjurors with boxes do it all the time. You see my point?"

"You have a cynical turn of mind, Mister . . . Kieran," Sarda said, sounding mildly admonishing.

"I told you, I'm paid to have. I just can't get out of the habit."

"Then I'll set your mind at rest. A big trans-system like Three Cs employs some pretty hard-boiled, cynical people too. They wouldn't put money into something like this until they were certain, either." The waitress came back, and Sarda paused to take his glass. He took a draft and looked back at Kieran. "There was what I guess you'd call a macabre kind of ceremony conducted down in the T-Lab yesterday. It involved several independent scientists and medical people, a legal notarizing official, plus representatives from Three Cs and their main interested funding organization. We—"

Kieran raised a hand to spare Sarda having to go through the details. "You went down with them while they opened up the door in the T-Lab. And they verified that the item being kept on ice down there..."

"It's more of a field-induced suspension these days."

"Whatever. But they verified that it's an authentic original of you."

Sarda nodded. "Documents to that effect are available for anyone having an appropriate interest from now on." The purpose, Kieran could see, would be to avoid having to keep two of them around forever as proof that the process worked.

"When did this happen yesterday?" Kieran asked curiously.

"In the afternoon. That was why I had to get back after lunch. It was one of the things we wrap up under 'tests.'"

"And it all went okay? Everyone was happy?"

"Just fine."

None of which explained Sarda's agitation that morning. Kieran eyed him questioningly. "So?"

Sarda shifted position, taking a moment to collect his thoughts. "Exactly what the deal is with Three Cs doesn't really matter. But let me tell you something about my own arrangement with Quantonix. That was something of an experience I went through. Even after all the rats and monkeys had come out of it okay, it's still not exactly the kind of thing you have to deal with every day."

"You don't have to tell me, Leo," Kieran agreed with feeling. "Even after hearing your spiel yesterday, I've been telling June that I wouldn't buy it."

"And the Quantonix directors understand that." Sarda waved briefly with a hand. "Oh, sure, I know that traditionally the inventor is supposed to be his own guinea pig, but this is in a different ballpark than some new vaccine or a headache pill. So they agreed to some additional remuneration—a bonus for taking the risk."

"But payable only upon a successful demonstration of the process," Kieran guessed. That was how he would have stipulated it.

"Yes. Payable yesterday, on satisfactory completion of the certification documents that I just told you about."

"And it was paid as agreed?"

"Oh, sure."

"Can I ask how much?"

"Two million initially. More later when certain conditions are met." Kieran nodded in a way that said Sarda could have done worse. "And then there are advance options on certain movie rights and media exclusives—the word was discreetly leaked in the appropriate places. The first guy to do this is a guaranteed celebrity when the whole thing breaks publicly."

Kieran nodded again. "And that makes you another . . . what?"

"Oh, you're getting close to about another three."

"Million?"

"Right."

So five in all. That could add considerably to one's quality of life, Kieran supposed. "So what's the problem?" he asked.

"It's gone."

Kieran had one of his rare moments of not being immediate on the uptake. "What has?"

"The money. All of it. I've been cleaned out." Sarda waited, but just at that instant Kieran could only blink. Sarda spread his hands. "It's impossible, but it happened. It was lodged in a secure account that I'd set up for the purpose at the Lowell Barham Bank, with personalized passwords and identity codes, all the usual ID procedures that banks insist on. But none of it did any good. This morning it was gone in untraceable withdrawals. The bank insists everything was processed legitimately, with authenticated signatures and authorizations. They're denying any responsibility."

Kieran stared at him disbelievingly. His mind had resumed working again; already, the germ of what could be an explanation was suggesting itself, but it seemed too bizarre. Check out the alternatives first, he told himself.

Sarda went on, "With the deal just about to close, we can't afford word getting out that there might be any kind of problem. We want to keep the regular authorities and agencies out of it. So my question is, is this the kind of 'mysterious thing' that you investigate?" He drank from his glass and sat back, giving Kieran as long as he needed to think about it.

Kieran looked down at Guinness, stretched out by the table in an attitude of having decided there was nothing of immediate interest going on in the world—but with an eye left open just to be sure. Kieran flipped him a pretzel. Guinness snapped it out of the air, moving just his head, then settled down again with a few contented thumps of his tail against the floor.

"Some dog you have there," Sarda commented.

"Oh yes. He can be a good friend to have around." Clearly, someone had known a lot about Sarda's affairs. Someone he had confided in too much, possibly? Finally, Kieran said, "I can imagine a lot of stress, a lot of fear, to put it bluntly, in facing the thought of going through something like that."

"Well, yeah . . . Like I just said. They didn't offer that kind of compensation for nothing."

"Was there anyone you can think of that you talked to about it?" Kieran asked. That would have been a fairly common reaction. "Someone that you confided in about how you felt?"

Sarda seemed about to answer, and then looked puzzled, as if suddenly finding he had nothing to say. In the end he just answered vaguely. "I don't know. You'd think there would have been. . . . But no, I really can't think of anyone."

"You just bottled up the fears and doubts? Kept them to yourself?"

Sarda shrugged. "Uh-huh. I guess I must have."

"It seems a little odd. I could see that of an introvert. You don't strike me as that type."

"What else can I tell you?"

Kieran drank slowly, all the time looking across at Sarda, inviting him to see the obvious. When no response seemed forthcoming, he said, to help things along a little, "Only one person could have known those codes and passwords, passed all the ID checks, Leo."

Sarda shook his head, refusing to consider it. "It's too crazy," he insisted.

"Is it? The original was . . . what, at midnight last night? How is it deactivated?"

"Plasma decomposition. It's virtually instantaneous."

Kieran asked the question that he had been wondering. "Who presses the button or whatever?"

"It's automatic—the final phase of a timed sequence that I initialized myself when we commenced the process four days ago," Sarda answered.

So that was how they had gotten around the problem. Kieran noted that Sarda referred unhesitatingly to "myself."

"So there's nothing left now, right? No way of knowing what got vaporized," Kieran said.

"Uh . . . right."

"How convenient."

Kieran let the implication speak for itself. Sarda might have had an erratic component, but he was no fool. He had probably arrived at the inevitable conclusion himself already but needed to hear it from somebody else before he could accept it. The original was still alive and well, loose in the city somewhere. And it had a grudge.

"But it doesn't make any sense," Sarda protested. "All the tests show I'm indistinguishable by any measure anyone can come up with. So if the original had worked out some kind of plan like this before he went in, I ought to know about it. But I don't. So how could it be him?"

"That's what we have to find out," Kieran replied.

Sarda looked at him uncertainly. "Does that mean you'll help?" he asked.

Kieran was too curious to walk away now. The Sarda he was talking to came across as personable enough, even if just at the moment probably not exactly at his most composed ever; the Sarda who had fleeced him had to be a very different person. Yet they were supposed to be indistinguishable. "I suppose I'd like to know the answers too," he said.

"Don't you usually expect to get paid for something like this?" Sarda asked.

"There's nothing usual about it, Leo, I assure you."

"You know what I mean, Mr. Thane."

"Would it be worth something to you?"

Sarda frowned, then showed both hands in a gesture that asked what other way was there to answer. "Well, if you recover five million for me, I guess yes, that would have to be worth something."

"Then let's talk about it when it's recovered," Kieran suggested.

# 8

The center panel of the mural design on June's living-area wall was switched to viewscreen mode and showed a replay of people waiting in front of the reconstitution chamber in the R-Lab at Quantonix. A frizzy-haired figure in a gray lab smock, whom Kieran had met during his visit there and recognized as Stewart Perrel, chief physician on the TX Project, swung open the access door and leaned inside. A moment later he turned to call back over his shoulder, "He's okay! It worked fine! Leo's okay!" Relieved murmurs came from the company. Then Sarda, draped in a surgical smock, was helped out to a chorus of congratulations and applause.

"So Sarda was brought out from Earth about a year ago to run the project," Kieran said, keeping his eyes on the screen and selecting parts to zoom into close-up. It was mid afternoon, the same day. Kieran had called June, saying they had a problem, and asked her to meet him back at the apartment. He didn't really expect to see anything new since they had rerun the recording several times, but there was always the chance. "Was it a typical sunsider deal?"

June nodded from where she was curled up at an end of the eggshell-blue couch with Teddy stretched out alongside in that attitude of perfect laziness and contentment that only cats and teenagers, before being smitten by culturally instructed adulation of avarice, can achieve. A precarious truce had been reached with regard to Guinness, who just at the moment had been taken for a romp along the lakeshore by some children from the neighboring terraces. "He'd been trying to get something going there, but the problems would have tied up city blocks of lawyers for

47

the next hundred years," she said. "He came out on an exclusive retainer. Five million on top of what he'd have collected in a year, in the bank before any deal with a principal was finalized, wasn't a bad offer." Kieran nodded. As the technical brains of the business, Sarda would also have been cut into a share of the proceeds later, when the proven technology was sold. With the sunsider not getting involved in the hassles of producing and marketing the actual goods, everything beyond paying off the costs of the research would be pure profit. That was where the real payoff lay.

Kieran cut off the replay and swivelled the recliner to face June across the room. "If it wasn't Sarda-the-First that the bell tolled for at midnight, then it must have been something else that was substituted. A client from a morgue somewhere, perhaps, who was past caring where it all led?"

"That's what I was wondering," June said. "But surely a body in suspension like that would be monitored. Wouldn't substituting a corpse set off all kinds of alarms?"

"Not necessarily. The sensors would feed into a monitoring computer. All you'd need to do would be to change the software to make it carry on reporting normal readings, whatever the sensors were registering."

June conceded with a nod. "Of course. Okay . . ."

Kieran went on, "Someone else must have done the switching. So we have an accomplice. It has to be someone with the medical background to do the body switching and take care of resuscitating the original; also enough computer savvy to reprogram the monitoring system without setting off bells." He stared at June invitingly to make the connection.

"Ah! Is this where the missing mystery woman enters: Elaine, the tall and slim, of the curly black hair?"

"Maybe. But the funny thing is, Sarda-Two doesn't know anything about any such arrangement with anybody. Yet he's supposed to have the same memories as the Sarda who would have made them. They're supposed to be the same person."

June frowned. "What was that man's name at the restaurant, again?"

"Walter—of the Trevany kind."

"Walter Trevany. That was it."

"How did that incident strike you?" Kieran asked curiously.

"Eerie," June pronounced. "He hadn't made a mistake. As he said at the time, Sarda's hardly the faceless kind of person that you forget easily."

"And he knew Leo's name."

"So was Sarda lying for some reason?" June shook her head. "I don't think so. He came across to me as genuine enough."

"Me too," Kieran said. "And when I talked to him today, he admitted to having rising fears about the whole thing as D-Day came nearer, but he couldn't recall voicing them to anyone. I thought that was odd too. He seems the type who would have." He made a plucking motion in the air to materialize a coin between thumb and forefinger, tossed it toward his other hand which apparently caught it, and showed both hands empty again. Then he looked back at June challengingly to make what she could of it.

She went over what they had covered as if reciting a checklist. "No recollection of the woman that Trevany saw him with in the bar. Must have had an accomplice but doesn't know anything about it. You'd have thought there'd be somebody he confided in, but he can't recall anyone." Her look said the question was obvious, wasn't it? "Are we talking about the same person here?"

Kieran opened his palms to reveal not one coin but two. "You tell me."

"Girlfriend, accomplice, and confidante," June mused.

"And he doesn't remember any of them."

The dark, impenetrable eyes held Kieran's searchingly. "Is there a pattern here, Sir Knight? I see a strong suggestion of selective amnesia at work. Is that the way your mind's working too?"

"It makes you wonder, doesn't it? Let's try and put ourselves in his position. However successful the animal tests appeared, he can't get inside their heads and know how it might have affected them in other ways. He's the one who's taking all the risks. And all he's standing to get out of it in return is the prospect of going down in history as Plasma Man. It's Sarda Mark Two who's going to get all the accolades, walk out to a cool five million, and probably end up a billionaire later. How would you feel about it?"

"About the same as you. But he argued pretty solidly for this rationale that he pitched at us about only speeding up what happens naturally," June pointed out.

"Too much so, if you ask me," Kieran replied. "I got the feeling he was working to convince himself more than anyone."

"Hmm . . . Okay, maybe. . . ."

"Then let's suppose so. Isn't it possible that inwardly, despite all the rationalizing, subconsciously he couldn't really buy that line. So maybe he decided to take insurance, and at the same time extract dues that *he'd* earned, and his risk-free alter ego, who walks forth into fame and fortune, hadn't." Kieran contemplated one of the coins as he rolled it edge over edge across the backs of his outstretched fingers and back again, indicating that the case rested. Then he flipped it up and caught it, palmed it onto the back of his other hand, and looked at June questioningly.

"Heads," she obliged.

He lifted his hand to reveal nothing.

"It makes sense," June conceded. "As much as anything, anyway. So where do we go next?"

Kieran got up from the recliner and crossed over to the liquor cabinet while he considered their options. "Vodka tonic with a slice of lime," he pronounced.

"Right. How did you know?"

"I didn't. Power of suggestion at work." Kieran began fixing the drinks, an Irish Bushmills whiskey straight for himself—expensive import; June had probably gotten it in just for him. "The only lead we've got to Sarda-One is through this Elaine. Sarda-Two ought to know everything we need to locate her, but all his recollections of her have been erased somehow. Or . . ." he looked at June pointedly, "they're still in there somewhere but are blocked."

"So if we knew how his amnesia was engineered, there might be a way to undo it," she said, taking his meaning.

"And *when* was it engineered? It couldn't have been before Sarda-One went into the copier, because he'd need to retain enough about what was going on in order to clean out Sarda-Two's bank account. But it couldn't have been after Sarda-Two came out at the other end, because if he came out knowing what was going on, he'd have promptly stopped it. So how was it done?"

June accepted a glass as Kieran moved over to her. "Some kind of drug, maybe?" she offered, looking up at him.

"Not selective enough. Too uncontrollable and unpredictable. We're looking for something that would work precisely . . . surgically." He took an approving sip of his Irish, swilling it around in his mouth before swallowing, then sat down on the other end of the couch.

June thought again. "Then how about something almost surgical? Could they have manipulated the regeneration of the neural circuitry so that selected memory configurations were eliminated?"

"That sounds more like it," Kieran agreed. "And a project like TX would include the right know-how if it were possible. . . ." He nodded, warming more to the idea. "*Is* something like that possible? You know, I'm really not sure."

June took the twist of lime from the glass and squeezed it over her drink while going back in her mind over the things she had read and heard on the subject. "I'm not either," she confessed finally.

"Who's the neuro-circuitry expert, then?" Kieran asked. "It doesn't sound like Sarda's specialty."

"No. It would be Tom Norgent. Memory extraction and implanting was his department."

"And you've gotten to know him in your work at Quantonix?"

"Sure . . . kind of."

"Hmm . . ." Kieran drummed on the rim of his glass with his fingertips, glanced at the clock displayed in part of the mural, and looked at June. "If Sarda-One is collecting already, there might not be a lot of time before he vanishes. The only other lead we have is this Trevany character. If I have a try at tracking him down, can you get back to the firm this afternoon and talk to Norgent? If news and publicity is your department, it shouldn't be hard to find a line."

"Okay." One of June's attractions was her easy way of agreeing, without the compulsion so many people seemed to have for finding complications with anything anyone else proposed. She finished her drink and left within minutes.

Kieran used his handset to call the Oasis, where Trevany had said he was staying. The name was registered, sure enough, but there was no reply from the room. Kieran tried the General Net Personal Code Directory and obtained numbers for a flotilla of Trevanys. A minute or two later he was talking to one who was listed as currently on Mars and in Lowell City.

"Hello. Is this the Walter Trevany who's booked in at the Oasis hotel?"

"Yes, it is. Who might this be?"

"The name's Kieran Thane. We've met in a kind of way, but it won't mean anything to you."

"Oh?"

"Yesterday, you recognized Leo Sarda in the Oasis restaurant. He was with a couple of people. I was one of them."

"Oh, that. Yes . . . Is that his name? I only knew him as Leo. What was going on there? I hadn't made any mistake."

"I know. He's been having some problems lately. That was what I wanted to talk to you about, Mr. Trevany. You might be able to help us."

"Are you a doctor or something?"

"You could say that." Which was true. Trevany just had. "I was wondering if we could get together, whenever would be convenient."

"Well . . . I'm kinda busy for the next few days. Then we'll be heading out on a field expedition."

"Oh, yes—you said you're a geologist."

"I'm not sure when I could be available. There's always a mess of last-minute things that hit you when you're organizing something like this. I won't be coming back to Lowell tonight."

"Where are you at the moment?" Kieran asked.

"At a place called Stony Flats. It's about twenty miles north of the main canyon—one of the early bases. We're fitting out a mobile lab to go to a base camp that we've got up in the Tharsis region."

"Maybe I could come out there instead."

"You're sure?"

"Why not? I'm the one with the questions."

"You'd need to drive. Are you mobile?"

"That's something I was planning on taking care of anyway," Kieran said. He thought rapidly. There was enough time to find himself a vehicle and get out there. "How about if I make it late this afternoon?" he suggested.

"That sounds good. I'll give you directions on how to get here. . . ."

Kieran finished the call and put the comset back in his jacket pocket. "Come on," he said to Guinness. "It's time we stopped by and paid our respects to Brother Mahom."

# ⫷ 9 ⫸

June picked her way through to Tom Norgent's paper-strewn desk and work terminal, located amid the clutter of electrical racking, pipe mazes, and other equipment surrounding the reconstitution chamber in the R-Lab. A few other people were working in the vicinity, but the frenzy of activity that had characterized the previous couple of days had largely abated.

Tom was in his sixties, with a grizzled beard, button-nosed, Mars-tanned face, and a balding scalp merging with his forehead to leave an atoll reef of whitish hair fringing the back and sides. He greeted her in shirt sleeves and loose khaki pants, pulling a folding chair out from a gap by a table with charts and manuals on top, and having to clear some boxes and a piece of instrumentation out of the way to make room.

June had dealt with him intermittently through her time with the project, finding him genial enough, if a bit inclined toward fussiness—Santa Claus out of uniform, fresh from a beard trim. During the ride back into Quantonix, the thought had crossed her mind that Elaine might not have been the only person involved in this, and if Sarda's partial amnesia had indeed been brought about by neural manipulation, it would have needed precisely the kind of inside expertise that Norgent possessed. All the same, although she had learned to be wary of external impressions, she found it all but impossible to picture him in the role of accessory to dire conspiracy and intrigue.

"I was wondering when it would be my turn to get the treatment," he said after he had sat down and cleared space on the desk for his elbows. "Leo says you've been squeezing everyone else's brains like lemons. . . . Do you know where Leo is, by the way? Max said he went rushing off this morning with some kind of personal problem, and we haven't seen him since."

June shook her head. "I've just got back in."

"Where's that friend you had here the other day—Kieran, was it?"

"Oh, out on business. He's thinking of getting a place here. He moves around a lot—has places everywhere."

June produced a paper pad from the folder she had set by the chair, and a pen from an inside pocket. Tom seemed surprised. "What? Aren't I going to be taped or something?"

"Some things, I like to do the old-fashioned way." That seemed to put him more at ease, and he settled more comfortably. June went on, "I've never really had a chance to get into the neural dynamics: transferring the activity pattern that defines a personality from one neural system to another. I was hoping you could point me in the right direction to finding out more about it."

"Ah, yes." Tom was obviously on home ground. "That was the other big breakthrough that made TX possible, along with data-mining the DNA. I take it Leo's been through all that with you?"

"Pretty much."

"But of course, DNA can't supply the brain modifications acquired after conception—every experience from the beginning of growth can alter how neurons connect up and communicate. Indeed, they have to. That's what makes us who we are."

June nodded. "Right. I follow that."

Tom unclasped his hands to show a palm. "But it turns out that a mathematical map of the neural connection pattern is sufficient. It contains all the information you need to regenerate the personality. That means you can infer what you need from the wave functions without having to specify detail at the molecular level. That makes the problem tractable."

"In the same kind of way that the expanded DNA information lets you interpolate most of the physical structure."

"Well . . . yes, pretty close."

"Okay, that's from one brain to another. But how about the other possibility that people have been bandying about for years: uploading a mind into a totally different kind of system—holotronic or something? Do the TX processes get you any nearer to something like that?"

Tom wrinkled his nose. "In principle I guess it could work.

But to upload it into another kind of system . . . ? I don't know of anything other than a biological nervous system that could be complex enough to express the code, and at the same time be sufficiently modifiable in the way it would have to. Right now, that would be a tough one."

June detected no hint of the wariness that she would have expected in somebody skirting a potentially dangerous topic. She edged closer to the subject that she had come here to learn about. "How about transferring parts of someone's psyche, then, Tom? You know, maybe some special skill or knowledge that they have? You see it in movies, where something that a person has learned is extracted and written into a machine or whatever."

This time Tom shook his head. "It makes good stories, sure. But our knowledge of memory mapping simply isn't up to it at this point in the game. We don't have any way of telling what parts of the total pattern correspond to any particular skill or piece of knowledge, like what you're talking about."

"There's no way of identifying what would need to be selected?" June checked.

"Exactly. It's not a simple one-to-one relationship, where you can say this bunch of connections defines that function or concept. Everything interacts with everything—like the way genes affect each other and turn each other on and off. It would be like having a book in Chinese. I can copy the entire thing onto another stack of paper, or into an electronic memory, photo film, magnetic image, anything you want. That's no problem. But don't ask me what any particular piece of it means."

"So would it be the same the other way around too?" June asked, as if the thought had just occurred to her. She kept her voice even. "It wouldn't be possible to delete anything selectively either? For example, so that the Leo who gets reconstituted here ends up missing memories that the original Leo possessed downstairs?"

"No . . ." Tom frowned, seeming to find it an odd and curious question. "Why would anyone want to do that?" His eyes betrayed no inkling of alarm or suspicion. He mulled over the suggestion for a second or two, and then his mouth curled in a parody of a grin, revealing uneven teeth. "Why, has Leo been forgetting things? What kind of stuff are you writing, June? This is starting to sound more like one of those thrillers with people getting brainwashed—" At that moment, his phone beeped.

Ignoring his pocket unit, he reached out to activate the flatscreen on one side of his desk. A female voice that sounded like Herbert Morch's secretary upstairs answered.

"Tom, I've got Herbert for you."

He gestured toward the screen. "Excuse me for a moment, June. Rank is being pulled."

"Mind if I have another look at the machine?"

"Go right ahead."

With all the activity around it through the final days, June had never really had a chance to see the reconstitution chamber since its last details were added. Stewart Perrel had shown her and Kieran the finished object briefly, but the lab had been crowded and distracting then.

She set her note pad on the desk, got up, and sauntered over between consoles and a droning coolant pump. The inside of the chamber was cramped and close, full of sensors, scanning arrays, tubes, and cabling to the point where it seemed a human body couldn't be squeezed in among it all. Kieran had said it put him in mind of some of the early space capsules he had seen in museums. The volume where the form was reconstituted had to be enclosed because of the strict environmental controls that were needed, and the positioning requirements necessitated limb, body, and head restraints. Leo had described how his most vivid sensation on regaining consciousness had been the heat and the clamminess in there. Not for the squeamish or the claustrophobic, June decided.

The walls of the chamber were bedecked with pipe and cable clamps, boxes and gadgets—even the inside of the access door, with its collection of labels and warnings: EXTERNAL LATCH OVER-RIDE ACTIVE; CHECK PRES EQ; TEMP ALARM . . . She leaned in and stared around. Whatever motives may have taken possession of the original Sarda sometime before the crucial day, the guy had guts, Kieran had declared—he'd given him that.

Something registered as odd about the inside of the door. And that was ridiculous, because this was the first time June had studied it in any detail. Yet the strange feeling persisted that something was missing. But how was she supposed to know how it should have been? It could only be from the replays of Leo's exit that she and Kieran had watched earlier that afternoon. Something was different.

She looked back across the lab. Tom was still engrossed, talking to Herbert on the screen. June took out her comset and keyed in the code to access her personal net files, obtained a directory on the unit's miniature screen, and routed the replay through. The image was too small to resolve any detail. She slid out the spectacles from their pouch at the back of the case, put them on, and brought up a high-resolution image that she was able to manipulate like the version on the mural panel in the apartment. As she stepped through the frames, she saw what had triggered something in her recollections. In a close-up of Sarda emerging from the chamber, the interior of the access door that swung open behind him showed a patch of color that was not on the inside of the door that June was looking at now. She zoomed in, and the patch expanded to become a curiously vivid design of a purple disk inside a silver outer ring containing a spiral pattern of colors. June moved the spectacles down her nose and was able to identify the place on the inside of the door that it had occupied. There was nothing like it there now. Touching it with a fingertip, she felt a faint stickiness of what could have been a remnant of adhesive. Something had been there, sure enough.

She was still staring at the spot bemusedly when Tom joined her again. "I've been shut up in there myself a few times when we were building and calibrating it," he commented, looking past June's shoulder. "Pretty daunting, if you want my opinion. Better Leo than me."

"Well, he's through it now," June said. "Time for him to be celebrating and relaxing, I'd imagine. It must have been pretty tense for him." Keeping her tone chatty, she remarked, "Too bad he doesn't have a Mrs. Sarda or current ladyfriend to share it with . . . at least, I've never heard him talk of one."

"I think he mentioned somebody once or twice several weeks back, but I guess that must have passed. He's been too busy most of the time." Tom looked curious. "Why?"

"Oh . . . just feminine nosiness, I guess." June stared at the inside of the door as if there were something mildly puzzling, and then pointed to the space she had been looking at. "Am I imagining something, Tom? Leo showed me and Kieran the chamber when he was here a couple of days ago. The place was full of people and it was all a bit hectic, so I could be mistaken. But was that

space empty before? I seem to remember something being there—
a kind of colored graphic design."

Tom looked at the spot and shrugged. "I can't say I remember anything." Evidently he considered it a matter of no consequence. He turned his head and nodded back in the direction of his desk. "Anyway, where were we? I'm afraid I'm going to have to wrap this up pretty soon for now, June. Something urgent has come up. But we can continue again another time."

"No problem. Let me know when you're free again. It's been interesting. Thanks."

Tom was okay, June decided as she went back to her own part of the building. Selective erasure by manipulating the neural codes wasn't feasible. Mentally, she crossed it off the list of things to be pursued further.

Kieran sometimes said that Sherlock Holmes had been wrong in his much-repeated quote that "When you have eliminated the impossible, then what is left must be the truth." When the impossible was eliminated, what was left was the possible. Only in the simple, artificial world in which Holmes existed did that always leave a single, straightforward alternative to be considered. In the real world it almost always left several, all equally plausible. The problem lay in finding which was correct. Sometimes it left nothing at all, which meant starting out again, all over. Real police work, and real science, began where Holmes left off.

She wondered how Kieran was doing in following up with Trevany. That seemed an even more slender hope. And they didn't have a lot of time.

# ⋙ 10 ⋘

"Well, I'll be! What gives, partner? I didn't even know they'd let you back on the planet."

Mahom Alazahad was six foot three at least, a coal-black Sudanese with the shoulders of a bull, chest of a gorilla, and handshake like a power vise. He greeted Kieran in a loose purple robe embroidered with flourishes of silver thread, a bright red fez sitting in a nest of fuzzy hair, and a grin like an organ keyboard splitting his ample, fleshy features. On a previous visit, Kieran had denied having anything to do with a series of strange misfortunes that befell a security company that had been getting over-zealous in persuading Alazahad of his need for business protection.

"Good to see you too, Mahom. How's the machinery moving?"

"Oh, you know how it is. Just trundlin' along. How about you? Still seeing that gorgeous woman you got—lives out on Nineveh, by the lake?"

"You bet."

"And how are you doing, guy?" Mahom leaned down to administer Guinness a couple of powerful pats on the shoulder. "Hey, lookin' good, boy! Lookin' good. Is this man still causing all kinds of trouble?"

"Actually, I'm here for purely domestic and respectable reasons this time," Kieran said, letting his gaze wander around the vehicles lined up on the lot, and the collection of miscellaneous machinery in the yard by the office building behind.

"Yeah, right. That's how it always starts."

"I do believe I detect skepticism." Kieran looked pained.

59

"Who from? Me? What are you talking about? Okay, so, what's going on?"

Kieran led the way over toward a selection of pricey but better equipped, high-performance models that he had spotted, grouped to the side for the more discerning. "It's time I found myself somewhere a bit more permanent here, Mahom—Mars is the center of a lot that's going on. That means I'll need to be able to get around. What have you got?"

"You name it. If I haven't got it, I can get it—and for you, Knight, a better deal than you're gonna find anyplace else. What did you have in mind? I've got a hot contact in personal flymos right now."

"Leave the flymobile for later. Let's stick to wheels for the moment."

"I hear you."

"Fast but maneuverable. A good looker is always nice, but no fake cosmetics. Something tough that'll handle well off the road and deal with the soft patches. Full satellite com and nav, emergency backup on all essential systems. Probably gas or hydrazide turbine-electric. Military-spec shocks and suspension; pivot axle; individual wheel drives are a must. Forget induction pickup, optimizing overrides, and any smart automatics."

They stopped in front of a Euromco Brigadier: gold sheen with dark strip inlays, sleek but with rugged foundations, tan upholstery. Kieran looked it over, then looked at Mahom inquiringly. Mahom shook his head. "Rich kid's toy. Okay for picnics and day trips around the domes. But the forced-flow oxidizer will kill your range out on the surface." He put a hand on Kieran's shoulder to draw him to the dark blue Kodiak next to it. Guinness stiffened and growled a warning note.

"It's okay. Just say hello again for a second," Kieran said. Mahom stretched down a hamlike hand for Guinness to check over with his nose. "Friend," Kieran told Guinness. "Remember? Keep it in your filing system this time. Friend, okay?" Guinness wagged his tail, evidently happy.

"Degenerate hydrogen reactor driving a closed-cycle turbine," Mahom said. "That's the way things are going to go. One recharge will last a year. Take you around the planet."

"When they get it right. I heard this is practically a prototype." It was a new technology being pushed by one of the

Martian home manufacturers running on a stretched budget and high hopes—but allegedly they knew their stuff.

"It's solid enough," Mahom said. "But the competition is making them cut back too much on costs for the home-grown models here. They've put the know-how into a new, deluxe production design that'll be coming out of the lunar factories." He winked knowingly. "Loaded. Got double-sealed shells. Terran government subsidies picking up the tab. The word isn't generally out yet, but I got an advance order in for a few. What I'll do is rent you this until the first ones show up. You can get the feel of how it works, make up your mind then. Should be around a month. Does that sound good?"

Kieran walked slowly around the Kodiak, taking in the light yet robust frame, generous ground clearance, splayed wheelbase for stability at speed. A chrome logo affixed to the trunk carried the proud message: SUPPLIED BY ALAZAHAD MACHINE. The dynamics of gravity wells made it actually cheaper to ship loads from the lunar surface to Mars than from Earth to Luna. And if governments back on Earth were trying to extend political influence to the Moon by making their taxpayers help him buy a car, why should he turn it down?

"The new one'll have a version with collapsible rear seats that'll turn the back end into practically a hatch-top truck," Mahom said, following him with his eyes. "You won't beat that for versatility. CO-two compressor-reservoir boosted cooling, specially developed for Mars. For you, fifteen percent off the regular price. Flat four hundred a month on the rental in the meantime. That's a steal all by itself."

Kieran opened the two doors on the side nearest him and leaned in to look and poke around. The interior was finished in soft black with gray trim, comfortable and spacious, though with minimal extras as Mahom had said. Guinness bounded in and took possession of the passenger seat, panting and looking back at Kieran as if to ask what they were waiting for. He seemed to have made *his* mind up, at least.

"I have to go out to Stony Flats this afternoon," Kieran said, straightening back up. "Let me take it out there for a test drive, and I'll let you know tomorrow after I get back. How's that?"

"Sounds like we've got a deal, Knight. I just need to take a swipe of your license in the office, and we'll pick up the key. Then you're on your way."

They crossed the rear yard through a mix of commercial vehicles and various wheeled, tracked, and balloon-tired, earth-moving, digging, and drilling contraptions—even one on legs. There was a Chinese army personnel carrier that had found its way to Mars through God-alone-knew-what machinations, and numerous partly dismantled bodies and frames that would never, of their own accord, move again. Just before they reached the office door, Mahom beckoned Kieran over to a door in a square concrete building behind the office shack, which he unlocked. He flipped on the light inside to reveal racks and shelves packed with handguns, shotguns, assault rifles, submachine weapons, several plasma cannon, a row of machine guns, and seemingly every form of ammunition conceived by man, ranging from twelve-clips for automatics to hand-launched antiarmor projectiles and grenades. "I wondered if you needed to do any shopping in the accessories department too, while you're at it," he explained, beaming.

"Mahom, I'm just driving out to see a geologist, not starting a war. But if I ever decide to, I promise I'll let you know."

"Okay. Just checking." Mahom turned out the light and locked the door again. "But in the meantime I'll be looking into getting a good flymo for you. I haven't forgotten about it."

"I'm sure you haven't, Mahom," Kieran agreed with a sigh.

# ≷ 11 ≷

A road climbing a series of hairpin bends through one of the side canyons, then upward between crumbling buttes of wind-worn rock and sandy hills, led out onto the more open plain. The air was hazy, the sky above, a curious pale pink that seemed faintly luminescent. For the first ten miles or so, the landscape was being submerged by a rising tide of interconnecting living complexes, bubble towns, industrial buildings, and farm canopies, all tied together with a thickening web of roadways, tracks, power grids and pipelines—the ground-level testimony to the spreading of humanity that Kieran had seen in his descent from orbit. Farther out, the desert reasserted itself to preside over a scattering of domes and isolated structures. Kieran remembered scenes he had seen in Japan, where cities flowed away into the distance until the details of individual houses merged and were lost in continuous ribbons that looked like glaciers filling the valleys between the mountains. He wondered if it would be like that here one day.

Stony Flats was the new, hardly-more-inspired name for what had once been designated Marineris Central 2, one of the original bases from the first phase of manned landings and consolidation on Mars. Since then, the early huddle of domes and dugouts had grown to become a collection of transport depots, maintenance hangars and freight buildings clustered beside an airfield that had a rail link to the Cherbourg spaceport. This was where off-planet shipments through Cherbourg connected to the surface air, road, and rail network. Kieran called ahead and was directed along a ravine to one of several truck-size airlock doors built into the base of the escarpment on one side. Above the locks, the slope was cut into terraces of building frontages with windows looking toward the airfield, where long-winged, gooney-bird-like soarers and thrust-assisted STOL/VTOL transports came and went, stirring up flustered clouds of pink Martian dust.

After negotiating the double-lock doors, Kieran drove into a brightly lit, concrete-walled cavern containing a number of ground vehicles with people working around them in the main floor space, a workshop area to one side, and a row of enclosed offices on the other. Large double doors opened through from the center of the wall at the rear. He identified the gray-headed figure of Walter Trevany, wearing dirt-stained olive coveralls, standing with a man and a woman, both younger, in front of a large, square-built truck suggesting a military version of a miniature mobile home or RV. Its side doors were open, and a litter of boxes and equipment lay around outside. Trevany watched the Kodiak draw to a halt and came over as Kieran got out to be greeted by the noise of riveting from the far side and the intermittent flashes of welding in a screened-off corner of the workshop area.

"Dr. Thane . . . ? Ah, yes. I remember your face now."

"Hi."

"You found us all right, then?"

"No problem. Your directions were fine."

"Oh . . . You're not alone." There was uneasiness on Trevany's face as he stooped to peer into the car.

"Stay," Kieran told Guinness, who was watching him inquiringly, ready to get out. Guinness emitted a resigned snort, shook his head, and settled back down. Trevany looked relieved. "Not keen on dogs?" Kieran said.

"Oh, I don't mind them. In fact, I've had a few. But in here . . ." Trevany swept an arm to indicate the surroundings. "Machines and things. People would get nervous."

"I understand." Kieran stood looking over the vehicle with interest. Trevany had described it over the phone as a mobile lab. There were a lot of electronics inside, a desk extending from one wall with chairs facing on either side, a work area with bench space, closets, tool and instrument racks.

"I'm only recently in from Earth," Trevany said, following Kieran's gaze. "Which is why I've been staying at the Oasis. I'm joining some colleagues who have been setting up a base camp out in the highlands at Tharsis, as I think I said. This lab will be leaving for there in the next few days."

Kieran nodded. The region lay about nine hundred miles to the west of Lowell City, a little north of the equator. "What are you up to out there?" he asked curiously.

"Are you much into Martian geology?"

"Some."

"Basically, we're part of a revisionist school that's challenging the orthodox thinking about Mars and its history. It all got bogged down in the same dogma that held everything up on Earth for a couple of centuries: the conviction of slow, uniform change—that everything can be explained by the same processes we see going on today, at the same rates, if you extrapolate them back far enough."

"So I take it that you and others in the business don't think so," Kieran said.

Trevany shook his head. "Everywhere you look, the evidence is staring you in the face that the whole planet was torn up by violent upheaval in the recent past—tens of thousands of years, thousands maybe; not billions. It used to have oceans and a denser atmosphere. What happened to them? Even by the orthodox establishment's own figures for meteorite infall, wind erosion, and dust transport, the water channels and most of the craters should have been erased long ago. They're new, not even begun to be worn down in a lot of places. Even the place we're in right now is part of a floodplain. And look at the systems of crustal cracks and fissures. Something jolted the whole planet, maybe wrenched it into a different orbit."

"Do you think that could be connected with the catastrophe that some scientists say hit Earth around twelve thousand years back . . . whatever it was?" Kieran asked.

Trevany looked surprised, as if he hadn't expected such a question. "Nothing's proved yet. But what do I think?" He bunched his mouth and nodded. "If I had to bet, I'd say they were both part of the same thing."

"So, what about the advanced culture that existed before then?" Kieran asked.

"The Technolithic."

"Yes. Where do you think it originated?" Besides the form that the cataclysm had taken and exactly when it had happened, that was another aspect that different schools of opinion clashed and debated over. Some accepted this early culture as having been native to Earth; others, less inhibited and more iconoclastic, believed that it had come from elsewhere.

"I'd say the jury is still out on that one," Trevany said. "But you never know. Things that turn up in places like this, for instance, could throw more light on it." Kieran got the feeling that the geologist could have said more. Suddenly, he was curious to know what the expedition to the Tharsis region was hoping to achieve and what was going on at the base camp that Trevany had mentioned. But Trevany halted things there with a shrug. "Anyway, that's not what you came here to talk about. Do you want to come inside, out of the noise? Maybe you could use a cup of coffee or something?"

"Sounds good."

They began walking toward the row of offices. "So what kind of a problem has Leo been having?" Trevany asked. "Sarda, you said his name was over the phone, right?"

"That's right. How much did he tell you about what he does?"

"Not a lot. It sounded like some kind of biological research."

They came into the office. There was an empty desk, a table strewn with folders, drawings, and papers. Maps and charts filled the walls between shelves full of oddments and boxes. A girl working at a screen shifted her eyes to nod at them perfunctorily. Trevany led Kieran across to a side table with a coffee maker, fixings, and some snack offerings.

"He's with a sunsider outfit," Kieran said as Trevany poured two cups. "They're into a line of neurological work—figuring out how memory, behavior, and things like that are coded. It involves probing around in the brain with fields and imagers, seeing what you can extract and change." Not quite accurate, but it sounded like the kind of thing a doctor would be into. Trevany nodded in the way of someone who had heard about such things but couldn't contribute much, and offered one of the cups. Kieran took it, declining cream or sweetener. "It seems that some of Sarda's memories have been affected. We're trying to map the damage and see what can be done to fix it."

"What a strange situation to be in," Trevany commented.

"It's a strange kind of work," Kieran said.

"Very well. So how can I help?"

"By answering a few questions, if you can. They may sound odd, but we have our reasons for asking them."

"Okay."

Kieran paused, indicating with a movement of his eyes the girl working at the screen. Trevany nodded that he understood and led the way into a smaller, empty office at the end, closing the door.

"You said you met Sarda there before?" Kieran resumed.

"Yes, in the bar at the Oasis, right outside the restaurant. I'd seen them at breakfast too, although we hadn't spoken then."

"'Them'? You mean him and this woman he was with? You said her name was Elaine."

"Elaine, right. We were at close tables in the bar one evening. I recognized them as guests too, and started talking. You know how it is—new here; it's natural to want to get to know people."

"Sure. How did they seem? Sociable? Friendly enough?"

"*He* did—as much as you'd expect. But the woman seemed reluctant to talk. Kept drawing him away. That was why I was surprised when he acted the way he did in the restaurant."

"Hmm." Kieran pondered on the information. "Did they say what they were doing there?" he asked finally.

"Just that they stayed there sometimes. It's not exactly the kind of situation you quiz people about when you don't know them."

Kieran paused for a moment, then said in the tone of someone finally deciding to share a confidence, "We're trying to find this Elaine. Sarda has blanked out completely, and we think she can provide us with important information. Can you describe her as best you can remember?"

Trevany thought hard but couldn't add much to what he had said previously. "She was tall and slim-looking, black hair, curly—up high, off her neck, not long. Kind of a pointy-nosed face."

"What was she wearing?"

"Seemed to like black. Shiny pants, tight. A black top with it. It could have been a shirt, coat, or sweater. I can't really remember."

"Anything else?"

"Nope. I don't think so. That's about it. Sorry . . . I don't think I can have been a lot of help."

"I appreciate it anyhow. . . ." Kieran paused to think back over what had been said. "Actually, you have helped—quite a lot.

What date was it when you talked to them in the bar? Can you remember?"

Trevany frowned. "Can't recall the exact day. But it was during the second week I was there. So it would have been between the thirteenth and seventeenth . . . somewhere in there."

Kieran produced a calling card and handed it across. It bore just his name with the initials KT emboldened, a General Net personal code, and a cartoonlike figure bearing a sword and shield. "Would you let me know if you think of anything else?"

"Sure." Trevany studied the card curiously. "What kind of a doctor is this?"

"It's an old symbolic representation of the hospitaler Knights of St. John. The tradition goes all the way back to the crusades. Very prestigious."

"Oh yes. I think I might have heard something about that."

"Very possibly," Kieran agreed, smiling enigmatically.

What Trevany had said that Kieran found interesting was that Sarda and Elaine had been hotel guests. That implied they were more than just casual acquaintances. Yet that afternoon, at Kieran's urging, Sarda had gone through his records and belongings but could find no trace of any Elaine in his life: not a picture, address, phone number, memento. But then again, if his original self had been part of the conspiracy, he would have removed all such traces, Kieran supposed.

However, hotel guests have to pay the bills. If Sarda was keeping a low profile at the time, as Kieran guessed would have been the case, then in order not to leave any paper trail that could point to him, there was a good chance that Elaine would have covered the charges. So even if evidence of her existence had been removed from Sarda's personal environment, it might still be in the hotel's records. "Worth a try," he told Guinness as they drove back through darkening shadows down the twisting canyon road into Lowell. "If you don't buy a ticket, you don't get a prize. Isn't that right, now?" Guinness blinked, yawned, and returned his attention to watching the landscape outside.

Once inside the pressured zone, Kieran followed the highway along Gorky and turned off at the Cherbourg tunnel exit leading beneath the plateau to the underground levels of the spaceport, its service facilities, and the Oasis hotel.

# ⁑ 12 ⁑

Kieran and Guinness arrived at the Oasis bar to find business warming up for the evening. Patti, whom he and June had met at the pool in Nineveh three days before, was on duty as he had hoped, and recognized him as he slid onto an empty bar seat. She had auburn hair tied in a ponytail and was wearing a white top with shorts. "You did! You remembered!" she exclaimed, looking down over the bar. "Hi, Guinness! Did you come all this way to see me?" Guinness thumped his tail on the table behind, read the tone, and returned a look that asked how she could ever have thought otherwise.

"You're lucky," Kieran said. "He was practically adopted by a gang of kids over in Nineveh."

"We don't have any stout—see, I remembered. What else can I get for you?"

"Let's see. What haven't I tried before?" Kieran scanned his eye along the shelves and settled for a glass of a local brew called Olympus.

"So is that where you live, Nineveh?" Patti asked as she poured. "It's a nice area. I had a boyfriend out that way not long ago."

"I'm staying there. Visiting," Kieran said.

"With that person you were with—June?"

"Uh-huh. Her cat and Guinness are in the process of disputing territorial claims."

"I liked her." Patti frowned and tried to remember, but had to give up. "Sorry. You're . . . ? I know it started with a K."

"'Kieran' to most people who like me. All kinds of things to the rest. Some of the names, you've never heard of. Shouldn't want to, either."

69

"Kieran, that's right." Patti set the glass down on a coaster. Kieran tried a taste and nodded. "So what brings you to Mars?" she asked. "What do you do?"

"Oh . . . a bit of whatever needs doing. Right wrongs; slay dragons; rescue damsels; vanquish villains . . ."

"And check out bars," Patti completed. Kieran waved a hand to say "whatever." "I'm a cat person too," Patti said. "What kind of a cat does June have?"

"All black, kind of in between long-hair and short. Mean and ornery most of the time. I prefer them that way. A real cat—not rubbing up all over you all the time."

"A he or a she?"

"A she. Her name's Teddy."

"Teddy?"

"Well, it's actually Nefertiti. But June says she could hardly go around calling her Titty, could she?"

Patti stifled a laugh and looked away, shaking her head. Two more customers had come in and were waiting a short distance away. "I'll be back in a moment." She straightened up and moved along the bar to serve them.

Kieran took a handful of peanuts from a glass and flipped one to Guinness. "So I think we'll use you for the bait, will we?" he said as the dog gulped it out of existence and waited for another. "Yes, it's about time you did something to earn your keep again. We will, so. Look your best—pitiful and appealing, now."

Patti came back and watched as Guinness caught another couple of peanuts. "Would you like to take him off my hands for a few hours from time to time—out somewhere for walks or something?" Kieran asked nonchalantly, keeping his eyes on the dog.

"Are you serious?"

"Oh, sure, why not? I'm here on business, so he has plenty of spare time. I get the feeling you'd enjoy it."

"Could I *really*? That would be terrific!" Patti looked down over the bar, still seeming unsure if it was a joke. Guinness looked back and blinked, doing his best to look pitiful and appealing.

Kieran let his voice fall. "If I said okay, then is there a chance you could do me a little favor that I'm in need of?" he said.

A flash of suspicion crossed Patti's face, then cleared as she realized it wasn't a proposition. "What kind of favor?" she asked.

"At the pool the other day, you said you were a trainee here—rotating around to get some experience at all the jobs."

"That's right. What about it?"

"Have you done the front desk yet? Taken care of the accounts and so on?"

"Sure. That was the last thing I worked before the bar. Why?"

Kieran straightened back onto the bar seat to lean closer. "There was a couple staying here about a week ago—between the thirteenth and seventeenth. I only have the woman's first name. I need to locate her. She might have paid their bill. If so, it'll be in the accounting records."

Patti looked uneasy now. "What are you asking me to do?"

"Check the payment slips between those dates and see if any of them match her first name. Let me have the details of any that do."

"But that's confidential. You could get me fired."

"Then I'll make sure you're better off than you would have been if you weren't fired."

"What are you? Some kind of investigator?"

"You could say that." Kieran's tone was serious now. "Look, this guy is a friend of mine. The woman has embezzled quite a sum of money from him. If we recover it, I'll make sure that your part is generously appreciated." He waited, read the uncertainty still lingering on Patti's face, and added, "And he's a good friend of Guinness's too. If the thought of a healthy lining in your bank account doesn't grab you enough, then do it for him. Look at those eyes. How could you refuse a face like that?"

Patti wrestled inwardly for a few seconds more, then gave up with a sigh. She looked around instinctively to make sure no one was within hearing. "I'm not promising."

"I never asked you to. Just see what you can do."

"What's the name?"

Kieran took one of his cards and wrote *Elaine* on the back, and the dates in question. For good measure, and just in case he was mistaken in his guess, he added *Leonard Sarda* too. "Either of them," he said. "Call the number on the other side if you come up with anything."

Patti took the card, glanced at it quickly, and put it away in a pocket of her shorts. Guinness looked up at her and thumped his tail trustingly in a way that told her he knew she'd do what she could.

✧      ✧      ✧

When Kieran checked with Sarda later, the problem had been getting worse. Charges that he knew nothing about had been mounting on various of Sarda's accounts. On trying to use one of his cards, he had been told he'd instructed its cancellation and replacement that morning. The bank was beginning to doubt his stability. He couldn't make an issue of it for fear of stories getting out that might adversely affect confidence in the project.

# ⋙ 13 ⋘

June looked at Kieran reproachfully over the dinner dishes on the table in the apartment. "You used Guinness? What a deplorable debaser of young innocents you turn out to be. You'll be pimping next."

"Shameless," Kieran agreed shamelessly. "Although I think the demand on Mars must be pretty near saturated already. Ah well, not to worry. Now I can always be a geologist." He had summarized his conversation with Trevany and the work that his team was engaged in.

"What do you think of all these different accounts we get of what happened to Earth twelve thousand years ago—and now Mars, by the sound of it?" June asked him. "I've heard, let's see . . . the giant-comet-that-became-Venus theory; the some-other-comet-but-not-Venus theory; wobbling crust; unbalanced ice caps; war between alien visitors; ancient civilization that screwed up in a big way . . . And I'm sure there are more. Which one do you subscribe to? Any?"

"They're like religions: I love 'em all." Kieran emptied the last of the wine into their glasses. "Diversity is a sign of health and vigor. It's appropriate to the way things are happening out here. Obsession with conformity in everything, and trying to impose it—that was what stifled Earth."

They collected their glasses and took them over to sprawl facing each other from opposite ends of the couch, legs intertwined comfortably. "So how's Mahom these days?" June inquired.

"Still in one piece, strangely enough. He's got a whole arsenal out back there. It wouldn't surprise me if he's made customers out of those heavies who tried to put the squeeze on him a while back."

73

June took a drink. "So what do you think of the Kodiak?"

"Impressed. I'll be interested to see this new range from Luna that he talked about. . . . The only thing, though, it looked blue. But when you get out in the sun it's more of a hideous French-hooker-panties color—kind of a dark purple."

"And how would you know what color panties French hookers wear?" June asked.

"Purely by repute. Didn't you know? In any case, I'm extraordinarily well and widely read."

"I heard somewhere that there isn't a word in English that rhymes with purple," June said distantly.

"Nonsense. A modicum of ingenuity and erudition produces rhymes with anything," Kieran assured her.

"Go on, then. Give me one," June challenged.

Kieran lifted his glass to hold it poised between fingertips, contemplated it with a faraway expression for some seconds, then looked up and offered:

> "When you're choking, turning purple
> A hearty slap and one good burp'll
> Usually fix it."

"Kieran, you're impossible," June sighed. "Okay, they say the same thing about 'silver' too. I bet—" A tone from Kieran's comset interrupted.

"Always, just when you've gotten comfortable." He got up from the couch and crossed to the breakfast bar, where he had put the unit. "Hello?"

"Hello? Is this Kieran Thane?"

"Hi, Patti," he answered, recognizing the voice. "That was quick. Don't tell me you've got something already?"

"I was right here, so I figured maybe there was something in the bar tabs. And there was."

"You'll make a professional for sure. And?"

"There was nothing on the guy. But I got two for the woman's name that you gave me. The card details were all I could get from here. I copied them into my phone. Can I download them?"

"Sure." Kieran keyed in the code to accept a transfer, and moments later the display confirmed its completion.

"Will you need more from the registration records, like you said?" Patti asked. "That might be a bit more difficult."

"Let's see where we get with this first," Kieran said. "But either way, I think you've earned a bonus. We'll give it to you when you pick up Guinness. What do you want to do, collect him here sometime? You said you know this area."

"Okay . . . but I'm not sure when. It would depend on my next time off. And when Grace can get out too."

"Anytime. I'll wait until I hear from you then."

"Well, I'm still working right now, so got to go. I'll let you know." Patti hung up.

Kieran turned back toward June, who had been following, and announced, "Nothing on Sarda. But two Elaines settled bar bills during the week that Trevany said. I've got the card details in here." He waved the phone. "Can you do your stuff on it?" Researching hard-to-find information was part of June's business. She had her own ways of tracking people down.

"Let me see." June got up, took the phone from him, and carried it over to the office corner of the living area. She sat down at the com system, activated a screen, copied in the details from Kieran's phone, and quickly became absorbed in taking things from there. Kieran stretched out on the couch again and dove into the *Kodiak Owner's Manual*.

After ten minutes or so, he looked up and stared across at June's back as inspiration struck.

> "Gold and silver,
>   Presents wilvir-,
>   Ginity tend to,
>   Put an end to."

He waited. June ignored him. Wasted talent, he told himself, and returned to his book.

"Aha!" June announced thirty minutes or so later.

"Are we in business?"

"Listen to this." June half-turned her head, reading from the screen. "The first is an Elaine Dorcavitz. I've got a log of other payments showing she was just here on a short visit, passing through. She's from a remote habitat out in the Belt, already left Mars."

"Scratch one Elaine," Kieran pronounced. "But my psychic radar detects emanations of excitement concerning the other."

"Elaine Corley," June supplied. "Address: 14B Watergardens, Embarcadero! I've got a picture."

Kieran got up and went to look over June's shoulder, stroking the side of her neck absently. Embarcadero was the wider, southwest-turning canyon arm of Lowell, formed by the merging of Gorky and Nineveh beyond the Trapezium. It consisted of a professional business park and expensive residences and boulevards built around a network of waterways.

The woman looking out from the screen had black hair, short and curly. Her face was pale, high-boned, with a tapering chin and thin around the lips—not unattractive for those who liked their women intense and serious. She looked about right. But there was only one way to be surer.

"Let's see if Walter can verify it," Kieran said. "Can you open me another channel?" June gave him a line on another screen and copied through the image. While Kieran called Trevany's number, June carried on delving further into the records she could access on Elaine Corley.

Trevany's face appeared on the screen that Kieran was using. "Hello? Oh, it's you again, Dr. Thane." June turned her head at the mention of the title, rolled her eyes upward briefly, and went back to what she was doing.

"Yes," Kieran said. "I hope it isn't late for you."

"No way. We're going to be up all night on this. What can I do for you?"

"I've got a picture here of who I think is the Elaine you saw with Sarda at the Oasis. I'd like you to have a look at it."

"That was quick work." Trevany looked surprised.

"I said you'd been more help than you thought. Anyway, here it is." Kieran got the prompt and sent the image.

"That's her," Trevany said without hesitation.

"You're sure? No doubt?"

"No question about it. Well, I'm glad you seem to have solved your problem, Doctor. I hope Sarda recovers."

"Thanks. And good luck with your field work. We'll be in there rooting for you, waiting for the orthodoxy to crumble."

"Well, it might take some time yet," Trevany said with a sigh.

As Kieran cleared down, June nudged him with her elbow.

She read: "Elaine Lydia Corley. Profession, nursing practitioner. Specialty qualification, neural physiology." June glanced up and sideways. Kieran whistled softly. "And listen to *this*. Currently listed as the professional partner of a Henry Balmer, associated with the Lowell Medical Center as well as running a private practice. And of all things, Balmer is registered as a psychiatric hypnotist!" June sat back and turned from the screen. "Could it be we have a way of selectively erasing slabs of memory here?"

Kieran hoisted her effortlessly to her feet, turned her around, and kissed her. "Lovely, I do believe you've cracked it!" he exclaimed. "I always thought you were a true genius. It must rub off. I think we should call Leo and get him over here right away."

# ⤜ **14** ⤛

Sarda stared at the features of Elaine Corley being presented on the screen and shook his head. He had listened to the account of Kieran's doings, heard Trevany's story, and was still incredulous. "Nothing. Not a thing," he declared. "If I hadn't heard what you've just told me, I'd be quite confident in saying I've never seen her before in my life."

"So she isn't someone you've known for some time, and just your memories of her recent involvement in this scam are erased," Kieran checked from the couch. "You must have met her fairly recently. All recollection of her existence has gone."

"That's the way it looks," Sarda agreed, turning back toward him.

Also, if Sarda had known her for some time, others would surely have been aware of her—such as Tom Norgent, Kieran reflected. "And you don't know Henry Balmer," he said.

"No. Never heard of him." Sarda shook his head. "Hypnosis. To tell you the truth, I've always been skeptical of the claims that it could do things like this. So that's how you think they did it? Some kind of posthypnotic suggestion, triggered before I came out of the reconstitution chamber."

"It had to be the graphic design that disappeared from the inside of the chamber door," June said from her desk area. "It would have been one of the first things you saw when you became conscious—and you couldn't communicate anything you might have known in the moments before it took effect, because you were still inside." She looked across at Kieran.

"Neat, eh?" he said.

There was a silence while June finished keying something in, waited, and contemplated the result. Then she turned in her chair to face them. "Then it seems we're close to being able to reconstruct what happened," she said. "Leo and Elaine met fairly recently, maybe socially." She looked at Sarda. "You told Kieran you were under a lot of emotional stress as the time got nearer—and I can believe it. Could you see yourself looking for company to help with the . . . how should I put it—tension-easing?"

Sarda stared at her moodily for a moment; then his expression eased to a faint smile. "I suppose that would have been more-or-less in character," he agreed gruffly.

"Could you have talked to somebody like her about the fears and misgivings you told Kieran about?" June asked. "It would seem understandable enough to me." It was a delicate question. She was asking him, in effect, if he might have discussed sensitive details of the project with an outsider whom, when all was said and done, he couldn't have known too much about. Everyone in the room knew that people did such things. It was a different matter to admit to it openly, though.

Sarda considered the question. "I guess something like that would probably depend on the relationship—you know, how close people get to each other. . . ." He glanced at Kieran, who was listening but saying little. "Oh damn, why am I trying to rationalize? Yes, I could have talked to her about it, sure."

"Including that there was five million in it up-front for you if you came through okay?" June said.

"Well . . . maybe after a couple of drinks? . . . Yes, it's possible."

June looked from one to the other in a way that asked what more needed to be said. "So Elaine goes back and tells Balmer, and they come up with the idea that the original Sarda doesn't have to go through with the negative side of it at all. With a little bit of help, he can preserve himself. And more. For a share of the proceeds, they can help him collect the dues that he's figuring should be his anyway, since he's taking the risks. It makes sense . . ." Sarda made a face that said he wasn't so sure. June broke off and looked at him questioningly.

"That mightn't be the way it was," he pointed out. "It could have been me. I might have come up with the idea after I found out that Elaine works with a medical hypnotist, and offered them a share because I needed the help. Or maybe I thought the whole idea up, tracked Balmer down as a necessary accomplice, and Elaine was drawn in later. See my point? Maybe you're not being fair to them."

Kieran found himself warming toward Sarda. And yet he could only conclude that the other Sarda—the original—must have been a very different animal. It was as if, in some Jekyll-and-Hyde kind of way, the process brought out different aspects of the same personality. Or maybe it was the different psychological factors operating before and after.

June hesitated and thought about it. "But it works the same either way," she observed. "Balmer sets Sarda up with a post-hypnotic suggestion that will cause him to forget everything concerning the plan moments before he comes out of the machine. Elaine switches a body from somewhere for the original Sarda, connects it up, and inserts a patch of simulation code into the monitoring computer so that it carries on generating the right readings. It would probably be late in the evening on the day we had lunch—after the authentication procedure. Then she goes upstairs to the R-Lab and removes the graphic . . ." June looked inquiringly at Sarda. "Would she be able to get into Quantonix to do it?"

"With authorization from me to enter the building, and given the right access codes? The place was quiet that night. Yes, I could see it being possible."

June turned to Kieran with an air of finality, as if that ought to clinch everything. Sarda's expression said that he couldn't fault it. They waited expectantly. Kieran stared back at them with an enigmatic expression. There was a short silence. "What do you think?" June asked finally.

Kieran took a few more seconds to be sure of his thoughts. "I think there has to be more to it," he said. After giving them a moment to register that they were not home and dry yet, he explained, "A three-way split of the five million that had been lodged in the Lowell Barham Bank? Yes, it's enough to get you through a cold winter or two, I'll give you that. But would it really justify established, professional people getting involved in the complications and risks of something like that? And why is Sarda-One still here, fooling with cards and credit accounts? If he cleaned Leo out as soon as the payments were in the bank, why stay around waiting for something to mess up? Why didn't he just grab what he'd got and run?"

"Maybe . . . to create more mischief first," June offered. "Getting even with his envied alter ego . . . I don't know, Kieran."

"I can't see it." Kieran shook his head.

"So what do you think?" Sarda asked him. It was a strange question—asking Kieran to guess what he himself might be up to.

"There must be more to it," Kieran said again. "They're holding out for bigger pickings yet. But time isn't on our side for finding out what. As soon as whatever it is is in the bag, they'll be gone."

Sarda suddenly looked worried. "Then what else is there to do? We have to confront them right away with what we've got. Call in the fraud people."

"And do what?" Kieran asked. "What have you got? No evidence. Sarda-One stays in hiding, and you've got nothing except a crazy story."

Sarda colored. "I've got a hole in my bank account where five million used to be. Isn't that enough?"

"So somebody smart figured out how to bust a security system," Kieran said. "That's happened before. Do you think that Crime Investigation is going to need a theory about walking duplicate people and suppressed memories to explain it?"

Sarda glanced appealingly at June, as if for support, then back at Kieran. "But . . . what else is there to do? You've just said, we have to move fast."

Sarda was looking desperate now, but Kieran remained unruffled. His eyes twinkled with the light of something new that had occurred to him, which was proving irresistible. June saw the signs of one of his schemes about to be hatched. "The only ones who know what's going on are Sarda-One, Elaine, and Balmer," Kieran replied. "And the only way we have for finding out fast is getting them to tell us."

Sarda shook his head, confused. "How in Hell are we supposed to do that?" he demanded.

"Do what they did and turn it around at them," Kieran answered. "We use *you* to impersonate yourself, Leo. Have you ever been on the stage?"

Sarda shook his head. "No." He looked nonplussed.

Kieran grinned in a way that radiated reassurance and seemed to promise that they were going to enjoy themselves. "Then let's start your dramatic coaching right away," he said.

## ≋ **15** ≋

Elaine lit a dreamer, inhaled, and waited while the first calming fingers began creeping from her lungs into the tissues of her body like water percolating through desert sand to find the roots of a thirsty plant. Then she crossed the living area of her home in Embarcadero to the veranda window and stood looking down at the canal and water gardens below, drawing in and exhaling several more times before feeling the full effect.

Having to try to act normally to keep up appearances had been bad enough during the regular day. Now, being on her own while Balmer met with a banking contact in town to arrange disposal of the proceeds, and Sarda lying low, she was finding it tougher. Step by step, she had felt herself being drawn into an entanglement that had progressed from trying to help someone who hadn't deserved the bizarre situation he had gotten himself into, to collusion in embezzlement and fraud, and now outright theft on a major scale, with somebody she was no longer sure she wanted any part of at all. She wasn't comfortable, but the feverish pace they were committed to allowed no time to extricate herself. All in all, she was very nervous.

She was no longer sure, even, where she planned to head for if they pulled it off. Earth had little appeal for her—fine if you moved among the privileged ranks of traditional social sets who lived above the rules, or the supporting castes of acolytes and technicians who engineered their comforts; but not for outsiders. Her misgivings about any kind of future with Sarda had grown worse by the day, and even with a third split of the cool billion that Balmer was hoping to net, she didn't know enough about the ways of the Belt or the outer systems to feel anything but apprehension at the thought of trying to make it in places like that alone. Continuing any kind of partnership with Balmer wasn't an option. She admitted to herself that it had been only ambition and an unseemly dose of career-consciousness on her part that had kept her with him this long; and after watching the prospect of big money drive him like a mania to concocting the scheme they were all now committed to, it would be all she could do to see it through to whatever end lay ahead. In odd moments she had even caught herself wondering if she—and Sarda, for that matter—could ever feel safe with Balmer out there in control of a third of a billion, knowing that they shared his secret. So what sort of paranoia was possessing her now?

Some friends of hers were crossing a bridge over the canal below. One looked up in the direction of Elaine's window. Elaine stepped back, not wanting to be seen. Two months ago, such a thing would have been unthinkable. What was this business doing to her already?

The house system beeped an incoming call. Elaine moved back across the room and sat down to take it on the screen by the corner recliner. It was Sarda. Elaine was perplexed. "Leo? What do you want? You know we're supposed to stay strictly off any communications. . . ." She noticed the background; it looked like a residence. It wasn't the second-rate lodging out near the far end of Gorky, where he was hiding out, away from anywhere he might be recognized, until the time came for him to play his role. "Where are you?" she asked him.

Sarda ignored the question. Concern was written all over his face. "There's a problem. I have to talk to you right away. Never mind whatever we said before. Everything's changed."

"Has Henry—"

"Never mind Henry. This just concerns us. I need to see you now. Can you meet me?"

A protest started to form on Elaine's lips, but she stifled it before it could turn into words. There was something different about him, in his voice and in his eyes. Even in those few seconds she could feel it. For the first time in weeks she felt herself responding to the person she had laughed and loved with, then found herself falling for . . . only to watch him turn into a stranger. Something had happened—something concerning *them,* not Balmer's insane scheme. That had to be what Leo wanted to talk about. She gave a quick nod. "Where?"

"You can get out by car okay?"

That seemed an odd question. Leo knew that she drove. She nodded again. "Of course."

"There's a strip of commercial places called Beacon Way, on the north side of Gorky near the Cherbourg tunnel. I'll meet you at an auto, truck and mobile plant dealer's there called Alazahad Machine. It's closed, but I'll be in the office. Don't tell anyone. Come alone. Shall we say half an hour?"

Again, it seemed an odd place to choose. Elaine hadn't known that Sarda had connections with places like that. But it made sense that he would want to avoid public places, she supposed. "Very well. Half an hour," she agreed.

It was dark when Elaine found the strip of small office units, industrial shops, and fenced lots that formed Beacon Way. The artificial illumination inside the city was phased to match the natural daylight cycle outside. Round-the-clock lighting had been tried in earlier days, but most people found they didn't like it.

A flashing sign of garish lights and colors announced the presence of Alazahad Machine. The place comprised a typical-looking office cabin and adjacent workshop tucked behind a distinctly non-typical assortment of vehicles and other equipment. A more solid-looking, windowless, concrete building stood immediately behind. Lights were showing in the office. A car was drawn up outside, standing apart from the stock models lined up along the front. Elaine drove in and parked next to it. It was empty, a Kodiak of some dark color impossible to discern under the flashing colors from above. A more sober mood had come over her on the way from Embarcadero. Perhaps her anxiety, wishful thinking, and the dreamer she'd been smoking had caused her to read too much into what she thought she had seen. Bracing herself to be prepared for a disappointment, she went inside.

But the person sprawled leisurely and smiling in the leather chair behind the desk in the chaotic office, his face thrown into relief by the sole light from the lamp standing at one end beside him, wasn't Leo at all. Dressed casually but elegantly in a blue jacket with white shirt, he was lean and tanned, with a regally cut face of strong jaw, sensitive mouth, and narrow nose and cheeks, the overall effect softened by wavy brown hair. His eyes were pale blue, fixing her with an intensity that was unsettling despite his relaxed posture and easygoing expression. "Elaine, I take it," he greeted cheerfully. "I'm so glad you could come. Sorry about the late hour and the mild deception. But as you yourself are only too well aware, we don't have a lot of time." He indicated a chair already drawn up on the far side of the desk. "Make yourself comfortable. There are some coffee self-brews if you'd like."

"Who are you? Where's Leo?"

"Kennilworth Troon, at your service. Or, I suppose it would be more precise to say, at Leo's. I'm representing him. You could say, as a kind of attorney."

"Whatever this is, I don't want any part of it." Elaine's reaction was automatic. What she meant was that she didn't want to be involved in anything deeper than she was in already. Before she had registered any conscious decision, she had turned and started opening the door. And then she stopped. He had called no warning, done nothing to stop her. She could sense him watching her. If she had been happy with the existing situation, she wouldn't be here. If Troon's appearance meant there was a way to change it—for better or worse as the case may be—there was only one way she was going to know. His manner was telling her that she was the one who stood to be affected. It was up to her. She closed the door and turned back. Troon waved again at the chair, still smiling, as if he had been waiting for her to arrive at the inevitable for herself.

"Would you like something?" he asked again as she sat down. Elaine shook her head. "Probably best. I'd imagine you've had enough stimulants and depressants today already, one way or another. It's the stress of these situations, you know. Plays havoc with the nervous system."

Elaine's faculties were regrouping after her initial confusion. "What kind of attorney are you?" she demanded. "Who ever heard of meeting for business in a place like this?"

"The owner is an old friend of mine. I can recommend him personally if you're ever interested in getting a good deal from inside the trade. You'd need to know how to bargain, though." Troon looked around. "Actually, you're right. It was something of a psychological ploy, I suppose. You'd hardly have expected Leo to suggest some public place, would you?"

How much did this man Troon know? Where did he fit in? Elaine couldn't even begin framing guesses. "Where is Leo?" she asked again.

Ignoring her question, Troon recited, "Elaine Lydia Corley. Current residence, 14B Watergardens, Embarcadero. Profession, nursing practitioner with a specialty in neural physiology." The clear blue eyes fixed on her, losing a shade of their playfulness. "Just the person who'd know how to resuscitate a body from stasis suspension and substitute one that was past caring; also, how to tell a monitoring computer to carry on reporting what it's supposed to be seeing . . . if anyone should want to do something strange like that. But there's no saying what some people might get up to, is there?"

Cold, clammy feelings slithered down Elaine's spine. Knots tightened in her stomach, and for a moment she thought she was going to be physically sick. When she tried to lick her lips, she found that her mouth had gone dry. She opened her purse on her knee, rummaged for the tube of "tigers," and shook one of the yellow-and-black capsules into her palm. Troon unfolded from the chair and walked across the office to pour a cup of water from a dispenser by the window. He was tall, powerfully built, but moved lightly with catlike economy of effort. Elaine popped the capsule into her mouth and took the cup when he offered it, but her hand shook, spilling some of the contents. Troon took the cup from her and held it while she sipped and swallowed. She nodded in acknowledgment. He set the cup down on the desk, went back around to the other side, and sat down.

"Also, the professional working partner of Henry Balmer," he resumed as if nothing had happened. "You know, I've always been fascinated by hypnosis. Can it really do all the things you hear about—deaden pain, make people ten times stronger, enable them to recall things they thought they'd forgotten? It's supposed to be capable of doing the opposite, too: people can be made to forget a whole chunk of their life, just on experiencing a post-hypnotic trigger . . ." Troon shrugged, as if trying to think of an example. "Maybe a graphic design that they've been programmed to respond to. Do you think it's possible, Elaine? Can Henry do things like that?" He paused, pointedly. "Or could the popular beliefs be overrating things a bit? Might it not work as well as it's supposed to sometimes?"

Elaine felt any inner resistance she might have mustered collapse in defeat. There was no point in trying to bluff or evade. He knew everything. And the only way he could have known was as he had just intimated: the posthypnotic suggestion hadn't worked properly; the other Sarda had come out of the process remembering. The whole scheme was blown. . . . She looked up to meet Troon's eyes as the implication hit her. He seemed to be waiting, as if reading her thoughts and giving her time to put the obvious conclusion together. At least, in his own strangely capricious way, he had shown grace enough to spare her a direct conflict from the beginning.

"He was the other Leo—the one that I talked to," she whispered.

"Of course. You've got your one hidden away somewhere. We've no way of tracing him."

The call had been a trick. She stared at the cup in front of her on the desk, and considered her options now. Troon waited. She could get up and leave, putting herself back in the situation that had been getting more unbearable by the hour; or she could wait and see what kind of alternative there was. Put that way, it didn't leave a lot of choice.

"Very well, Mr. Troon," she acknowledged. "What do you want?"

He nodded in a satisfied way; at the same time, his manner became businesslike. "I think you've worked out for yourself what happened. I can't guarantee anything, but obviously your best way to make things easiest for yourself would be to cooperate and come clean. We need to know where the original Sarda and Henry Balmer are now, and how far they've progressed with the rest of the plan. . . ."

Elaine had stopped listening somewhere around halfway through what Troon was saying. She gasped barely audibly and slumped back in the chair, shaking her head in protest. For what it meant was that the Leo she thought she had glimpsed again briefly on the screen less than an hour ago, the person she had felt for and wanted to preserve, was the one who now knew her only as a betrayer. Revenge would be his only motive now; restitution, his object. The only Sarda she had prospects of sharing the future with was the one at present in hiding—the one she had come to despise and reject.

All she knew was that she couldn't face the Leo that Troon

was presumably intending to confront her with now. Somehow she was on her feet, as if another power had taken over her body and she were just a spectator of its movements. "I'm sorry, I can't . . ." She clutched a hand to her mouth. "It's too much. . . ."

Troon watched, his eyes reading her intently; yet he remained sitting, unmoving. She turned, and the surroundings blurred into a tunnel of confused impressions leading her toward the door; then she was outside in sudden darkness beneath the flashing colored lights, and climbing into her car. She was vaguely aware of starting the motor, backing out from beside the Kodiak, expecting Troon or someone else to run out and stop her. But nothing happened. Then she was back on the roadway and heading in the direction of Lowell center. . . .

When her mind began functioning coherently again, she was through the Trapezium and halfway back to Embarcadero, with no clear recollection of getting there.

# ⇗ 16 ⇗

Sarda burst out of the side room opening off Alazahad's office just as Kieran turned the overhead light on from the switch by the door. "*What do you think you're doing?*" Sarda demanded shrilly, waving his arms in agitation at the door. "You let her go! Now she'll go straight to Balmer and the other me with the story. . . . And we still don't even know where they are!"

The outer door opened, and June came in with Mahom. They had been positioned outside in one of the cars lined up on the front of the lot. One press of the *recall* button on the phone in Kieran's pocket would have activated June's number, giving them the signal to pull up behind Elaine's car to prevent her from leaving. Evidently, Kieran had chosen not to. "What happened?" June asked, sending a puzzled look from him to Sarda.

"He . . . he let her go!" Sarda stammered. "He had her cold. I heard everything. She'd as good as confessed. Another half hour, and we'd have found out all we needed to nail them and get the money back."

"Yes, you could have gotten the money back . . . and lost her," Kieran said to Sarda. "I presumed you'd rather have both. Actually, I think you can do better still."

Sarda's sails crumpled, windless. "What are you talking about?" he retorted.

"Hey, trust the man," Mahom told him. "If I know anything, it's that the Knight has his reasons."

"You don't remember anything about her," Kieran said.

Sarda shook his head. "Of course I don't. All I *do* know is that I'm in a hole for five million, and you just let somebody walk away with it."

"That's the problem. You don't *know* how it was with you two." Kieran waved a hand at the comscreen on Alazahad's desk. "Replay that call you made to her earlier this evening and *look* at it," he said. "Look at what it's telling you. And I saw it all over her face here again just now."

"What? You saw what? What are you talking about?"

"She's in love with you, man! *You!* The Leo she used to know, before he started having ideas about getting even with his other self, and turned into someone else. She didn't get mixed up in this for a share of any money. She did it to keep the man she had *then*. Was she supposed to trust this process that everyone said would create the same person, identically? How could she? He didn't even trust it himself."

Sarda gave June a bemused look, asking if it made sense to her. For the moment she could only return a shrug. "But you didn't talk about anything like this," he objected, looking back at Kieran.

"I didn't have to. Her face and body language said it all—plus the fact that she came here. . . . She came because she thought she would find someone she'd lost."

"Well, maybe." Sarda seemed none the wiser. "But I still don't see what good it did, letting her go like that. Why do it?"

Kieran sighed patiently. "When you called her earlier, she assumed you had to be the original, as we intended. But even in that short time she saw the Leo that she'd known at the beginning, who didn't know anything about this scheme that got dreamed up later—because that's exactly who you are. She thought that the original had somehow reverted to what he had been. But then she realized that *her* Leo—the one she came here to find—is now the enemy, itching to get even." Kieran gestured toward Sarda in a way that said the proof couldn't be any plainer than that. "She couldn't deal with it for the moment, so she left. If we'd wheeled you in at that point, it would have created a fight between the two of you that could never have been mended. Oh, sure . . . a half hour with the hot irons and the thumbscrews, and we could probably have learned all we needed to take everything to Herbert and Max, stop whatever Elaine's friends are up to, and recover your five million. But whatever you and Elaine had would have been lost. And I happen to think it was something worth trying to hang onto, Leo."

June was staring at Kieran with a look that seemed to say that no matter how long she knew him, he would never cease to amaze her. Alazahad had no idea what was going on, and was happy to leave everything to the rest of them.

Sarda looked at Kieran uncertainly, apparently expecting more. Kieran's manner suggested that he'd said all that should be necessary. "So what happens now?" Sarda asked finally, at the same time glancing at June to ask if he had missed something.

"We wait for her to come back," Kieran said, as if it should have been obvious. "Well, not literally here, of course. I assume she'll call."

Sarda was still not really any nearer. "How do you know she'll do that?" he asked.

"Well, I don't in any mathematical sense. Call it an instinct derived from many years of intense application to the study of human nature. If all the—"

"*Wha-at?!*" Sarda emitted a strangled protest verging on a shriek. His eyes bulged; his yellow mane shook; his shaggy mustache took on life and bristled. "You're telling me now that this whole thing is based on nothing more than a *hunch* of yours?!"

"Instinct," Kieran corrected. "More refined, less impulsive. It carries imputations of greater sophistication and more solid groundings in reality. The weak part about relying on logic is always in the assumptions."

"Whatever—I don't care. But holy Christ . . . !" Sarda waved both hands while he sought for words. "What I'm telling you is, there's nothing to stop her going straight back and blowing everything. And all you're telling me is that you don't *think* she'll do that! That really makes me feel a lot better, Kieran. You're gambling five million of *my* money—"

"Mine too," Kieran pointed out. "You more or less insisted yourself that you expected me to have a stake in this."

"Making decisions concerning my personal life that I don't recall ever being invited to give an opinion about . . ."

"It was hardly a feasible option at the time."

"I don't know anything about this woman," Sarda fumed. "What if I don't *want* this romance that you're so touchingly keen on restoring?"

"If I'm right, we still stand to do a lot better. They have to be into this for more than just a split of five million. To find out what, we need Elaine as a willing ally through choice, not a reluctant snitch who was bullied into divulging the minimum she could get away with. I'm prepared to gamble that her feelings for the Leo-who-was will make that choice."

"And what if you're wrong?" Sarda asked dubiously.

Kieran clapped an arm cheerfully around his shoulder as they headed for the door, while Alazahad turned out the lights. "In that case, Leo, I know just the person to go to who can make us forget our sorrows and everything connected with them," he said.

They drove in the Kodiak through the tunnel connecting Gorky canyon to Nineveh, heading back to June's place, where Sarda had left his own vehicle. In his own mind, Kieran allowed that Elaine would need time to wrestle with her thoughts and reach a decision. In the meantime, he was trying anything to distract Sarda from constantly trying to come back to the subject.

"I was thinking over what you said about DNA being the program for a complete, self-assembling factory—much more complicated than any program people have ever written."

"Uh-huh." In the seat behind Kieran and June, Sarda returned from other ruminations. "Unimaginably more complicated. The whole set of plans needed to build a spaceliner wouldn't make a dent in it."

"So could a program like that just have written itself—out of random accidents, for no reason?"

"What makes you think it did?" Sarda asked.

Kieran shrugged. "That's what they taught everybody when I went to school."

"Outside of Earth, nobody in the business believes that anymore," Sarda said. "Start changing lines of the machine-tool codes for making spaceliner parts at random, and you'll end up with a pile of junk—if anything works at all. With what you're talking about, it's a lot of trillions times more guaranteed. In short, it's ridiculous." He seemed about to elaborate further, but then his eyes wandered away, and he pulled pensively at his mustache. "How can you be sure? I can't believe you just let her walk away. We're fooling ourselves. She's not gonna be coming back."

"Just give it until morning, Leo."

"We might not have until morning. They could pull out and be gone anytime."

"Not if they're involved in higher stakes. Nothing's going to happen tonight."

"But how—"

"So why are things different on Earth?" June asked Sarda, turning her head from the seat beside Kieran.

"What? Oh . . . it's the same as with a lot of things. They've all got turf and reputations to protect. I used to be an orthodox materialist once. But the more I thought about it, the more I came to see their line as being as dogmatic as the fundamentalism that it was invented to replace. That was why I decided to move out—to be part of an environment where questioning is permissible and it's okay to look at alternatives."

"So what do you think?" Kieran asked him. "Where did genetic codes come from?"

"Nobody knows. It's what a lot of scientists out there are trying to figure out. . . . But I'd guess there has to be some kind of intelligence at work. You can't get away from it."

"Sounds like you've got a religious side, Leo," June commented.

"Not really—not the way most people think of it, anyhow. But yeah, I think that the original religions—before they got corrupted and sold out to politics—encapsulated a lot of genuine ancient knowledge. The truth will turn out to be more exciting than anything people ever dreamed up."

For a while, Sarda fell quiet. Kieran waited hopefully for some even deeper philosophical revelations and speculation.

"And even if she wanted to, how could she get back? She doesn't have your real name, and you didn't give her a number."

"Love will find a way, Leo," Kieran sighed.

Sarda called from his office the first thing next morning, while Kieran and June were finishing breakfast. "I got a message from Elaine!" he announced. "She called my administrative assistant at home—either she knew the name already, or she tracked it down since last night. She wants to know how to contact Mr. Troon."

"Now do you believe in instinct and the arcane arts of divining human nature?" Kieran asked him.

"Okay, yeah, yeah. You were right; I was wrong . . . maybe. So what do I do?"

"Give your assistant my number and tell her to relay it back," Kieran replied.

Elaine was through in less than fifteen minutes. "I'm sorry about last night," she said, when Kieran answered. "I was confused and upset—but I think you knew that. I've been thinking about things, and I'd like to talk. It needs to be as soon as possible. Where can we meet?"

# ⅗ 17 ⅖

Elaine was noticeably red around the eyes and yawned intermittently—no doubt the result of a lot of thinking and not too much sleep. They met on a bench in a secluded corner of a leafy square on the administrative side of the Trapezium, facing a sculpture depicting a group of Lowell's space-suited founders from the early days. Events, it turned out, had followed roughly the lines that June and Kieran had surmised.

"I met Leo casually not all that long ago. It was at one of those dinner parties where everyone tries to impress everyone else with how much they're making. We were both bored and a bit repulsed by it all, and got to talking between ourselves about . . . well, the things Leo talks about. Interesting things, exciting things—things that have imagination and vision. I was captivated. We clicked, arranged to meet again . . . You know the kind of thing."

Kieran nodded. "This was how long before the experiment?"

"A couple of months, maybe. As we got to know each other, he told me more about his research and its implications. I was blown away. He was right on the cutting edge of this speed-of-light travel anywhere in the Solar System that people have been hearing about for years—and outside it too, one day, I guess." Elaine drew a long breath and exhaled. "He told me about the experiments they did with animals and things. Then, one day he told me he was scheduled to be the first human to try it. I started to get nervous, asking him how sure they could be that things mightn't be happening in animals that it wasn't easy to know about. . . . And eventually, I guess to try and be reassuring, he confided that it isn't quite the way everyone thinks—you know, that you disappear from one place and reassemble in another. What it actually does is make a copy. Did you know that? And so for things not to get completely crazy, you've got to get rid of the original. Once the process is running commercially, it'll be so fast that nobody will know the difference. But for the first experiment that Leo was going to be involved in, they kept the original in a suspended state—for a few days, until they could be sure. That was why he said I shouldn't worry."

"Yes, I do know that," Kieran answered. He looked at her curiously. "So did you worry?"

"Not at first. Leo had this line that said switching the personality to the duplicate was really no different from what happens naturally in the course of years ..."

"Yes, I've heard it. Leo told me."

"He made it sound believable, and I accepted it. . . . But as the time got nearer, he started to act less sure. It got to be as if he were trying to sell himself more. But inside, I could tell: he was scared."

"I would be too," Kieran said.

Elaine seemed relieved at not having to go into details. "Well, when he came up with this idea of switching bodies so he wouldn't really have to go through with it, I was more than just willing to help. It was after I told him I worked with a medical hypnotist. Obviously, a plan like that couldn't work if the copy came out knowing everything that had happened."

"You're saying that's all it was to begin with?" Kieran checked. "You just wanted to help the Leo that you *knew* stay around— and to keep him yourself. It didn't matter what he or anyone else said about this copy who was supposed to be identical."

Elaine nodded, brushing her eye with a knuckle. "That's it, exactly. I loved him. How could anyone not sympathize with his situation? As you just said, it was to keep him. That was all we wanted. We were just going to disappear and find a spot somewhere. The copy could get rich and famous—do whatever he liked."

"So when did the notion of cleaning out his bank start?" Kieran asked.

"That came later," Elaine said. "Something started to change in Leo. He became envious, malicious, saying that *he* had earned the money and taken all the risks; why should the other one walk away with the proceeds? I wasn't so happy about the idea. But

I couldn't help feeling for him in some ways. I attributed it to the strain he was under, and let myself be drawn into it."

Kieran waited. Elaine sat staring at the sculptures a short distance away. Her manner signaled that there was more, but she wasn't sure how to broach it. "Was it really worth it?" he asked, helping her a little. "I mean, okay, a third of five million isn't exactly peanuts, I know. . . ." He watched her as he spoke. She nodded an unconscious confirmation, her eyes still on the figures. That told Kieran that only the three people were involved. "But for established professionals like you and Henry? It wouldn't justify all the complications and risks."

Elaine sighed and turned her head, finally. "Once Balmer got involved, everything was moved up to higher stakes." She gestured appealingly, as if some defense or justification were called for. "He's one of those high-pressure, over-assertive people who will always take over something like that to get whatever they can. He persuaded us that we could go for much bigger money than what Leo was talking about. Leo was interested straightaway. . . . And I was so far into it by then, I just saw no alternative but to go along."

"There was no question of setting Leo up, then?" Kieran said. "Nothing 'personal' with Balmer—on your part?"

Elaine looked horrified. "God, no! Everything with Leo had been genuine. My relationship with Balmer was just professional . . . even a bit opportunist, I guess you could say. He knew all the right people, had the contacts. He was the perfect ticket to success and career advancement—if you could put up with the rest of him."

Kieran nodded. It was as he'd thought, but he'd needed to be sure. "So how did Balmer decide to up the stakes?" he asked.

"By doing an end run around Quantonix and the client they've got lined up, and selling the TX technology elsewhere. We're talking maybe a billion here, not five million." Elaine looked at Kieran, giving him a moment to think about it. "And with Leo handling the negotiations—the one who isn't supposed to exist—you've got the perfect front man."

Kieran had already seen where she was going. "The only person the customer deals with directly is Sarda-One," he said, voicing his thoughts as they fell into line. "Not you or Balmer. Sarda does all the talking because he has the technical expertise—it's his creation. And then he vanishes. If Quantonix realizes later that it's been sold out, and if it or its client starts proceedings, any pointers that they dig up incriminating Sarda will be taken as meaning Sarda-Two—because he's the only one who officially exists. And the beauty of it is that he won't be able to help them no matter what they try, because he doesn't know anything. His memory of it has been wiped." Kieran stared at her, his eyes shining with honest admiration. It was so ingenious that it felt almost a shame to have to spoil it. "Well, you've got to hand it to Brother Henry for originality, Elaine. I'll give him that."

Elaine threw out a hand wearily. "That's it. There's nothing else to say."

"So which outfit is Quantonix finalizing the deal with?" Kieran asked.

Elaine hesitated, then replied, "Three Cs. Both the Morches and the Leo who's getting all the attention stand to clear a billion each out of it." Kieran nodded. He already knew that, of course; but Elaine's answer provided a useful check on her believability.

Which brought them to the key question that Kieran had been leading up to. He made it sound easy and natural. "So who's Balmer setting this other deal up with?" he asked.

Elaine sighed as if asking, now that she was forced to spell it out, how she could have gotten drawn in to something like this. "Some people are here in Lowell who arrived in the last few days. Leo is due to meet with them later today at the Zodiac Commercial Bank to finalize the first phase of the deal. I don't know who they represent. Balmer handled that side of things himself. But the money's coming from some shady underside of the business."

"What's the first phase of the deal?" Kieran asked.

"It's set up as a series of progress payments," Elaine replied. "A testable portion of the technology to be supplied for a quarter-billion advance. The rest payable in stages as the previously-supplied parts are verified."

"And you're saying that Leo will be handing over the first batch of information today, in exchange for a quarter-billion up-front."

"That's right."

Kieran eased himself back on the bench and let his eyes wander idly over the square and small park to one side as he digested the information. It was along the same general lines that he'd come across before. Even if the technology eventually found its way back to one of the major communications providers, outfits like that wouldn't involve themselves directly in a flagrant ripping off of property that a rival was buying legitimately. They would deal through some nebulous intermediary, possibly created for the purpose and then liquidated to erase the trail. A bogus research program would be invented as having been conducted secretly somewhere, uncannily close to what Sarda had done at Quantonix, and the alleged results of it would duly become the possession of the highest bidder in some netherworld transactions. Tough luck for Three Cs—but they were in business and knew the risks. When time is ripe for such breakthroughs, these coincidences will happen.

And then, again, the client might not be a communications carrier at all, but somebody else with other interests entirely. Such as what? Kieran had to remind himself that what they were talking about here wasn't, first and foremost, the people-transmitter that the carriers were popularizing and scrambling to acquire first, but a *people-duplicator*. He was only beginning to reflect on the possible ramifications, when Elaine spoke again. Evidently, she had more to get out, now that she was able to talk.

"Leo changed in the time all this was developing. I watched him become a different person—hard, vengeful. When Balmer urged upping the ante and going for really big money, he was all for it. But when the other Leo called last night, it was like listening to the person I remembered. Even in those few moments, I could sense the difference. It was as if . . . as if opposite aspects of him polarized into two different people." She turned to look at Kieran. "He doesn't deserve any of this. I can't let it go through—what we planned for today. That's why I wanted to talk to you."

Kieran promptly forgot the line his mind had been turning to. His brow furrowed. "What are you saying? That you're giving up the chance to walk away with a third of the loot, and are prepared to take the consequences, just to straighten this out?"

Elaine nodded resolutely; but she was barely holding back tears. "It's what's right. . . . Deep down, I guess I never was the right material for this kind of thing." She shrugged. "That's all there is to it."

Kieran turned to stare at her. A faint smile puckered his mouth as he sensed a situation of opportunity beckoning. It was exactly the kind of people that Elaine had described, whose unenlightened existence he felt it his mission to better through a little moral guidance and introduction to the virtues of munificence and austerity. "Maybe we don't have to let you go through anything quite as bad as that, Elaine," he said softly.

She produced a handkerchief to stifle back sniffles. "What other way is there?"

"I presume the initial transfer will be made into an account in Sarda's name," Kieran said. "That way, he can vanish when the time's right, and there'll be no trail back to you or Balmer for the banking authorities to follow."

Elaine nodded. "You obviously know your way around these things."

"Do you still have the graphic that was inside the chamber door?" Kieran asked. "The pattern that triggered the posthypnotic command."

"No . . . But the image is stored. I could make a copy. Why?"

Kieran felt rising excitement at the glimmering of an idea that was forming. *The original Sarda would obviously have been through the same conditioning too!* "Tell me more about this meeting that Leo's attending at the Zodiac bank," he said. "What time is it scheduled to take place?"

# ≋ **18** ≋

In the lodging at the outer end of Gorky Avenue where he had been hiding since his unscheduled resuscitation, Leo Sarda checked through the collection of documents and data cartridges making up the phase-one delivery, and arranged them in his briefcase along with the downloaded papers from the bank. The room around him was cramped, cheaply furnished, and felt squalid—construction workers' accommodations just inside one of the main locks out to the surface. He would be glad to get out of it. But he'd had to stay away from places where he might be recognized.

"Lousy five million," he snarled as he clicked the lid of the briefcase shut. Balmer was right. He would have been insane to settle for that, while his other preening, celebrity self, along with Herbert and Max Morch, and their financial backers were getting set up to share out billions. Well, he would be putting that little item right very shortly now.

He zipped up his jacket, checked one last time over the oddments strewn on the steel-frame bed and side table that he had been using as a desk to be sure he'd forgotten nothing, and let himself out into the stairwell. Two flights down, he came to a gray-walled passage flanked by entrance doors to other units, which took him out onto the shallow-stepped walkway leading down to the concourse where the maglev line ended. As he approached the terminal, a tall, athletic-looking man in a dark business suit and tie with tan topcoat—conspicuously unusual attire for that part of town—stepped forward from where he had been standing by the entrance to the boarding platform. He was smiling cheerfully and carrying a brown document folder under one arm.

"Good morning. Dr. Sarda?"

"Who are you?" Nobody was supposed to know of Sarda's whereabouts except Balmer and Elaine.

"Kennilworth Troon is the name, from Zodiac Commercial Bank. Henry Balmer wanted to be sure you arrived without mishap, so they sent a car. It's waiting on the lower level."

Sarda was suspicious. If that were so, why hadn't they called earlier? Because they were afraid he might check? "I think not," he said, moving around the stranger in a wide arc and quickening his pace.

"*Guard!*" the man commanded. A large black dog that Sarda hadn't noticed before, sitting on its haunches a few yards farther on in his direct path, stood up and growled. Sarda halted and turned. The stranger shrugged apologetically. "Sorry and all that. But as you see, I must insist."

Sarda's hand flashed inside his jacket, but even as he drew out the phone, his thumb punching in the emergency code, an arm appeared from behind him, and a black fist the size of a boxing glove plucked the phone from his fingers. He turned to find a beaming giant in a silky green coat, his eyes and teeth standing out against a jet black face, his hair wild and frizzy. "What is this?" Sarda demanded, his gaze alternating nervously between one and the other.

"Shall we?" the man who had called himself Troon invited, indicating the stairs leading down to the road traffic level.

Troon led the way down, his manner as breezy as if he were trotting down steps to the beach for a swim. Sarda followed, with the huge black man keeping close behind, the evil-looking dog trailing. Who they were or what could be going on, Sarda couldn't imagine. A rival outfit trying to steal the TX data wouldn't make any sense. The part that Sarda was carrying to exchange for the initial payment wouldn't be any use to them without the rest.

A car was standing in an open area to one side of the traffic lanes—dark blue, sleek and luxurious compared to the norm on Mars, looking out of place among the utility autos, dump trucks, and surface rovers in this part of town. Sarda didn't recognize the model, but the trunk bore a chrome logo announcing the supplier. A woman—or, at least, a figure that Sarda took to be a woman from the little he could glimpse—wearing dark glasses, head wrapped in a scarf, and a fleece-lined suede jacket with the collar turned up, was at the wheel. Troon opened the rear door for Sarda to enter. The black slid in behind him, while Troon walked around to climb in the other side, and the dog hopped up beside the woman and turned to watch its charge dutifully. "There's nothing to worry about, Dr. Sarda," Troon assured him. "Just a few things we'd like you to identify." He slid a folder out from the document case that he was carrying and passed it across. Sarda took it, opened it . . . and found himself staring at a strangely vivid graphic image which drew his gaze in a way he was incapable of resisting—a purple disk inside a silver outer ring containing a spiral pattern of red, yellow, and aquamarine. It was doing something to his mind; he could sense his thoughts coming apart, being rearranged like the image in a kaleidoscope, pieces of the picture disappearing . . . but he was unable to look away.

And then whatever had taken hold of him seemed to release its grip. He sat back in the seat, blinking and shaking his head bemusedly.

"An interesting design, don't you think?" Troon said chattily beside him. "Ever seen it before, out of curiosity?"

At the sound of Troon's voice, Sarda was able to tear his eyes away. But now his confusion was total and all-immersing. He knew Troon's name, but he wasn't sure why . . . or where he was, or how he had gotten here. The people with him had intercepted him upstairs and said something about going to a bank, but he had no idea why he should be going to a bank. He realized that he wasn't even sure *when* this was. . . . He knew he had been holed up in a cheap room that he didn't recognize, but didn't know why; and there were disassociated recollections pertaining to the experiment. He could remember the preparations, and being wired up for the scanning procedure in the T-Lab. . . . But why couldn't he remember emerging from the process in the R-Lab? There was nothing coherent after then. How long ago had it been? Did it mean that the experiment had failed, somehow? What had happened to him? Where was he now? Who were these people?

"Does the name Henry Balmer mean anything?" Troon asked, watching him intently. "How about Elaine Corley?"

Sarda crumpled up the graphic that he was holding and threw it savagely back in Troon's lap. "What is this shit?" he demanded. "I don't have to talk to you people."

Troon made a sign toward another car parked a short distance away, which Sarda hadn't noticed previously, and a woman got out. There was another figure in there too: a man, wearing a hat pulled low, obscuring his face. Troon opened the window next to him as the woman came across. She was tall and slim with curly black hair, dressed in a patterned sweater and dark pants. "Recognize her?" Troon asked casually.

Sarda jutted his jaw obstinately as she peered into the car. "No, I don't. Why should I? Look, I've just about had it with these games. Is anybody gonna tell me what's going on around here?" The woman stared at him with an expression of disbelief on her face, then shook her head. She seemed distressed, pleading almost, in a strange kind of way. So, she had problems. Sarda had plenty of his own too, just at this moment. "Who are you staring at, lady?" he shot at her. "Look, I don't know you, okay? Is that it? Everybody satisfied?" Troon nodded to the woman. She turned and walked quickly back to the other car. "Right, that's enough. I'm outta here."

Sarda made to move, but Troon's restraining grip on his arm was like a steel clamp. At the same time, the black barred his way with an arm from the other side. In the front passenger seat, the dog growled. "I think not," Troon said, echoing Sarda's own words upstairs at the terminal. The sudden authority in his voice, quiet yet insistent, would have been enough on its own to make him desist. Sarda slumped back, still angry but defeated. "Actually, we're from your medical team," Troon said. "I've got some bad news for you, Leo. Something went wrong with the experiment. We haven't unraveled exactly what yet, but you've been acting strangely, forgetting things, and getting loose all over the place. Now I have to go, but these nice people are going to take you back in again. Try not to worry about it. It's all very comfortable and civilized." Sarda could only look at him, bewildered now. Gently but firmly, Troon took the briefcase that he had been carrying. Sarda wasn't sure why he had been carrying a briefcase. "It's all right, Leo. You won't be needing this. I'll make sure that everything goes back where it belongs."

And then, before Sarda could collect his wits enough to object, Troon was outside, closing the door, and striding across toward the other car. Before Troon reached it, the woman in the suede coat started the motor of the car that Sarda was in, and he felt them moving away.

The Lowell City offices of the Zodiac Commercial Bank were located in the commercial sector at the inner end of Gorky Avenue, where it joined the Trapezium. Kieran and Sarda-Two arrived ten minutes before the time that Sarda-One had scheduled to meet the delegates from the intermediary that Balmer had set up. They were received by a bank official called Walworth, who ushered them smilingly through to a conference room where four men were already waiting. He indicated coffee brewing on a side table, an assortment of other beverages and snacks, and after gushing at them to call if there was anything else they needed, left them to conclude their negotiations privately. He would rejoin them later to attend to the details.

Two of the men were dressed expensively but flashily, one in a loud striped suit with crimson shirt and white tie, the other in royal blue with glittery links, studs, and rings. They seemed ill at ease in the bank, glancing around surreptitiously as if suspicious of bugs or hidden cameras. The man with them was plainly dressed and more easily forgettable—the technical expert, to vet the contents of the briefcase, Kieran guessed. The fourth, soberly attired in a charcoal three-piece with plain blue shirt and tightly knotted tie, introduced the others as Mr. Brown, Mr. Black, and Mr. Green, and himself as their nameless attorney. He seemed disconcerted to find that Sarda was not alone. "Who's this?" he asked, indicating Kieran. "My understanding was that you were to be the sole contact."

"Kennilworth Troon, gentlemen," Kieran said, smiling pleasantly and extending a hand. "You will appreciate that Dr. Sarda's field of expertise is limited to strictly scientific matters. In a situation such as this, he naturally feels it prudent to avail himself of professional representation—as do your own clients." He placed the briefcase he had been carrying on the top of the table and opened it to reveal a standard comscreen inside the lid, and the interior filled with wads of neatly separated and labeled documents, several folders of papers, and a multiple container for high-density data cartridges. "I think you'll find everything in order," he informed the company breezily, and gestured toward the waiting chairs. "And now, shall we get started?"

## ⚛ **19** ⚛

For the twentieth time, Dr. Henry Balmer, M.D., M.M.C.M., M.S.M.H., F.C.P., paced tensely across the plushly carpeted office of his private practice in the Trapezium's upmarket Wells Place, glared down from the window overlooking an artificial stream bordered with shrubs, which farther on joined the Embarcadero waterways system, and for the twentieth time stomped back to the desk. He had a stocky, powerful build, white hair with a ruddy countenance, and immense eyebrows which he used for effect when switching on the penetrating stare that patients usually expected. Just now, however, the eyebrows were arched into anxious contortions above a dark frown as he drummed his fingers impatiently and stared at the comscreen.

He didn't like being in situations where he had done all there was to do, and the rest was up to others. He didn't like waiting for others, and he didn't like having to depend on them. The feeling of not being in control was something he was not used to. He especially didn't like having to put everything in the hands of a scientist when this kind of money was at stake. Scientists were financially and politically naive by nature—why else would they spend their lives hiding away from the real world and dealing with things instead of people? And the ones like Sarda, "visionaries" who sought to escape even from the reality of things, were the worst kind. But it had needed to be that way. Sarda was the only one of them who officially didn't exist, and could be made to vanish permanently and untraceably after the proceeds were netted.

He extended a finger uncertainly toward the *call* button of the format being displayed on the screen. But before it made contact,

106

the unit emitted a tone, and the intercom icon indicating his receptionist and assistant, Fay, in the outer office, began flashing. "Connect," Balmer ordered.

Fay's face appeared in a window. "I'm sorry, Dr. Balmer, I know you don't want to be disturbed this morning, but—"

"What is it?" he demanded irascibly.

"Mrs. Jescombe has been through again for the third time. She's sure her attacks are about to start again, and she's insisting—"

"*Insisting?* What do you mean, 'insisting'? *Nobody* calls me and insists, do you understand? I *told* you, I have other, extremely important business to attend to today. Deal with it and fix something with her for next week."

"But she says—"

"*There aren't any buts about it.* Kindly do the job that I pay you to do, which is using some initiative and trying to think and act like a professional. That means doing more than sitting there with your brain disengaged and relaying messages. A counter robot at any workman's flophouse could do that. Is that enough for you to understand?"

Fay swallowed visibly and nodded. "Yes, Doctor." Balmer cut the call and returned to the window. A dark blue car had turned off the throughway and was following the drive toward the front entrance of the building.

On top of everything else, Elaine had been acting strangely, having to be pushed all the time—and, he got the feeling, inwardly disapproving of just about everything. As if this thing weren't difficult enough already. It needed people who trusted him and who would do as they were told, not start questioning and losing their nerve at the crucial moment. Oh, sure, she'd been all confidence and full of herself when she attached herself to him, thinking she could just use his brains and his contacts, and then move on—did she really imagine he had never seen through that? But when she and her new scientist friend came to him with their half-baked idea, *he* had been the one who'd had to take charge and open their eyes to the potential that made it really worth the risks. He'd had the feeling then that she would never have the stomach to see it through. And lately, things between her and Sarda seemed to have been cooling. With a bit of subterfuge, maybe Elaine could be induced to be content and go her way with her third of the initial sum. She had played her part now, after all. If only Sarda had stayed with the plan and remained patient, instead of letting feelings of personal revenge get the better of him over a miserable five million. That made Sarda too unreliable for any long-term consideration. But Balmer needed him around for a while, until the progress payments were completed.

In the meantime, Elaine worried him. He hadn't been able to raise her, despite making calls all morning, and she had been curiously absent the evening before. He turned, went back to the desk yet again, and tried her number once more. A code on the screen announced that she was unavailable, even on priority. Balmer swore to himself, hoping that she hadn't broken down and done something stupid at this crucial moment. It had probably been a mistake to include her in the deal at all.

The intercom icon flashed again. "*Connect,*" he snapped at the machine, and then, "*Yes? What now?*" as Fay's face appeared, looking apprehensive.

"You have a visitor, Dr. Balmer."

"Who?"

"A Dr. Sarda. He's saying—"

"*Sarda?!* What's he doing here? He was supposed . . . I'll be right out."

Fay was already escorting Sarda across the outer office when Balmer emerged. There was a confused look on Sarda's face. Balmer caught him by the shoulder and ushered him toward the doorway into his own office. "What in Hell are you doing?" he muttered. "I told you not to come to this office. What's happened?"

Sarda looked at him blackly. "Am I supposed to know you? What happened with the experiment? He told me you'd be able to give me some answers."

"He? Who?" But Sarda was taking no notice, his eyes darting around the office as if for clues. Balmer looked questioningly at Fay, who was hovering uncertainly a few feet back. She glanced toward the waiting area on the far side of the reception desk.

"He was with another man. I guess he didn't stay—a big black guy. I never saw him before."

"*Jesus!*" Balmer pushed Sarda inside his office. "Get me Walworth at the Zodiac Commercial Bank, right away," he called back at Fay as he closed the door.

Sarda shook his arm away angrily. "What's this about? Everyone's talking about banks. I was told you had answers. Now it's looking to me like you don't know anything either. I want to know what in Hell's happening. Who are you? What place is this? And why was I brought here?"

"I'm Balmer, for God's sake."

"Is that supposed to mean something?"

"Elaine's professional partner. Yes?"

"Who is Elaine?"

Balmer shook his head. This couldn't be happening. "Look, you work for Quantonix, right?"

"I'm aware of that."

"And the TX Project?"

"What's your connection with the TX Project?"

"If you want answers, just answer my questions first, please."

"I went into the process. I don't remember coming out."

"*You* never did." Balmer groaned. "Are you telling me you know absolutely nothing about our—" The desk comscreen beeped. It was Fay.

"I've got a Mr. Morch calling from somewhere called Quantonix Researchers in Lowell. He says it's in connection with the visitor you have in there: Dr. Sarda. . . ."

"Yes, yes. Put him through."

The features appeared of a fleshy faced man with thinning hair combed straight back. "Dr. Balmer?"

"Yes."

"Hello. My name is Herbert Morch. I'm a director of Quantonix Researchers, here in the city. We're looking at applications of certain quantum physical effects."

"How come he doesn't know you if you're working with them?" Sarda asked Balmer.

Balmer licked his lip. "Just give me a moment," he muttered. Then, to the screen, louder, "Yes?"

"We've just received a call from an Elaine Corley, whom you apparently know. She tells us that a subject of one of our research programs is there with you right now and is experiencing some disorientation problems—a Dr. Leo Sarda. I don't know where you fit into things, Dr. Balmer, but this could be serious. We're on our way over right now. I'd appreciate it if you'd do whatever you can to keep Dr. Sarda comfortable, and if you can, please try not to let him leave the premises. We'll be there soon. Thank you." The screen blanked before Balmer could reply.

"How long ago was the TX—" Sarda began, but the screen immediately sounded a tone again.

"Mr. Walworth from Zodiac," Fay's voice announced over the image.

"Mr. Walworth? Look, I'm an associate of Dr. Sarda, who was due to meet some people there this morning. I'm just calling to say I'm sorry he couldn't make it. We had a slight hitch." Balmer forced an oily smile. "But everything's under control. Please apologize to our clients and ask them to bear with us."

Walworth looked puzzled. "I'm not sure I understand, Mister . . ."

"Er, Balmer. Dr. Balmer."

"Dr. Balmer, Dr. Sarda was here, on time, with Mr. Troon. Everything went smoothly. They left about fifteen minutes ago."

Balmer was beyond rational thinking by now. He pushed Sarda forward in front of the screen, gibbering almost incoherently. "I'll explain why in a moment. . . . The money . . . He'll recognize you. . . . Ask him if the funds went into your account."

Still not understanding, his face darkening with suspicion, Sarda confronted the screen. "You know me, right? Were some funds paid into an account that I have with you?"

"Yes, I know you of course, Dr. Sarda. . . ." Now it was Walworth's turn to be bewildered. "But if you're *with* Dr. Balmer, why does he think . . ." Walworth shook his head, evidently deciding that it was beyond him, or else none of a respectable bank official's business. "Anyway, yes, the funds were paid into your account here, and have been transferred onward in accordance with your further instructions. . . ."

# ≋ 20 ≋

Kieran stared distantly over the remains of the evening meal, while June attended to dishes in the kitchen area. There was no word in the English language that rhymed with "orange," she had claimed. A few feet away, Teddy hunched on one of the breakfast-bar stools, eying Guinness as he lay sprawled on the edge of the living area, chin resting on paws.

> "An Irishman green,
>     Can take the potheen,
>     But an Irishman orange,
>     Just falls to the flooranj-,
>     Ust doesn't seem able,
>     To stay at the table."

He looked triumphantly across. "Were we playing for forfeits?"
June shook her head despairingly. "Kieran, you're impossible."
"But surely it can't come as a surprise. You know that my creative genius knows no bounds. In fact, I'm considering a project to popularize Shakespeare in the American South by translating it into redneck. I thought the first sample might be *As Y'All Like It*. What do you think?"
"I refuse to think anything. I'm putting it down to nonadaptation to the gravity and the air mixture here. It can affect some people strangely, you know . . ." she looked at him hesitantly, "except that for you, I suppose, it isn't that strange."
"Scoff if you will. You'll regret it one day, when women are flocking around in a feeding frenzy after they put up a statue to me in Atlanta. Or maybe they'll give my name to an expressway

111

across Alabama and the Carolinas. Won't you feel proud to have known me, then?"

"Are you sure you wouldn't rather an airport?"

Kieran considered the suggestion gravely. "Well, okay . . . but I wouldn't settle for less than international."

Before June could reply, the room's sound system chimed for an incoming call. She took it on the comset that she had placed nearby, listened for a few seconds, and then switched the call to the mural screen in the living area for Kieran to join in too. "It's Leo and Elaine, from Phobos," she informed him. "Donna got them places on a Triplanetary lifting out tonight. They're just about to board."

"Splendid!" Kieran got up and moved to the couch to be in the wall unit's viewing angle. June joined him a moment later. The screen showed Sarda, minus mustache and with his hair trimmed and darkened, pointing a comset while he stood with Elaine, both wearing sunglasses-like imaging spectacles, reflected in one of the mirror panels provided in public places to afford two-way visual connection for handheld devices. Their old feelings had come back in a flood within hours of pulling off the stunt the day before. Kieran had urged them to get away from Lowell that same night, before any repercussions had a chance to catch up with them. They had been sitting out the day at the transfer terminal on Phobos while one of Kieran's ubiquitous "friends in the business" juggled with reservations and pulled wires.

"Hey, Kieran, so we're on our way," Sarda greeted. "TP Sirius clipper, lifting out at three-ten local standard for the Ceres sector. After then . . ." he shrugged, grinned, and gripped Elaine's hand, "who knows?"

"Well, I've no doubt that you'll both end up doing something interesting," Kieran said. "There's enough in the kitty to keep you comfortable for a while, anyhow. Just watch the deals out there. If it sounds too good to be true, then it probably is."

"I don't know how to thank you enough for what you did," Elaine said. "June, I'm so glad that you picked a man who's curious about everything."

"It can have its moments," June answered dryly.

"Our commission more than covered the costs," Kieran said. "So, you see, I'm just as brazen and commercial as the rest, really."

Sarda shook his head. "No, not like the rest. Never. You're something else . . . 'Knight.'"

"And how's Guinness?" Elaine asked.

"Fed, content, and at peace with the limited part of the world that interests him."

"We were thinking you should have called him Sirius," Elaine said. "The Dog Star. Get it? He is one."

Kieran smiled. "That's good. I wish I'd thought of it."

Sarda moved the spectacles a fraction to look around. "Well, it looks as if we're going to have to be moving. It's all been a rush here at the last minute, but I'm glad we had a moment to call. Thanks again from me too. It goes without saying that if there's ever anything we can do . . ."

"I'll want to know what you get into next," Kieran said. "So you'd better stay in touch from time to time. You've always got the number on the card."

"You can count on it," Sarda promised. "So . . . take care for now."

The two figures on the screen waved; then Sarda pressed a button on the unit he was holding, and the image vanished.

"And a happy-looking couple they make, doubtless destined to live so forever after, wherever they end up," Kieran pronounced. "A pity that people will still have to be shut up inside tin cans for weeks or more to get to places, though—for a while yet, anyhow. With Sarda-the-First walking around not knowing what day it is, the word's probably going around the business already that the process is fatally flawed somewhere. No one's going to be interested in touching it now. There simply isn't a marketable technology anymore."

"And it's probably just as well—until somebody comes up with a way of doing it right," June said. "They thought they could pull a fast one, and it backfired. Let's face it, Kieran, the world and beyond isn't ready for something like TX yet, and probably won't be for . . . I don't know, maybe a century. Look at the mess it got into with just one, carefully designed experiment. Even the guy who practically invented it ended up not being convinced. Look what it did to him." She shook her head. "You couldn't turn something like that loose on the public. Can you imagine it going on everywhere at the rate of millions a day? The whole Solar System would be turned into an insane asylum within a week."

"And that's not even part of it," Kieran said.

"What do you mean?" June asked.

"Something I've been thinking about on and off ever since Elaine and I talked about it in the park. We don't know that the deal Balmer was setting up was with another of the trans-system carriers at all. It could have been with interests having totally different aims."

"Other than a light-speed teleporter?"

"Exactly."

"Such as what?"

"How about what you told me it was in the first place?" Kieran suggested. "A people-duplicator. Think of all the things you could do with that. Your life insurance company keeps the record on file. If anything happens to the original, they can provide a replacement. Or if the talents of rare genius are priceless, then why not enrich the condition of the human race thousandsfolds by mass-producing them? Come to that, why expend effort selecting and training lots of near-good experts like sports stars, élite military, and so on, when you can concentrate on getting just a few right and then copy them? What kind of crazy social dynamics might result from people making two of themselves to share the load—or three, or four. . . . See—there's no end to it. That would make what you're talking about seem as sober as a convention of judges."

June frowned at him in the reflexive way that said there ought to be something wrong with it, but then seemed at a loss to pinpoint what. Her expression changed to one of perplexity. "Why does it always take someone else to point out the obvious?" she asked.

"Because it's always the last thing you think of," Kieran replied. "For the same reason that you always find things in the last place you look: Who's going to carry on looking for something after they've found it?" His voice took on a more ominous note. "But there's another side to it too. What if the wrong people got their hands on something like that? How about that bunch who wiped out the people on the *Far Ranger* and tried taking over Urbek, for instance? Knight's Pest Control Inc. might have taken care of them this time, but what if there were dozens of the leaders loose to start up all over again? See my point?"

"You're thinking that Balmer might have been selling to people like that somewhere?"

"It makes you wonder, doesn't it?"

"Then I'm even more sure that it's better with things the way they are for a long time yet." June leaned back along the couch with a faraway look on her face, stretching out a hand automatically as Teddy jumped up, wanting attention. "You know, the only thing I feel bad about is Herbert and Max. They put everything they had into it; worked as hard on their end of the operation as Leo did; compensated him for the risk he was taking. . . . It doesn't seem right that he and Elaine should fly away to start anew, while they're left to count the losses. It's just feels, some-how . . ." She caught the look on Kieran's face. "What's so funny? I don't happen to think they deserved it. They got it right, for heaven's sake, Kieran! Their project worked! Only now, they'll probably never even know."

"Well, there is one more little detail I didn't want to go into until I was sure the money transfers had gone through," Kieran said. "A quarter of a billion would be a bit much for Leo to handle. Sums like that do strange things to people, and always to the detriment of their personality. Take Brother Henry, for example . . . Oh, don't get me wrong. Leo and Elaine will have more than enough to keep the autochef stocked and start up their own operation—and if my instinct is anything to go by, it won't be long before Leo's into something far-out again. And naturally the KT retirement fund has benefitted not inconsiderably. . . . But on top of that, some time this afternoon, Herbert and Max should have found a substantial credit paid into Quantonix's account from an anonymous source that will be impossible to connect with anything that happened yesterday. It should be ample to get them going again. I just hope they pick something a bit less zany, and think it all the way through next time."

June threw her head back with a laugh of delight, then leaned forward to fling her arms around Kieran. "I should have known! It's just like those guys you played cards with at the terminal, coming in. You're just too soft to leave it any other way. Please don't ever stop being soft."

"Well, I guess it means I'll never end up running something like Three Cs," Kieran commented. "But I think I prefer life better this way, nonetheless." He eyed June circumspectly. "Would you be interested in a ten-million-a-year Three Cs CEO?"

She shook her head. "Too self-important and serious. It would probably mean hearing about nothing but money all the time. And besides, who'd think up the silly rhymes?"

Kieran leaned back and clasped his hands behind his head. "Fine. I've been here five days, and look what you've got me into already. So now what are we going to do about this vacation I was supposed to be coming here to have, where absolutely nothing untoward or out of the ordinary was going to happen?"

# THE KHAL OF TADZHIKSTAN

# ≋ 1 ≋

The residents' association of the complex of which Park View Apartments were part was considering a proposal for a neighborhood restaurant and bar with dance floor, to be added down by the lake. The dance floor could also be used for classes during the day. Of course there were objectors, who believed that such a construction would be a first step toward destroying the rural atmosphere of the area. A countergroup had formed and was collecting signatures of support.

Kieran tossed down his pen as June came over to the breakfast table with the coffee pot to refill their cups, reversed the sheet of paper that he had been writing on, and slid it next to the copy of the petition list that June had left laying out. "What do you think?" he asked. The paper showed his own renderings of the last six names to have been added.

June studied them. Each signature was reproduced flawlessly in its own distinctive style, as if photocopied. "Scary," she pronounced. "Remind me not to leave my checkbook laying around while you're here."

"The secret with forging a name is to do it upside down," Kieran informed her. "That way, the eye interprets it simply as a graphic. You don't see words, and so the letter-writing part of your brain isn't jumping in trying to write them its way."

"Have you ever heard of handwriting being hereditary?" June asked as she sat down. "Mine's practically the same as my mother's, yet we went to school and grew up in totally different places. I've heard other people say the same thing too."

"Hm. I really don't know. . . . Can't think of any obvious reason why it should be."

"Neither can I. That's why I was curious."

"That's something we should have asked Leo. It sounds like his department." Kieran picked up his coffee mug and sat back. He looked at June, his eyes twinkling mirthfully. "Speaking of which, I wonder how much sense they're managing to get out of Sarda-the-First back at the firm." June would be going in to Quantonix that morning. The news from the day before was that the incoherence of the Sarda who had been collected from Balmer's office, and his evident memory loss of practically everything that had happened since the experiment, were causing consternation. Everyone there naturally believed he was the one thought to have been transported through the process successfully, since none other was supposed to exist. It was generally assumed, therefore, that some calamitous flaw was revealing itself, and an air of gloom had settled over the project. Kieran hoped that his anonymous donation to the solvency fund would help make the gloom not quite as deep as it might otherwise have been.

"The last I heard, he was being thoroughly obnoxious and uncooperative," he said. "It's uncanny how different sides of him seem to have polarized into two different individuals. I wonder if—" A tone from Kieran's comset announced an incoming call. He reached across to lift the unit off the breakfast bar and drew out the handpiece.

"Hello. Knightlife Enterprises."

"Er, Dr. Thane?"

"This is he."

"Walter Trevany."

"Ah, Walter! Good morning, indeed!"

"The woman you sent me the picture of: Elaine. I've remembered something else. She was some kind of nurse. It's not a lot, but I said I'd let you know if anything more occurred to me."

"And I appreciate it. But actually, Walter, we've traced her. And a big part was thanks to you. I told you that what you said was more useful than you realized."

"Oh—I'm glad to hear it. So how is Leo now? Has his memory improved at all?"

"Well, a lot of people are currently working to help him in that direction," Kieran said truthfully. "Elaine was even more helpful than I'd hoped. We'll see what happens. So how is the expedition to Tharsis shaping up? You must be getting close to leaving."

A sigh came over the phone. "Oh . . . there's a mechanical problem with the Juggernaut. We're—"

"Juggernaut?"

"That's what we've christened the mobile lab. We're having trouble getting a part. Something always gets you at the last minute. I'm new here. Do you happen to know any good places to try?"

"Do you have Alazahad Machine on your list?"

"Yes, but I haven't tried that one yet. Are they good?"

"It's the place I rented the car from when I came out to see you. Mahom Alazahad, the owner, is an old friend of mine. He's also a magician. If anyone in Lowell has your part, it'll be him. Otherwise he'll conjure you one out of thin air."

"Thanks for the tip. We'll give it a shot."

"Mention my name. And good luck."

Kieran expected Trevany to clear down, but a short pause followed. Then Trevany said, "There was something else I wanted to ask. Our expedition's medic has had to drop out. His main work is in biological research. He thought he'd have some spare time, but it turned out that some work he's involved with in Lowell is at a crucial point. What kind of doctor are you? I wondered if it was something you'd be able to help out with at short notice. We could offer pretty good remuneration . . . if you were interested."

Kieran smiled. "It's nice of you to think of me. But to be frank, my calling to the curative arts is not of the physicians' kind. I suppose it would be better described as remedying wrongs that ought to be put right." June caught his eye with a questioning look.

"Oh . . . okay," Trevany said. "Maybe this Elaine might know someone, if she's a nurse."

"Possibly," Kieran said. "But I'm afraid she left Mars yesterday. She's going to be gone for a long time. But I know other people too, Walter. Let me ask around. If I come up with someone who might be able to take it on, I'll have them get in touch."

"Well, if it wouldn't be a lot of trouble . . ."

"Not at all. It's my turn to do the favor. Leave it to me."

"Thanks a lot. I'll be hoping to hear from someone then."

"Bye for now, Walter."

"So what was that about?" June asked after Kieran had cleared down. "I presume the 'Walter' was Walter Trevany."

"Yes. He had another detail about Elaine that he'd remembered. Also, they're having trouble finding a part to fix something on the Juggernaut—that's what they've called their mobile lab."

"Hm. I kind of like it."

"Anyway, I put him on to Mahom."

"So what was the bit about curative arts and physicians?" June asked. "I take it he still thinks you're a doctor."

Kieran explained the situation. "I'll try calling Donna for a start. She might be able to put me on to some ships' doctors who are laying over between trips right now. A jaunt out across the surface might be appealing. It sounds as if they could find themselves involved in some quite interesting things, too."

June looked at him thoughtfully while he drank from his cup and then began folding the paper with the forged signatures into an origami form. "Then why don't you?" she said finally.

"What?"

June leaned forward to the table, intent on making her point. "Perhaps you *ought* to disappear for a while. I'm probably going to be tied up for some time in whatever repercussions develop at Quantonix. But more importantly, it's very likely that there are people still here in Lowell who might recognize you—with very awkward consequences. Making yourself scarce might be a good idea." The movements of Kieran's hands slowed as he considered what she was saying. He looked up. There was, of course, one small detail that she couldn't have overlooked: he wasn't a doctor. As if reading his mind, she went on, "Didn't you have some training in that line when you were with the military? If what Walter needs is someone on hand for accidents, emergencies and that kind of thing, you might be able to fit the bill as a kind of corpsman. And backup is never far away these days. I think you should think about it."

Kieran sat back, rubbing his chin. The look on his face already said there was nothing to argue or disagree with. It also said he was becoming more taken with the thought by the moment. "I'd probably have to leave Guinness with you," he said at last. "Walter was a bit stodgy about having dogs around when I was out there. In any case, Guinness would have to be shut up inside all the time if he went. . . . I wonder if they'll ever make dog suits."

"That's not a problem. Patti and Grace could have him some of the time. They'd love it."

Kieran let the proposition shuffle through his head one last time. Then he picked up his comset again, drew out the handpiece, and called Trevany's number. "Walter," he said when Trevany answered. "Kieran Thane again. Look, I've been thinking more about this problem of yours. There's a chance I might be able to help after all. What kind of thing are you looking for, exactly? . . ."

# ≥ 2 ≼

Henry Balmer was a short, squat man with a fleshily jowled face, searing eyes set beneath immense eyebrows, hair combed straight back, and a dark, trimmed mustache. As was often the way with small men, he tended to overcompensate with aggressiveness what he lacked in stature. On the rare occasions when he found himself forced onto the defensive, his shoulders hunched protectively, imbuing him in form and manner with the salient attributes of a cannonball. Just at the moment, in Herbert Morch's office at Quantonix, confronted by Herbert and Max, and the project's chief physician, Stewart Perrel, he felt very much on the defensive indeed.

After Herbert Morch's call two days previously he had panicked, entrusting the bemused Sarda to the care of his receptionist, Fay, and deciding suddenly that Mrs. Jescombe was a patient with a critical condition who couldn't be ignored. Since then, he had gone into hiding, keeping away from his office and ignoring Fay's frantic calls, torn between a self-preservation instinct responding to distant places beckoning far from Mars, and a deeply rooted part of his nature that balked at the thought of walking out on any prospect that might remain of netting a quarter of a billion Zodiac Bank-underwritten, offworld, inner-system dollars. However, before he had reconciled his dilemma, a terse note in his mail system from "The Auditor," suggesting pointedly that his longer-term health might benefit from his making himself visible and condescending to communicate again, had induced his eventual appearance at Quantonix. That was where Sarda was, and about the only chance Balmer had of placating certain netherworldly go-betweens who weren't feeling amused just now depended on unlocking information that he hoped still resided somewhere inside Sarda's skull.

"If Leo Sarda has been a client of yours, we should have known about it, Dr. Balmer," Herbert said, looking disgruntled and not a little suspicious. "He's key in our main project here. You say he's been disturbed for some time. Then possibly that's the reason for the condition we're seeing now. But the project is being blamed. The market value of our whole program has collapsed to nothing."

Balmer forced a parody of a smile through clenched teeth, fighting down the urge to scream that if the people at Quantonix had kept adequate tabs on the Sarda they were supposed to have been dealing with, none of this would have happened. "A matter of professional ethics and client confidentiality. I sympathize with your situation, but . . ."—he shrugged—"your internal affairs here are hardly my affair. My obligation was to my patient."

"What kind of problems was he experiencing when he first came to you?" Stewart Perrel asked. Balmer had cited rising apprehension about the forthcoming experiment as the root cause of Sarda's becoming unhinged. Although not widely publicized, the nature of the TX Project was not a closely guarded secret that Sarda would never have discussed—hence, it was acceptable for Balmer to reveal that he had known about it. And if it helped give the Quantonix people a feeling of responsibility for what had gone wrong, then so much the better.

"Acute stress and anxiety," he answered. "Patches of memory loss with no coherent pattern. I interpreted it as a subconscious attempt to disown the old personality, anticipating the need to identify with the new one. The problem was reconciling internally what he had convinced himself he believed consciously."

"Hmm." Perrel looked perplexed. "It seems strange that none of this showed up in our tests." He was probably also put out at Sarda's having consulted an outsider and not the project's physician. "Did you know Leo previously, or something?"

"He was introduced by my professional partner, Elaine Corley. They had been friends for a while."

"He's never mentioned any such person to me."

"That was one of the things he'd forgotten when he appeared at my office. I attributed it to a complete breakdown."

"So it would seem. . . . And is she helping in any of this?"

Balmer fidgeted uncomfortably. "I, er, haven't heard from her for two days. She doesn't return calls."

"Strange," Perrel commented. He shook his head, seemingly not knowing what to make of it.

Balmer shrugged. "She was a highly strung woman under a lot of stress, if you want my opinion. A lot of this Sarda business was affecting her too. She'd been acting erratically in a number of ways. I can't say I'm totally surprised."

Herbert Morch began, "This is all very well, but the main—" then stopped as a commotion of rising voices culminating in protests from his secretary came from the outer office. Moments later, Sarda burst in, bulging-eyed and purple-faced. He glared around the room for a second, and then leaped at Balmer, seizing him by the lapels with both hands. "*It was a trick!*" he shouted. "The whole thing was a setup! *Where is it?* You'll tell me, Balmer, or I'll wring your neck!"

Perrel stepped forward to separate them, while Herbert jumped up and came around the desk. Delia, Herbert's secretary, watched helplessly from the doorway. "Get Sam Eason up here," Herbert called to Max. Max nodded, white-faced, and pulled out his comset.

"*He's mad! Get him off!*" Balmer yelled.

Herbert and Perrel pulled at Sarda's arms. "Let go of him, Leo!" Herbert barked. They dragged Sarda off, but he lunged back again as soon as they loosened their grip. Herbert forced himself between Sarda and Balmer, planting both hands restrainingly on Sarda's chest. "What are you raving about, Leo? What's gone?"

Sarda pointed an accusing finger over Herbert's shoulder. "The five million advance money that I banked! He knew about it! It's gone! He got the codes out of me while I was under. That's what it was all about!"

"You're insane! I don't know what you're talking about," Balmer bellowed back over Herbert's other shoulder. The duplicate Sarda who had vanished would already have known about that, of course. This one had evidently only just found out. That must have been another item included in the lost memories. The whole thing was preposterous. Sarda had robbed himself and didn't even know it.

"Well, this isn't the way to solve anything," Herbert said, half turning between them to address both. "Calm down, Leo. If it's true, I know it must be a shock. But I don't think Dr. Balmer would have appeared here like this if he were responsible, do you? Now why don't we sit down and discuss this like civilized people?"

"Who else could have done it?" Sarda seethed, but drew back grudgingly. Herbert had a point.

"Now," Herbert said, "tell us from the beginning, Leo. What's happened?"

Sarda glanced balefully at Balmer, who was edging away. "You know what the arrangement was, Herbert. Long before the experiment took place, we acknowledged that there were certain unique risks involved that . . ." He broke off as Sam Eason, Quantonix's security officer, appeared in the doorway behind Delia.

"What have we got? Some kind of a problem here?"

"Oh, I think everything's under control now, Sam," Herbert said. "There was some misunderstanding for a moment. Perhaps, if you'd just stick around outside with Delia for a few minutes . . ."

"Sure thing." Sam gave Sarda and Balmer a stern look to let them know the situation was entrusted to his department now, and withdrew, leaving the door ajar.

"If we—" Herbert began again, but Balmer put up a hand.

"It's no good trying to go over what we know," he said. "The answers are in the huge gaps of missing things that Leo *doesn't* know."

"It's going to take a lot of time and patience, Leo," Perrel told Sarda.

That was the last thing Balmer needed. He shook his head. "Not here. I was on the right track before the experiment happened and brought about the crisis. We need to get him away from here, back to my office—a different environment and associations, away from all the negative triggers that are operating here."

Herbert looked at Sarda appealingly. "Will you do that, Leo? It sounds as if it might be the best chance of getting a lead on what happened to your money."

"It might work . . . I guess." Sarda looked suspicious but apparently couldn't argue.

"Maybe Stewart should go too—to keep us involved, as it were," Max suggested. It was a veiled way of asking if Balmer would feel safe working with Sarda alone.

Balmer raised a hand hastily. "I appreciate the offer, gentlemen, but I have my own methods. They work best when fully removed from extraneous influences." Perrel seemed a bit disgruntled but left it at that.

"When would you want to start?" Herbert asked Balmer.

"The sooner, the better," Balmer replied. "Is there any reason why Dr. Sarda couldn't come back with me now?" Herbert looked inquiringly at Sarda. Sarda returned a resigned shrug.

"*Sam*," Herbert called to the outer office. Eason stuck his head in. "Leo Sarda will be leaving with Dr. Balmer right away. Could you go with them to reception, just to make sure they get off the premises okay?"

"Sure thing," Sam said, holding open the door.

Sarda opened his eyes and looked around. He was in the consulting room at Balmer's office, sitting in the black leather recliner that Balmer used for his patients. Balmer was standing in front of him, peering at him intently. Sarda was confused. He remembered coming here with Balmer from Quantonix, and acrimonious exchanges between them all the way. What Balmer had been doing at Quantonix, he wasn't sure. He remembered being enraged at discovering that the five million was gone from the account at the Lowell Barham Bank, and accusing Balmer of taking it. It didn't make any sense. That was the *other* Sarda's loss: the copy's—which had been the whole idea. It had been his own plan. Why would he accuse Balmer? Stewart Perrel had been there with the Morches, expressing concern at his supposedly forgetting things. Nothing made any sense.

"Leo?" Balmer's voice was curiously anxious. Sarda focused on him. "How are you feeling?"

"I feel . . . strange—as if I've been confused over things, but I'm not sure why." Sarda realized he had just awakened from a trance. This hadn't been scheduled. He also realized with alarm that he had no recollection of closing the deal—the big one. His expression darkened. He had never liked Balmer or trusted him. "What's going on?" he demanded.

"Just bear with me, Leo. What are the last things you remember?"

"Being back in Quantonix for the last couple of days before you showed up . . . That's crazy. What was I doing back there? Why wasn't the copy around? Lots of questions from Stewart, Tom Norgent, others . . . Stupid questions. It seems like I was having trouble remembering a lot of things. I don't know why. What have you been doing, Henry?"

Balmer seemed encouraged. He raised his hands placatingly. "Let's go back a bit further—before the experiment. You remember the plan to appropriate the five million? It was your fixation, Leo—after you and Elaine came to me with the proposal for resuscitating you. And then the more worthwhile one of cutting our own deal . . . ?"

Sarda nodded. "I went into the process. Then, I guess, there were a couple of days blank." That would have been while he was in stasis suspension.

"Yes, yes. Go on."

"I remember coming out of resuscitation; leaving the building with Elaine. . . . We met you, came back here for a while, and then you took me to that crummy place out at the end of Gorky, where I was holed up for days."

"I'm sorry, but it was necessary, Leo. We couldn't risk your being recognized and mistaken for the copy at that point."

Sarda looked around. "So where is Elaine?"

"Er, not here. She's out of town right now. We'll come to that later. So you remember the exchanges over technical details, setting up the meeting at Zodiac to close the deal. . . ."

"I left on time, went down to the maglev terminal . . ."

"And . . . ?" Balmer was taut, like an overwound spring on the verge of flying apart. He made tiny, impatient, circular motions with his hands.

Sarda frowned. That was where it got screwy. "I never got to the maglev. There was a guy there, turned out in a suit, like a lawyer or something. He gave some name—I don't remember it; 'Tune' or something. Said he was from Zodiac and would drive me there. It was supposed to have been your idea."

"Me? I don't know anything about it. What then?"

"I didn't believe him. But when I tried to pass, this other guy appeared from somewhere—huge guy, black. And they had a dog."

"Dog?"

"Big, black, like a police dog, or military. Mean looking. It belonged to the guy in the suit. He gave it orders. There was no way I could argue. They took me down to the traffic level. They had a car waiting. And then . . ." Sarda frowned. It was clear up to that point, but then everything became fragmented, like a jigsaw picture breaking up into pieces and gaps.

"What?" Balmer prompted.

"I'm not sure. . . . We sat in the car. There was another car parked not far away. Elaine was in it. She came across and looked in at me." Sarda drew a hand across his forehead as if wiping a piece of hair away. "She was upset. I'm not surprised. It's crazy—I didn't know who she was. She went back to the other car with the guy in the suit. . . . And the black guy from the car brought me here, to this office. You were in a panic, talking to Walworth at Zodiac. I couldn't understand what was going on then, but it's clear now. The deal went through, but we weren't a part of it." Something sickening seemed to open up in Sarda's stomach, and his anger came flooding back. He started to rise from the recliner. "What's happened, Henry? If you're pulling some kind of double-cross—"

"No, no, I assure you." Balmer eased him back down. "The man with the dog. He's the one we have to find."

"Are you telling me the money from that deal has gone missing too?" Sarda asked menacingly. "You'd better not be, because—" A call tone sounded from the comset in Balmer's jacket pocket. He snatched it out and answered.

"Yes? . . . Yes." Balmer's face paled. "I'm working on it now. I think we have the answer. It just needs a little time. . . ." He listened, then gulped visibly. "Yes, I understand. . . . No, of course not. . . . Three days."

"What—" Sarda began. Balmer cut him off with a wave. Sarda saw that he was sweating.

"This man with the dog. Can you describe him?"

"Well, as I said, he had a suit—dark; black, or maybe navy. Tall, with wavy hair. Easygoing, smiling kind of person. He had clear eyes, like blue ice—the kind that seem to look right through you."

Balmer gesticulated nervously. "Anything else? What about the person who was driving the car? Can you recall anything more about him or her? Or the car itself? Did you get its registration?"

"The driver was all wrapped up. I don't go around memorizing the registrations of every car I see. Do you?" Sarda thought back. "It was classy looking, dark colored. Not sure of the type . . ." Then Sarda remembered something. "But there was a sort of chrome logo on the trunk. It said something Machine. Funny name. Alice, or something like that." Sarda cast his mind back, trying to visualize it. Balmer fished out his comset again, activated it, and brought up a directory listing of vehicle dealers and renters in Lowell.

"Alazahad?" he offered.

Sarda nodded. "Good thinking, Henry. Yes, I'm pretty sure that was it: *Alazahad Machine.*"

"Let's try their web link, just out of curiosity," Balmer murmured. He operated the comset again and watched for a response. "Hm. Owner and proprietor, Mahom Alazahad." He entered another command, studied the result, and then directed a copy to the larger screen on the desk to one side of the room. Then he looked at Sarda inquiringly.

Sarda took in the face: coal black, massively proportioned, smiling broadly beneath a red fez nesting in a wild bush of fuzzy hair. The caption beneath read: THE MR. WHEELS OF UNBEATABLE DEALS. When Sarda had seen him, he was wearing a silky green coat.

"That's him!" he pronounced without hesitation.

# ⅀ 3 ⅀

Solomon Leppo had been born on Mars and raised in a settlement called Americyon, founded among the southern highlands in the early days to put into practice the ideals of communal living and sharing. There, apart from household furnishings and personal effects, the community had owned everything. Private quarters were allowed only for married couples and families; the rest slept in dormitories, ate together, relaxed and exercised together, and worked together in roles assigned via a military-style command system that employed ranks and uniforms. The expectation was that everyone would find fulfillment through universal recognition of their contributions according to their inclinations and abilities, great or humble. Solomon departed at the age of fifteen by stowing away with a passing Arab caravan of surface crawlers and trailers that had camped nearby on their way to make a home somewhere. He eventually ended up at Lowell, where he found work as a trainee fitter in a machine shop. From there he had progressed to equipment servicing and repair, and now, at nineteen, was making good money as Mahom Alazahad's resident mechanic.

The key to everything that had appeal in life, he had decided, was *money*. Sure, like some people said, it wasn't everything; but all the other things depended on it. In all his long years of observing life and forming insights as to how the limited time that it offered could best be enjoyed, he had come to identify three things at the bottom of it all that mattered: *girls*—at Americyon, betrothals were by approval that depended more on social needs than what the individuals involved thought about it, and the likelihood of his getting approval of any kind had been a joke; *things*,

132

like clothes he picked himself, a place to live that he'd decided *he* liked, or a snazzy set of wheels to drive around on—for instance, any of the numbers in the front row lined up across Mahom's lot; and *freedom*, which in Solomon's vocabulary meant being able to devote his energies to pursuing the first two, as opposed to having to do what somebody else—such as the superintending tribunal at Americyon—decided he would do. But simply being free to pursue one's ends didn't amount to much without the necessary wherewithal to achieve them. In short, it all boiled down to money. True, you couldn't take it with you at the end of the act; but where else could you go without it?

He looked up from reconnecting the turbine compressor gearing in a Mars-assembled "Camel" tractor in the workshop, as the sound came of a car turning in from Beacon Way. A shiny black Metrosine, flashing silver and white wheels and outside trim, drew up in front of the door of the office building. Solomon had seen it around town a few times. Three men got out, all soberly and more expensively dressed than the norm for Mars, and went inside. Several seconds later, Phil Verlan, Mahom's sales manager, appeared from among some parked vehicles and sauntered in the side door, drawn by the scent of possible prospective customers.

Now, *that* was what he meant by money, Solomon told himself as he settled back to what he was doing. Doing things in *style* was what pulled the interesting chicks. In a place like Mars, a good mechanic would always be able to pay the rent, take care of the bills, and would never need to look very long for a job; but it would never lead to the kind of life that had style. Working for Mahom, however, opened up other possibilities that went beyond just fixing trucks, autos, and other weird kinds of machines that appeared in the yard. The "Stores" building at the back contained enough hardware to equip a revolution. With his mechanical and workshop skills and some applied study, Solomon could use his time here to start himself on the way to becoming a weaponry and ammunition expert. Now, *that* was something that could command really good money. The people who had what it took kept big places on their payrolls for those who helped them hang onto it.

Having grown up on Mars, Solomon had difficulty imagining what life must be like on Earth, with every square inch of land controlled by a government that laid down rules you couldn't argue with, and nowhere much different for anybody to go. Here, there was an "Administrative Congress" in Lowell, a "Security Council" at Osaka, in the Tharsis region, a "Directorate" at Zerolon, on the planet's far side above Hellas, and other kinds of setups at other lesser places, all of which performed more or less the same kind of function in spelling out a few basic rules that few people would argue with, and backing them up with the muscle and firepower to make sure they stuck. For instance, you didn't walk in and take anything you fancied of anyone else's just because you happened to be bigger and meaner, or blow someone away for disagreeing with your opinions. And that seemed to make sense. It was businesses and industries that had built Lowell, so they should have the right to spend their money keeping enough law and order for people to want to live and work there. And anyone who didn't like it was free to find somewhere in the Outlands or self-run settlements—such as Americyon—that suited them, and take their chances.

Some people said things couldn't last like this; that the territories being organized around places like Lowell, Osaka, Zerolon, and likewise the others, would expand outward bit by bit, maybe gobbling up the little guys, until their borders all met up and there wasn't anywhere left in between; then they'd either settle down, or that would be when the really serious trouble would start. But either way, the eventual appearance of the same general pattern that had taken over Earth would be only a matter of time—but that would be far in the future as far as Solomon Leppo was concerned. And in the meantime, for those with the savvy and expertise, there was money to be made hiring out to a hundred variants of the protection, security, and enforcement business. And making the right kind of name in that department could do wonders for supplying life with the chicks and the things too.

He had just tightened the flange bolts and was starting to reconnect the sensors, when a shadow darkened the open doorway of the shop. Solomon looked up as a figure that he hadn't heard approaching entered and stopped to look around casually. The man had dark hair, styled into a crest, that should have been showing some graying for his age—probably rejuvenated—and the kind of even, golden tan that you got in the classier gyms and spas—not blotchy from spending too long outside under the raw Martian sky. He was dressed in a dark suit that fluoresced silver ripples where it creased, and a gray turtleneck shirt. "Hi, kid," he greeted.

Solomon used a rag to wipe the worst of the grease from his hands and straightened up. "Can I help you?"

"So how's it going?"

The friendly approach, eh? Solomon maintained a neutral air, keeping his options open. "You mean the tractor? Nowhere till I'm done fixing it."

The man grunted approvingly. "Quick thinker. Got humor, too. You could go a long way."

"I plan to . . . when I'm ready. So what are you, some kind of headhunter? I didn't know they went looking for auto mechs. Something must have happened in this business lately that nobody told me about."

"Sorry, it's not your turn today. But yeah, I guess you could say we're sort of headhunting. Three days ago, a guy that we'd very much like to talk to was out at Wuhan in a car that came from this place. Kind of tall, wavy brown hair, lean, fit-looking . . . Also has a dog—kind of big, black with some light brown around the face. I was wondering if you'd seen him around, like when he was here to pick up the car. It's a business thing. Anything you've got would be worth something."

Whoever these people were, or why they were looking for the man with the dog, the message came through clearly that it was *they* who asked the questions. Solomon thought back, then shook his head. "Wish I could help. What kind of a car?"

"Kodiak, dark color—blue or black. The car had this place's name in chrome on the trunk."

"Yes, I know the car. It was rented out four or five days back. But it must have been my day off or something. I wasn't here when it went out." Solomon shook his head and shrugged. "That's all I can tell you."

The man seemed to accept it as a matter of routine. He produced a wallet from inside his jacket and extracted a calling card. His hands were strong but well manicured, with several rings that glittered expensively. The card bore the name Lee Mullen, described as a "Financial Expediter," along with a mail drop and net code. While Solomon was studying it, a twenty slid across on top. He hesitated, then took the bill and tucked it in his shirt pocket.

"Everybody could use a little extra, huh?" Mullen said. "If you remember anything else, or if he shows up again, I'd appreciate a call. Like I said, it'll be worth your while."

"If I hear anything, you've got it."

"You could go a long way, kid," the man said again. Then he turned, and sauntered back toward the office.

# 4

In the center compartment immediately behind the driving cab of the Juggernaut, now in the final phase of being fitted out at Stony Flats, Kieran checked the pincer-shaped sutures that he had clamped along the gash on the back of Harry Quong's hand after cleaning it, then sprayed a fast-setting coagulant along the wound. Both would dry up and flake off when the healing was complete. Harry was the vehicle and equipment technician included in Walter Trevany's expedition out to Tharsis. He had hit his hand on a heat exchanger cooling fin when his foot slipped on a greasy stepping plate. Mahom had found Trevany the part he needed. The Juggernaut would be leaving first thing next morning.

"Is that comfortable?" Kieran asked. "I'll put a pad over to protect it while it's soft. After two days you won't need it."

"It feels fine, Doc." Harry watched as Kieran selected what he needed from the medical box opened on the table. "Is that what we're supposed to call you? Walter said you were a quick fix when Pierre had to drop out. Something about being a military medic once?"

"Not even that, to be honest, Harry," Kieran answered. "Back in my impetuous days of youth, I did a few years with an SAF regiment. It was part of the cross-training you got." Spaceborne Assault Forces were a breed of combat soldier that specialized in defending and penetrating all manner of vessels and structures in the face of problems peculiar to the space environment; also in making rapid descents and deployments from orbit. The term referred to a category of military competence rather than describing the armed services of any particular political or other entity. SAF units were formed by governments, commercial enterprises,

137

and other organizations, and recruited by mercenary forces available for hire to anybody striving to enforce claims, seize opportunities, or simply protect themselves in the salmagundi of rivalries and alliances scattered across the Solar System.

Harry looked impressed. "Who were you with?"

"Oh, for the most part, a conglomerate effort in one of the Belt sectors that was organized against claim jumpers. Then some merc strikes to take out launch bases being set up on Ganymede. I'm not sure we were the good guys in that one, though. So these days I just work for me."

"Why did you do it?" Harry asked.

"To prove I was a tough kid, of course. That's when they know they've got you."

"In my book, that makes you all the more useful to have along. I hear this place can have its wild moments."

Kieran secured the edges of the pad with adhesive tape and looked up. "There. Try not to wave it about too much." As he began tidying up, he asked, out of curiosity, "What kind of biological research was Pierre involved in, that made him drop out?"

"Oh, nano stuff—pieces of molecules that come together inside body cells."

"What for?"

"Something to do with remote-controlling metabolic chemistry. You'd need to talk to Dennis and Jean when we get to Troy. They know more about it. Pierre was a friend of theirs." "Troy" was the name that Hamil had given to the base camp at Tharsis. Dennis Curry and Jean Graas, together as a couple by the sound of things, were geologists with the group that had remained at Troy with Hamil while Juanita and Harry came back to Lowell to meet Trevany and the others from Earth, and collect the Juggernaut. Harry examined the finished dressing on his hand and seemed satisfied. "So what should we call you?"

"Why not just 'Kieran'?" Kieran suggested. "I also go by 'Knight'—from the initials."

Harry considered the options. "Is it okay if I stick with 'Doc' anyway?"

"It's fine by me—but you know it pushes one of Rudi's buttons."

"I know. That's why I like it."

Rudi Magelsberg was the group's scientific technician. He had greeted Trevany's announcement of the new addition to the team with reservations regarding Kieran's suitability for the job, although without going as far as open criticism. Kieran interpreted Harry's stance as a way of telling him that he had one solid supporter on board at least.

Feet sounded on the metal steps below the outer door of the side lock. It opened to admit Trevany, wearing a khaki bush shirt and tan jeans streaked and stained from the previous few days' work. He came through the open inner door and glanced at Harry's hand while Kieran stood up and moved to the galley sink to wash his hands. "I'm glad we didn't waste any time. You're earning your keep already," Trevany commented.

"I'll try not to lose anybody," Kieran promised.

"This guy's okay," Harry told Trevany. "It's not as if we're scheduling any transplants or heart surgery."

"How does the hand feel?" Trevany asked.

"Pretty good."

"Will you be able to work with it, do you think?"

"Sure, no problem."

"First Pierre, now this already. And we haven't even left yet." Trevany shook his head. "Don't tell me there's a jinx or something on this expedition."

"I didn't think scientists believed in jinxes," Kieran said, reaching for a towel.

"I didn't, once. Now I've seen too many strange things to scoff at anything. Who was it who said that a man can't begin to learn that which he thinks he already knows?"

"Epictetus, I think, wasn't it?"

"Hm. I do believe you're right." Trevany looked mildly surprised.

"Well, I've got a few things left to do," Harry said, getting up. "Thanks for patching me up, Doc . . . er, Knight. Let's hope that's about the worst you have to do, eh? Glad to have you aboard." He left the way Trevany had entered, closing the outer door behind him. The sounds of objects rattling and being put into drawers and closets came from the lab section behind the bunk area to the rear, where Juanita Anavarez, Trevany's Peruvian scientific partner, was inventorying instruments and equipment.

Kieran put the items he had been using back in the medical box. "So, Walter," he said as he closed and fastened the lid, "what's it all about? The expedition. I'm going to know in a matter of days anyway, and you've no idea what the curiosity is doing to my tranquility."

Trevany lowered himself onto one of the end seats and eased back to rest himself, his hands braced on the table. "Do you remember when you first came out here—when you were looking for leads on that woman, Elaine Corley? You were curious about Earth's ancient Technolithic culture."

"Right," Kieran said over his shoulder as he pushed the box back into its stowage space above the bench seat. "Whether their disappearance was connected with whatever happened on Mars."

"They're called that because of the huge stone edifices they built in places like the Middle East, northern India, Central and South America—with a technical skill that was lost. The constructions were all works of the same, or very closely related, people."

"So it wasn't the pharaohs who built the pyramids?" Kieran said. It wasn't the first time he'd heard the suggestion. "There was an old song that said it was the Irish, but I never really believed it." He sat down, interested now, at the other end of the table, facing Trevany.

"Oh, the pharaohs built some," Trevany replied. "The Sahure Pyramid, for example, dates from the Fifth Dynasty around 2450 B.C. It's a dilapidated ruin, with little to tell it apart from a mound of desert rubble—nothing like the Giza complex, built from blocks weighing tens, hundreds of tons in some cases, cut and laid with machine precision. You see what it means? The later Egyptians tried to copy structures that they found, which went back to far earlier than the Dynastic Period. But they didn't know how. The knowledge was gone."

"It's what a lot of the books still say, though, isn't it?" Kieran said.

"Ah, the tyranny of nineteenth-century English Egyptologists, reaching down through time." Trevany showed his teeth. "The Giza pyramids are supposedly from the Fourth Dynasty—the big one was allegedly put up by Khufu—Cheops—around 2550. Do you really think standards could have declined that much in so short a time?"

"Sounds pretty drastic, all right," Kieran agreed. "So why do you say 'allegedly'? What are the reasons for believing it wasn't?"

"The whole case rests on one piece of evidence. You can judge for yourself how solid it is. Want to hear the story?"

Kieran made himself comfortable. "Sure, I never turn down a story."

"The Victorians figured life as a progression from primitive beginnings through steady improvement all the way to the ultimate expression of excellence in the form of eminent Victorians—which was obviously the purpose of the exercise," Trevany said. "That meant there couldn't have been any advanced cultures earlier—and especially not if they weren't white. Ergo, these structures we're talking about must have been built during the Dynastic Period."

"Even though the technology was obviously from a different time?"

Trevany waved a hand. "It doesn't matter. We're defending a dogma here. Did you think this was science or something? But they could never produce any actual evidence to prove it, which kind of embarrassed some people. According to the orthodox line, the pyramids were built as tombs, and only as tombs. Yet never once was a body or a mummy actually found in one—except for a few bones in the smaller Menkaure Pyramid that were later shown to be from the early Christian era. Intrusive burial of that kind was a fairly common practice. None of the burial treasures or artifacts that Egyptians reveled in, either. All completely bare. The official explanation has always attributed it to tomb robbers, at the latest around 2000 B.C. But again it was only an answer invented to fit the assumptions. And not a very credible one, really, when you take a hard look at it."

Trevany got up from the seat and selected a marker pen from the tray beneath a white board fixed to the wall above one end of the table—it seemed scientists became uncomfortable when they were not close to something to scribble on. He drew a triangle representing the cross section of a pyramid and then a passage descending from low on one face to a point deep in the bedrock below the center. While he was doing this, Juanita Anavarez came through from the lab at the rear holding a printed list in her hand, and stopped to listen. She was dark-skinned, with straight hair that she tried futilely to induce into waves, and large, brown, questioning eyes. Kieran had found her to be precise and businesslike in the way she went about her work.

Trevany went on, "The mystery begins in the ninth century A.D. A Muslim governor of Cairo organized a team of quarriers to tunnel into the north face of the Khufu Pyramid, telling them they'd find treasure."

"That's the big one, right?" Kieran said.

Trevany nodded, then added the letters *DC* to the passage-way he had sketched. "As luck would have it, they joined up with the 'descending corridor,' which had been known in Roman times but later forgotten. Their work dislodged a granite plug from the opening to another corridor *ascending* in the same general direction." He added this and denoted it with *AC*. "But there was a problem. The lower end was blocked by a series of solid granite plugs that had clearly been there since the time of construction, so they were forced to tunnel around to rejoin the ascending corridor higher up—through the softer limestone that the main structure was built from. But you see the point. They had to bypass an obstacle that had *never before been breached!* They continued up through a wider section called the Grand Gallery—which in itself presents enough engineering impossibilities—and reached the so-called King's Chamber, in the heart of the pyramid. They uncovered other corridors and chambers too, but the upshot was that they found absolutely nothing in them, apart from a granite coffer in the King's Chamber, which was later decided, on not very strong grounds, to be a sarcophagus." Trevany showed an empty hand. "So was the place emptied of all the treasures and things that were supposed to be there, as the Egyptologists claimed? But nobody had ever gotten past the granite plugs. Or was it more prob-able that it had been empty all along, since the time it was sealed?"

"Unless there was another way in," Kieran offered.

Trevany regarded him curiously for a second or two, as if weighing up something that might confuse the issue. "As a matter of fact, there was," he said finally. He drew in a narrow connection from a point farther down the descending corridor, rising to the base of the Grand Gallery, and labeled it *WS*. "It's called a well shaft for want of anything better—not discovered until the nine-teenth century. It rises almost vertically a hundred-sixty feet through bedrock, and then more than twenty limestone courses of the pyramid itself. Yes, it's a bypass around the granite plugs. . . .

But the upper end had been found before the connection to the descending corridor. It was choked with debris, sealed at the lower end, and only three feet across, with some awkward vertical sections. Is it really feasible that this could have been the way for getting out the treasures of Khufu, the greatest pharaoh of the magnificent Fourth Dynasty? Surely not things like the statues and shrines that were found filling the places that we know really were tombs—mostly in the Valley of the Kings. But *nothing*? None of the litter that robbers typically leave? Not a shard of a broken pot, not a scrap of cloth or a piece of a tool?" Trevany shook his head. "It's just not credible."

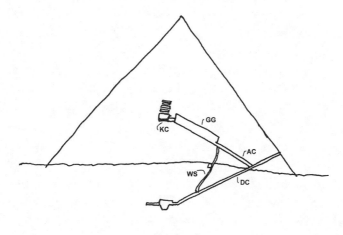

Figure 1

Juanita put in, "The Egyptians were lavish at decorating everything they did—with hieroglyphics, figures, inscriptions, ornamentation. But these structures are bare and built with precision. They suggest more, instruments or machines of some kind rather than monuments. It's incredibly difficult to get the face angles of a construction that big and massive sufficiently accurate for the apex to be over the center. But they did it exactly. The corners are square to within a few arc minutes. I could go on."

Kieran stared up at Trevany's drawing and reflected on what he had heard. "But you did say there's a piece of evidence that the orthodox case rests on," he said.

Trevany smiled thinly. "If you can call it that. In—" He looked at Juanita. "When did Davison find the first relieving chamber?"

"1765," she supplied.

Trevany turned back toward Kieran. "An Englishman. He found a chamber above the King's—apparently there to relieve and redirect stress from the overbearing structure. Again it was empty and bare."

"Advanced engineering," Juanita commented.

Trevany went on, "About seventy years later, another Englishman, Colonel Vyse, was ending a costly and fruitless archeological season, and getting a lot of flak from back home. He needed a major find to justify it all. And guess what."

Kieran smiled. "Don't tell me. Just too convenient?"

"You be the judge. He cut his way into four more relieving chambers above the one that Davison had found. . . . And there, and nowhere else in the entire Great Pyramid, were hieroglyphics claimed to be 'quarry marks,' indicating Khufu to have been the builder. It was greeted as one of the greatest finds for years— exactly what the experts had been waiting for." Trevany gave Kieran a moment to think about it. "As you say, just too convenient, eh?"

Kieran was astounded. "And that's it? It became an article of faith? Nobody's questioned it since?"

"Not in the official halls of academia . . . And never mind when it was later shown that several of the hieroglyphics had been painted upside down, and others used ungrammatically. It didn't matter. The theory had been proved."

"So you're saying they go back much further, to the Technolithic culture," Kieran concluded.

"Yes—way, way back."

"And in America," Juanita said. "Peoples like the Inca and the Maya, they didn't build the huge megaliths there. They *told* the Spaniards that they found them, sometimes buried in jungle. They're all from the same lost race."

Kieran wondered if they were getting back to the thread they had started with. "So what does that have to do with your being here on Mars?" he asked them. "What have they found out at Tharsis? Are you saying there are signs of the same race here too?"

"We're not sure," Trevany said. "Whatever it is, Hamil out at Troy is excited." Hamil Hashikar was the archeologist in charge of the expedition. "But let's not make the same mistake of jumping to what fits our expectations, and wait and see." His eyes were gleaming, all the same. Kieran had the feeling Trevany knew more than he was letting on. But he would just have to be patient, he supposed.

Just then, his phone beeped. He took it out and answered. The caller was Mahom Alazahad. "I'll be a minute," Kieran told the other two.

Juanita moved forward to show Trevany the list she was holding. "Some of the attachments are missing from the kit for the small drill. I think we should turn them in and get another set. I'll do it this afternoon. . . ."

"What is it, Mahom?" Kieran asked into the phone.

"I just wanted to let you know. Three guys were here asking about you. Showed up in a big Metrosine—suits and rings, cool daddy-os, heavy with the juice. They knew about your dog, described you as a lawyer type. Sounded to me like it could have been from when we snatched that guy at the Wuhan terminal. Just so's you know, Knight. You take it easy wherever you're at. And watch out. Okay?"

# 5

Fractal patterns. Structures similar to themselves over a wide range of scales, making it impossible to tell if a coastline is that of a driveway puddle or a continent; a forking discharge that of a laboratory spark or a lightning bolt.

Kieran stared out from the bench seat to the right of the Juggernaut's driver's station at the chutes of red-brown sand and scree funneling down between crumbling buttresses of scarp to the right, and then spreading out like river deltas to invade the edge of the plain that they were following. From the correct angle, with nothing familiar to set the scale, the formation would have looked just like a child's sandcastle yielding to the first brushes of the incoming tide, or the side of a storm gully in southern California. So were these the scars and deposits of water action, too—immense, surging, scouring bodies of water in the process of being torn or boiled off the planet? Mars had possessed oceans once, and a different atmosphere, Walter said. Theories and arguments abounded as to where they had gone and why, but the truth was that nobody knew. If conditions had once been so very different, what else might have been very different?

Harry Quong was sprawled in the c-com station behind the two front seats, staring at an infinity somewhere ahead and lost in thoughts of his own. It was Rudi Magelsberg's turn to take a spell at driving. Kieran had guessed initially that he was of German origin somewhere along the line, but Rudi said it was Austrian—not that things like that meant very much in the fluctuating patchwork of Martian society. All the same, he looked the Nordic part, with short-cropped blond hair, almost white, a lofty brow, lean, high-boned features, and a pointy chin and mouth. Right now, he was wearing white shorts that revealed tanned legs generously endowed with blond hair, a bright red shirt, a floppy bush hat, and gold-rimmed sunglasses. Kieran could see why his drive for getting things done and obsession with doing them right could make him a valuable asset on a scientific expedition. But at the same time, the "right" way in Rudi's vocabulary tended to mean *his* way. Kieran had seen from times spent in spacecraft how inability to yield on the small things could prove the detonator in a confined community. So far, however, apart from his initial coolness toward Kieran's credentials, there had been nothing to suggest a future problem in the bud. Kieran could only hope things stayed that way. He had weathered worse if they didn't.

"So, is this your first time on Mars, Mr. Thane?" Rudi asked, keeping his eyes ahead as the Juggernaut lurched and swayed over sand and rubble. The thought flitted through Kieran's mind that maybe he should have his answers printed as a handout for every new person he met.

"No." (So what brings you here this time?) "I'm visiting an old friend. But also thinking it's maybe time to get myself a place here, too." (Any particular area in mind?) "Probably somewhere in Lowell center."

"It looks quite acceptable from what I have seen. But I don't pretend to have seen that much. Did you know that Lowell has become famous in the last several days—at least within a certain specialized scientific circle? Or maybe I should say, notorious."

"Has it?" Kieran feigned surprise. "Why? What's happened?"

"Apparently, one of the sunsider research operations thought they'd solved the teleportation problem that's been talked about for years. They actually put a human through the process—one of the scientists. At first everybody thought it had worked. He was supposedly acting normally and everything. Then, suddenly, half his memories disappeared, and he went crazy. I never thought it could work, anyway."

"I wouldn't walk into a thing like that, even if they said it did," Harry Quong drawled from behind.

"How did you hear about it?" Kieran asked Rudi curiously.

"I have a brother who's a financial exec with one of the big trans-system carriers. He says there's panic in all their boardrooms right now. Me? I'll stay with archeology."

"Interesting," Kieran commented.

The smell of cooking had begun wafting through the open bulkhead door from the galley, at the forward end of the center compartment immediately behind the cab. "Ah, suddenly I'm hungry," Rudi declared. "Do you need to eat now, Harry? Or can you take over while I go back and get something?"

"I can wait," Harry said. "It's about time you took a break, anyhow."

"I'll get out of your way," Kieran told them. He rose, squeezed himself through the gap between the armrest at the end of the bench seat and the hull, and moved to the door while Harry waited before going forward to change places with Rudi. On the far side of the bulkhead, Katrina Ersohn, the sixth member of the expedition, was pouring batter to prepare another pancake to go on the stack she had started. There was already a steel dish with strips of grilled bacon—large slices; Martian pigs grew bigger in the lower gravity. Katrina glanced up with a quick smile as Kieran came through.

"Boy, that didn't need any announcing!"

"A hungry hoard is about to descend," Kieran pronounced. "Can't say I blame 'em. That looks good."

"I wonder if I get credits for this, too."

Slightly pudgy, pale-skinned with faint freckles across her nose, and with mousy hair that defied her efforts to comb it straight, curling instead into waves that would have delighted Juanita, Katrina was a graduate student from a private European college that had put up a significant part of Trevany's funding to have her included in the expedition. Like Trevany and Rudi, she was a recent arrival from Earth.

"How are you finding things here so far?" Kieran asked her.

She answered while carrying on with what she was doing. "I didn't really get a chance to see too much. Everything seems so unruly and chaotic. . . ."

"Unruled might be a better word."

"But also, it's so . . . *alive*." Katrina nodded as she flipped the pancake with a spatula—the size of the galley didn't go with aerial dynamic stunts. "If I had to, I think I could get used to it."

"Be careful. You might end up finding you don't want to go back."

"I've heard of that happening. Is it really true? Don't people miss things like the oceans, forests, walking in cities under an open sky? They never feel the need for those things again?"

"Lots of people have never known them," Kieran pointed out. "But of those that have, yes, most of them probably do. But on the other hand, they get intoxicated by the freedom, the ruggedness, the vastness out here. Some say they find it's like going back into a pressure cooker." He watched her for a moment, and then came back suddenly from one of his inexplicable tangents. "Do you dance?"

She laughed. "What, in here? You're crazy."

"On Mars it's a new experience. A fast Viennese waltz makes you feel like an ethereal being whirling among clouds. . . ." Rudi appeared in the doorway from the driver's cab. "I bet a month of it would even make a romantic out of Rudi," Kieran said.

"What's this?" Rudi asked.

"Viennese waltzes," Katrina said. "Shouldn't you be an expert?"

"Actually, I consider myself quite proficient," Rudi agreed.

Kieran decided not to risk provoking him with a response. "Want me to tell Walter and Juanita that grub's nearly ready?" he asked Katrina as she began cracking eggs into a jug for scrambling.

"Sure."

Kieran went back through the living and bunking area, and past the rear bulkhead into the lab section, which took up at least a third of the vehicle's length. The rear window was unshuttered, providing a view of the supplies and equipment trailer rocking and bumping at the end of its tow bar, with the Martian wilderness creeping by behind. An arrangement of glass tubes and vessels connected to a piece of apparatus on one of the side benches, where Trevany and Juanita had been carrying out some kind of chemical test or calibration. Just at the moment, however, they were engrossed with an image on one of the screens at the c-com terminal in the far corner. It showed part of a surface of irregularly shaped blocks interlocked together in an unusual pattern. A figure in a light-duty Martian EV suit stood at lower left, its hand resting on one of the larger blocks at the base.

"I hope you're near a good stopping place," Kieran told them. "Katrina's just about to dish out food. Pancakes, eggs, and bacon. It looks good."

Trevany looked over and made a gesture at the screen. "Not

quite. We're through to Hamil, waiting for him to come back with something. . . . That's him there, in the suit. You asked the other day what this is all about. I didn't want to go on then about things that might not be what they seemed. But this is from this morning at Troy. Does it say anything to you?"

Kieran studied the curious mixture of shapes and sizes more closely. The lines defining them couldn't be natural, he realized. This wasn't some kind of formation. It had been *built*. No two of the stones were the same, some having maybe a dozen or more faces, angles, and notches making up their complex polygonal outlines, yet all dovetailing together to form a peculiarly striking jigsaw effect. And they were immense. The stone that Hamil's hand was resting on stood more than twice his height.

"It's got Murphy Construction Company written all over it," Kieran said. "Jeez, they get everywhere."

"Just north of Cuzco in Peru, there is an ancient citadel called Sacsayhuaman," Juanita said. "Conventionally, it's supposed to have been built by the Incas, but a lot of us have never believed that. Some of the blocks weigh hundreds of tons, yet they're fitted like machine parts. And you see the same thing at another place not far away called Machu Picchu, somehow built at the top of an impossibly inaccessible mountain. Both places use a highly distinctive system of blocks with irregular angles interlocking three-dimensionally; also, a form of reentrant-cut, right-angle block for internal corners. Uncannily similar designs turn up in other places far across the world. A coincidence? Then you find they use the same unusual way of cutting huge gateways out of a single block of rock." Juanita made a deprecating face. "Maybe the Incas were spread out farther than everyone thought, eh?" She turned to follow Kieran's gaze, still taking in the screen. "And now, here we have it again. Or something that looks so extraordinarily close, that from an image, at least, I can't tell the difference."

It was one of the rare times in his life when Kieran felt truly overwhelmed. If his emotions were a fraction of what this must be producing in the scientists, their powers of self-control were astounding. "What are you saying?" he asked them. His flippancy had vanished. "Does it mean that the Technolithic Culture *was* alien after all—the way some people have always thought?"

"I'm not saying anything at this point," Trevany said. "As I told you the other day, I'm not jumping to anything. Premature commitment causes more problems in science than anything I know. But at least, now you have a better idea of what we're doing."

At that moment, a window showing Hamil's face opened on the screen. He was brown-skinned with saggy chins and a wisp of gray beard, but with an easygoing, jovial disposition—at least, from the few times that Kieran had talked to him—that was conveyed principally by large, animated eyes. "No, we don't have those counts yet," he said. "I'll send them through later. . . . Oh, hello, Knight. So what do you think of this? I assume Walter and Juanita have given you the news."

"Just this moment," Kieran said. "I don't think I've really had a chance to digest it."

"It's big. I promise you, it's big," Hamil said. "What do Rudi and the others think?"

"We're just about to go forward and join them to eat," Trevany answered. "I was meaning to tell them then. My God, one thing at a time, Hamil! Don't you ever let up? Is it going to be like this all the time when we get there?"

Hamil grinned unapologetically. "What else is life good for if not to get things done? Don't you think so, Knight?"

Kieran pursed his lips. "It's probably the best chance you're going to get," he agreed.

"Aha! A natural philosopher too. He'll fit in well, Walter."

"Yes, well, before you start getting philosophical, our lunch is waiting," Trevany said. "I'm sure it's going to be a lively one."

"Enjoy your meal. I'll probably have the figures to you before you're finished." Hamil vanished, leaving his other image, dwarfed by the mysterious orchestration in stone.

# ≥ 6 ≤

A major construction and mining concern called Zorken Consolidated, which had hollowed asteroids, dug tunnels, bridged chasms, and made domed cities out of craters across the central parts of the Solar System, had conducted a pilot survey and made test borings for a possible new space complex in the Tharsis region. The engineers and crew had then pulled out pending a decision on whether to take the project further. While the data were being evaluated, Hamil and Juanita had arrived with a small archeological and geological field team and set up camp to investigate the workings that Zorken's survey team had left.

The Troy camp consisted of two trailers accommodating the scientists and a five-man work force, a three-compartment inflatable-frame cabin affording a messroom and work space, and a couple of shacks left by the Zorken workers. One of the latter was pressurized; the other was not, but provided a convenient shelter for power generators and an air recirculation plant. Now, in addition, there was the Juggernaut. The structures and vehicles were clustered at one end of a clear area amid boulders and rubble on an irregular shelf a hundred or so yards wide, halfway down the broken side of a mesa formation upon which the space complex would stand—like Cherbourg, at Lowell. The mesa side overlooked a crumpled valley floor rising to orange bluffs on the far side, which one day, perhaps, would hold a new metropolis. A road bulldozed out of the shallower lower slopes reached the shelf via four steeply-angled segments connected by reversing strips—the side was too steep to construct hairpins. From the ends of the shelf, narrower trails explored the shattered mesa sides, while in the center, a slanting cut carrying an

open-cage elevator, again left by Zorken Consolidated, gave access
to the mesa top. Above the far end of the shelf from the camp,
an improbable rock formation the size of a small house, actually wider at the top than its base, propped by several lesser rocks
wedged beneath, balanced on the very edge of the precipice.
Dubbed the "Citadel," it was, according to Hamil, another example
of the work of one-time water, not an effect of wind erosion as
the conventional explanation maintained.

Looking round and diminutive even in a Martian surface suit,
Hamil led the way with Jean Graas, one of the geologists from the
original group, along a trail that led on from where the left end
of the shelf petered out among rockfalls and vertical blocks separated from the main face. Rising and falling around mounds of
debris, skirting drops into gulleys forty or fifty feet below, it must
have been treacherous initially, but had since been widened and
cut for regular use, with rope handrails installed at the worst spots.
Kieran and Katrina followed next, Trevany and Rudi behind them,
and Dennis Curry, also from the original team, bringing up the
rear. Dennis and Jean had met through their shared professional
interests, and Kieran could see them ending up as a husband–wife
team one day. Juanita and Harry had remained at camp to fin-
ish some chores. They already knew the layout and would see the
newer finds later.

Hamil waved an arm to indicate the mass of the plateau loom-
ing above them. His voice came through the speaker in Kieran's
helmet. "The overburden above the site is over five hundred feet
deep. Below the first couple of feet of surface, the layerings and
grain alignments are characteristic of cementing by finer bind-
ing particles under the action of fluids, not wind deposition."
So they were looking at the aftermath of immense flooding,
Kieran thought to himself, translating into everyday language.
And comparatively recent at that, if the archeological finds were
below.

"Where are the oceans that did it, eh?" Trevany said, puffing
audibly on the circuit despite the low Martian gravity.

"Exactly, Walter."

"How long will it be before the establishment back on Earth
accepts it?" Jean Graas's voice asked.

Rudi chimed in, sounding derisive. "What makes you think
they ever will? They've got enough evidence staring them in the

face of the same thing happening there, but they refuse to see it. Why should this be any different?"

"What evidence do you mean?" Kieran asked curiously.

"Huge sediments laid down rapidly—thousands of meters thick in some places. Not slow over millions of years," Rudi answered.

"Uniformitarian chronology is dead," another voice commented. It sounded like Dennis Curry.

"If oceanic deposits were due to slow, uniform accumulations, they would get steadily thicker with increasing distance from the ridges as the sea floors spread." Rudi again. "In fact that's what some textbooks originally claimed before the facts were in, because they were so sure it would be true. But when they got around to actually doing the drillings, they found the opposite. The thickest deposits were at the ridges and along the edges of continental shelves. Practically nothing on the sea floors far from the ridges, where it should have been."

"But just the places where planetwide flood surges would be slowed by obstructions and shed their sedimentary loads," Kieran completed aloud. It made sense to him—but then, he wasn't an academic indoctrinated with assumptions that were incompatible with the notion.

"Exactly," Hamil replied. "You have many interests for a busy doctor. Where did you graduate med school, out of curiosity?"

"We have to talk about that, Hamil," Trevany interjected hastily.

Before them, a pinnacle of rock leaning away from the main massif rose thirty or forty feet above their heads, its sides weathered into horizontal grooves and ribs that revealed the strata it had formed from. The trail ended at a leveled terrace skirting the fissure separating the pinnacle from the face, where an assortment of canisters, boxes, and other pieces of equipment lay scattered around. What they had seen of the pinnacle turned out to be only the top part, Kieran saw as they spread out along the edge. The fissure plummeted downward as a narrowing wedge of space that was quickly lost in shadow relieved only by the yellow glows of artificial lighting lower down that told nothing of their depth. Kieran estimated that the lights had to be somewhere near the level of the valley floor below the mesa, although inaccessible from there directly.

A concrete platform set into the lip of the drop carried a motorized hoist mechanism and winding drum with a projecting girder structure and guide wheels, over which a cable descended alongside two vertical rails attached to the rock. A track of lighter colored dust among the rocks extended from the hoist platform to the far side of the terrace, probably indicating where rubble brought up from below had been carried to the edge and dumped.

Hamil was talking inside his helmet, presumably on another channel. Then his voice came through, cautioning: "Stand clear of the machinery, everyone." Moments later, the hoist began running. Hamil extended an arm to indicate the fissure below. "Zorken started one of their slant bores from the bottom as a shortcut for getting samples from deep under the plateau. The excavations that they opened up down there attracted our interest too. When we got to poking around on our own, we started to uncover things like pieces of what looked like paving, and stones that couldn't have been shaped naturally. That was when Walter decided to come out from Earth and join us."

"I'd been following what was going on. Juanita and I are old colleagues," Trevany commented. "I'd already been talking with Katrina's college about getting them to sponsor some field work. Rudi contacted me to say he wanted to come along too. He had the background for this kind of work."

"And Gottfried," Rudi said.

"Oh, yes. Of course there's him."

"Who's Gottfried?" Kieran asked.

"He's a small, tracked, remote-controlled robot that I had made for field work out in the Middle East," Rudi replied. "Ideal for exploring things like narrow shafts and awkward places. There is an autonomous mode of operation too—good for mapping areas of terrain or exploring larger spaces. You might see him. He's down where we're going."

The elevator appeared from below in the form of a railed metal platform six feet or so square with the hoist cable attached to the side running on the guide rails. Two men were riding it, clad in double-skinned heavy-duty suits streaked with orange and brown dust. As the elevator stopped level with the concrete edge, one of them opened the inner section of guardrail like a gate, and together they manhandled off a rubber-tired tip wagon filled with sand and rubble. One had a wizened face with a straggly gray mustache; the other was black.

Hamil clapped the older one on the shoulder and turned to

the others. "Hah, people! Here are two of the gang that we depend on for getting the real work done in this operation. This is Zeke. The one with the heavy tan is Lou. Gentlemen, here are our new arrivals, Dr. Walter Trevany, Rudi Magelsberg, Katrina Ersohn. And this is Kieran Thane whom I told you about, who's come in as Pierre's replacement. We're all a family here."

"I guess we'll all get to know each other later," Zeke muttered as he moved through, steering the front end of the wagon.

Lou nodded a round of acknowledgments at the company as he followed. "Nothing personal, Doc," he said as he passed Kieran. "But I hope our relationship stays strictly nonprofessional."

"I need to check something with Zeke," Dennis said, stepping aside and looking toward Hamil. "I'll follow you on down."

While Zeke and Lou trundled the wagon across the terrace toward the dump point, followed by Dennis, the others crowded onto the elevator. Hamil closed the gate and pressed a button, and they began descending.

The rock flowed by, the rumbling and squeaking of the pinch rollers on the rails sounding faint and distant through the thin Martian air. The far wall edged closer as the fissure narrowed; then shadow fell abruptly, framing a receding patch of pale pink sky above. As darkness closed in around, Kieran reflected yet again on what it was about his life that always seemed to draw him into situations of the strange and unexpected. He had come to Mars in all innocence to visit an old friend and follow a unique scientific experiment. Now here he was, plunging down a hole in the Martian desert, once again involved in something totally unconnected with the purpose he had started out with, wondering what twists would lead him where this time. Somebody had remarked to him once that his life was like a lightning conductor.

Light reasserted itself as the elevator passed the first of the lamps on the sides of what had by now became little more than a broad slot through the rock. More lamps appeared and the light grew stronger, revealing the face wall breaking into fault lines and fractures where the pinnacle had torn away. The elevator stopped in what appeared to be a cavern extending under the face beneath a jumble of standing flakes choked with debris and jammed boulders that had fallen from above. The cleave planes and bore holes from blasting showed that it was artificial—or at least, had been artificially enlarged. Another tip wagon stood by a pile of rubble, presumably hauled from farther within. More tools and equipment, stacks of adjustable steel roof props and scaffolding parts, and a humming motor-generator with cables snaking off toward the rear of the cavern filled the rest of the space around the elevator. Hamil raised a gate opposite the one via which they had entered and beckoned the others out. They followed silently, the chatter of the trail above gone now, conscious of moving from one world and its time into another, far removed.

The left side of the cavern ended in a square-cut alcove, clearly artificial, where a section of steel pipe several feet long and a foot or more in diameter, capped by a red plastic plug, protruded up at an angle from the floor. "That's the original Zorken bore shaft," Hamil told the others, waving as he led the way past it and into a low, rising gallery of open floor interrupted by roof props, extending farther back, under the plateau. "But what got our attention when we began exploring the surroundings was this. We were lucky in finding just a trace that the Zorken people had uncovered but not recognized. We've opened up a lot more of it since then."

He stopped before a cleared section of floor and indicated it with a gesture of both hands. The others drew up on either side. The area was formed from roughly rectangular, convex-faced slabs, lying regularly with the edges aligned in both directions. To the rear, they disappeared under a layer of rock that looked as if it had covered them and been cut back. At the front, where the group was standing, the slabs ended at an erratic edge where the underlying rock had fallen away into the fissure behind. A trench had been cut to one side, presumably to investigate the foundation and underpinnings.

"Hm. Not unlike several pillow lavas that I've seen," Rudi's voice commented dubiously.

"These are metamorphic, not igneous," Hamil answered.

"And when you probe down under, you can see there are no plumes. They were cut and laid," Jean Graas added.

"Hm," Rudi said again. But even he couldn't argue.

They moved on, still ascending at a mild angle, into the narrowing rear part of the gallery, where Hamil stopped again to let them examine a series of large stones of various shapes and angles that had been set on one side. There were long and short rectangular blocks, several broken curved pieces suggestive of sections of arch, some round pieces, and a few with markings from which encrusting rock had been painstakingly removed, looking tantalizingly as if they could be symbols of some kind. But whether they were or not, it was plain even to Kieran's unschooled eye that these objects had been fashioned. Trevany recognized a couple of instances of indentation marks similar to ones found in South America and Egypt for accepting I-shaped metal pieces to clamp adjacent blocks together. Hamil confirmed that was what he thought they were too. Another broken fragment of rounded rock was surely part of a humanlike chin and nose.

An opening at the back of the gallery, looking at first like a tunnel mouth, turned out to be the entrance to a chamber from which several shafts and crawlways radiated away, some rising, others descending. Hamil led the way, single file now, along a shaft which required only moderate stooping, through another opening. The far side opened up suddenly, in a way that came as a surprise after the warren that had preceded it, into a space that was high but narrow, braced by props mounted horizontally. The rock on one side had been cut into a rising series of ramps and ledges bearing scaffolding, cable boxes, and lights. But it was the other side that captured everyone's attention as the party crowded in to straighten up and stand in awe along the rubble-strewn strip of floor between. They were gazing up at the wall that Kieran had seen on the screen in the Juggernaut.

"We broke through, and here it was, uncovered by a fall that appears to have taken place at some time," Hamil told them. "We haven't had to do much digging at all."

That explained how it could have been news two days ago, yet unburied to an extent that should have required weeks of digging. The space was more confined than the view on the screen had suggested, comprising for the most part a vertical rock fault that revealed part of the wall all the way to its top, where it ended in a line of corbeling at about twenty-five feet. It was smooth and unweathered, grayer and lighter than the surrounding rock. To the left, the wall disappeared behind a line of obscuring rock slanting down to an opening that looked like a pilot tunnel following the base. Just outside the opening was a small, turretlike vehicle, not much bigger than a shoe box, running on what looked like rubber tracks. It was equipped with a lamp, a miniature camera on a pivoting arm, and a variety of sensors, manipulators, and appendages.

"Is that friend Gottfried?" Kieran asked, gesturing.

"Yes," Rudi confirmed. "He'll be in action again later today."

The right-hand side of the wall was buried behind fallen rock extending to the roof, but cleared enough in the lower parts to reveal the ends of several massive stone steps and part of a vertical corner that could have been one side of a gateway. As Trevany and Juanita had said of the mysterious constructions found back on Earth, the way these huge stones fitted was strangely complex yet precise. Kieran tried to imagine what sequence of measuring, cutting, testing, trimming, repositioning and remeasuring would be necessary to achieve such results. He couldn't. Yet, according to the orthodox wisdom that still prevailed upon Earth, it was supposed to have been achieved by cultures that hadn't advanced beyond levers and pulleys, by means of earth ramps and rollers. Trevany scoffed that such explanations were the confident inventions of Egyptologists sitting in university offices; "Construction engineers," he said, "just shook their heads."

So what did it mean? If a close affinity with constructions back on Earth were confirmed, had some lost alien race visited both worlds in the distant past, either from elsewhere in the Solar System or from some other system entirely, and left their enigmatic signatures at enormous expense of effort for purposes yet to be divined? Could they, as some believed, have been the progenitors or creators of the human race? Alternatively, might they have been some advanced but forgotten race of Earth itself, perished in a calamity of interplanetary proportions that had erased virtually all traces of their existence? Or even from Mars, wiped out along with its continents and its oceans? The research that would grow from these beginnings would continue possibly for lifetimes. How much of the planet might eventually be involved in what might eventually be turned up was for anyone to guess. But already, Kieran could see that in terms of additions and revisions to human knowledge, the return over the years was going to be incalculable.

"How about that, Rudi?" Katrina asked with a hint of piquancy. "Does it remind you of any pillow lavas that you've seen?" She winked at Kieran through her visor.

"Hm . . ." Rudi answered. He shuffled awkwardly in his suit.

"It appears we have a lot of work ahead of us. Priceless work, I might add. If my guess is right, this will overturn the conventional school completely."

"Then let's bear that in mind when we set to it," Hamil said to them all. "And think about science. Leave all the petty rivalries and jealousies back where they belong, eh? That was what people came out here to get away from."

# ⅀ **7** ⅀

The flymobile stood in the shed that Solomon Leppo and his buddy, Casey Phibb, rented as a garage and workshop in the tangle of commercial and industrial premises lying along Gorky Avenue toward the terminal domes at Wuhan. It had previously belonged to the son of a wealthy agricultural grower who operated one of the roofed-crater farms. The son hadn't been able to decide whether he wanted a racing machine or a party wagon for his friends. As a consequence, after commissioning a series of unusual and expensive modifications, he had ended up with a curious combination of both that featured a six-seat basic layout with fan-ram hybrid supercompressors, stressed double bubble mainframe, stall-sensing geometry modifiers, and twist-wing aerodynamics. Then he had crashed it, expensively and spectacularly, and as a result of his being either scared off from further sporting ambitions by the experience, or prevailed upon to settle for a lifestyle more agreeable to friends, relatives, and insurance companies, the wreck found its way to the rear yard of Alazahad Machine.

There, it posed Mahom with something of a problem: too heavy and commodious to interest serious racing enthusiasts, yet unconventional enough to dissuade the practical buyers—was its incongruous mix of specifications worth the investment of refurbishing in the hope of an unlikely sale? Mahom had just about written it off for parts, when Solomon Leppo announced that it would be ideal for a project he had been conceiving and offered to take it off Mahom's hands in return for a weekend's overtime. Shrugging, mystified, but never surprised by anything that the human animal might do or desire, Mahom had agreed, happy to cross the liability off his books.

"Not a flymo, Casey. A protection machine! Your flying body-guard. Five years from now, nobody who really is somebody will be going anywhere in anything else, anymore than they'd leave home without their muscle escort." Leppo spoke while he put tools back in the rack above the bench, brushed chaff and drillings from the past three hours' work into a pan, and emptied it into the trash bin underneath. "Ya gotta think new things—innovation. That's the way to break into where the big money is. Create a demand—a new market. It's no use busting your ass for the crumbs left over from what everyone else has already cleaned out."

Casey worked as an engine and flight systems technician in the transportation depot at Stony Flats. He surveyed the modified flymobile from an oily steel stool, where he sat munching a microwaved roast-beef sandwich held in a paper napkin by a casu-ally wiped oily hand. They had christened it the *Guardian Angel*. Painted blue and white with silver sidelines, it was to be their demonstration model. Adding space-grade lightweight armor clad-ding around the cabin and at critical points had been fairly straightforward, as was duplicating the flight and security elec-tronics in a hidden compartment—deactivating the locator call-back was always the first precaution when stealing or hijacking vehicles. The center-mounted, forward-firing automatic cannon would be trickier, involving another deal with Mahom and some advice, but fortunately he was the kind who tended to let the world be and didn't ask questions. The current project was a pair of rear-mounted tubes for passive infrared and electronic, or laser/radar designated infantry-class homing missiles. Leppo also had plans for target-acquisition and incoming-tracking radar, along with a sophisticated countermeasures package, but they would need parts he was still trying to locate among Mahom's various sources. In the meantime, they had something that was at least flying again.

"This is all good experience we're clocking up, Sol," Casey agreed. "It'll double the ticket I can go hawking around. But do you really think we're going to get big packers with wads lin-ing up for them? I mean, it's not just a question of the iron and the specs. You have to know names, and they have to know you. It's as much a social thing too, know what I mean? You have to have the contacts."

"There's ways," Leppo insisted. "Maybe we don't even have to look further than Mahom. He knows political people, military people, lots with money, some you don't wanna talk about, others you never imagined. They talk to each other. See how it works? All you have to do is get a toe in the door here and there, do a good job and show 'em something that'll make their eyes open, and before you know it they'll be coming to you." He pressed a button to dispense a coffee from the battered autochef on its shelf by the laser needle-drill. "Especially when some of them are rivals like the pirate narc and med dealers, or maybe the security agencies' big-name clients. When one decides to upgrade on equipment"—he gestured in the direction of the *Angel*—"then pretty soon all the rest will have to too, right?"

Casey regarded the rear body section as he chewed. It was opened to expose the just-installed six-shot reloading mechanism. "The tail baffles need adjusting for more clearance," he commented.

Leppo went on, "I mean, do you think I plan on crawling about in grease traps like this place for the rest of time? That's not what gets the classy chicks interested, Case. The secret is living with *style*. . . ." Leppo paused to sip from his mug, then added absently, "Some guys like that showed up at the lot the other day."

"Guys like what?"

"With style—you know, living a cool act, man. Looked like they hang out in the best places, probably with chicks everywhere just itchin' to be a part of the scene. They showed up in a big shiny Metro—suits, manicures, clips and rings loaded with ice. One of them stopped by the shop."

"What did they want?" Casey asked.

"They were looking for some guy—said it was business, but I think something heavier was going on. He'd been in Wuhan a couple of days before with a big black dog, driving a rented Kodiak from the firm. That was why they came there."

Casey thought back, then turned his eyes toward Leppo curiously. "Big guy? Lean, tough-looking. Friendly smile, but could probably tear you apart if he had to?"

Leppo looked surprised. "That'd fit. Why?"

"I saw him. He came out to Stony Flats, it must have been, aw . . . about a week ago. Had a dog like that with him. Dark-colored Kodiak—kind of a funny purpley blue?"

"That's it." Leppo was interested. "What was he doing out there?"

"He came out to see some scientists who were fitting out a rig for a surface trip somewhere. I don't know what it was about. Then he showed up again just before they were due to go, and left with them—didn't have the dog that time, though. Somebody said he was some kind of doctor."

Leppo blinked. Life didn't come up with breaks like this every day. "A surface trip?" he repeated. "You don't know where they were going, do you?"

"No. But I could probably find out by making a call. Why the big interest?"

"Oh . . . I just promised the guy I'd let him know if anything turned up," Leppo replied vaguely. "And yeah, Case. I'd appreciate it if you would make that call."

Fifteen minutes later, as Casey began preparing brackets to mount the firing circuit control, Leppo said there was something he needed from his car parked in the alleyway outside. He went out to it, got in and closed the door, and used his comset to call the number on the calling card that he retrieved from his wallet. A man's voice replied unilluminatingly, "Enterprises." Leppo recognized it.

"Mr. Mullen?"

"Who wants him?"

"This is Sol Leppo. I talked to you when you were at Alazahad Machine out on Beacon Way. You were asking about a man with a dog. I said I'd get back if I heard anything. Okay, I think I can tell you where he went. . . ."

# ≋ 8 ≋

A mood of exhilaration gripped the camp, infecting even the work detail hired to handle the brunt of the digging and clearing. In addition to Zeke and Lou, they were Shayne, a burly Canadian, Nailikar, of some distant Asiatic ancestry, and Chas Ryan, the crew's foreman. When they weren't at work down the "Hole," bringing up the excavation debris, playing cards, or catching up on movie fare over chilled cans of Olympus home-brewed beer, they asked questions of the scientists about background to the work and listened with widening interest to accounts of ancient Terran constructions and their mysteries, and theories concerning Earth's turbulent history in recent times. They even came up with speculations of their own. Chas wondered if the Technolithic culture might have had foreknowledge of whatever had befallen them, and erected their huge, virtually indestructible monuments as a testimony of who they were and when they had existed, written in language that any advanced race coming later would eventually be able to decode. Hamil confirmed that many scientists thought the same thing and believed they had made beginnings in unraveling the code. Zeke thought that the "gods" of Biblical and other ancient creation stories might have been space beings. But that wasn't really original. From time to time, the media would air some new angle or other on notions heard for years that the tussles between good and fallen "angels," or the Greek Olympians and Titans, and so on, were accounts of ancient power struggles and rebellions involving other-worldly visitors, described by early humans who had no other way of interpreting what they were witnessing. Kieran had expected a comparatively drab interlude of staying out of circulation while the heat

165

died down in Lowell. On the contrary, in every aspect, the company and the subject were proving a new source of fascination for his ever-restless curiosity.

It was a variation of an old puzzle, guaranteed to split opinions down the middle and generate controversy at a vicarage afternoon tea party. Kieran laid three cards facedown on the long table in the messroom of the inflatable-frame cabin. "Okay, it's simple," he told Chas Ryan and Harry Quong, sitting opposite him on the bench seat that ran along one wall. "Just one of them's a king. Which one?"

"You mean just make a guess?" Harry checked.

"Yes," Kieran said. He hadn't shown the faces and then made elaborate passes or flourishes; this obviously wasn't the classic three-card trick.

"And you know which one, right?" Chas queried.

"Of course."

Harry shrugged, ran his eye over the row, then pointed. "That one."

Kieran looked inquiringly at Chas. "Good enough for me," Chas responded. "I'll say that one too."

"Fine. Well, *I* know it isn't this one." Kieran turned over one of the other two cards to reveal it as the three of diamonds. "The question is this: For the best chance of being right, what should you do? Stay with your choice? Change to the other one? Or doesn't it matter?" He sat back to let them ponder. Juanita was in a foldaway chair in the corner, going through some papers. The others were either away down the Hole, busy in the Juggernaut lab, or otherwise out on some chore around the camp.

"It can't make any difference," Harry said. "There's two cards left. It's fifty-fifty. Stick or change. It doesn't matter."

Chas hesitated for a moment longer, than nodded. "I agree. It's not gonna change your odds."

Kieran gave them a few seconds to reconsider, smiling waggishly. "Actually, it does," he said. "You should change your bet. The odds of winning are twice as good." This was where the fun part started. Even mathematicians often couldn't see it—and they tended to be the most belligerent in defending their view. The interesting challenge, Kieran had found, was picking the right way of explaining it, depending on his judgment of the personality he was dealing with. An argument or analogy that made the answer immediately clear to one person would be unfathomable to another.

Chas shook his head. "I can't see it. Like Harry said, you've got two left. It's either one or the other. We don't know which, even if you might. So how can anything we decide make a difference?" Harry seemed less sure, but at the same time completely unsure why. He rubbed his chin and stared at the two face-down cards as if waiting for a revelation.

Kieran studied their faces, as if divining the way to play a poker hand. "When you made your choice, the odds were one in three that it was the right one," he offered. "That can't have changed. So the odds for the other card here—the one you didn't pick—must be two in three. Change your choice and you double your chances."

Chas brooded, then shook his head again. "That was then. This is different. We've got two cards. It's fifty-fifty."

From the entry chamber that served the cabin's three rooms came the sound of the pump starting up to fill the outside lock. Juanita had pushed her glasses down her nose and was following the conversation over the paper she had been reading. "Think of it this way," she suggested. "Suppose your first choice had been out of the whole pack instead of just three cards. Kieran knows which is the king. He's used that knowledge to throw out fifty for you and left just the king and one other. Do you still think the king is likely to be the one you picked?"

Light dawned in Harry's eyes. "Ri-ght! *Now* I see it!" It was Chas's turn to look uncertain.

Before it could go any further, the sound of boots stamping and dust being brushed off a suit came from outside the room. Then the door opened and Dennis came in, already removing his helmet. He was in his early thirties, sandy-haired with a fresh, open face, the kind of pragmatic academic who preferred getting out in the world and doing things rather than theorizing. His preoccupation with his work left him with a total disinterest in politics, which with his generally amiable nature meant he got along with just about anybody. Dennis had worked with Trevany previously on Earth. For the past couple of years, however, he and Jean Graas had been exploring various parts of the Martian surface with Hamil and Juanita.

"How are things going?" Juanita asked him.

"Steady. Shayne and Zeke have cleared the top of the E-2 object. It's definitely a gate. The amazing thing is, it's monolithic. Walter estimates that on Earth that one piece would weigh over two hundred tons. And places we know back there have designs just like it."

Chas leaned back from the table and spread his hands. "So how did they build with things like that? I mean, I've worked on enough construction projects to know what it takes. I've heard these stories about how they were supposed to have done it with lots of guys hauling ropes, but with me it doesn't wash. Once something like those things is down, it's down. So how could they end up with them put together like stacking toys?"

"There was an Inca king who wondered the same thing," Juanita commented. "So he decided to see if he could emulate it by bringing just one boulder of comparable size to add to the citadel at Sacsayhuaman in Peru. According to a Spanish account from the sixteenth century, he had twenty thousand Indians hauling it across the mountains. It broke loose over a precipice and crushed something like three thousand men. That was the end of the experiment—their only known attempt to duplicate the feats they're supposed to have achieved all over the area. Not very convincing, you see."

"You mean that whatever the original techniques were, the Incas of that time had no knowledge or experience of them," Kieran translated.

"Exactly," Dennis said. "And now this. It gets more interesting, doesn't it?"

Just then, the call beep sounded from the c-com unit on the wall near where Juanita was sitting. She reached across to accept. The screen showed the head and shoulders of Walter Trevany, inside the Juggernaut, which was now drawn alongside the cabin and connected by a short, flexible-wall tunnel to avoid the hassle of suiting up every time somebody needed to get from one to the other. His expression was uncertain, with a hint of worry. "Just to let you know, we picked up something approaching on radar a few minutes ago," he announced. "It looks like we might be having visitors. I don't know who. Hamil's on his way up from the Hole. If anyone else wants to show their face, we'll see you outside."

✧          ✧          ✧

Clad in a light-duty surface suit, Kieran stood with Dennis and Juanita on the edge of the open area next to the huddle of shacks and vehicles. Trevany and Jean Graas were nearby with Hamil. All heads behind the helmet visors were gazing upward at the "Mule" transporter circling now after interrupting its descent, presumably on seeing the signs of occupation. It was a dark metallic gray, with a boxlike, square-sectioned body, high tail assembly with triple fins, and stubby wings situated amidships carrying large engine nacelles at their ends—a standard model used for hauling people and freight all over Mars. A voice came through in Kieran's helmet on the local air-traffic channel that they were all tuned to. His wrist-screen showed the smooth-skinned face of a man in his mid to late thirties, hair light yellow, with the neck ring of a flight EV suit visible below his chin. He hadn't introduced himself.

"This area has been retained under the terms of a use registration certificate filed by Zorken Consolidated. You are in violation of the generally acknowledged code. Identify yourselves and state your purpose here."

Hamil answered. "This is Hamil Hashikar speaking, professor of archeology. We are an independent archeological research expedition supported by a diversity of private and academic interests. Your activity here has been suspended. The pilot diggings that were left offered an invaluable opportunity of a kind that science doesn't get very often." All typical of the way he could imagine Hamil working, Kieran thought to himself. Easygoing and genial, never stopping to doubt as he sauntered through life that the things that mattered to him wouldn't automatically hold the same significance for everyone else. Unless he absolutely had to, Hamil wouldn't sacrifice available field time getting approvals from inflated bureaucrats or bogging down under pedantic and irritating procedures.

"You've got the rest of the planet to go exploring in," the voice on the channel said. "This area has been declared a retained territory. We're here to prepare for the resumption of work by Zorken. You will be required to vacate."

"I have a feeling that might change if we could talk to you," Hamil replied. "But it's not exactly convenient at this distance."

The Mule banked into a turn and came lower, straightening out to make a slow pass over the camp—low enough for Kieran to feel the pulsations of its engines and make out the white-on-orange ZC logos painted on the tail fins. The occupants were no doubt checking for signs of weapons or anything out of order in the surroundings. "Very well," the yellow-haired man answered finally. "Keep clear of the landing area."

The craft slowed into a vertical descent immediately in front of the camp, its engine note rising, though still sounding distant in the rarified air, and settled amid swirls of dust and sand. The sound and the flurries died. There was a short pause. Then the Mule's access steps hinged down with a section of the hull, and three suited figures emerged. They stopped at the bottom of the steps to look around and assess the party waiting for them, and then came over. The yellow-haired man was in the center, leading. With him were a thin-lipped, pallid-faced woman with straight, gray-streaked hair cropped short, and an Asian with a short, pointed Charlie Chan beard. Hamil, looking characteristically jovial, extended a gloved hand.

"Hamil Hashikar."

The yellow-haired man ignored it and remained unsmiling. "I don't think such displays would be appropriate to the circumstances. My name is Banks. I represent Zorken Consolidated. My exact capacity doesn't matter. As I have already informed you, these workings are certified under a use registration. Under the adopted Martian codes, you have no claim here. There is nothing more to discuss."

Hamil made a placatory gesture. Kieran had already written off any attempt to reason at this stage as pointless, but Hamil was missing that fact. He went on, "But you don't understand, Mr. Banks. What we have found here could rank among the most important archeological discoveries of the century. We need to get in touch with whoever has ultimate responsibility for your project here."

Banks closed his eyes and sighed. "I think it's *you* who doesn't understand. A whole new space complex is going up here. Do you think someone's going to stop that so you can dig up rocks to argue about?"

"Hardly. But how about a whole lost civilization?"

"How much is it likely to add to our profitability account? I can't see anyone getting wildly interested."

"But what I'm talking about could have profound connections

with our own origins on Earth too...." Hamil's voice was rising with incredulity. He looked from one to another of the three
faces regarding him stonily through their visors. The futility of
trying to get anything across that might evoke a more receptive
attitude finally registered with him. He shook his head, at a loss
for how to continue. A strained silence persisted for several
seconds. Jean moved closer to Dennis.

Then Juanita exploded. *"Philistines! Barbarians!* Is that all you
can think about—your precious accounting balances and prof-
its? Don't you understand what he's telling you? We're talking
about events that may have determined the beginnings of the
human race!"

"Information that's priceless," Trevany put in, sounding bewildered. "Priceless..."

"Really?" Banks sneered. "In that case, if enough people agree
with you, you shouldn't have any trouble raising a figure that'll
buy us out. We're always open to offers." He shot a look at Juanita.
"You see—perfectly reasonable people." His face darkened. "In
the meantime, I want you and your equipment out of here. We've
got work to do, and you're in the way. If you refuse to leave peace-
ably, we'll be forced to resort to employing stronger measures."

# ⋺ **9** ⋹

Henry Balmer lived in a small but luxurious condominium contained in a system of glass-walled levels spanning the canyon above where the Trapezium joined Embarcadero, and known collectively as "Crystal Bridge." The search to trace Sarda's missing money was being conducted by the Investigative Department of Lowell's Administrative Congress, which kept their attention away from the real problem. The syndicate that the deputation sent to the Zodiac Bank represented were demanding the return of the quarter billion they had advanced for what the industry buzz was now dismissing as a technology too plagued with problems to be worth the investment. Although finding it was technically Balmer and Sarda's problem, the syndicate was making its people and resources available to the task. Given the choice, it preferred cash in the bank to bodies on mortuary slabs—at best a deterrent of debatable efficacy to others when all else failed.

Leo Sarda sat in the corner recliner, tugging at his mustache with a thumb and forefinger. At Stewart Perrel's suggestion, he was taking a week's convalescent leave from Quantonix, not least because as far as anyone else could tell, the therapy with Balmer seemed to be working, albeit still with some remaining gaps in Sarda's memories from the period immediately following the experiment. That, of course, was because the events he was supposed to remember from that time had been experienced by the other Sarda—the one who had gone missing—whom nobody at Quantonix knew about. Hence, the syndicate had a pretext for the time it needed to find out what had happened to the other Sarda and Elaine. So far, it had drawn a complete blank, even with Balmer's numerous and diverse contacts to draw on.

Whoever had engineered the pair's disappearance had done a thorough job.

"We were set up from the start," Balmer said darkly, standing at the sliding glass door at the rear of the living area, unable to keep still. Outside was a small conservatory with tropical flowers and plants, and beyond, a reinforced picture window presenting a stunning view over the roofs of Embarcadero and along the canyon toward the main Marineris rift. "Probably since before the experiment. Obviously, you couldn't have been involved, or you would remember it. So it has to have been Elaine. This double cross was never her doing. It was the work of professionals who know the business. So they must have been involved from the beginning."

"Before the experiment?" Sarda repeated. "So what are you saying? The whole line of hers about using you to keep me around was part of the scam? She had something like this figured out all that way back?"

"Of course she must have." Balmer turned from the window. His eyes glared across the room from beneath the huge eyebrows. "She sold you the idea in order to create a victim figure they could work on. Then she must have poisoned your mind with fears, and resentments toward the other Sarda, who would risk nothing. Well, didn't she?"

Sarda nodded at the suggestion. He had to have been put up to it. Already, he was sure, he could remember her provocative words and sultry urgings for him to claim what was rightfully his. "And I walked right into it," he muttered blackly.

"I always knew she'd latched onto me for what she could get out of it," Balmer said. "But I have to admit I didn't see all the way through her either. An opportunist, yes; but I never realized she could be *that* much of one."

Sarda showed a hand. "And this pained, moral high tone she put on, suggesting it was *me* who was being unethical . . . when all the time she was working to clean out both of us."

Balmer breathed heavily. "It almost makes you want to lose faith in—" The chime from the front door interrupted. "Who's this?" He raised his voice slightly. "House manager. Door view." The wall screen opposite the couch activated to show two figures standing outside. One, tanned, suave, was Lee Mullen, a local "facilitator" engaged by the syndicate to help with its inquiries. The other was dark-skinned and bearded, also expensively dressed in a suit. Balmer didn't recognize him. "Function, door open," he said, moving in the direction of the hall. Mullen and the other man stepped inside just as Balmer came through the doorway to meet them.

"Hi, Doc," Mullen greeted. He looked past Balmer, into the living area, where Sarda had risen from the recliner. "Well, say, the other guy's here too. That makes it easier. We've got a few things to discuss," he told them. "But first, I just wanted to let you know that we've come up lucky on the guy with the dog. Seems like he's a doctor too—going under the name of Thane. He took off a week ago with a party that went out in the desert to dig up rocks. We're sending some friends out there to bring him back for a talk. So don't you two get any ideas on going anywhere, okay? We want you around to make sure he gets asked the right questions. People back at the Firm are getting very anxious about this. . . ."

Low and sleek, like a blue-and-white shark out of water, the *Guardian Angel* stood in front of the workshop behind the office at Alazahad Machine, where Solomon Leppo had towed it to be fitted with its automatic cannon from Mahom's miniature armory. Phil Verlan, the sales manager, stood, arms folded, contemplating it alongside Mahom, while Leppo and Mack, an avionics-specialist friend of Mahom's, finished installing the fire-control box inside an access hatch forward of the driving compartment.

"So what do you reckon, Phil?" Mahom asked, giving Verlan a picket-fence grin of pearly teeth. "Sol says there's gonna be a big market one day."

"Who with?" Verlan replied. "Are we planning on expanding into the military supply business?"

"Private security," Leppo said over his shoulder as he held the cover panel while Mack gunned in the fixing screws. "There's no Mars law here yet that everyone agrees on, and the place is filling up. People who matter are already organizing their own protection and alliance deals. Five years from now they'll all be wanting one."

"Is that the way it's gonna go, Phil?" Mahom asked Verlan. "Should we be thinking about taking options?" All prospective business ranked equally in Mahom's estimation. Passing judgments on what ought or ought not to be didn't figure into his way of calculating.

"Let me sound out a few contacts before I answer that," Verlan said. He glanced at his watch. "Speaking of which, I'm supposed to be meeting a couple of guys, and I'm running late already. I need to pick up some things from the office, too."

"I'll walk back in with you," Mahom said.

"Keep at it, Sol," Verlan tossed back as he and Mahom walked away. "You could be onto something there, all right. I'll start doing some sounding around on it, like I said."

"We can't lose. You'll see," Leppo called after them confidently. Mack began replacing items in the toolbox from his truck, parked a few yards away. "That should be fine when the sights are calibrated. We'll fly it out to the range at Stony Flats tomorrow for some test firings. Suppose I stop by at ten?"

"That'll work fine," Leppo said. "I'll get Casey over. He works out that way anyhow."

"A couple of boxes of tracer and one minipack of live should be enough. Mahom's got them in the back. I already checked."

"Will do. I'll square it with him as soon as you're gone."

"Okay." Mack closed the toolbox and straightened up expectantly. "What was it we said . . . ?" Leppo felt inside his jacket and took out the envelope that had been delivered from Mullen. He opened it and peeled out four inner-system fifty-dollar bills. Mack checked them, then folded and stuffed them into a back pocket of his jeans. "Okay, Sol. So we'll see you here again tomorrow."

"Ten."

"On the dot." Mack hoisted up the toolbox and walked over to his truck. Leppo watched while he climbed in, started up, and drove off along Beacon Way.

The envelope was still in Leppo's hand. He stared at it for several seconds before returning it slowly to his inside jacket pocket. It was money, yes; and he had long considered money to be the key to everything else that was desirable. But blood money, very possibly? The thought wasn't comfortable at all. He was still wrestling with it when the sound of a motor started on the far side of the office shack; moments later, Phil Verlan's auto came into sight and turned onto Beacon Way, heading in the opposite direction from the one Mack had taken. Leppo felt the envelope in his jacket again. Then he walked up to the office and let himself in by the side door.

Mahom was fiddling with the adjustment of a drawer in his desk that wasn't closing properly. "You got Phil thinking now, Sol," he chuckled. "Whatever gave you the idea of getting involved with people who wanna start private wars?"

Leppo shrugged. "I just think protection is going to get big around here."

"Well, you came to a good place to do your apprenticeship. Was that the idea?"

"Hey, what you pay me for always comes first. You know that."

"Oh, I'm not complaining. You do good work. It sounds like pretty sharp thinking to me. I never held that against anybody. That's what you need to do to get along."

There was a short silence. Leppo walked over to the water fountain and poured himself a cup. "What happened to that blue Kodiak that was out front?" he asked without looking back. "I haven't seen it around. Did we sell it?"

"Rented it. Someone might be interested in one of the lux DH models coming from the lunar plants. The Kodiak'll give him a taste of DH and get him around in the meantime."

"Anyone we know?" Leppo forced his voice to remain casually curious.

"Oh, a real good friend. One of the best."

Leppo's stomach tightened. "Oh, really?"

Mahom nodded his massive, frizzy mane. "They call him the Knight. He comes and goes, gets involved in all kinds of situations you wouldn't believe. Real smart—but always straight. Sides with what's right, especially when it's some little guy who needs help. Has fun getting a piece of the action from the big takers. A while ago, long before you started here, I was being leaned on by a heavy-style protection operation who would have cut me down to being a rent collector for my own place. It was the Knight who fixed them then." Mahom cackled again at the recollection and drew the drawer out experimentally. "Fixed 'em so good that they ain't around anymore. I don't know where he is right now, but maybe when he's back this way you might want to talk to him about private security. He'd give you some angles you never thought of." Mahom nodded, satisfied, and slid the drawer home again. "One of the best," he said again. "You won't ever meet a better friend than that one, Sol."

✧        ✦        ✧

Leppo had a date that night with a girl called Mitzi, whom he had known casually for a while. Partway through the evening, she remarked that Leppo didn't seem to be his usual talkative self. Was there something wrong? Leppo replied that it was nothing to do with them. He had a business problem that was worrying him.

# ⫷ **10** ⫸

The atmosphere in the inflatable triple cabin was stuffy with the unusual number of bodies crowded inside, and heavy from the sense of uncertainty hanging over the expedition. After a strained night during which Banks was no doubt awaiting instructions, he had retaken possession of the two shacks left by Zorken and moved the Mule alongside them. The cluster formed its own small camp apart from the scientific expedition's, enclosed inside a perimeter of metal stakes linked by infrared beams to detect intruders. There could be no real argument, since the shacks were unquestionably Zorken's property. Hence, the expedition had seen no option but to concede and vacate them. The next challenge would probably be to contest their access to the Hole. Accordingly, in case worse should come to worst, Hamil had gone down there with Juanita to photograph and record the findings to date. In this, Kieran noted, Hamil had also removed the most fierily disposed member from the immediate scene while a chance remained of working something out diplomatically. To this latter end, Trevany and Jean had gone across to the Mule with the aim of establishing some grounds for reciprocal accommodation. Hamil's reasoning was that Trevany's standing as an investigator come specially from Earth might underline the importance of the finds. Harry Quong and Chas Ryan were outside, reinstalling the electrical and air recirculation equipment displaced from the shack in one of the two trailers. The rest of the expedition, doubtless reflecting the human tendency to group together in anxious times, had collected in the messroom of the inflatable-frame shack to await events. They were Kieran, Dennis, Rudi, Katrina, and the five site workers. The need for

178

the services of the latter was effectively suspended for the time being.

"Harry told me once that Pierre was a good friend of you and Jean," Kieran said to Dennis. They were sitting a little apart from the rest, who were immersed in a discussion of legalities and land rights.

Dennis nodded. "Jean knows him from way back. They used to belong to some European student club."

"Apparently, you know something about the work Pierre's involved with in Lowell—some kind of nano-scale biological research."

"Self-assembling artificial molecular structures. Why?"

"Oh . . . I'm just curious about everything, I suppose. Harry said something about pieces coming together inside body cells. Is that where the self-assembling comes into it?"

"Right. The components are small enough to be taken in through ingestion or inhalation, and get transported into the body cells via the regular mechanism." Dennis paused with an inquiring look that asked if the concepts were familiar. Kieran nodded for him to go on. "There, they use the cells' metabolic machinery to assemble into protein synthesizers."

"You mean like artificial ribosomes?"

"Exactly. But the unique thing is, they can be directed remotely," Dennis said. Kieran looked puzzled. Dennis explained, "As to what proteins to synthesize. Part of the structure is actually a resonant molecular circuit that decodes externally applied electronic signals. So the kind of proteins that get made inside the cell can be programmed from the outside."

"That's a new one on me," Kieran said.

"Neat, eh?"

"So what would you use it for?"

Dennis made a tossing-away gesture. "They're not sure of all the possibilities yet. One might be remote-directing a regimen of medication. Instead of having to hope you've got all the right drugs with you for whatever problems you might run into, the instructions to make whatever you need can be transmitted from a diagnostic center far away. Think how useful that could be with people scattered around the Solar System getting themselves into all kinds of messes."

Kieran was intrigued, and sat back to see what other lines he could think of. But before he could come up with anything, Rudi turned and called across from the long table where the others were gathered. "Hey, Sir Knight, you tell us—how do things like this work here? If there's no overall authority to issue land titles, then Zorken can't actually *own* this site." He made a careless gesture with an open hand. "So they were here before us and sank a few shafts. What of it? That doesn't sound like much of a case to me. They went away and left it. You can't have people going around making claims on anywhere, just because they happen to have been there before."

"They filed a certificate stating that the area was being productively used," Kieran replied. "It's a bit loose, but the various forms of governing authorities and what-have-you around Mars generally recognize it."

"What did Banks mean when he told Hamil that Zorken would back his claim with force if need be?" Katrina asked. "Surely it can't work as a free-for-all?"

"You said you were looking at properties to buy recently," Rudi said to Kieran. "Okay, who controls those rights? If you pay a real estate agency for a place somewhere, who enforces your claim if somebody shows up one day and says it's theirs because they were there first?" He showed both hands. "It's ridiculous. That would be chaotic."

"Most of the time, people manage to muddle through," was all Kieran could say. It didn't sound very satisfying but there was no neat and tidy answer to give. "You have to be here for a while to get a feel of how it works. There's no easy way to explain it."

"But what about when being reasonable and understanding doesn't work?" Rudi persisted. "Do they bring in the paid security agencies that we hear about, and it turns into a private war? Is that what Banks was talking about? I came here as an archeologist, not to join somebody's infantry."

Lou, the black man on the work team, said, "There might have been a few scuffles and differences now and again. But there's never been any real attempt to stake out a big slice of territory by force. . . ." He glanced at his companions. "None that I've ever heard of, anyhow."

"That's only because there's a lot of empty space out there, yet," Zeke said. "When there's plenty of everything for everybody, that's when folks can get along. The bickering starts when something or other they all want gets in short supply. I seen it all before in other places. Either some kind of system has to come out of it all that can lay it down for everyone as to what's what, or else there's gonna be a lot of trouble one day before it straightens itself out."

"Took long enough to get a world system back on Earth," Shayne pointed out. "And even now it isn't as complete as they wanted it. They managed somehow for a long time before that, though."

"Right, and look at the amount of trouble they went through doing it, too," Zeke countered. Rudi looked at Kieran, as if for a verdict.

"That might not be the only way," Kieran said. "There are lots of experiments going on all around. I'd say to wait a bit longer and see what happens."

"That doesn't do a lot to help us in the meantime," Rudi observed. Kieran couldn't argue.

"So what are we supposed to do?" Katrina asked. "There isn't any kind of ultimate police or court system that we can appeal to. I think I agree with Rudi. It's ridiculous."

"Perhaps you wouldn't want to," Kieran cautioned. "Squatters' rights mightn't apply. You could find that Zorken has the better case."

"So are we supposed to organize some kind of credible counterthreat—raise our own army?" Rudi demanded derisively. "That's preposterous!"

"It doesn't strike me as Hamil's way in any case," Katrina said.

"And it might be a waste of time wondering about it," Kieran told them. "Why don't we wait first, and see what Walter and Jean have to say when they come back?" From his initial assessment of Banks, he didn't expect very much—but it had to be tried. And assuming that Banks would be acting under orders from his principals, the brief amount of research that Kieran had been able to do via the net didn't lead him to hold out much hope for any change of attitude from that direction either.

The headquarters of Zorken Consolidated's vastly spread operations was a large artificial structure called Asgard that cycled in an eccentric orbit between the Belt and a perihelion that precessed between Earth and Mars. Currently it was approaching and would cross the orbit of Mars quite closely within the next two weeks. Zorken had a predatory history of acquisitions and hostile mergers, and in the free economic conditions that reigned beyond Earth's region of influence, hadn't shrunk on several occasions from employing armed force in dealing with inconveniently active rivals. Once, they had invaded and permanently taken over an asteroid holding of a customer they deemed wayward on payments. Now, they had evidently set their sights on developing this location at Tharsis, and Kieran couldn't see them altering their policy out of goodwill towards a shoestring-funded scientific group whose work held no prospect of any benefit relevant to Zorken's interests.

"Well, I don't see that anyone can expect us to stick around if it's going to turn into some kind of range war," Shayne declared. "Our contracts didn't say nothing about anything like that."

Lou nodded uncomfortably. "I think I have to agree with that."

"Don't go getting yourselves all jumpy too hasty," Zeke told them. "That's just what they want. Things aren't gonna get like that anytime soon. Folks out here might like their independence, but they have a way of acting together real quick when someone starts getting too heavy-handed. These Zorken people might be mean, but they're smart enough to know that. It'll be talk and bluff for a long while." Kieran wasn't so sure he agreed, but any advice not to panic was good advice. He let it ride.

Nailikar, who was watching the c-com unit mounted on the wall at the end of the table, looked around suddenly. The screen was showing the view from an outside camera trained on the parked Mule a few hundred feet away. "They're coming out now," he announced. Conversation ceased as everyone moved to get a better view. Two suited figures were descending the Mule's access steps. Nailikar brought up a zoom window showing their heads and shoulders in close-up as they began walking back toward the expedition's camp. Trevany was not looking happy behind the visor of his helmet; Jean, about the same. "Base here, Walter, we're reading you," Nailikar said. "How'd it go?"

Trevany shook his head. A heavy sigh came over the audio. "We tried, guys. Offered to give them a tour. The upshot is they think it's quaint, but they're not interested—it's just a pile of old rocks. Their orders from head office are to wheel in some persuasion if we don't move. I don't know what we do now. I'm new here. Wait until Hamil and the others get back up from the Hole, I guess."

But even from where he was sitting, Kieran could read the dejection written across his face. This wasn't a situation that these people were equipped or experienced to handle, he could see. As Katrina had said, trying to match force with force wouldn't be Hamil's way; furthermore, a group such as this, divorced from Terran scientific orthodoxy, would have little recourse to institutions or political connections capable of initiating some defense from that quarter either.

It was a job, then, he decided, for the Knight.

# ⇒ 11 ⇐

The first requirement of any job was adequate information. While the scientists went into a cycle of debating around repeating circles, Kieran ensconced himself in the Juggernaut and began familiarizing himself with as much as was publicly on record concerning Zorken Consolidated's plans for the area. To his surprise, it turned out that the project to develop a spaceport at Tharsis was on hold indefinitely. The results of the pilot survey were stated as deeming the site unsuitable, although no further details were given. Zorken had already filed intentions to proceed with investigating possible alternative sites. And that made Kieran immediately both curious and suspicious. If they were no longer interested in the Tharsis site for the original reasons, then what did they want it for? It might help, he decided, to know something more about the kind of people that Banks had brought with him.

A code that Donna at Triplanetary had supplied him with a while ago gave him access to the spacelines' passenger lists of recent arrivals on Mars. Kieran located the Zorken group without much difficulty, all on tickets charged to the corporation: Justin Banks; Gertrude Heissen; Tran Xedeidang; Clarence Porter. Whoever else was with the Mule—crew, more employees, agents and consultants—must have been brought in locally. That was all that the spaceline records could tell him. Building meaty bodies around such scanty bones was part of the magic that June excelled at. In any case, it gave Kieran a reason to call her. She answered from her apartment in Nineveh.

"Well, hi! A face from the wilderness. I was beginning to wonder if you'd decided to take up a life as an ascetic recluse out there."

184

"Oh, there are times when it sounds tempting, but fortunately they don't last," Kieran replied. "How are things in the vast metropolis?"

"Metropolitan. Sarda's been retired from the limelight at Quantonix—the story is, to rest up and concentrate on getting straightened out."

"At Doctor Balmer's spa and cure-all."

"Exactly. More likely it's to concentrate on finding where the money went before the money people's patience runs out."

"They've been covering the territory. I got a call from Mahom a few days back, saying that some unworthies had been out at the lot asking about me. I don't think it was because of concern over my health and happiness."

June's eyebrows rose. "Really? Then maybe my concern for it, and getting you out of sight wasn't such a bad thing after all."

"Seems like it."

"How did they get a lead on you at Mahom's?" June asked.

"I'm not sure. Sometimes my popularity just runs ahead of me."

June dismissed it with a toss of her head as one of those facts of existence surrounding Kieran that would never be explained. "So how's the budding archeologist? Have you decided yet that your whole life so far has been misguided, and discovered your true calling to be a search for solitude, serenity, and peace of the soul?"

"Not quite. But we've run into some complications."

"Now why doesn't that surprise me?"

"What they've found here as far as the scientific side goes is staggering: constructions from some long-lost culture. No question about it. But even more astounding is that they show every sign of being related to the Technolithic structures on Earth. I can see now why Walter rushed out here."

The frivolity vanished from June's face. "You're serious?" The question was reflexive. Even with all Kieran's quirks and convolutions, she knew when he was and was not joking. "So what's the complication?"

"A big construction and mining outfit from the Belt, called Zorken Consolidated, has first dibs on the site, and they're not letting a few rocks and ideas of dead aliens get in the way of the holy flow of dollars. Some of their people showed up here and are waving an eviction notice with threats."

June nodded in a way that called for no elaboration. "What are they staking it out for?" she asked curiously.

"That's the funny part. The original plan was for another spaceport. But I've just checked with the registries in Lowell, and that plan has already been shelved. So who are these people from Zorken and what do they want? I've got four names who arrived from off-planet out of the spaceline lists. Will you get what you can on them for me?"

"Sure. Shoot them through."

Kieran clicked a button to send off the list. "And how is the new lord of your manor making out?"

"Guinness? Oh, he's out somewhere with Patti from the Oasis and her friend. I think you might be lucky if you get him back." Kieran was about to respond, and then a distant look came over his face suddenly. June waited. "What is it?" she asked.

"Guinness . . . That could be it. He was with us when we intercepted Sarda-One on his way to the bank. Balmer has probably restored his memories by now. Guinness would have given something different for people going around asking questions to latch on to."

"So how would they connect from there to Mahom's place?" June asked.

Kieran thought for a moment longer, then shook his head. "I don't know. Anyhow, it doesn't make any difference now. I've got some more things I want to check. Get back to me with whatever you come up with on these four as soon as you can, would you, Lovely Lady?"

"Flattery will get you most places you want to go. Okay, Kieran, I'll get on to it right away."

Like celebrities and political leaders, high executives in business tended to be driven by egos whose sense of importance was served by having their success stories, views on life, pearls of wisdom, and whatever other contributions they felt might be valuable to posterity, widely circulated for worldly consumption. In short, they were hardly publicity shy, and since they suffered from no shortage of the wherewithal and influence to gain visibility, were always happy to oblige media foragers looking for some fill or another angle on a story. This made it not especially difficult to put together surprisingly detailed pictures from interviews, gossip columns, profile pieces, and other sources available across the General Net. This, Kieran proceeded to do, garnishing the result with a few extra inside details gleaned through calls to contacts he had acquired in media research departments and elsewhere.

Zorken's chief executive and president was one Hamilton Horatio Gilder, who at 58 had held the position for eight years after promotion from vice president of the Legal Division—it was interesting that Zorken needed a full legal *division*, whereas most of even the larger-scale operations were able to make do with a department. Before that, he had climbed through the ranks from a background of finance, law, and business administration in a demonstration of loyalty and treachery surgically applied in appropriate directions in a way that would have earned a no-fault rating from Machiavelli. He had carved his way to the top—at least, so the adulatory testimonials said—without benefit of family connections or the impetus of previously entrenched wealth, but now presided over a dynasty of interlocking marriages and other forms of individual contract that owned the lion's bite of Zorken-controlled assets across the Central Solar System. The clan disported themselves in residences scattered through the Belt and the Jovian moons, and had been featured in articles depicting life among the fashionable on the beaches of western Florida, mountain resorts in Bavaria, and the pleasure city of Durban, South Africa.

Gilder himself had three offspring, none of them from the brief marriage he had attempted at an early age, declining to repeat the experience since. In this he represented a departure from the staid conformity still generally expected of senior executives, but far from offering contrition, he apparently reveled in the image of rebelliousness and untamed individualism that it gave him. "Moral high ground is just a refuge for the mediocre," he had told a journalist when the subject came up in an interview. The oldest daughter, Deirdre, 36, had withdrawn into a recluse religious order out in the Belt, and as a consequence wasn't alluded to much in the "Who's Where" reviews or the glitter pages. The antics and affairs of the 27-year-old playboy son, Achilles, however, received plenty of coverage. And then there was Marissa, 24, beautiful, beguiling, and doted upon, her wedding due that week, to be held at the corporate space-based citadel, Asgard, when it approached close to Mars.

It had been Hamilton Gilder, personally, who instigated the seizure of a delinquent customer's asteroidal minerals-extraction facility—and, it turned out, several similar actions that hadn't received the same publicity. In defense he had quoted Feliks Dzerzhinski, founder of the Soviet political police in the early 20th century: "Trust is good, but control is better." Gilder seemed to like airing quotes and being quoted. A couple of others that Kieran took as indicative of his broad philosophy of life were Collis Huntington, the long-gone U.S. railroad tycoon's: "Whatever isn't nailed down is mine. Whatever I can pry up isn't nailed down." And Charles Dickens: "Do other men, for they would do you." There was also: "Our work is business. Assuring freedom and justice has never been the money community's job," attributed to Gilder, but suspiciously close, Kieran was sure, to something he'd come across somewhere else.

Like many figures who worried that one day their power might wane, Gilder was concerned about health and dispensed advice on promoting it. Germs weren't the prime cause of anything, he maintained. Diseases happened when bodies already stressed and damaged for other reasons were no longer able to keep them in check. Attacking germs with drugs was just another way of misdirecting efforts on symptoms. The real causes lay with states of mind. If mere emotional extremes or exposure to the object of a phobia or a mania could produce physical changes, such as sweating, palpitations, flushing or paling, that were readily visible in moments, then what greater effects could be wrought by deeply rooted mental attitudes that persisted for months, years, or an entire lifetime? One of his favorite lines was, "There's a reality behind what you see that you have to connect with." Then, pointing to his head, "Learning to control what's in there is the key to controlling everything else."

And that was the lead into Hamilton Horatio Gilder's fundamental world view, which he used as his explanation or justification for everything else. Much of it seemed to have come from Marissa. Kieran wondered if she might have been influenced at an earlier age by the apparently spiritual and mystical leanings of Deirdre—but that wasn't the issue here.

Gilder believed that some higher force or powers guided the

universe's fortunes, and that he and a certain select few enjoyed a privileged rapport with them. That, of course, accounted for his methods and successes without implying any recourse to the baser instincts that his critics were wont to invoke. It was simply that Gilder was in tune with the way of things. He didn't pretend to understand whatever laws drove the tides of human events in the complex patterns they moved in, but like any skillful navigator who knows the elements, he rode with them, claiming superior guidance and approbation for just about anything that suited his inclinations.

As an apology for grabbing what was going and sending others to the wall, it was a better construct than materialism and Darwin. Instead of pleading the absence of any law, Gilder embodied an even Higher Law. And of course he justified it with a quote: "It's the duty of any free person to live for their own sake, not for others. Exploitation isn't a mark of a depraved or primitive society. It's a consequence of following the natural compulsion to greatness and growth." This time Kieran recognized it as a steal from Nietzsche. Out of curiosity, he looked up references to the Gilderism that he'd been suspicious of earlier about freedom and justice never having been the money community's job. Sure enough, it was from Albert Camus.

He was still ruminating on how to put this newfound knowledge to use, when a call came through on his comset. He channeled it to the main screen he was using, expecting it to be June calling back. But the caller turned out to be somebody who preferred keeping to audio only. "Is this Kieran Thane?" a voice asked. It sounded like a young man's. "The guy they call the Knight?"

"This is he."

"You have a dog, right? And you're driving a rented Kodiak?"

Kieran's brow creased. "Who are you, and what is this?"

"A friend. I just wanted to warn you that the guys who are looking for you know where you are. I told them . . . but I didn't know who you were then. I guess what I'm trying to say is I'm sorry. I'm trying to put things right."

Kieran's mind worked furiously. He had already said to June that Guinness must have been a giveaway. But even if someone had noticed the car and traced it to Alazahad Machine—which would explain Mahom's call before the expedition left Stony Flats— how would this person have gotten Kieran's net code? Only by rummaging through Mahom's directory or records. Kieran decided to gamble. "Come on," he challenged. "You work for Alazahad Machine, correct? So I can place you with one call to Mahom. You might as well show yourself and let us talk in a civilized fashion without the melodramatics."

A few seconds went by. Then the screen came on to show a character maybe in his early twenties, with a lean, swarthy face and wispy black hair, wearing a yellow bandana. He looked sheepish, apprehensive, yet at the same time visibly amazed. "How did you know?"

"I think I'm the one with the prerogative to be doing the asking," Kieran said pleasantly. "But first, how about a name, since you already know mine? Then let's have it from the beginning. Some people showed up at Alazahad's, asking about a man with a dog. . . ."

And so the story came out. Kieran had no doubt that Heaven was sending him an opportunity—in his own way, he sometimes believed in guiding higher powers too. His mind went back to the glimmerings of an idea that had begun to form about how Gilder, despite all his convictions—or maybe because of them— might prove the weak spot. "Okay, Solomon," he said when Leppo had finished, "I always admire a straight confession. But absolution will cost you more than three Hail Marys."

"What?" Leppo asked guardedly.

"You know those Aerobot 6-Cs? Mahom has a couple of them in that arsenal of his out back."

"Sure." Aerobots were a type of small flying drone, used for miscellaneous errands and deliveries all over Mars.

"I've got a small list of items from the store that I could use out here. Square things with Mahom, and then I'd like you to send them out right away. I'll get back to you shortly with an approach path and landing code. Would you do that?" Kieran's expression and tone conveyed that if Leppo did the sensible thing, he could find he had a strong and valuable friend for life—just as Mahom had. But he really didn't want this person as a foe.

Leppo swallowed visibly and nodded. "Sure," he said. "What do you need?"

# ⇟ **12** ⇞

After he had finished talking to Leppo, Kieran went back to the inflatable-frame cabin, where he set Harry Quong the task of downloading available plans for construction and standard communications equipment of the Mule general purpose, low altitude, medium-haul transporter. By then it was late in the afternoon. While the others took a break from their debating to move around, some going outside to stretch cramped limbs, he sprawled out with a pen and note pad in an easy chair in the corner of the messroom and lost himself in thought, intermittently adding to a growing web of jottings and doodles copiously sprinkled with arrows, query marks, and exclamation points. Almost an hour later, he chewed on his pen and stared at a summary account of his labors in the form of the lines:

> *Replete with empire, fame, and wealth,*
> *Hamilton frets for mind and health.*
> *Seeking after higher things,*
> *That guide the fates of priests and kings.*
> *Would such a soul fear ancient powers,*
> *Locked in pyramids and towers?*

Then he got up, poured himself a mug of coffee, and went over to where Dennis Curry was sitting with Jean at the end of the long table.

"Hi, guys."

"Well, it's nice to see you're among us again," Dennis said. "You looked as if you were composing your life's memoirs or something."

"Just collecting thoughts." Kieran pulled up a chair and sat down opposite them. "About that nano work of Pierre's that we mentioned this morning."

"What about it?"

"I assume that these remote-programmable protein synthesizers can self-assemble in any cell of the body. If they're taken in through ingestion or respiration, there's no way they can discriminate."

"That's my understanding," Dennis agreed.

"Yet you couldn't have them switching on in every cell in the body when they get a signal. It would be too crude. You'd swamp the system. There would have to be a way of selecting which cells you want activated."

"Correct. There's some way they react to enzyme activity and know which kind of cell they're in. So part of the signal instructs which cells to activate." Dennis looked at Jean. "Wasn't that how it worked?"

"Something like that. I'm not sure I remember the details. We'd have to ask Pierre."

"Why are you interested?" Dennis asked Kieran.

But Kieran was still too absorbed in his line of thought to reply directly. "So you could instruct them to start making some specific kind of protein only in a certain, specified kind of target cell? Harmless colored protein—a pigment?"

"Well . . . yes. That's the idea," Dennis said.

"How close are you two to Pierre?" Kieran asked them. "Harry said Jean knows him from years back."

"That's right," Jean said. "Back on Earth. We were in the same bunch of students who hung around together, went on hikes, camping trips, tours abroad, things like that—the things kids do." She sent Dennis a mystified look.

"Do you think he'd let you have access to this technology?" Kieran asked. "Maybe to help test it out in an impromptu field trial?"

Jean frowned. Dennis looked askance. "Well, wait a minute," he cautioned. "I don't know about that. As far as I know, it's still a nonpublicized piece of private research. . . ."

"It's not even his to decide about," Jean said. "What are you asking him to do, steal it?" She shook her head. "Why should he do a thing like that?"

"What was his interest in your work here?" Kieran asked, trying another angle. "Was he on board just as the medic? I get the feeling his involvement went deeper than that."

"That's true," Jean agreed. "Earth's early history and the mysteries of the Technolithics had always been one of his passions. When we told him about the expedition, he was wild to get a place on it. We talked to Hamil. Hamil said that if we recommended Pierre it was good enough for him, and arranged for Pierre to travel out from Lowell with Walter. Pierre was devastated when he had to call it off—even more so now he's heard what we're finding here."

"He knows about it all, then?" Kieran said.

"Yes, we kept him informed," Dennis confirmed. "As we've said, we're good friends. There was no reason not to."

"So he'd be pretty upset to learn that the whole thing might be over."

"Devastated," Jean said again.

Kieran gave them a moment to reconsider what he had said earlier. "Then why don't we give him a chance to help save it?" he suggested.

Dennis and Jean exchanged looks that were puzzled but at the same time interested. "I'm not sure I follow," Dennis said.

"Pierre is in Lowell now, yes?" Kieran said. "I want us to call him, and for you to introduce me so I can ask him a few more questions about this work of his. Then, if it's what it sounds like it could be, I'd like to offer that we try a sample out for him . . . but leave that part to me." Kieran rose to his feet, as if what he was proposing were as natural and everyday as calling a friend to set up lunch. "Let's go through to the Jug and call him from there. It'll be more private."

The face staring back from the screen in the Juggernaut's center compartment was in its thirties, boyish but stubble-chinned, with intense dark eyes and a mop of black hair that hung in a curlicue over the forehead. Kieran's first impressions of Pierre were that he was of the reflective sort, not overly given to words, serious in disposition, probably a romantic at heart—all of them good signs. Also, Pierre evidently had faith in Dennis and Jean's judgment, showing equanimity over their telling Kieran as much as they had about his work—but being understandably curious.

Kieran posed the questions that he had listed, mainly concerning the coding system used and how it would be sent. The answers turned out to be surprisingly simple: the molecular receivers would respond to a pulse modulation impressed on a low-intensity, radio-frequency field surrounding the body. For remote direction to produce medical pharmaceuticals internally, the present intention was to send a signal to a body transducer worn by the patient, maybe on a belt, carried in a pocket, or worn as a bracelet or pendant. "But it wouldn't have to be in contact?" Kieran checked. That was correct. A field from any equivalent transmitter would do, as long as the local field strength was sufficient. It sounded promising. Now Kieran came to the crucial part. He mustered the look of one about to divulge sensitive secrets.

"You've been pretty direct, Pierre. Thanks," he acknowledged. "Now let me tell you why I'm interested. I'm not with the expedition just as your replacement. There's a political aspect to what's going on that Hamil couldn't really talk about before Walter got here." Which was perfectly true: neither Hamil nor anyone else had known about it. "Some people have shown up from one of the big construction conglomerates. They're claiming first rights to the area, and if they succeed, they'll obliterate everything. There'll be nothing to show for the expedition, nothing on record. It will all be lost."

Pierre looked aghast. "*No!*" he protested. "Such a thing would be criminal! It could never happen!"

"Tell Juanita," Kieran replied. "Ask her what the oil industry did to dozens of unexcavated Olmec sites in Mexico a hundred years back."

For the first time, Pierre seemed to lose some of his composure, shifting his gaze agitatedly from one to another of the three images confronting him. "They must be stopped!" he said.

"That's what I'm here to find an angle on, if I can," Kieran told him.

Pierre studied him, seeming to go back in his mind over what had been said. "Are you saying there's something I can do? My work here can help somehow?"

"Maybe—if you don't mind bending a rule or two," Kieran said cheerfully. He made it sound like conspiring to do no more than keeping secret a birthday surprise. "And then again, it might even contribute something back. As I said before, you might think of it as helping the firm out by staging a small, unofficial field trial. . . ."

After they had finished, Kieran put a call through to Solomon Leppo. "Have you sent the drone off with those things yet?" he asked him.

"I've cleared it with Mahom and got the stuff you listed. I was leaving it till after dark, like you said," Leppo answered.

"Good," Kieran said. "Hold it a little longer. There'll be one more item. Someone will be contacting you. She'll deliver it. Let me know when you're set to go."

June called back with profiles of the four people that Zorken had sent to Mars. Justin Banks, from what everyone had seen, the senior member of the group, was listed in Zorken's organizational tree as an executive project leader, reporting to a Thornton Velte, projects appraisals director for the Mining Division and one of Hamilton Gilder's inner clique. That Banks represented the corporation's mining interests, not construction or engineering, was surely significant—all the more so when taken in conjunction with the backgrounds of the three people who had come with him. Gertrude Heissen, who had to have been the thin-lipped, pale-faced woman present with Banks at the first meeting with Hamil, was described as a corporate mineralogist. The bearded Asian with them was almost certainly Tran Xedeidang, a geochemist also employed by Zorken. The fourth Mars arrival, Clarence Porter, not seen on that occasion, was an outside consultant specializing in petrological magnetism and radiation.

"Great stuff!" Kieran complimented. "Now it's starting to make more sense. Look, there's one more thing I'd like you to do. There's a guy in Lowell who's into biological nano-research. He has a package that I need sent out here. Can you pick it up from him and deliver it to Mahom's mechanic out on Beacon Way? He's going to ship it out with some other stuff that's waiting."

"What are you up to now, Kieran?" June asked suspiciously.

"Remote-programming body cells to change color. What do you think? It could open up a whole new world of body art. How would you like a completely different medium of self-expression?"

"Right now, I don't think I'm even up to hearing about it. Just give me the details," June sighed.

❖     ❖     ❖

Hamil confirmed that the expedition's own work had found an abnormally high radiation background in the plateau area. He hadn't mentioned it to Kieran before because it hadn't seemed relevant. But the clear implication seemed to be that what was holding the interest of Zorken Consolidated in this part of the Tharsis region was minerals potential. "It makes sense," Kieran said when he reviewed his findings with the scientists. "Extract what's under the ground first. Then use your land rights for development afterward."

"Very efficient. Very thorough," Hamil conceded. "So do you have an answer to it? You seem to have been very busy."

The others were following with solemn faces. Kieran cast an eye around the circle, then said to them all, "Going back to these Technolithic structures and sites back on Earth . . . You sometimes hear legends of 'curses' and 'perils' associated with these things—mysteries that popular fears get built around, which are said to defy explanation. I'd like to know more. What can you tell me about them?"

Some of the listeners looked taken aback, but gradually they opened up. The talk went on to cover strange accidents said by some to have befallen desecraters of tombs; alignments of structures supposedly modeling astronomical configurations and the precessional cycle of the equinoxes; peculiar ratios of height and base measurements coming out at precise multiples of pi, giving rise to speculation that both Egyptian and Central American pyramids were planar representations of a hemisphere of the Earth. Katrina mentioned that the French sites at Quimper, Tombeau de Geant, and Istres marked a triangle in exact proportion to a side of the Cheops Pyramid but fourteen million times larger. Personally, she didn't assign any particular significance to this—it was just an observation that some had drawn attention to; but that was the kind of thing Kieran had asked for. Jean Graas described the mysterious ground drawings of Nazca, in Peru, which made sense only when viewed from high altitudes—and how they could have been marked out so precisely without direction from such a vantage point was also difficult to imagine.

"What's the point of this?" Rudi asked with a trace of irritation after it had gone on for a while. "This kind of thing is mainly fanciful imagination and wishful thinking. How is it supposed to help us in our present situation?"

"I'm not sure yet. Just some thoughts I'm toying with," Kieran replied vaguely.

Trevany hesitated for a few seconds. "There is another story that goes back to the 1960s," he said finally. "I've never had reason to check the details personally, but it involved an American physicist called Louis Alvarez. He set up a cosmic ray detector inside the Khafre Pyramid at Giza in an attempt to locate hidden chambers containing archives of scientific records that were supposed to exist. Penetrating radiation should show a greater intensity if it encounters hollow spaces than if it goes all the way through solid rock. By analyzing the patterns from many different directions, he hoped to map the internal structure. But the results were so garbled that nobody could make sense of them. Even the outer faces and edges couldn't be distinguished. It was as if some other source inside or under the pyramid was interfering with the readings. The equipment was taken outside, dismantled and checked, and worked just fine. But back inside again, it did the same thing. As far as I know, no one has ever been able to explain it." Trevany looked at the others to invite dissent. They shrugged or shook their heads.

His remarks prompted Juanita to follow. "There's another strange thing that they found at Teotihuacan."

Kieran thought back over the things he had heard in the previous few days. "That was . . . the City of the Gods, in Mexico, right?"

She nodded. "A little north of Mexico City—supposed to be Quetzlcoatl's capital. One of the structures there is known as the Pyramid of the Sun. Back in the early years of the twentieth century, they found a thick, continuous sheet of mica sandwiched between two of the upper levels. What it was doing there was never established. It was stripped out and sold before anyone got a chance to examine it properly."

"Mica? That's what's used for capacitors and high-voltage insulation," Kieran said.

"Yes, exactly."

"As a moderator in nuclear reactors too," Dennis added. "It's opaque to fast neutrons."

Harry Quong looked dubious. "Too convenient," he commented.

"Stories about things that vanish like that make me wonder if they ever existed at all."

"Weren't there more, though?" Trevany said to Juanita. "There's one somewhere that's called the Mica Temple, isn't there?"

She nodded. "It's another building in the same place. Two massive sheets of mica are laid one above the other under a floor paved with heavy rock slabs." She shot a look at Harry. "And yes, they're still there: each ninety feet square, carefully cut and laid— and that takes a lot of skill."

"Nobody's figured out their purpose?" Kieran said.

Juanita shrugged. "They have no decorative function—and were out of sight anyway. . . . But the strange thing is that mica from different places varies in trace element composition and is fairly easy to identify. This particular type occurs only in Brazil, two thousand miles away. It seems that the builders had some definite need in going to the trouble of bringing it there. Other varieties are available locally."

"Interesting," Kieran mused. Just at that moment, he had nothing to add.

"What's the point, though?" Rudi asked again. "Are you wondering if it might be possible to scare those Zorken people off with legends and fables?"

"Maybe," Kieran said.

"No chance!" Rudi shook his head and jabbed a finger in the direction where the Mule was parked outside. "You've seen the kind of person Banks is. He's never going to believe anything like that."

"That isn't the point," Kieran replied evenly. "Think of him as a conduit back to their big chief in the head office, who's a very different kind of person. The object is to get to him. It's what *he* believes that matters." He gazed around the circle of curious faces. "I don't know where this will lead, but it's the best I can think of that might be worth a try. You're all at a stop for the time being, and that might be good because it will involve enough work to keep all of us busy." He looked toward Hamil for endorsement. Hamil stared back at him for a moment, then returned a consenting nod. Kieran, it seemed, was becoming the de facto leader of the group.

The Aerobot from Leppo arrived a couple of hours later, coming in as Kieran had instructed on a low approach along the valley from the direction opposite to the Zorken camp, landing a few hundred feet back below the ridgeline undetected by the Mule's radar. Kieran checked the items that it had brought and was satisfied. Then he got Hamil to put a call across to Justin Banks in the Mule, saying that there was a person here with the expedition that Banks really needed to meet and talk with face-to-face. By then, the time was approaching midnight. As Kieran had anticipated, Banks preserved his symbolic authority by decreeing that it would have to wait until the following morning.

And that suited Kieran's plan fine.

After the two camps had settled down for the night, Rudi sent out his little tracked robot, Gottfried, to a hollow between two rocks that had been noted by daylight, where it was able to pass under the lowest beam of the Zorken camp's security perimeter. The robot was equipped with a telescopic arm terminating in a jointed three-claw hand, which it used to unscrew the cap of the external fill pipe to the Mule's amply sized drinking-water tank. It then inserted a tube, through which it pumped a measured amount of the liquid solution that had been supplied by Pierre.

# ⋙ 13 ⋘

Clad in a surface suit, Kieran crossed the few hundred feet of ground separating the two camps. Neither he nor Hamil wanted direct confrontation at this point, and he passed Chas Ryan, Lou and Zeke, laying out and inventorying equipment in anticipation of the expedition's having to pull out. A camera mounted inside the opened outer door of the Mule scrutinized him as he approached. He mounted the steps to the access lock, waited for it to close and pressurize, and when the inner door opened, entered the main cabin.

The Mule was designed for inhospitable environments, and as such provided extended-term living accommodations besides being simply a vehicle. In some ways a flying version of the Juggernaut with freight space instead of lab facilities, it possessed a full galley and surface-endurance life support system, with the main cabin functioning both as dayroom and sleeping quarters. Observation from the other camp had shown Banks and his group to be generally keeping to the Mule, availing themselves of its superior comforts compared to the shacks. Kieran guessed that the shacks were being left for the military contingent that he was expecting, who would be using more basically equipped, less commodious vehicles.

The same trio who had met Hamil were waiting in the cabin: Banks, Gertrude Heissen, and Tran Xedeidang. Clarence Porter had left on foot about half an hour previously with one of the three crewmen identified so far. The two others were probably in the nose section, Kieran guessed. That could be a problem, because he wanted to get in there. Banks watched with a sour expression while Kieran removed his helmet and gloves and placed

200

them on a side ledge before sitting down uninvited and settling back with as much comfort as a light-duty suit, even with its flat, compact back unit, would permit. Kieran had dusted his hair a little grayer and added some line work that added a few years to his face.

"Mr. Keziah Turle," Banks acknowledged.

"*Doctor*, if you don't mind."

Banks shrugged. "As you wish. Now, would you get to the point? Your professor said there were matters you need to discuss directly. I can't imagine what they might be, but you have our attention."

"I'm not actually a member of Professor Hashikar's expedition," Kieran began. "Archeology, geology, and so forth are not my kind of specialty. I'm more, what you might call an external consultant, brought in because of my expertise in the more . . ." he paused, as if weighing how to phrase a delicate but significant matter, "*esoteric* aspects of the discoveries here." He looked at Banks expectantly.

"Go on," Banks said in a neutral voice. His two companions remained stone-faced. Kieran treated them to the smile of one accustomed to gently leading others into new conceptual territory.

"I'm sure you've all heard of the ancient Technolithic culture of Earth," Kieran said. His voice took on a mildly quavering, reverberating tone, as if revering hidden secrets of the universe. "Long before any civilization of ours existed, they built the pyramids of Egypt, the lost cities of the Hindu Kush, the engineering miracles of Mexico and Peru. They wrought feats that defy gravity itself, wonders that Zorken Consolidated with all the resources and knowledge at its command would be unable to match, even today." He rose to his feet, as if unable to contain the excitement surging through him, turned a full circle, extending both hands, and pointed downward with a trembling finger. "And now, beneath this very spot where we are—"

"Yes, yes," Banks interrupted impatiently. "We've been through all that with your—what's his name?—Trevany. If you're about to tell us again about structures here that you think were made by the same aliens, ancestors—whatever your theory is—then you can save your breath. We have the prior claim on this area, which, as I have already advised you, we are prepared to enforce. I'm sorry if that frustrates your immediate hopes, but we're a business enterprise, not a philanthropic society with academic sympathies. If these Technolithic people were here, no doubt there will be other signs of them all over Mars—and probably other places too, from what you seem to be saying. I can only suggest that you show patience and tenacity in the best tradition of your profession. But you can't expect serious development and commerce to halt every time you find a few rocks that nobody else is interested in. If that were allowed, the race would never have gotten off Earth at all."

Kieran shook his head emphatically. "No, you misunderstand. I told you, my field is outside the academic disciplines of Dr. Trevany and his colleagues." He made a flourish—and in the process swept his helmet and gloves off the shelf he had put them on and onto the floor. Banks and the others watched disdainfully while he fussed around gathering them together again and stood up, regaining his composure. "I didn't come here to plead, or to belabor you with scientific details. I came here to warn you."

Banks blinked. His face showed reaction for the first time. "Warn us?"

Kieran's eyes gleamed, fixing on each of the three in turn. He moved a pace toward the cabin center, causing Xedeidang to pull back in his seat, and gestured with an extended arm. "Study the histories down through the centuries of those who violated the places made sacred by the Technolithics. How these things happened, we don't know, but the records and testimonies of those who were there, and who saw, are clear. Strange accidents and misfortunes befell them. Lives that were successful and prosperous fell into ruin. Inexplicable *diseases* ravaged their bodies. . . ." That one was thrown in for Gilder's benefit. "Others went insane, committed suicide, turned violently upon each other. . . ."

Xedeidang looked perplexedly at Banks, silently saying they had a madman aboard and asking what to do. He started to pull his leg back as Kieran turned to retrace his course; Kieran tried to evade by altering his step, went off balance, and steadied himself against the bulkhead.

"This is preposterous," Gertrude Heissen muttered at Banks.

Kieran straightened up and resumed. "You don't understand. Your experience is confined to the materialistic processes that your scientists tell you are all there is to the universe. But they have barely glimpsed a fraction of it. The Technolithic peoples, whoever they were, wherever they came from, had knowledge of powers that we can only guess at. The structures they built were not tombs and monuments as has been told. Materials are found in them that we use only in our most advanced scientific creations. They were precision *machines*—instruments involving forces unknown to us today, serving purposes that we are unable to imagine." Kieran stabbed a finger in the direction of the ground outside again. "And down there, beneath where we are standing, is an example of—"

"This has gone far enough," Banks cut it. "We've heard as much as we're prepared to. Whether you're officially a member of Professor Hashikar's staff or not, go back and tell him that if—"

But Kieran seemed to have worked himself up into too much of a frenzy to hear. He whirled, throwing out a hand and causing Heissen to duck in alarm, gazed rapturously upward as if for inspiration, in the process backing into an empty seat by the folding table serving the area and sitting down heavily in it. But his verve and vigor were undiminished. "Communicate back with those who sent you here, and have them end your mission. Strange powers operate in these places, manifesting themselves as radiation fields and magnetic disturbances. They exist here!" As if Banks and the others didn't already know. "They *know* those who come with malevolent intent. They can distinguish. *Leave while you are still safe!* Things happen that scientists cannot explain. Their instruments stop functioning. Even as you sit here—" Kieran turned his head toward the door leading forward, as if a thought had just struck him. "The instruments in this aircraft, maybe. Wouldn't that make you think? Can I ask your crew?" Before anyone realized what he was doing or could stop him, Kieran got up suddenly, pulled open the door, and stepped through into the nose section. Two surprised faces jerked around to greet him from the crew positions. "Excuse me, gentlemen, but can I ask you—"

"What the hell?" one of them demanded.

"*Get him out of there!*" Banks's voice shouted from behind. "He has no authorization. He's not wanted in here at all."

But Kieran tripped on the step up to the flight deck and went down on a knee. He braced a hand against one of the consoles to raise himself, but it slipped off and shot between it and an adjacent unit, causing him to sprawl sideways. Rough hands hauled him back onto his feet and ejected him back into the main cabin. "I just wanted to ask them about—"

"*Get him helmeted up and off the plane!*" Banks yelled. "If I hear one more word out of him, just throw him out as he is. I've had enough!"

It was a rueful-looking Kieran who stumped back down the Mule's access stairs several minutes later and returned to the inflatable-frame cabin. But the smile that broke out across his face as soon as he got inside was unnecessary. Harry Quong was already tuning in to the two bugs—from the items sent by Leppo—that Kieran had planted, one in the main cabin of the Mule, the other underneath the c-com operator's table in the nose compartment. The first was bringing tirades from Banks, still incensed over the "lunatic"; the latter, a resumption of ratings of girls in various bars in Lowell and Osaka that Kieran's intrusion into the crew compartment had evidently interrupted.

In his contrived fall, Kieran had also found the cable shown in the installation drawings obtained by Harry Quong, which connected the c-com panel to the amplifier-driver unit feeding the antenna system, which was where message encryption and decryption were performed. Hence, messages traveling through the cable itself were not encrypted. Kieran had attached to the cable a small clip-on collar that would pick up the external magnetic fields generated by incoming and outgoing signals and transmit encodings of them to the Juggernaut via one of the devices that Chas and his crew had buried outside—it hadn't been by accident that they had picked the area between the two camps to sort their equipment. So now the team had a tap into the Mule's external communications link as well as bugs inside it.

Banks would no doubt forward a report of Kieran's antics to his boss, Thornton Velte, at Asgard, which was the whole idea, and hopefully the essence of it would find its way to Gilder. If so, Gilder would probably order a check on the net to see what information on Keziah Turle could be dredged up. But that was okay—they would find him to be mildly eccentric and excitable, but highly regarded within his own circle. For most of the night Trevany, Juanita, and Dennis had been writing biographical and background notes, extracts from supposedly published papers, and other inspirations, and posting them on a net site that June had created for the purpose on behalf of the fictitious personality.

The tap on the Mule's communications link quickly revealed that the use of supporting military had been approved from Asgard, and a force would be arriving later that day. In anticipation of this, the devices placed by Chas and his men included several remote-controllable miniature radio signal and interference transmitters near the area where the military's aircraft would probably be positioned after it arrived. Meanwhile, Hamil, Juanita, and Dennis, after informing Banks that they needed a final visit to the Hole to tidy up their notes and recordings, had placed several more among the excavations. Also, while there, they had gone around touching up selected spots with fluorescent dyes from the Juggernaut's lab that would activate at varying periods after being excited with ultraviolet light—which Kieran said would be emitted by the security devices that he predicted the military would deploy. Not especially surprisingly, the response from Banks had been aloof indifference. Finally, Rudi had sent Gottfried up among the crags overlooking the shelf to dispense a number of canisters that Kieran and Harry Quong had contrived for emitting smoke and releasing pressurized volatile liquids.

There was nothing more they could do for the time being but wait. Or maybe, Kieran suggested, they could always try praying to the protective spirits of the Ancients.

# 14

Rudi bit off a piece of a chocolate-peanut snack bar, chewed moodily for a while, then downed a swig of reconstituted fruit juice and looked at the others around the table in the Juggernaut's central compartment. He was disgruntled over what he saw as too ready a surrender to bluster. "I mean, seriously, what could they do at the end of it all?" he asked, singling out Kieran with his gaze. "Drag us all outside and shoot us? Surely overt violence against an undefended minority wouldn't be tolerated. Things can't work that way."

"Is that how it works anywhere, Rudi?" Kieran asked from where he was lounging by the forward doorway into the driver's cabin. He shook his head. "People looking to start trouble don't immediately resort to armed force. They provoke and escalate until it becomes appropriate. Situations like that get ugly and distressing for everyone involved. We all want to avoid that."

"I thought that people here were supposed to have a way of acting together when something threatens their common interest," Rudi said.

"The common interest could be best served by respecting first claims," Trevany reminded him. "Don't assume that everyone would be sympathetic to our position. Creating a fuss might not be the way to go."

Rudi looked indignant. "But . . . but we're talking crass commercialism versus knowledge that could be invaluable. I mean, what's there to argue with? You've only—"

Trevany cut him off with a shake of his head. "Most people wouldn't see it that way. They're interested in what relates to *them*. Rights of use do. Academic claims to privilege don't."

"I'm not asking for privileges," Rudi insisted. "Just some recognition of fundamental values."

"But that's how they'd see it."

Juanita, who had been following, commented, "The system here is based on tenacious defense of—how would you put it?—things you know are yours."

"Property ownership rights," Trevany supplied.

"Yes. That doesn't mean just being allowed to hold a technical title to something, that someone else can grant or take away. It means you possess a *monopoly* on deciding how the property gets used, sold, exchanged, or whatever." She shrugged. "That's what Zorken is doing. And if pushed to decide, Mars would probably side with their right to do it."

Rudi made a face and waved a hand. "Yes, but can't this kind of thing be worked out by reasonable compromise? It's the using of coercion that I'm objecting to." The others stared at him, then looked at Kieran to take it.

"When you talk about monopoly, you're implying an ability at the bottom of it all to enforce it," he said. "When a dispute arises that agreeable compromise can't settle, and arbitration fails, then people will resort to fighting it out until some view or other is able to prevail." He nodded at Juanita to endorse the point she had made. "In other words, until monopoly privileges are reasserted. And territory is the most fundamental property right of all, from the space occupied by your body, through the wider domains of personal living space, homes, towns, nations. . . . Exercising a monopoly on territory means securing it from rival claims. That means being able to bring sufficient force to bear to defend it."

"All right, I take your point," Rudi said. "But at the same time, I think you're making mine. You own your house and the belongings in it because nobody else has an equal right to walk in and camp down with impunity, yes? But what gives you that right is the recognition of your monopoly under *one system of law* which exercises the force. Shared ownership of territory—or jurisdiction by competing defensive agencies, which amounts to the same thing—isn't a workable arrangement. Stable households exist when there's one head that the others are prepared to acknowledge. Otherwise the community fights or fragments. And the same happens with larger territories too. When national group marriages break down, the solutions are division of living space, divorce, or murder in the form of migration, revolution, or war until territorial monopolies of some kind stabilize. But that isn't what you've got here."

"You're right," Kieran agreed. "It hasn't happened yet on Mars. Too much room; too few people. But when the boundaries start running up against each other, then it'll all start to shake itself out."

"Yes, and in the meantime we've got this situation where the only alternatives seem to be either to find our own private army, or be run off like poachers."

Kieran pursed his lips and responded with one of his enigmatic smiles. "Oh, I wouldn't jump to conclusions too hastily, Rudi," he said. "There are always other ways. Why else do you think we've all been so busy?"

Harry, who had been watching the communications panel in the driver's compartment, appeared in the doorway. "It looks like they're here," he announced. "Two blips on radar coming in from the northeast. An outgoing message from the Mule to Asgard confirms their backup is on approach now."

The force consisted of a "Venning" troop carrier with rated capacity of twenty men plus equipment, mounting support artillery in the form of a multiple munitions delivery turret behind the cockpit and underslung automatic cannon, accompanied by a command/scout flyer carrying missiles and laser pods. They landed where Kieran had predicted, between the two camps but closer to the Mule. Deployment was brisk and businesslike. A detachment in armored combat gear emerged from the troop carrier to cordon off the archeologists' cabin and vehicles and secure the perimeter around the Mule, while another went down to clear and post guards in the Hole workings. While this was going on, officers from the command flyer entered the Mule to report to Banks and confer, as Kieran and the others were able to follow via the bugs planted there. There were no great surprises. Shortly afterward, Banks came through on local band inside the Juggernaut to issue his ultimatum: the team had four hours to complete its wrapping up and depart. If they were not gone from the shelf by that time, they would be forcibly removed.

Hamil and Walter went across to the Mule to plead their case again and demand that they be permitted to talk directly with the top management at Asgard who were responsible for the Tharsis project. It was a token protest, probably expected, urged by Kieran for appearance's sake. And, as expected, it was refused. Banks was delegated full authority, and his decision stood. They now had three and a half hours.

Chas and his crew deflated the three-room cabin and packed it into its trailer, stowed the remaining items, and a little before the deadline, a procession consisting of the Juggernaut and two trailers with their hauling vehicles alternated forward and back on the sloping road sections to descend the mesa side below the shelf. They drove away across the valley floor and halted at a spot between two and three miles away, outside the boundary that Zorken had demarcated.

Back at the Troy site, Gottfried had been left to provide mobile eyes and sensors from a vantage point high on the slopes above, not far below the Citadel rock. The tap on the Mule's communications line brought Banks's report back to Asgard that the operation had been carried out successfully, on time, and without trouble. The ensuing message traffic expressed satisfaction and revived plans for a more comprehensive survey of the minerals potential under the plateau—which had been the original objective of Banks's mission. It also brought Banks's boss, Thornton Velte, responding to the Keziah Turle stunt, since Gilder himself was preoccupied with preparations for his daughter Marissa's wedding, guests for which were assembling at the Oasis hotel before being transported up from Lowell as Asgard approached. While Velte dismissed it all as nonsense, Turle's apparently authentic background had impressed Gilder. But there had been no thought of reconsidering—not that Kieran had expected any at this point. Gilder was still focused fully on business. He hadn't made any connection with the Higher Powers which in another compartment of his mind he believed governed the workings of the universe.

"So we'll just have to help him make the connection," Kieran said when Harry replayed the latest snippets relayed from the Mule. He told Dennis to go ahead and transmit a set of the codes supplied by Pierre, which would activate groups of the protein synthesizers now present in the bodies of the Mule's occupants. Some of the selected cell types were dermal, while others lay in the digestive tract.

"So what if it does cause Gilder to do some thinking," Rudi said. "I can't see the military people being very impressed. They're our main problem now."

"I know the psychology of the rank and file," Kieran told him. "They're like mercenary military anywhere, rootless and insecure underneath all the imagery. It makes them suggestible and superstitious—like old-time sailors."

Rudi eyed him dubiously. "And you think you can exploit something like that to our advantage?"

"You'd be surprised," Kieran said, and smiled gaily.

# ≋ 15 ≋

*Crunch . . . crunch . . . crunch . . . crunch.*

The sound of Trooper Slezansky's footsteps came hollowly through his own suit as he slowly patrolled through the warren of caverns and diggings below the camp. This far underground, it shouldn't have made any difference that his and Delaney's was the 2:00 A.M. to 4:00 A.M. watch, but the gloom and somberness of the surroundings somehow intensified the bleak feelings that came with the hour. He had turned his local area channel off because of intermittent interference from somewhere that had become persistently more irritating, cutting himself off from base except for emergency band. Maybe that was adding to the sense of isolation that he was feeling.

Still, he'd had worse assignments in his time, before taking a tour with the Lowell-based enforcer service that had sent them here on this job. The mission to take out that bandit stronghold on an asteroid out in the Belt somewhere, for instance. The officers who were supposed to know about these things hadn't allowed for alliances among the enemy, and a counterattack from the rear had cost some good men. Thieves protecting each other. The incursion force that Slezansky was with had to pull out, and he'd never found out what the final outcome was. And then there was the fringe settlement that they had defended, who then wouldn't pay, or whatever the disagreement afterward had been about, and the protecting force had turned around and taken what they said they were due. That had left a bad taste in his mouth for a long time. But the job to be done was the job, was the job. . . .

The passage Slezansky was following opened into a wedge-shaped chamber that narrowed into shadows above the dim glow from a couple of the lights strung on a cable running along one wall. He stopped to run his flashlamp around and up, revealing a slab of rock leaning drunkenly across the space overhead. It looked as if it had fallen away from one side of a fissure extending upward into darkness beyond. Slezansky wasn't sure if it was his eyes playing tricks, but he thought he could see wisps of greenish light among the rocks and crevices up there. Should there be lights down underneath a plateau on what was supposed to be a dead planet? He didn't know. But it seemed eerie. He swung the flashlamp beam over tumbled rocks looking like skulls sticking out of the sand; shadows twisting and writhing upward out of sight among the silent, brooding pillars. . . . This whole place was eerie.

He carried on through to a larger cavern of branching passages and shafts, past the partly uncovered remains of what looked like something that had been built by somebody, to the place where they had placed the monitor panels for the security systems deployed through the area. The routine check showed all ultraviolet transmitters and sensors functioning; motion detectors reset by his ID signal after registering to his progress; infrared fences live and intact. He updated the log and tried local again to report to base, but again the transmission was swamped before he had exchanged more than a few words. He delivered his opinion in the form of some chosen and well-practiced obscenities, killed the circuit, and carried on.

At least, there were no plasma bolts here, or smart munitions homing on you out in a void with no cover you could trust. Running a few professors, or whoever they were, out from where they had no business being had a lot more going for it than some of the action he'd seen. He needed to think seriously about getting out of this business while he was young enough to make a go of something else and still in one piece to do it. Something where he could market the skills he'd picked up, but less violent and with a lower wastage factor. A corporate security outfit, maybe, or a private bodyguard; even a bouncer somewhere. But in the meantime the pay was good, so the life had its compensations. Horrocks and Malotto could laugh if they wanted when he talked about his plans and how he'd have it made one day. He'd show them.

They tried to unnerve him with jokes about the unreality of

his plans, or maybe air rumors about a job they were due to go on. Even on this one. Horrocks had told him about some kind of fortune-teller or wise guy who was with the professors, calling Major Cobert, the unit's CO, and saying that the workings were haunted by spirits of ancient alien builders . . . or something like that. Slezansky wasn't sure if it was true, or just something they'd made up to rattle him.

He came to the gallery leading back toward the entrance cuttings. As he rounded a corner into brighter light, a grotesque shape flew at him, speeding silently over the walls and across the ceiling. Stifling a shout of alarm, Slezansky recoiled against the wall, at the same time fumbling to unsling his weapon; then he realized it was Delaney's shadow being cast ahead as he advanced from the direction of the main access shaft, patrolling his half of the route. Flustered at the thought of appearing foolish, Slezansky hastily pulled the rifle back onto the shoulder grip of his suit and moved forward. But Delaney hadn't even noticed. The expression on his face, when Slezansky flickered the flashlamp briefly across his visor, was distracted and tense.

"What is it?" Slezansky asked—communications worked in this kind of proximity.

"Something strange . . . I'm not sure. This whole place. Come see what you make of this."

Delaney led the way back along the gallery, then into an opening on one side, beyond which a wide, irregular cavern lay between an undulating floor of boulders and rubble, and a roof of rock shapes hanging low and oppressive in the dim light from the gallery. He stood to one side, letting Slezansky peer past him. Even though Delaney's figure was in shadow, Slezansky could sense the other trooper watching him, waiting for his reaction. Slezansky's brow knotted as the doubts and premonitions that he had felt earlier came flooding back.

This place they were in was no mere hole dug into something dead, like a disused tunnel or an old mine. The very rocks around them were *alive*. As his eyes accommodated from the brighter gallery they had left, he could make out strange, softly glowing tongues of violet and blue, and in other places, ghostly background streaks of yellow, pink, and green, adding an ethereal depth to the surroundings and throwing intervening edges into starkly outlined silhouette.

"What do you make of it?" Delaney's voice asked again.

Slezansky was about to reply, when he became aware of other sounds on the circuit—not more static or interference, but something that swelled and faded in sighing cadence like the surging of an ocean, distant yet hypnotically insistent, as if bringing fragments of voices from the far reaches of space or of time. What they were saying was beyond comprehensibility. Or—he could *feel*, now, the presence of the ancient beings who had created this place—was it something that required the comprehension of a different, totally alien kind of mind?

Slezansky stared fearfully, as if expecting apparitions from the past to arise out of the rocks, and glanced back the way they had come, unconsciously checking that their way out was clear. "How long do we have left on this watch?" he asked. His voice had turned dry and croaky.

"A little under an hour," Delaney replied.

"I say we go back up now," Slezansky said. "Tell 'em we've got a communications glitch."

Delaney didn't argue.

By the time they returned to the Venning troop carrier, Slezansky was already feeling that they had overreacted. But it turned out that the atmosphere there was far from settled either. Communications problems had been intermittently affecting the long-range link too, not just local channels. And the Zorken scientists in the Mule were puzzling over strange emissions of vapor and colored mists from places on the slopes above the camp. It seemed that things like that shouldn't be happening. Even Horrocks didn't have a wisecrack or disparaging remark to offer. There was a rumor that the fruitcake who was with the professors that the troops had kicked out had called the Zorken bigwigs at their headquarters to warn about some kind of plague breaking out.

"Maybe there's something to it," Malotto hazarded when he heard Delaney and Slezansky's account of their experiences below. "I'll tell you one thing: I don't like the sound of this."

Horrocks rallied himself enough to retort, "What kind of troopers do you call yourselves, getting jumpy over a few lights and some puffs of smoke? Haven't you ever been down a cave before? I'll believe it when we start coming down with the plague that the lunatic out there was raving about."

Delaney thought about it, then nodded decisively. "Yeah." He had chirped up noticeably since being back in daylight and among familiar faces. "Yeah," he said again. "I go along with that too."

An hour later, Major Cobert came back from the Mule and announced that its occupants weren't feeling or looking very good at all. Every one of them, including the flight crew, were complaining of nausea, fever, and diarrhea. Cobert described their appearance as "seasick."

A little under three miles away, Kieran and the others had followed Cobert's dialogue with Banks and the other Zorken people via the bugs planted inside the Mule. The tap on the external antenna line brought an outgoing message to Asgard describing the latest developments. Shortly afterward, Kieran, bypassing Banks, called Cobert in the military scout vehicle directly, citing his position as the archeological team's doctor, whom he decided to christen Kineas O'Toole. Making free use of military jargon from his own previous experience, he stated that he had heard via the medical grapevine that the Mule's occupants were afflicted by a sickness. Cobert was flabbergasted. "But Banks only reported it back to his management within the last half hour," he protested.

"The medical community takes pride in the efficiency of our communications," Kieran agreed modestly. He went on to recite the symptoms; Cobert confirmed them.

"What is it?" he inquired gravely.

Kieran mustered his most studied professional look. "Probably *pulmonary lenticular encolitis*—otherwise known as closed-cabin infection," he replied. "I've seen a lot of it out in the Belt and on long-duration trips. It's a microbe that gets into the bloodstream via the lungs, caused by an unbalance in the chemistry of closed recirculation systems. Very infectious."

"How serious is it?" Cobert asked.

"Disfiguring and debilitating, but not permanently. They'll look bad for a while, though. . . ." Kieran paused, as if considering a delicate matter. "Was anyone from your unit over there recently—in the Mule?"

"I only just got back myself. . ." Cobert's voice trailed off as he saw what Kieran was implying. "Do you think I might have brought it back here?"

"It's very likely."

"Oh no!" The major's face fell. He groaned.

"But there's a chance I could stop it—if we move fast. It incubates in no time."

"How?"

"I'm an old space medic. I carry the right antibiotics. If I get over there and give you and your men a shot right away."

"Sounds good. I'll clear it with Banks."

"Why?"

"He's the Zorken chief here."

Kieran made a face. "I would prefer not to lose any time, Major. You know what corporate bureaucracies can be like. He probably can't wipe his nose without permission from head office. Better to keep it between ourselves. Anyway, who's in command of the unit there—you or him?"

A pained look crossed Cobert's face, but he took the point. He nodded. "Very well, Dr. O'Toole. Get over here as quickly as you can."

And so, Kieran drove back to the Troy site on one of the Juggernaut's "scooters," approaching the two military flyers on the blind side of the Mule. For good measure, Harry and Dennis back in the Juggernaut timed more interference and some spectacular communications effects just as he arrived, to provide a distraction.

The "preventative" that Kieran administered contained, of course, a measured amount of Pierre's concoction in each dose. Zorken's military force was thus set up to be rendered ineffective whenever the moment suited.

And the plan was advanced that much further, accordingly.

# ≋ 16 ≋

Justin Banks looked ghastly. His face had a greenish, gangrenous hue and was mottled with purplish, warty blotches. He looked something like a corpse that had clawed its way out from under a tombstone in a horror movie. Even Kieran was impressed as he took in the unhappy visage framed in an image window on one of the Juggernaut's screens. The codes that he and Dennis had figured out from the information supplied by Pierre had worked well enough indeed—and then some.

Kieran himself, cast as the wild-eyed persona of Keziah Turle, was speaking from another window. "It is as the testaments of old describe: The Plague of Akhnaton has come upon ye! '*And their skins became as the diseased flesh that clothes the undead; their eyes became as limpid, yellow swamps. . . .*' You who would not heed the warnings passed down through the ages must now bear the price. . . ." It was the message he had sent earlier to Gilder personally, and which to his admitted surprise had evidently gotten through. Gilder, appearing alongside Thornton Velte in the two remaining windows, was replaying the message for Velte's and Banks's benefit.

"How do you know that anyone of old ever said it?" Velte challenged. "Turle could be making it up. I've got people checking for some other references. They haven't come up with anything."

"He does seem to be a man of obscure and specialized knowledge," Gilder commented.

"Too much of a coincidence," Banks mumbled. "Didn't you say you got this before any symptoms developed here?"

"How could he have known about it, Thornton?" Gilder asked Velte.

Velte's mouth twisted while he searched for an explanation. "Wasn't he in the vehicle there?" he said finally. "He could have spread something around. Who let him in? What kind of security are we operating down there?"

"Boy, if he only knew how close he is," Kieran murmured to the others with him, enjoying the show.

"Is Gilder going to buy it?" Harry asked.

"Someone like him doesn't bend so soon," Juanita said.

"He looks like he's taking it more seriously than Velte, though," Walter put in.

"Right now, he doesn't want to get involved," Hamil told them. "He's too preoccupied with his daughter's wedding."

On the screen, Gilder seemed to accept that this was not going to lead anywhere immediately. He glanced around moodily, as if searching for a different tack. "What's this about trouble among the military force down there?" he asked.

"Major Cobert says they're on edge over the interference problems we've been having, and the fluorescent effects down in the workings," Banks replied. "Also, the gas emanations. Somehow they've gotten it into their heads that we're all in a tizzy about it."

"Hm. So where are we?" Gilder asked.

"Clarence agrees that the fluorescence is surprising—but it would hardly be the first time that a theory needed updating. Tran admits he's mystified by the emanations. They shouldn't be there."

"Can't somebody go up there and look?" Velte asked irascibly.

Banks raised a discolored face appealingly toward the camera. "It isn't something that's exactly top of our list right now, Thornton," he said, admonishing his immediate chief rather than the boss directly.

Gilder shuffled uncomfortably. "Well, I'm too wrapped up in other business right now. We've got those squatters out of the way, at least, so that's something. Thornton, can you take charge of this and get to the bottom of what's going on down there? Fly a doctor in from Lowell. It's probably just some kind of bug that's gone around. I've always said these small-scale systems are closed petri dishes. This idea about that Turle zealot bringing something in strikes me as too farfetched. From what I've heard, he doesn't have the coordination to get a hat on his head. Talk to Cobert too, and tell him that if he can't maintain discipline in his unit we'll have it replaced."

"Leave it to me, Hamilton," Velte replied.

An ambulance bearing medical specialists arrived from Lowell less than an hour later. On seeing the condition of the Mule's occupants, Farquist, the doctor in charge, confessed himself baffled. He'd never seen nor heard the likes of this before; neither did the literature contain a description of anything resembling it. Preliminary scans and biological tests using the equipment aboard the ambulance yielded nonsense results. After consulting remotely with various specialists and getting nowhere, Farquist told Banks that he proposed calling out a larger transporter to take all of the Mule's occupants back to Lowell and have them placed under observation there. By this time, Banks and the others were feeling too miserable to care. Then Major Cobert reported from the Venning carrier that he and his men weren't feeling or looking too spiffy either.

A grin of pranksterly delight adorned Kieran's face as he watched the latest exchanges within the enemy camp.

"*What?*" Banks managed, in the nearest he could manage that would otherwise probably have been close to a shriek. "He was there? You let him in? Why wasn't I consulted?"

"The health of the men of *my* unit was at issue," Cobert's voice replied distantly and primly—Kieran didn't have a tap on the local link to the Venning, so he had to make do with a relayed transmission of the audio coming through inside the Mule. "*I* decided that the possible risk of undue delay by involving external parties was unacceptable."

"Do I have to remind you that you are under *our* commission?" Banks seethed.

"Matters subject to direct military orders are still my prerogative," Cobert retorted.

"Who was this doctor of theirs, again?" Farquist asked, from inside the Mule with Banks.

"You said his name was what?" Banks queried.

"O'Toole," Cobert answered.

"Never heard of him," Farquist growled.

"You don't mean Turle?"

"I said, O'Toole."

"What did he look like?"

"From what you can tell in a suit: tall, well built, lean face—tanned, brown hair. Late thirties, maybe forties."

"Not graying hair, more fifties-ish?"

"No. I've just told you."

"Hmph."

"There isn't any *pulmonary lenticular encolitis* listed in the references," Farquist said. "It doesn't even make sense. And I've never heard of closed-cabin infection."

Velte, who had been following with rising exasperation on a link from Asgard, interrupted. "This isn't going to get us anywhere. Toole, Turle, whatever his name is—get him over there and have him account for himself in person. It's the only way we'll make any sense out of this. The whole thing is turning into a farce."

"I'll call Hashikar and—" Banks began.

"No!" Velte snapped. "Why tip them off and give them a chance to think up something else? Just send a squad out there and grab him. Are you there, Major?"

"I hear you," Cobert's voice answered.

"How bad are things with your men at the moment? Are they up to it?"

"Queasy, but soldiers have fought with worse. Best to do it now, before they deteriorate further."

"Let's get on with it, then," Velte directed.

At that moment another voice, sounding as if it were coming through on an internal speaker, announced, "*Attention, attention! Possible hostile alert. Approaching radar contact thirty kilometers, one-ninety degrees low, not responding to ID INT. Fire team to stations.*"

Clad in a light orange flight suit, Lee Mullen sat up front in the folding jump seat behind the pilot and c-com op. Behind, in the main body of the Airchief pickup skimming in from the south, the ten armed heavies that he had recruited for the raid to seize Thane and bring him in sat in two impassive lines along the sides. It should be a cinch, all had agreed. A quick swoop; just a bunch of geekspeaks and schoolteachers on a caravan tour . . . They'd be on the ground, have him out, and be away before the first graybeard had finished talking.

The pilot turned his head and indicated forward with a nod. "Coming into view now."

"*Squad ready,*" the c-com op said over the cabin intercom. "*Target in sight. Helmets secure. Final kit and weapons check.*"

Mullen craned forward to look. The terrain was as they had seen on the graphic reconstruction from the information given by the people at Stony Flats: a high plateau with a steep side facing a broad, flat valley with hills beyond. The scientists' camp was where the contact had said it would be: on a rocky shelf halfway up, reached by a zigzag road.

"Three . . . no, four aircraft," the pilot commented. He sounded surprised. "Wasn't this supposed to be an overland trip?"

"They must be having visitors," the c-com op said.

"Too bad we'll have to spoil the party . . . So where are the trucks?"

"Aren't they the two square shapes at the back?"

"Those look more like portashacks to me." The pilot turned inquiringly to Mullen again. "Maybe we should circle first and check it out."

"Fast in and out," Mullen reminded him. "It's not worth losing surprise over. Stick to the plan. We're going straight in."

"You're the man who's telling it. Approach vector set. LZ select confirmed. Descent program activated. We're going on it."

"*Thirty seconds. Release latches. Be ready to go.*" A short pause, then, "*Somebody must be sick. That's an ambulance down there.*"

The plateau top flattened ahead of them, then rose above. The shelf grew and unfolded below. And then, suddenly, from the c-com op again, "*Break off! Evade! Evade! We're taking fire! Bursts ahead, starboard!*"

Mullen clutched at the seatback in front of him and his head swam as the pilot flipped to manual and sent the Airchief into a stomach-wrenching, climbing turn. Balls of flaring orange swept by outside. Confusion broke out in the rear as unrestrained bodies that had been poised ready to move fell and collided to the accompaniment of shouted curses. A pattern of crimson blotches appeared in the mid-ground between the veering craft and the rocky shelf—detonated short as warning shots. Even so, several scattered *cracks* sounded of fragments striking the structure.

"What kind of schoolteachers are those?" the pilot snarled over his shoulder. "I thought you said this was gonna be a picnic. The operation's off. We don't have anything to take on that kind of artillery."

Mullen found that his mouth had gone dry. It had been a long time since he'd been in any kind of firing line. "That little creep! Somebody else bought him! We were set up! He'll fry when I get back! Nobody crosses me and walks away! Okay, let's go home."

Kieran and the others had followed what they could of the action from the little that Gottfried, still perched on the slopes above the shelf, had been able to capture through his lenses. They were as unable to make sense of it as anybody at the Troy site, as the commotion coming in over the monitoring taps showed. To cap it all, in the midst of frantic calls from Banks to Asgard asking for instructions, Farquist joined in, making it shrilly clear that he and his medics hadn't come here to get involved in a private war and demanding to know what was going on—as if anyone there could tell them.

Kieran decided that he had created about as much mischief here as he was likely to. It was time to carry the good fight to other quarters. He was fascinated by Pierre's self-assembling nano-synthesizers, and was certain that therein lay the means to make Gilder finally crack. But to do it he needed to get to Gilder directly, and the way to do that was not here. But possibly the wedding group assembling in Lowell might offer opportunities. Accordingly, he called Solomon Leppo and told him to get out to Tharsis in any kind of flyer he could lay his hands on and take Kieran back right away.

Leppo arrived with a partner called Casey, sooner than Kieran had dared hope, in a sleek flymobile "special" they had modified themselves. Kieran left with them for Lowell just as Cobert's snatch squad was taking off from Troy to come and get him. He told Hamil and Walter that he'd just have to leave them to deal with Banks and Cobert for the time being, and come up with something to account for his disappearance. But then again, a coherent explanation for the antics of an eccentric like Keziah Turle was hardly something that could reasonably be demanded. Like Jesus Christ, the twentieth century's General MacArthur, and the Schwarzenegger Terminator of the old movies, he assured them that he would be back.

# 17

It was good to be back. Lowell felt urban and cosmopolitan, strange as that sounded for what was itself just a microscopic part of humanity gathered under a collection of domes and dugouts surrounded by desert. But it was a big step up from being confined in vehicles, portable cabins, and surface suits.

Since there was a chance that June's place might be watched, Kieran called to let her know he was in town and then checked in at the Oasis—which was, after all, where all the action was happening that he hoped to use to his advantage. After treating himself to some clean clothes from the lobby-level shops and consigning his grubby desert wear to the hotel laundry, he showered, shaved, and relaxed for half an hour with a touch of Vivaldi and a Bushmills Black Bush straight. Then, feeling refreshed, rejuvenated, jaunty, and invigorated, he went down to the bar to reconnoiter the situation and consider his options from here. As luck would have it, Patti was working the shift. Her face lit up as she recognized him.

"Hey, Kieran! Welcome back. June said you were away on business for a while. Did you get it all done?"

"The away part, anyhow."

"So, Olympus again?"

"Sure. You've cut your hair. What happened to the ponytail?"

Patti took a glass and began filling it. "Oh, it just got to be too much bother. It just doesn't hang right in the gravity."

"So I take it Guinness has been behaving? He's still taking you and Grace for walks?"

"Yes. He's terrific. Half our friends are fighting over him now.

223

Does that mean you haven't seen them yet since you got back? How come?"

"I haven't been back there. I'm checked in here right now."

"Oh! That doesn't mean that you guys are fighting or something, does it?" Patti looked horrified.

Kieran grinned and shook his head. "Nothing like that. I just have reasons for being here rather than there for a while."

"Well, I'm glad about that. You two seemed to be right together." Patti set the glass down with a coaster. "Although, something a bit odd happened. I don't know if it was important or not, but Grace said that when she and another of the girls were out with Guinness, two guys in a car pulled up and wanted to know who the owner was. They sounded kind of . . . mean. Grace didn't want to get into complications so she just said he was hers. Was that okay?"

"Hmm . . . Yes, sure."

"Back in a moment." Patti moved away to serve some other customers.

Kieran sat back on the stool to rest against a partition and looked around. Maybe it wouldn't be such a good idea to walk around here brazenly as himself, he decided.

The bar was busier than what had been the norm. And there was an atmosphere of boisterous familiarity among the people present, as if most of them knew each other—unlike typical guests and travelers, who tended to confine themselves to ones, twos, and small groups. "Seems you've got a party going on here," Kieran commented when Patti came back.

"People have been coming in from all over for some big wedding that's being held off-planet," she told him. "They'll be leaving late tomorrow—but they're loaded."

"Who's getting married? Any idea?"

"Hamilton Gilder's daughter, Marissa. Where have you been? You know who *he* is, right? His face is on the net often enough."

"The big chief of Zorken Consolidated, isn't he? The construction and mining outfit."

"Right. They have this place in orbit that's swinging close by Mars right now. That's where the wedding is going to be."

"Who's she marrying?" Kieran asked, although he already knew.

"Mervyn Quinn." Who was a superstar of role-taking movies. "But his group is getting together over in Zerolon, somewhere—

you know, the old tradition about staying separate beforehand. I guess they'll be going up on a different ship."

Kieran nodded, sipped his beer, and fell silent for a moment, as if digesting the new information. "What's she like close up— the delectable Marissa?" he asked. "She looks pretty good in the shots I've seen of her."

"You know, Kieran, I haven't even seen her. She's too special to be seen down here in the bar. They've taken a whole floor upstairs, and she practically stays in one of the suites up there— you know, with their own security people watching the doors and elevators." Patti shook her head as she began replacing clean glasses in an overhead rack. "I don't think I'd like to have to live like that, whatever she's worth. I'd rather work down here and be able to talk to people like you."

"And walk Guinness," Kieran reminded her.

"Of course. Can you imagine Marissa Gilder being allowed out to do something like that?"

After he had finished his drink, Kieran sauntered around inconspicuously, taking in what there was to be seen, at the same time pondering on how to become invisible without losing touch of what was going on. There were groups of wedding guests everywhere, beginning the process of letting their hair down for the big occasion. Harried hotel staff bustled back and forth, while in private rooms teams of hired caterers, florists, suppliers, and buying agents organized the profusion of gifts and trappings that would be transported up to Asgard along with the guests. To relieve the air of business utility and work-a-day officiousness that normally reigned there, and create a festive mood that would bring alive reminiscences of Earth, a South Pacific theme had been decided on. Troupes of Hawaiian and Polynesian dancers and musicians had been imported for the event; the menus gave foretastes of dishes prepared from yams, tropical fruits, luau meats, brought to perfection with spicy ingredients from all over Oceania; there were more budding flowers from local hothouses and nurseries than probably existed in one place anywhere else on Mars.

Kieran drifted in on one of the florists and started chatting with her. Her name was Marion. She explained that the flowers were genetically adapted for shipping in the budding stage at low temperatures, which would enable them to bloom full and fresh when warmed on arrival. She showed him a species of such delayed-flowering lilies that had been selected for inclusion in the garlands and bouquets on account of their enhanced fragrance, which they achieved by expelling their scent actively. That was interesting, Kieran commented. He hadn't known about that before. "They create atmosphere for you—literally," Marion said, running a finger over a bundle of the buds fondly. "They'll be the last things to be packed tomorrow."

Kieran wandered around the hotel thoughtfully for the next half hour. Then he went back up to his room and retrieved from the Juggernaut's data files the figures that Pierre had supplied for the externally applied electrical field strength needed to activate nano-synthesizers incorporated in body cells. Armed with that information, he placed a call to an old friend and communications specialist to inquire if, and if so, how a digital code could be multiplexed into a regular phone signal in such a way as to pulse the receiving voice coil to generate that order of field gradient. The system advised him that the recipient was almost a light-hour away in the Belt, and the reply would be forwarded. A short while later, Kieran reappeared downstairs in the room to the rear of the lobby area, where Marion and several assistants in white work coats were still wrapping and boxing budding blooms, tying posies, and arranging assorted sprigs of greenery.

"Any chance I could steal a few of those lilies?" Kieran inquired casually. "I'm due to meet a special date in a couple of days' time. Wouldn't fresh-flowering lilies go off just great in a place like this!"

"Don't tell me you're a romantic at heart underneath it all," Marion said.

"And what's wrong with that? Sure, it comes with the name. Look around, you've got hundreds of them."

Marion shook her head with a smile and gave him a bunch. "Here. Don't say I never do anyone a favor."

"You see, I know a fairy godmother when I see one." Kieran examined the flowers. "How long beforehand would I need to start warming them up?"

"About eight hours gives the best results."

"Uh-huh." He peeled back the furled outer petals of one of

the buds and studied it. "How does the ejection mechanism work?" he asked curiously.

"Why do you need to know that?"

"I'm an engineer. Engineers can't look at anything without taking it apart and wanting to know how it works."

"Tell me about it. I was married to one once." Marion opened the inner layers to uncover the structures of the pistil and stamen, and gave him a mini tutorial on the pollination process and how it related to scent manufacture.

Kieran watched and listened intently. "My word!" he commented when she was done. "It makes you glad to be a vertebrate, doesn't it?"

Marion ignored the remark. "Good luck with your date. If you don't make out, you won't be able to blame it on us for not trying to help."

"Much appreciated, indeed." Kieran walked away, smiling.

Back in his room, the first thing he did was put the lily buds from Marion in the room's refrigerator. Then he called Pierre to say where he was and that he would need a further supply of nano-synthesizer solution the following morning, prepared with a base that would disperse rapidly in air. He also asked Pierre's recommendation for a substance carrying a distinctive odor that would behave similarly. Having settled on a type, he ordered some from a local medical supplies company, to be delivered to the Oasis immediately by courier, along with an assortment of medical syringes, and asked the hotel's room service to bring a half-dozen extra wastepaper bins to his room. He called Solomon Leppo, telling him to be at the hotel the next morning too, and then Mahom Alazahad to ask if he could organize a private fire team for possible use at short notice from among his nefarious contacts. With the irrationality and flaring tempers that seemed to be in evidence everywhere, and especially after the show of force at Troy, Kieran felt that having some protection ready on hand for Hamil and the others out at Tharsis wouldn't be a bad investment.

Finally, he called June again with a shopping list of further items that he needed: a white work coat of the kind worn by lab techs and in plant nurseries, and some kind of memento from the Martian desert. "You know, a piece of polished rock, or a

mineral with a striking pattern—the kind of thing they make
into ashtrays and souvenirs. And it needs a fancy box to put it
in, suitable for a wedding gift, along with a blank card." From
theatrical suppliers, Asiatic-style stores, costumers, or anywhere
else she could think of, he wanted an Eastern outfit: loose,
pajama-style trousers; Turkish dolman jacket or similar; tarboosh
or other suitable headgear, along with appropriate shirt, slippers
and accessories; to go with it, a stage makeup kit and a selection of wigs—dark through white, showing various stages of
graying. Kieran concluded: "Put some of my own clothes at the
apartment in one of my bags, leave it in a baggage locker at the
spaceport, and send me the key code. And, lastly, I want you to
book a reservation at the Oasis for me."

"You're already there."

"Well, not me, this other character. Come on, stop acting obtuse.
Let's have him arriving tomorrow, let's say for two nights."

"And who would this be for?" June asked.

"I'm not sure yet," Kieran confessed.

"I need a name to make the reservation."

Kieran frowned and thought for a few seconds. Then his face
broadened into the kind of smile that came with a sudden
inspiration that he couldn't resist. "The Khal of Tadzhikstan," he
announced with a verbal flourish. "What do you think? Like it?"

June groaned. "Dare I ask what this is about?" she hazarded.

"He's going to be our way of getting to Brother Hamilton,
otherwise known as He-Who-Seeks-After-Higher-Powers," Kieran
informed her. "And the person he can do it through is right here,
at the Oasis. You know, Lovely, I'm almost beginning to believe
in a Higher Helping Hand somewhere myself."

When the syringes and test solution arrived, Kieran settled
down with a pen, note pad, and a sample batch of lilies from
the refrigerator to experiment with. He tried various ways of
introducing the liquid using the different syringes, noting down
the details and then carefully unraveling the buds to inspect the
results. After discarding the failures, he found four methods that
avoided internal damage or spoiling the external appearance.
Using a numbered label to identify each, he repeated each of the
four procedures on a new, untouched bud, and then laid them out
around the room to thaw overnight, each covered by an upturned

wastepaper bin. Beyond that, there was little he could do until
the packages that June was organizing began arriving. Kieran went
downstairs to have dinner and learn what he could through dis-
creet questioning about the wedding party's composition, security arrangements, schedule for the following day, and anything
else that might be useful.

The last thing he did that evening was call Walter Trevany out
in the Juggernaut for the latest eavesdropping news from Troy.
Major Cobert and all his men were now showing clear signs of
Banks & Co.'s condition, and Dr. Farquist had been advised that
the entire contingent—Zorken people and the military force—
would be moved to a hospital in Lowell before the end of the
day for further observation.

Everyone—in Asgard, at Troy, and in Hamil's group—was
equally mystified as to who had been in the Airchief that had
been driven off at Troy earlier, and what they had wanted. Trevany
believed that whoever it was had presumed the camp to be still
occupied by the archeological expedition that had been there
previously, but it left him none the wiser as to who or why. Kieran
had a pretty good idea where the intruders were from and what—
or more accurately, who—they had come looking for. Tomorrow morning would be a good time for him to disappear again
for a while, he decided.

# ⤳ **18** ⤲

When Kieran checked his mail the next morning, a reply had come back from the communications-expert friend out in the Belt. The frequencies that Kieran had specified for activating the nano-synthesizers were outside the bandwidth of regular phones, so their coils couldn't be pulsed in the way Kieran had proposed. However, a power oscillator circuit associated with the graphics might work, but it would require an external piece of hardware called a multiplex modulator, or "muxmod," to inject the signal into a data channel while the phone was in use. The message detailed several models and wished Kieran good luck. Kieran then called Pierre, who confirmed that he had prepared an additional quantity of the solution as requested. Kieran told him to have it delivered to the room of the "Khal of Tadzhikstan" at the Oasis hotel before the end of the morning. Pierre was beginning to know Kieran sufficiently by now to not even bother asking. Kieran passed on the information he had obtained concerning remote activation of the nano codes via the phone system, along with the details of the muxmod that it would need. Pierre promised to look around and see what he could find.

Kieran showered, shaved, dressed, and downed a snack breakfast from the room's autochef unit, by which time it was close to eight hours after he had set out his four selected lily buds to thaw. He had spaced three well apart around the room and one in the bathroom, so that when he removed the bins covering them, he was able to get a good indication of how effective each had been in dispersing its scent. Samples 1 and 3, although visually undamaged, hadn't worked at all; 2 yielded a strong scent, and 4 a distinct but milder one. He chose 2, consulted his notes for the procedure that he had followed in treating it, and was able to practice more with several fresh samples from the refrigerator before Solomon Leppo arrived. Leppo stood looking around in bemusement at the room's collection of medical gadgets, mutilated flowers, and trash bins. "This isn't from some kind of party you had last night," he decided.

"Don't worry," Kieran told him cheerfully. "We're not getting ready for a funeral. I'm going to give you a crash course on the new science of botanical surgery."

"Surgery? On plants? That's a new one."

"I've just invented it. Then, when you've graduated—which had better be in under an hour, since I've got a lot to do— you'll be performing your new art live this afternoon. Now this is what we're doing. In a room at the back downstairs, they'll be packing delayed-opening flowers that are being sent up to Asgard for the wedding." Kieran picked up one of the sprays that he had saved. "The flowers will include bundles of lilies like these. Follow hard and concentrate on what I'm about to show you, Solomon, my good friend, because there won't be any second chance. . . ."

Kieran demonstrated the technique that he had settled on, describing its purpose, repeating it with several of the lily buds and breaking them open to show Leppo the results. He then had Leppo try his hand, doing it over until he seemed to have the hang of it. Kieran then gave him the syringe, the remaining test liquid, and the rest of the buds. "Take these away and practice until you can get it right every time," he said. "I'll meet you down in the lobby at two o'clock this afternoon. Make sure you've got the syringe with you. We'll take it from there."

"Does anything ever run sane and normal around you for long?" Leppo asked, shaking his head.

"I've let it sometimes, just out of curiosity, but it tends to get boring," Kieran replied. "Piece of philosophy: if any two days of your life are the same, one of them was unnecessary."

The packages from June had all arrived by this time. Kieran spent the next hour using the makeup kit and wardrobe to transform his appearance. When he was satisfied with the graying, brown-eyed, swarthy-skinned patriarch of indeterminate central Asian origins staring back at him from the mirror, he turned his attention to the gift item that she had picked.

It was a carved Martian Cross, cut and polished from a gray-green native rock that Kieran recognized as an igneous type similar to dolomite, found below the red layer—which was essentially a surface feature now generally accepted as having blanketed Mars from an external source some time in the not-so-distant past. The design borrowed elements from the Maltese and Celtic crosses, combining them in a distinctive angular style in some ways suggestive of Navajo sand-pictures. It had originated with one of the religious sects that had come to Mars in the early settlement days, and had since been adopted as a generic symbol of the culture, like the Japanese sun or the Irish shamrock. It was ideal—just what he wanted. The box with it was of a silver alloy inlaid with patterns built from polished grains of variously colored local stones and minerals, some of them quite rare and pricey. Inside, it was padded and lined with a satiny maroon material.

Again more than satisfied, Kieran called Walter Trevany for an update on intercepts from Asgard via Troy. The most interesting snippet was an exchange between Velte and Banks, in which Velte confided that while talking to Marissa down on Mars within the last hour, Hamilton Gilder had told her about the affliction that had broken out among the survey group at Tharsis and their military support unit, and the rumor that it was somehow connected with the ancient builders whose works were being violated.

"She was the influence that got him into all this in the first place," Velte remonstrated. "If Hamilton starts listening to her now, we could get bogged down forever."

"There isn't much I can do from here," Banks grumbled. "I've still got squabbling doctors who can't even agree what it is. Anyway, you're up there with him. I'm not."

"But it's the squabbling doctors that we need to play down," Velte replied. "If anyone checks with you, don't open up that can of worms. Tell them there's no question that a perfectly rational explanation lies behind it all. It's just going to take a little time. If Hamilton goes off on one of his tangents, he'll be throwing wrenches in everywhere."

"Okay, Thornton. You can count on me," Banks promised. But Kieran got the feeling that Banks might be starting to wonder himself now.

"Perfect," Kieran muttered to himself as he cut the connection from Trevany.

Taking the blank card that June had enclosed with the cross, he opened it and penned inside in a flourishing hand:

> *Let this guardian talisman watch over your future together,*
> *From he who watches the future.*
> *K. of T.*

He placed the card on top of the cross, closed the box, and set it to one side. Then he used his comset to compose a message which read:

> *The most profuse greetings, Marissa.*
>
> *Your forgiveness if this form of address seems inappropriate from one who has not met you; but then, in a way, I have—on the planes into which our psyches do indeed extend, and where they interact. You may not have become conscious of it yet at your early stage of material life, but you possess rare gifts of insight and understanding which one day will play their part in the further growth and enlightenment of the soul, which is the reason for our Earthly journey.*
>
> *But I write now on a matter of a more immediate and serious nature, which concerns the disfigurement suffered by your father's agents and their defenders, which he revealed to you today. Your father seeks the truth, but he is in danger of being misled by those close to him who will never see and cannot believe. The Plague of Akhnaton is a warning from the creators of the ancient mysteries. Empires have fallen, armies have been destroyed, cities crumbled to ruins . . . of those who would not heed.*
>
> *I have come from afar to instruct you in the workings of the realms that have been hidden, and to beseech your cooperation now, while there is time, before calamity befalls us. I will be arriving before noon.*
>
> > *Earnestly,*
> > *He who is known as:*
> > *The Khal of Tadzhikstan*

Kieran read the message through, complimented himself, and despatched it over an external channel to the Oasis hotel with a request for it to be printed out, sealed, and delivered to Ms. Marissa Gilder.

Which took care of everything on his list for the time being. He cleared away the evidence of his horticultural experimenting before leaving the room to be serviced, wrapped himself in a topcoat with the hat in a pocket to be less conspicuous, even among Lowell's exotic display of styles and garbs, and taking the Martian Cross in its box and the white work coat, left the Oasis by a rear service exit to the parking area.

He strolled through to the spaceport terminal and went to the baggage locker that June had indicated. Two of his bags from the apartment were there, along with a short, ornately embroidered cloak that June had evidently decided to add—the ideal thing to set off the rest of the outfit. Kieran changed it for the topcoat, put the topcoat inside one of the bags along with the white work coat, and then went out onto the concourse to hail one of the electric runaround cars used for local public transportation. Minutes later, he was conspicuously set down at the main lobby entrance to the Oasis, where, leaving a bellman to take care of the bags, he swept inside in full regalia to announce himself. His reservation was confirmed; also, he was informed, he had a message waiting. The desk clerk presented him with a stiff, rose-pink envelope. The note inside read:

> *Please come to my suite on the penthouse floor as soon as is convenient. Present this to the security guard at the elevator.*
> *Marissa Gilder*

Meanwhile, in an apartment suite on Embarcadero that had been rented by visiting clients of the Zodiac Commercial Bank, Lee Mullen was taking a call from a henchman who had spotted Solomon Leppo coming out of the Oasis hotel earlier and followed him to an address in Gorky, where he was still ensconced.

"Don't let him out of your sight," Mullen instructed. "I'll send more of the guys over. If he makes a move before they get there, call me."

"Wait." Henry Balmer, who happened to be with Mullen,

raised a cautioning hand. "You've got Leppo now any time you want him. But Thane might not still be out there in the desert—especially after that fiasco yesterday. If he's back here, Leppo could lead us to him."

Mullen held his reaction to returning a sour look. "Nobody crosses me and walks," he said, repeating what had become his regular theme lately. "Thane is your problem. Of course he's still out in the desert. You weren't there. Why else would they be hiding behind all that artillery that nearly blew us away?"

"You don't *know* that," Balmer retorted. "Thane is also the problem of the people who are paying you. A big problem. Your job is to cover all bases. I don't think they'd like it if they found you'd let someone who crossed *them* walk."

Mullen considered the point darkly, then turned back to the screen.

"Don't pick him up yet," he told the caller. "Just keep a tight tail on him for now. We need to see where he goes."

"Gotcha," the caller confirmed.

# ≷ **19** ≷

Marissa Gilder was curvy, bouncy, and petite, with round blue eyes that seemed practiced in widening to convey awe, wonder, or simply an intensity of fixation that constituted her means of ensuring the attention and special treatment that she was accustomed to. Except that, in this instance, perhaps, the awe that she was directing in Kieran's direction was more solidly grounded and not just contrived as a manipulative device. Her hair was blond, shoulder-length, and bouncy like her person, with a reflective tint that gave it a mobile golden sheen. Her face lived up to the images that the media had made popular: saucily pretty with an upturned nose, pouty mouth, rounded cheeks tapering to a button chin, all no doubt coaxed to a high point of subtly enhanced sensuousness and allurement by the coordinated efforts of an expensively retained team of beauticians and stylists. She received Kieran in a loose, sleeveless cream dress with gold spangles, suitably adorned with an exposition of gold rings, bracelets, necklace, and a hair comb.

The suite itself was a riot of flowers, cards, gifts on display, and unopened packages, with trays of candies and tidbits, a selection of cold snacks, and a corner bar for visitors in the suite's outer room. Hotel staff bustled in and out at intervals, bringing clothes to already bulging closets and removing others for packing in anticipation of departure that evening. Two Zorken security men in dark suits sat in the outer room, keeping a wary eye on Kieran through the open doorway. He had been checked for weapons on arrival, before being brought into Marissa's presence. Even so, she sat at a greater distance back from him than would have been normal for the circumstances, in the center

236

of a couch at the far end of a low table. So far, she had followed his words with the raptness of somebody who has wandered for a lifetime, finally finding her guru. She was stunned by his awareness of events that had transpired between herself and her father, faraway on Asgard, that very morning. The plague that Kieran had named, although unknown to any of the medical authorities that had been consulted, had been described identically by another savant out in the desert with the scientific group that the Zorken people had evicted. Kieran replied modestly that obviously the same truth would manifest itself to everyone in touch with ultimate reality.

By this time, Marissa had recovered from her initial display of wonder. How much of it was genuine, and how much a Socratic way of drawing people out, Kieran hadn't yet decided. She watched him take a sip from the glass of vodka tonic he had accepted and met his eyes curiously. "I always thought people like you didn't touch alcohol and such," she commented.

Kieran waved a hand dismissively. "Imitators obsessed with externals and trivia. Such things affect me to the degree that I allow them to. The truly empowered mind controls its body and itself totally."

Marissa seemed impressed. "You must be from a very rare kind."

"Haven't we already established that?"

"So why are you here?"

"I told you in my letter: to enlist your help in warning your father and his agents against the consequences of interfering with the workings of a superior science that this culture does not yet understand."

"What's a 'khal'? I tried looking it up but couldn't find it."

"It's related to 'khan,' which means ruler or leader, but relates more to the world of the spiritual than of mundane human affairs."

"I see."

"An obscure central Asian word."

Marissa stared at him, her eyes round and searching, as if expecting a sudden revelation. "Is this superior science the 'hidden realms' that your letter talked about?" she asked.

"Yes, exactly."

"It said you were coming to instruct about them. Very well, I'm listening."

Kieran made an expansive motion with his hands, then brought them together as if illustrating the challenge of having to sweep much into a small space. "The universe that today's science imagines to be all is but an infinitesimal part of what exists. The vaster reality contains all that has happened, will happen, and could happen—all of it equally real, just as all the frames of a movie are equally real. Consciousness provides the illumination that focuses on one part, creating what we think of as the 'present.'"

Marissa looked intrigued. "Is this the many-worlds picture that they get out of quantum mechanics? I know something about it."

"I prefer not getting tied down to such restrictive language. Scientists have uncovered the workings of the backstage machinery that creates the illusion, but they see it only as technicians. They miss the point of what the performance is about."

"You mean it serves a purpose."

"Of course."

"What?"

"A learning environment. The fleeting lives that mortals experience are courses charted through the totality of possibilities by personas that souls create, in such circumstances and of such natures as the soul needs to heal and to grow. When the experience is complete, the persona is discarded but the lesson remains imprinted. You could think of them as characters in a role-playing game."

"You're talking about whoever created and directed the movie—what *their* purpose was," Marissa observed.

"A good way to put it," Kieran agreed.

"I *knew* it! So tell me more."

"The branchings that lead to all possible outcomes make morally meaningful choices possible. We can decide the kind of future we steer toward."

"Um . . ." Marissa needed to think about that. "More than a rock or a fish can, anyway," she said finally.

"You are correct. Ability to direct will is what really evolves. With the progressive emergence of consciousness, pure randomness gives way to volition."

Marissa was following intently. This was clearly a subject that fascinated her. As an imaginative and clearly far from stupid, doted-on daughter, Kieran could see how she could be an influence on

Hamilton. "But not just as individuals," she said. "We're social animals too, right? So we create ways of steering collectively."

Kieran sat forward and nodded emphatically. "*But* . . . there was a culture of old that could shape their future in more ways than just by their collective policies and actions. They were able to manipulate *the probabilities of physical reality* to favor outcomes that they deemed desirable. Do you see what that means?" He allowed a few seconds for effect. "To anyone who didn't know what was going on, it would appear as if chains of improbabilities and unlikely coincidences were conspiring to drive events in unlikely directions. Strange happenings; inexplicable accidents . . ." He gave her the most gurulike glare that he could muster, intense and fixating, and let her think about it.

The blue eyes widened and rounded. "Accidents happening to people who interfered. Strange 'curses.'" Marissa's voice fell almost to a whisper. "*Plagues* . . ."

Kieran nodded gravely. "Except that they wouldn't be curses or anything mystical. Just misinterpretations of a deeper working of reality . . . And the Ancients left the power behind them in their works. That's what your father's agents in the desert are up against. And the consequences will spread back to those who sent them if the warning is ignored."

Marissa was sold. It wasn't so much that anything Kieran had said would withstand rigorous scrutiny or a skeptical demand for evidence. But as a result of the very aimlessness that much of her life entailed—doubly frustrating for an active mind like hers—it was something *exciting* for a change, something that she *wanted* to be true.

"What do you want me to do?" she asked.

"We need to help your father gain the same insight that you have begun to glimpse," Kieran told her.

Back in the Khal's room, Kieran found that the package containing the solution of nano-synthesizer assembly molecules from Pierre had been delivered. Since he still had time to spare before he was due to meet Leppo, he ordered a grilled mahi salad with a half carafe of chablis and ate it in the room while reviewing published information on Zorken's management structure and key people. Then, donning his cloak again and putting the bottle of solution, the white work coat, and the box containing the Martian

Cross in a plastic laundry bag from the room's supplies, he took the elevator back down to the lobby level and wandered through to the room he had been in the previous evening, where the flowers for shipment were being prepared and packed. He found Marion at a desk, checking lists on a screen and singing out instructions to relays of white-coated assistants and hotel staff, coming and going. She didn't recognize him.

"Ah! You must be the madam to whom I was guided. I am told you are the one to speak with here. I have just arrived today from afar."

Marion took in his appearance and garb, and suddenly she was all attention. "You must be the person who was with Marissa Gilder this morning. I heard about you."

This was even better than Kieran had hoped. "The same," he acknowledged graciously. "We are old acquaintances."

"It's Mister . . . ?"

"Khal. Strictly, it's *the* Khal, but I am easy about these things."

Marion nodded knowingly. "So, what can I do for you?"

"I have a gift for her to take with her, naturally. But it would be incomplete without a floral tribute to our friendship. Could you oblige?"

"But of course. Do you have the gift with you?"

"In my room upstairs. I can be back with it in a few minutes."

"Sure, that would be just fine."

Kieran smiled in a way that was mildly apologetic. "I will probably need some help in choosing the right arrangement. It isn't exactly my field of expertise, you understand."

"I'll be happy to take care of it personally."

"Would you be able to wrap it too?"

"Certainly."

"You are too kind, madam."

"The least I can do."

Kieran appeared in the lobby just before 2:00 to find it busy with wedding guests checking out and meeting in lunch groups, or leaving early for the spaceport. Leppo was already there, standing in front of the store near the reception desk; so was Casey, Kieran noted—watching from one of the seats inside the main entrance. Kieran ambled over to stand nonchalantly a few feet away. Leppo glanced at him briefly as he approached, then took no further notice. Kieran joined him in scanning the throng of faces. After a minute or more he murmured quietly, "Two rules if you're going to be working with me, Sol, old chum. One, I'm always on time. Two, be prepared for the unexpected."

Leppo's head jerked around. He still had to stare for a second or two before he could believe it. "I don't believe it," he blurted, all the same.

"You've got the syringe?" Kieran asked him.

Leppo patted a bulge in his coat pocket. "It's here, cleaned and working."

"How did the practice go? Have you got it pat now?"

"Every time."

"Fine. Here you are, then." Kieran extracted the box with the Martian Cross from the laundry bag that he was carrying, leaving the coat and the solution inside, and passed the bag to Leppo. Leppo nodded, tucked it under an arm, and walked away in the direction of the men's washroom. Kieran, carrying the box, headed back toward the rear of the lobby. Casey was half in and half up from his seat, staring uncertainly after the bizarre character who had appeared from nowhere, whom his partner had talked to. Kieran left him to make what he could of it. Marion was waiting for him when he came back.

"It's beautiful!" she exclaimed when Kieran showed her the cross. "A Martian design. I take it that's a native rock?"

"More than just that," Kieran said. "It has emanations. I believe it reradiates the influence of associations from long ago."

"Really?" Marion allowed a moment of hushed reverence. "So, did you have any particular kind of arrangement in mind?"

"For the flowers? I leave that entirely to you."

Marion cocked her head to study the sprays and bunches arrayed around them. "Let's see . . . I think first, a crystal vase like that one to build it in . . ."

"Splendid."

"And a white motif for a wedding. Something a little exotic . . . ? White orchids with Casablanca lilies, maybe with some snapdragon too."

In the background, Leppo, wearing the white coat, came into the room behind another of the assistants. He identified the table of lilies that Kieran had briefed him on and moved casually over to it. "Not too pale," Kieran said. "To me that would carry suggestions of a deathly shade. We should have a touch of color."

"How about a blush of Bridal Pink Rose?" Marion pointed. "And variegated ivy with white and green in the leaf, like that."

"Perfect! And a background of more green to set it off."

Leppo had turned his back on the room and begun working rapidly, his shoulders hunched.

"Mixed ferns for body and support: maidenhair and Ming," Marion pronounced.

"Could we add some of that?" Kieran pointed. "What is it?"

"Yes, lily grass. A spray to flow and move with the trailing orchids. An excellent choice. You must be a natural."

"It's really you. I pick up influences too—like the rock."

"Now you're being flattering. . . ."

Mullen reported the latest to "Mr. Z," one of two "expediters" from the Firm, who were being sent to oversee the situation in Lowell and recover the lost quarter billion inner-system dollars. They were still a day or so out, inbound for Phobos.

"He went back to the Oasis and met up with his buddy, then kept an appointment. But it wasn't with Thane. It was some Ali Baba screwball in a pyjama suit that showed up there this morning—seems like he knows the Gilder girl."

"No connection with Thane?" the face on the screen checked.

"Nah. He's still out in the desert with the professors . . ." Mullen turned his head to mutter at Balmer, who was following disconsolately, "like I said all along."

"How is the recruiting progressing?" Z inquired.

"They'll be up to strength by the time you get here. Two troop carriers and a gunship, loaded, plus command car." The other thing Mullen had been doing was raise reinforcements to go back to Tharsis for Thane. If the other side wanted to play it tough, that was fine with the Firm. He went on, "I figure Leppo knows the score out there. He set us up. He's at the Oasis now with his partner. I've got Brown and Black there with three soldiers. What do you want us to do?"

Z considered the situation for a few seconds. "Where is this force being assembled?" he asked.

"A warehouse at a place called Stony Flats—that's a few miles outside the city. The flyers will leave from there to go out over the desert."

"Leppo and the other are serving no useful purpose loose and could pose a risk," Z pronounced. "Grab them now, but keep them there where you are for a while to cool off. Then bring them out to Stony Flats when we arrive, and we'll all have a talk."

"You've got it." Mullen treated Balmer to a satisfied look as he cut off the screen and clicked in the code to make a call. "Sorry, Doc, but your guess didn't pan out. We're playing it our way now. And this time, you and Leo can come along for the ride too. I wouldn't want you two to think you were missing out on anything."

It was done. The doctored lilies had been packed and were being consigned to carry their message, and the final groups of wedding guests were departing for the shuttles up to Phobos. There was little more for Kieran to do now until they arrived at Asgard, and the ceremony and reception took place, which wouldn't be until the next day. With the more immediate things taken care of, his concern turned back to Hamil and the people out at Tharsis. He had planned to go next with Leppo and Casey to Alazahad's to check what progress Mahom had made in raising a protection force.

Still arrayed as the Khal of Tadzhikstan, Kieran arrived at the elevators on his way to the lower parking level, where they had arranged to meet. It was one of those rare times in life when everything seemed to be going smoothly, he reflected as he waited for the car to arrive. And that in itself was enough to keep him on guard. It had been his experience that events never continued in such a manner for long; such deceptive calms were inevitably the prelude to the sudden bursting of a storm.

The reaffirmation that little in life ever changed came as soon as the doors opened. Two of the three men inside were none other than "Mr. Brown" and "Mr. Black," whom Kieran had last seen in the conference room at the Zodiac Commercial Bank. The third's face was unfamiliar, but he was obviously with the others and of similar ilk. "Gentlemen," Kieran acknowledged, stepping inside and smiling pleasantly. The button for the lower parking level was lit. Kieran pressed the main lobby button and turned to face the doors as they closed.

All the way down, he could feel Black's eyes traveling over him like the beam for a body scan. He could read the thoughts from behind as if they were being transmitted telepathically: *There's something familiar about that guy. Where have I seen him?* But obviously it didn't click.

On the lobby level, Kieran got out and headed for the stairwell down, at the same time tearing his comset from his pocket and thumbing Leppo's code. "Hel—" Leppo's voice began, but Kieran cut him off.

"Sol, it's the Knight. Watch out. There are bad guys here, and they're heading your way. It could be a coincidence, but I don't . . ."

The connection had gone dead.

As Kieran moved cautiously out from a stairwell door to a landing overlooking the parking level, he saw why. The three men from the elevator had joined two others, who were with Leppo and Casey in one of the rows between the vehicles, and from their positions and attitudes, Kieran guessed, holding them at gunpoint. Even as he watched, keeping well back in the doorway, the captives were bundled into a shiny black Metrosine. Two of the others squeezed in after them, the remaining three up front. The car backed out and left in swishing display of opulent engineering and luxury. Kieran could do nothing but watch as it disappeared down the exit ramp, heading for the tunnel onto Gorky.

# ≷20≶

Mahom Alazahad looked Kieran up and down with a wide, approving grin. It was getting late in the afternoon. "Well, I'll be . . . It took me a second to be sure, but, yep, it's you all right, Knight. So what's going on? Looks like you decided to come over to the sophisticated side of the race."

"Special effects, Mahom. I've taken it on as a new vocation to become the spiritual savior of the chief of Zorken Consolidated."

Mahom looked appalled. "The big construction outfit? You're kidding! But, no . . . you're not kidding. Don't tell me you're thinking of taking on a Zorken army with those troops you asked me to rustle up. I thought they were supposed to be just standby protection for these friends of yours out at Tharsis."

"Don't worry," Kieran told him. "I'm not into the interplanetary war business yet."

"So what gives?"

As they walked to the office, Kieran added as much as was pertinent to what he had told Mahom when he called from the Oasis the previous evening. Mahom poured two coffees from the pot by the window while he listened. Kieran finished with a summary of the latest developments, including what had happened to Leppo and Casey.

"Sol has this way of rushing into things, like a lot of kids with ambitions," Mahom said. "But he's okay. Do I take it our first priority now is to find where he's at and bust him out?"

Kieran nodded. "The light wasn't too good, and I was at the wrong angle. I couldn't get the car's registration."

"Probably fake, anyhow," Mahom grunted. "But that shouldn't

be a problem. There aren't that many snazzy black Metrosines in this city. And if these are guys from some off-planet syndicate looking for a wad of loot that went missing like you think, it'll either be a rental, or registered with an owner on a pretty narrowed-down list. If we come up with a probable, we can find it if we get its locator code out of the security company's database." Mahom winked. "Otherwise it might depend on eyes out on the streets."

There was little Kieran could do but wait. He had thought that after the wedding party left, he might risk showing himself at June's, but with the syndicate out and almost certainly looking for him he decided against it. He was on his way back to the Oasis, when Pierre called to say he had obtained a multiplex modulator of the kind Kieran had specified, and they needed to get together to rehearse how they would use it. Since there was no point in advertising Pierre's involvement by having Kieran go to where he was, they arranged to meet at the hotel.

Pierre had with him an artificial culture of cells containing the assembled protein synthesizers and molecular-circuit receivers for activating them, along with portable equipment to analyze the codes picked up by the receivers and how the synthesizers responded. Through several hours of trial-and-error testing, they called the room's number from a pocket comset fed by the muxmod and established the settings needed to generate the required external field pattern. By the time they had gotten it right, they could call the room, and under cover of an innocuous regular connection, transmit a protein-director code to the synthesizers inside the cells of the culture sample placed close to the receiving screen. To be sure it wasn't an accidental result due to all the equipment being in the same room, Kieran took the muxmod down to one of the public booths in the lobby and made several calls from there, which proved successful. As a finale, he routed a call *through* Pierre's comset, with the muxmod attached. Hence, they could piggyback the codes onto a call from a third party being routed through to the called number. The call carrying the code to the target didn't have to originate from the phone that the muxmod was connected to.

By this time, a new possibility had suggested itself to Kieran's ever fertile mind. "Let's put it to a live test before we go active with Asgard," he said to Pierre upon returning to the room. "Can you set up codes to deactivate the synthesizers that we initiated among those guys out at Troy?"

"*Deactivate* them?" Pierre looked mystified.

"Yes. I want to test the effectiveness in selecting a target subject." Kieran meant the individual who would be actually at the receiving screen, as opposed to others who might be close by. "And it will add to the image. Hasn't one of the best ways of turning nonbelievers around always been a demonstration of mystical healing? We're about to expand the business."

A half hour later, Kieran was looking at the frightful, green-purple visage of Justin Banks at the Troy site. Banks was still in the Mule transporter but outfitted in a lightweight suit as if he were about to leave; also, there were figures in the background who looked like medics. It seemed that Kieran had caught them just as they were about to be moved to the hospital at Lowell.

"Who the hell are you?" Banks demanded, taking in the garish, smiling form that had appeared on an incoming message screen.

"Profoundest greetings to you. I am he who is known as the Khal of Tadzhikstan, at present in Lowell, who only as recently as this morning had the honor of an audience with your Lady Marissa." Kieran glanced across the room at Pierre, who was juggling numbers on a screen plugged into the muxmod, which in turn was feeding into the room system's data port.

"Oh God, not another one," Banks groaned.

"Who is that?" Kieran heard one of the doctors mutter in the background.

"I'm not sure. I haven't seen him before. We've been having trouble from—"

"I have come at the behest of the seer Keziah, who is with the party nearby to you in the desert. Deserts are no stranger to me. Neither is the affliction that you suffer. But the tidings I bring you are joyous! Your transgressions were committed out of ignorance and not malice, and are therefore to be forgiven. I bring to you the healing powers from our Earthly home of the spirit."

"Isn't there ever going to be an escape from you people? Look, for the last time . . ."

Pierre was nodding and sending a thumbs-up. Kieran responded in kind, his hand below the viewing angle from the screen's pickup. "Whether you believe or not at the present time is immaterial. You will." He pointed a quavering finger, at the same time fixating with a mystical stare. "To give proof, I have selected *you, Justin Banks*, to be the sole receiver, for now, of relief from the curse that is known as the Plague of Akhnaton. *Thy skin shall henceforth be restored and its blemishes vanish. The sickness shall be gone from thy stomach and thy bowels. The aches that have blighted thee shall ease and fade. Thy—*"

"Bullshit," Banks snarled, and cut the connection.

"It seemed to go through okay," Pierre told Kieran.

"We'll soon see," Kieran said.

Minutes later, Trevany called from the Juggernaut out at Tharsis. "Bravo," he complimented when Kieran answered.

"What do you mean?"

"We just watched your performance with Banks." Kieran had talked to Trevany from his hotel room after becoming the Khal that morning, so Trevany was familiar with his new appearance.

"Like it?" Kieran said. "It looked as if they're just leaving for Lowell."

"That's right," Trevany confirmed. "Lowell sent an airbus to collect them. Their own vehicles are staying there for the time being, until they've been checked over. Now would you mind filling us in on the rest of it?"

"As I just told Pierre, who's here with me, we're going into the mystical healing business."

"You're going to make them better?"

"Just Banks."

"How can it be that selective?"

"Pierre and I think we've figured out a way. So this is a test before trying it with Asgard—but think of the impact it could have on Hamilton if it works. Also, it might have the very real effect of changing Banks into a convert—or at least, give him a lot to think about." Just then, a call came in on Kieran's comset. He flipped the unit out and accepted to find that the caller was Mahom. "Look, Walter, I've just got another call that might be something I've been waiting for. Can I get back to you on this?"

"Sure." Trevany disappeared. Kieran redirected Mahom to the room's larger screen.

"Mahom. What news?"

"I think we've got it. It's owned by a city hire franchise, on lease to a guy called Lee Mullen, who organizes local muscle and does caretaking."

Kieran nodded. It sounded like the kind of person he'd expect the syndicate to mobilize until their own people arrived to take over. "Where is it?" he asked.

"At an address in Embarcadero. The people I've put there have counted seven bodies coming and going who aren't Sol or Casey."

"You haven't positively identified Sol and Casey there?" Kieran checked.

"Not as yet. But they have to be there. It's going to be a tough one to crack, though. No clear plan of action right now. The troops are checking it out and going through the options. The best thing for now is just to keep watching the place for a while longer to see what comes up."

Kieran nodded reluctantly. "Do we know where Sol and Casey's flymo is?" he asked.

"The skylock at Cherbourg." Mahom meant the upper-level flyer parking area with locks out to the atmosphere. Flyers weren't used within the covered-over confines of Lowell itself. When Leppo and Casey wanted to work on it in their shop, they moved it there by road.

"Okay, well I guess I'll have to leave it with you," Kieran conceded. "It's been a rough day here, too. We'll be wanting to turn in after we've eaten something. Let me know if anything new develops, okay?"

"You've got it, Knight," Mahom promised.

# ⇉ 21 ⇇

Asgard was an inside-out planet a little under a mile in diameter. An artificial sun keeping a regular day-night cycle hung in
the center; the surface where everything happened—apart from
arriving and departing spacecraft—was on the inside. The
enclosed space and the force induced by slowly spinning the structure thus took the place of mass and gravity in retaining an
atmosphere and keeping people and everything else on the
ground. The regularly inhabited part, consisting of residential and
commercial areas, and the corporation's business and technical
facilities, extended around the equatorial belt; heavy installations,
industrial plant, and docking areas were located around the poles.
The space between was largely devoted to test sites for new
engineering methods and construction techniques, with several
open landscaped areas for recreation.

The reception was held in the ballroom of the complex
known as the Constellation Suites—a part of the residential
sector containing accommodation, catering, pool, and sports
facilities, intended for use by visiting business people, relatives,
and friends. It was a splendid affair indeed, with over two
thousand guests arrayed in thematic South Sea costumes, garlands, robes, and hula-hula skirts, as well as colorful and glittery
conventional styles. Marissa and Mervyn, respectively blushing
and handsome, cut cake, tossed garter and bouquet, smiled,
posed, and received lines of congratulations and tributes.
Hamilton delivered a speech laced with jokes and witty anec-
dotes targeted at some of those present, proposed toasts, and
got in a few quotes; performers and musicians, including a full
orchestra and two choirs, entertained; lavish food offerings

graced the tables; profusions of flowers decked the walls, the halls, and the people. There were lots of flowers.

When the formal parts were over, Hamilton joined his daughter for the first waltz to commence the remainder of the day's festivities. He might spend a lot of his life in first-class seats and at conference tables these days, but he could still glide a step or two. Adoring matrons in jeweled gowns and tiaras gazed on admiringly; friends and patrons of the corporation, and henchmen from the organization chart's ionospheric levels smiled; management lackeys and their spouses, and assorted hangers-on tried to look as if they felt they fitted in. Hamilton Gilder was a happy man. He liked life when he and his tribespeople were the center of attraction, and just at this moment, the island headquarters-in-space of the empire he had created seemed like the center of the universe. Yet, a part of him was worried. It was a worry that he had talked about only with Thornton Velte and one or two others of his innermost clique. And Marissa, of course—but then, it was she who had brought the matter to him in the first place. Ever since then, she and Mervyn had been so in demand that this was the first moment he had found to have a word with her away from other ears after having any time to think about it.

"You really think this Khal is the real thing?" he murmured, smiling through his teeth at the onlookers as he led Marissa through an underarm twirl and smoothly back into a *one*-two-three box step. "He might know what it is that's broken out down there?"

"It was uncanny, Dad. He knew things that you and I had said over the link from here less than an hour before—things that *nobody* could have known. And those eyes! I could tell from them alone."

"I always said you had this intuition."

"That's what he told me too. His note said I have rare gifts of insight and understanding."

"So, should I halt this project, do you think? Thornton's told me that I'd be out of my mind. It would lose us a lot of friends— big friends."

"There are higher things to existence, Dad."

Hamilton nodded and reminded himself. It would still be a tough decision. Thornton and the others didn't know the things he knew. He'd tried to share his insights at times, but he knew now that such efforts would always be futile. Seed could only take in ground that was ready.

They toured the floor in a series of vigorous Viennese whirls. People applauded. "And he told you it could start here too?" Hamilton said, just a touch breathlessly. "I shouldn't have mentioned that to Thornton."

"Why? Don't you believe it? The Ancients were able to manipulate physical probabilities, remember? Impossible things can happen."

"Oh, *I* know what can happen. But Thornton and the others are settled that this guy's a crazy."

"Just be careful, Dad. Don't forget, you're the prime instigator."

"I am being careful. . . . Look, that hideous Krentz woman is waving. Wave back at her and smile. Her husband is a patent attorney who does us favors. . . ."

Forty minutes later, Hamilton was summoned away from a plate of roast guinea fowl and dressed pork to an incoming call from a person on a list that his staff had been told were to be put through, wherever he was, whatever he was doing. He went to take it in an office along a corridor, away from the noise from the ballroom.

From the first moment, the Khal was every bit as colorful and riveting as Marissa's description had prepared him to expect. The clear brown eyes seemed to emit a light that was not of the screen. The expression on the aged yet ageless countenance was infinitely deep and all-seeing. Already, Hamilton felt as if his thoughts were being read like words on a poster. "I thought I might be hearing from you," he said. "Your name was given priority status."

The Khal nodded, as if that were indeed what he had been wondering. "A wise decision. And first, allow me to add my congratulations to all those that have been heaped upon you. May your charming daughter and her husband live lives that are long, happy, and prosperous."

"Well, thanks." Hamilton eyed the figure with a mixture of awe and curiosity. As with Marissa, an inner part of him rejoiced at finally finding what was surely the doorway to Truth that he had always known existed; at the same time, he was wondering through habit what might be the best way to get this guy on the payroll. "She showed me your gift. It's splendid—so unusual. We have it on display at the reception."

"A modest token. I am honored that you are pleased." The Khal looked aside, as if checking for anyone who might overhear. His voice dropped to a conspiratorial note. Instinctively, Hamilton leaned closer to the screen. The Khal went on, "But I must also speak of more serious things. Heed the warning that was given through me. Your agents here on Mars scoffed when the seer who is with Professor Hashikar and the scientists at Tharsis tried to tell them. The doctors at Lowell will have no more success than Farquist had. This plague is not of their ken."

Hamilton was startled. "How did you know his name—and that they were being taken to Lowell? I've only just found out about that myself."

The Khal looked at him in a way that said he shouldn't need to ask. "I want you to know this in advance. You have detractors there who demand proof. So that you can allay their doubts—and also any that you yourself may still be harboring— your agent, Banks, has been selected as a demonstration that these events are being driven by powers beyond the reach of all the specialists and their equipment. From him and him alone, the affliction will be lifted. When these words come true, then all will believe."

"You can really do this?"

"Not I. The powers of old, for which I am merely a conduit to the present time."

"Of course."

Hamilton realized that he had actually spoken reverently.

Thornton Velte got a call shortly afterward from a youngish man with a stubbly chin and a mop of black hair, who said he was a doctor with the emergency team at Lowell entrusted with Justin Banks and his companions. He understood that Velte was Bank's superior at Asgard. He was sorry to interrupt Velte at a wedding, but this was a medical matter. Velte said he understood. Could Velte authorize the transfer of company medical records for the individuals involved? Of course, Velte agreed—although it seemed a little strange, since Banks could just as easily have instructed that himself. Maybe the disease had progressed, and

Banks was more incapacitated than Velte had realized. The doctor went on to ask some routine questions, which irritated Velte because it seemed they were questions that could more easily have been asked of those on the spot. Also, he got irritated at the doctor's tendency to mumble. Velte had to press his face close to the screen to make out what he was saying.

Deirdre, Hamilton's older, recluse daughter, didn't attend but sent a message of congratulations from her religious retreat out in the Belt. Achilles, the playboy son, received a call at a mobile bar by the poolside, where he was cavorting with a couple of the bridesmaids. It was from a good-looking woman with long, black hair and a sultry voice who said she was from the Mars office of a spacemobile rental company based in the Jovian system, and had a query concerning a reservation he had made for the following month. Achilles was puzzled, since he couldn't recall any such reservation, and getting testy because she had somehow bypassed the incoming filters, and this was eating into his fun time. Wasn't this Mr. Achilles Glider . . . ? No, *Gilder*. Yet she seemed to have his account number and ID code. The woman could only apologize, presume there had been an unprecedented mix-up somewhere, and promise to straighten things out. Achilles wouldn't need to do anything if he heard no more, she assured him. By that time he had been on the line for over four minutes.

Several minutes later, a woman who looked uncannily like the one who had called Achilles was put through to Mervyn Quinn, the handsome, superstar groom of the occasion. She had told the staff member filtering calls that she was a director with one of the major media networks focusing on the event, and she seemed to have the right credentials; but once connected, she confessed to him with a beguiling charm that she represented a fan group of over a million members and had "cheated a little" to ask for a few words on this big day that they were all sharing from afar. Mervyn's vanity was as massaged by the thought of a million idolizing fans as major network coverage, and he spoke for a full six minutes.

The same "doctor" from Lowell called one of Hamilton Gilder's vice presidents, whose name was Slessor Lomax, asking the same kinds of questions as he had put to Thornton Velte, but this time about the military contingent that had been taken to Lowell along with the Zorken group. Lomax was mystified because it was the kind of information that should come from the mercenary organization that employed them, not from Zorken. It seemed to take the doctor an inordinately long time to grasp the point, whereupon he hung up with apologies.

It had been Slessor Lomax who first proposed and later ordered the use of military force at Troy.

# ≥ 22 ≤

A scream pierced the night, coming from the lakeside chalet in the grounds of the Constellation Suites, where the bride and groom were staying. Apprehensive domestic staff fluttered around the door, while behind them, guests who had been awakened or in the vicinity looked on. Word went around that a doctor had been called and was on the way. The head steward strode forward brandishing a master key, but just then the door opened and Marissa appeared in a pink velvet robe. Normally calm and controlled, she could only indicate the direction behind her with frantic nods of her head, at the same time gnawing her knuckle distraughtly. "It's Mervyn! He's got it! It's here! Oh, my God . . . !"

While one of the night maids guided Marissa back to a chair and tried to calm her down, the head steward went through to the bedroom suite, followed by several of the guests. They found Mervyn Quinn staring, horrified, into the mirror wall behind the gilded bathroom sink and vanity unit. His face was sickly yellow, showing hints of a greenish tint in places.

"Where is he? What's going on?" a voice demanded from the hallway outside.

"The doctor and a nurse are here," someone announced.

"We should call Hamilton," one of the guests said.

"Huh . . . ? Wha . . ." The call note from the comset by the bed dragged Hamilton Gilder up from the depths of a sleep fortified by copious administrations of champagne and century-old brandy.

"I'm sorry to disturb you, Mr. Gilder. This is Dr. Dante, duty

256

physician at Constellation Suites. We have an emergency, I'm afraid. It concerns your son-in-law, Mr. Quinn."

The news brought Gilder abruptly back to wakefulness. "Mervyn? What's happened?"

"He's feeling nauseous and has a facial discoloration. My first guess would be that he might have eaten something that disagreed with him, but Ms. Gilder insists that it's some kind of plague. To be honest, it's her that I'm more worried about."

"Marissa?"

"She's very disturbed."

"I'll be right over."

Gilder cut the connection, swung himself out of bed, and hurried through to the dressing room to pull on some pants. He grabbed a shirt and detoured back via the bathroom to splash water on his face. As he straightened up to reach for a brush to run through his hair, he froze at the sight of the face peering blearily back at him from the mirror.

"*Jesus Christ!*" he breathed, staring disbelievingly.

Thornton Velte was still up, drinking with a group of cronies in the subdued light of an alcove outside the ballroom. In a visit to the men's room, someone had remarked that he was looking a bit pasty, but Velte dismissed it with a laugh and the comment that none of them was getting any younger. By the time he wandered out to get some air in the new light of Asgard's dawning sun, his condition had advanced several hours. A fellow guest gasped at his appearance and took him back inside to see himself in a mirror. Stunned but still rigidly disbelieving, Velte made his way with a couple of attending colleagues to the medical room, where they found Mervyn and Hamilton suffering from the same affliction. Minutes later, a gibbering Achilles Gilder called in from his own suite, whence his ladyfriend of the evening had just fled in terror. Slessor Lomax joined them within the hour.

Food poisoning was the doctors' first suspicion, but it became less plausible as further checking showed the condition to be confined to just those five cases. One of the doctors recognized the symptoms as the ones affecting the corporation people and their military detail down on Mars, upon which the security head from the Oasis recalled the eccentric Asiatic who had visited Marissa there. Velte needed no further proof that the Martian

Cross the Khal had given her to bring up to Asgard was the culprit. "It's impregnated with something or releasing something," he fumed as the facts strung themselves together before his eyes. "Get it over to the labs and find out what's in it. Take it apart down to the last molecule if you have to."

They X-rayed the Cross, electromeasured it, sonogrammed it, broke it in pieces, ground parts of it to powder, and subjected samples to neutron activation tests, fluorescence tests, gas and liquid chromatography, various types of spectroscopy, nuclear magnetic resonance tests, a battery of solution assays, and biometric imaging. And they found . . . nothing. For the moment the experts were baffled.

"But *we* know it *was* the Cross, although not operating through any of the mechanisms they're looking for, don't we, Dad?" Marissa said when they got a chance to talk alone. She was having trouble keeping horror from showing on her face as she looked at him. "You have to ask the Khal for guidance. He's the only person who'll know anything." Hamilton had his assistant call the Oasis hotel down at Lowell, but she was informed that the guest of that name had checked out without leaving any contact information.

"I still think you're jumping to unwarranted conclusions," Velte maintained stonily, despite his own condition. "Something broke out on Mars, and a lot of people here have just come up from Mars. There's bound to be a simple connection. What's the latest on the ones they've got at the hospital down there?"

Hamilton had Asgard's medical chief call the unit down at Lowell who were dealing with the syndrome. And the startling news from there was that Justin Banks—and *only* Justin Banks— was magically recovering.

"Now what do you have to say?" Gilder stormed at Velte, finally losing his patience. "*Everything* he said has come true! No, I can't explain it, you can't explain it, and neither can anyone else here. But there isn't a single fact known to science that couldn't be explained at some time." It was one of those rare times where Thornton Velte found himself too shocked and bemused to say anything.

"What do you want to do?" Gilder's assistant asked.

Gilder thought furiously for several seconds. Marissa watched him anxiously. "Get a fast transfer ship ready for immediate descent to Mars," he ordered. "The only hope now is that other mystic that the Khal talked about. We'll go down there, and we'll talk with him directly."

"Does that mean you'll let them have the site?" Marissa asked.

Hamilton squared his jaw stubbornly. "I didn't say that. Let's see if this guy can get rid of whatever this is first. It's still a big investment to throw away. Then we'll play it by ear. There might be ways of getting to him yet—just like anyone else."

The eight-man squad that Mahom had recruited was taking it easy outside until plans were sufficiently advanced to hold a detailed briefing. Inside Mahom's office, Kieran sat across from the desk, staring at pictures of the building that Leppo and Casey were being held in, along with floor and site plans purloined from a city architect's office. Since it suited him to keep Kieran Thane invisible for a while longer, and he didn't know when circumstances might require the reappearance of the Khal, he had changed into casual clothes but kept the swarthy Asiatic features and grizzled hair. The squad's commander, Major Everit, small, brown skinned, dapperly turned out in a dark jumpsuit with black beret and calf-length boots, went once again through what seemed to be the only option.

"Speed and surprise. A distraction phone call, diversions front and back, and then straight in behind stun and flash grenades, and grab them. It's a high-density location. The geography doesn't give any maneuvering options."

Kieran wasn't overenamored. Hard in and brutal. It lacked the finesse and use of misdirection and deception that appealed to him. But for once he was at a loss to come up with anything better. He shook his head dubiously. "Right in the middle of a residential zone. It's bound to spark instant reactions. Even if you spring them, what are the odds going to be of getting yourselves out?"

"Speed and surprise," Everit said again. "We'll be gone before any enforcement gets near the block."

"And then what?" Kieran asked. "You still have to get out of Lowell. All they have to do is seal the locks."

"There are other ways out of Lowell."

Kieran looked at Mahom. "I wanted these guys more to keep an eye on Hamil and his people at Tharsis. For this we need something more subtle—quiet and easy. You know my style."

Mahom shrugged, showing two empty ham-like palms and a pair of bulging eyes. "We looked at it from all the angles, Knight. There aren't other options. There isn't the time."

Kieran stared back at the pictures and charts. He was still contemplating them, when an incoming call came for Mahom. It was from one of the spies he had stationed around the block from where Leppo and Casey were being held. People were coming out and getting into the Metrosine. A screen showed the picture. There were six of them. Both Balmer and Sarda were there. Kieran also recognized Brown, Black, and the other man he had glimpsed with them in the elevator at the Oasis. Mullen, whom Mahom had previously identified, was with them. Brown drove. A quick tally of the numbers logged coming and going indicated that only three were left inside guarding the two prisoners. It gave much better odds than those Everit had been assuming.

"If we're going to do it, this is the time," Everit said. "We won't see this again any time soon." Mahom looked inquiringly at Kieran. Kieran nodded reluctantly. Everit went outside and called his men inside to brief them.

As things transpired, it now seemed they had plenty of time. Tracking the vehicle's locator code, which one of Mahom's contacts had extracted from the leasing company's records, showed the car progressing through the Trapezium and along Gorky to exit to the surface at the Wuhan end. It soon became clear that it was heading for Stony Flats. Kieran puzzled over what might draw Balmer, Sarda, and practically the syndicate's entire coterie at Lowell, out to a place like that.

By the time the Metrosine arrived at a spot identified from the map as a warehouse shed at the back end of the airfield, owned by a company that imported hydrocarbon distillates from the Belt, Everit had run his men through the plan several times, and they were preparing to move out. Kieran used Mahom's desk c-com to buy five minutes of priority time from one of the commercial surface surveillance satellite operators, and when one was next passing over, directed a high-resolution scan of the buildings Mahom had picked out from the map image. Sure enough, the black Metrosine was parked under a glass-roofed annex at the rear of two of them, reached by an alley between. More interestingly, some shapes next to the Metrosine, if he wasn't very much mistaken, were a couple of general personnel carriers painted in desert camouflage, a distinctly warlike profile suggestive of a gunship, and a smaller flyer. Somebody else out there, it seemed, was also putting together a private militia. But theirs had the appearance and firepower of an attack force. Kieran was still pondering on what it could mean when Everit and his team departed in a plain civilian bus. The only thing that made any kind of sense was that whoever had sent the abortive mission to Troy that had almost gotten shot down were getting set to try again. What to do? Recall Everit and get him out to Tharsis before the Stony Flats force made its move? Or gamble on seizing the chance to get Leppo and Casey out while the opposition was minimal?

But then the situation changed again, and the second option went away. Mahom's spy in Embarcadero called again to say that five more people were coming out. The accompanying view showed, sure enough, the remaining three guards marching Leppo and Casey to another vehicle that had been parked nearby, which then left, going the same way as the Metrosine had. Mahom's man fell in to follow at a distance, and it soon began to look as if the second car was heading through for Wuhan, and hence out onto the surface to join the others at Stony Flats.

"Mahom, what's the fastest way to get Everit and his team outside in a flyer?" Kieran asked suddenly as the meaning became clear.

"Their outfit is geared for fast response. They keep an air-APC on permanent standby ready at the Cherbourg skylock." The Sudanese frowned. "Why? What's going through your mind, Knight?"

"Get them onto it right away! The syndicate still wants its money back. They think I'm at Tharsis—and probably two other people who are far away off-planet by now. They're sending out another team to grab us. But they also think Leppo set them up last time, and therefore he's in with us and knows the story. They want to grill him before they go in." Kieran turned from the screen while Mahom clicked on Everit's call code. "See what it means, Mahom? We don't have to risk a lot of noise and commotion in the city at all. If we move fast, we can spring them outside—right there on the road to Stony Flats!"

# $\gtrless$ **23** $\lessgtr$

Wedged in the rear seat between Casey and one of the guards, with another armed guard sitting facing them while the third drove, Solomon Leppo stared gloomily out at the complex of levels and spaces beneath the tangle of intersecting domes that formed Wuhan. What he had gotten them both into now, he didn't know. He no longer had any doubts that the Knight was straight enough; but he was also somebody who didn't play with trivia, and extremely complex. Whatever aspect of the Knight's business this was part of was way over Leppo's depth.

His stomach still ached, his ribs felt raw, and his cheeks burned from the drubbing Mullen had given him to express his displeasure—and Leppo had the chilling feeling that worse was to come. Mullen was convinced that Leppo had somehow set him up and almost gotten him killed, and he just wouldn't buy Leppo's insistence that he didn't know what Mullen was talking about. He didn't know what any of those who had gone on ahead earlier—apparently to meet some important people who had arrived from off-planet—were talking about. Two of them hadn't seemed to be "with" the others at all, but acted as if they were in as much trouble as Leppo and Casey seemed to be. The short, flabby one with the black mustache and freaky eyes, that somebody had called Balmer, had wanted to know how big a split off the quarter-billion dollars Leppo had been offered. Trying to tell him that he'd never heard of any quarter-billion dollars was a waste of time. They seemed to think that the Knight was still out in the desert where Leppo and Casey had collected him from. Why else, they had argued, would the site out there be defended? They also seemed to think that a couple named Elaine and Sarda were there too. Leppo didn't know who Elaine might be, but he thought that the other of the pair—the yellow-haired one—was supposed to be Sarda. Maybe he had a brother or something. Leppo wasn't able to make any sense of it. He was starting to have acute second thoughts about this really being how he wanted to tackle the task of making substantial money. There had to be other ways, more conducive to health and longevity, than this.

They came to the approach lane of the Wuhan exit lock and joined a short line of vehicles waiting to make egress to the surface. "Looks like we're going on an outside trip," Casey murmured needlessly.

"Didn't someone say Stony Flats?"

"Shuddup," the guard next to Leppo growled, elbowing his bruised ribs painfully. Leppo shut up.

They moved forward with the next batch of vehicles. The inner doors closed behind them; the lock emptied, then refilled with Martian atmosphere. Once outside, the other traffic quickly dispersed among the clutter of roadways and constructions extending along the canyon bottom beyond the extremity of the city. This thinned as the road began rising, until, by the time they came to the series of steep hairpins carrying the road up to the open desert, the signs of habitation had given way to dry, crumbling slopes of sand and rock, with a line of tired pink crags above in the distance. As they gained height, more of the Martian landscape unfolded beyond the canyon. And then, suddenly, on rounding the last of the climbing bends, they almost ran into the skeleton of a tow trailer blocking the road. It lay across at a crazy, tilted angle, one end gouging into the sand mound bounding the roadside as if it had been dropped from the sky. The driver braked hard, throwing the occupants forward.

"Where the hell did that come from?" the guard next to Leppo called to the driver, pulling himself up on the door pillar hand grip.

"I don't know. It's . . ."

The driver's voice dried up. He looked from side to side. Figures in EV combat garb were rising from behind rocks and out of the gulleys, their weapons trained on the car. Two were holding emergency life-bags. It was an indication that they meant business. A few shots would be enough to decompress the vehicle. They would then storm in and cocoon the occupants, unconscious, or at least incapacitated. Resistance was out of the question. Nobody inside could even bring a defensive gun to bear.

"We've got no chance," the driver threw back over his shoulder. "What do I do?"

"Call them," the one beside Leppo said tightly. The sound of engines growing louder came from overhead, and moments later an airborne armored personnel carrier with mercenary markings landed ten yards or so behind the car. The driver picked up the headband carrying his stem mike. "Okay, okay. Hold your fire. You've got us cold. What do you want?"

"Very sensible," a voice agreed over the speaker. "You've got two good friends of ours in there. Get them into breather sets and jackets, and send them out. Then, if you behave yourselves, as far as we're concerned, the other three of you can be on your way. You've got three minutes. Fair enough?"

Leppo turned in his seat and looked back disbelievingly at the jaunty, red-suited figure that had come out from the APC and seemed to be doing the talking. He'd recognized that voice the moment it started speaking. And the face behind the visor—still brown, but familiar enough by now—confirmed it.

It was the Knight!

The APC rose slowly until the slack was almost gone from the line connecting it to the trailer frame blocking the road. "Slow . . ." Major Everit gauged the distance from a screen showing the vertical view below. "Hold it there," he instructed the pilot beside him. "Now, slow again . . ."

"Taking weight," the pilot confirmed. "Okay, I've got it. . . . It's good."

"Fine. Get rid of it."

The APC lifted the frame clear, hovered for a moment, and then moved slowly forward to release the suspended load over the downward slope below the road. The car with the three guards inside waited warily; then, when nothing further happened, it began edging forward. Mahom watched it through a window as the APC resumed its ascent.

"I'm not so sure we should be letting them go like that," he muttered to Kieran, sitting across from him behind the flight deck. "The first thing they're gonna do is call ahead with the bad news." Kieran hadn't ordered the vehicle's phone or the guards' personal phones to be disabled to buy extra time. Deliberately leaving people out on the Martian surface without communications just wasn't done.

"They'd just have been in the way here," Kieran answered. "And the Stony Flats celestial choir is no doubt tracking them. If the car had stayed there much longer, they'd know something was wrong, anyway."

Next to the pilot, Major Everit was looking perturbed. "Two troop carriers and a gunship rigged for ground suppression," he said, turning to Kieran. "We don't have the firepower to take on something like that. We were commissioned as a light defense force."

"It's bluff," Kieran assured him. "They want me and a couple of other people they think are down there. They won't just come roaring in with guns blazing."

"So what do you need us for? If you're not there, they'll go away again."

"A show of force on the ground—so those goons don't take it into their heads to start slapping any scientists around."

Everit still didn't seem happy. "I don't like asking my men to face odds like that. If we had firepower to offset that gunship . . ."

"There's the *Guardian Angel*," Leppo said from the seat behind, where he and Casey were listening.

"What's the *Guardian Angel*?" Everit asked.

Kieran turned his head abruptly, wondering why he hadn't thought of it. "Sol and Casey's flymo," he said to Everit.

"Flymo?" The major started to scoff, but Leppo defended their creation indignantly.

"More than a just flymo, Major. Man, it's got lock-on auto-cannon, rear-firing laser or radar homing missiles, target acquisition and incoming tracking radar . . ."

"Not fully tested ye—" Casey started to blurt, but Leppo kicked his foot beneath the seat.

"Mil D-spec countermeasures package . . ."

"Where is this machine?" Everit asked.

"Right under the roof at the Cherbourg skylock," Leppo said. "We could be there in minutes."

"Fight bluff with counterbluff," Kieran said. "Put there by Providence. You said that was what you needed. Okay, let's go for it. You can drop us off at Cherbourg and then carry straight on to Tharsis. We'll follow as soon as we get the *Angel* airborne."

Everit was looking dazed. "You'll get used to it," Mahom told him, grinning. "Things kind of happen when the Knight's around."

"Alter course for Cherbourg," Everit told the pilot resignedly.

The pilot entered a code into the navcomp, which flashed a request to Cherbourg Local Area Traffic Control for an inbound slot in the skylock schedule. A few seconds later the associated comscreen responded: *CONFIRMED AND HOLDING. ESTI-MATED COMPLETION 6 MINUTES.*

Consternation had broken out in the partitioned office at the rear of the warehouse at Stony Flats, where Lee Mullen and the Firm's local team had been updating the two expediters who just arrived via Phobos to take charge. A call had come in reporting that Leppo and his partner had been hijacked en route by an unidentified military unit that came down out of the sky. The guy who seemed to be in charge of the grab wore a red suit and had a brown face. There was even a picture that one of the guards had managed to snap with his phone as the rescuers and their two charges were embarking.

The mention of a brown face triggered Mr. Black's recollection of the brief encounter in the hotel elevator. "Let me see him," he demanded. An enlarged version of the face in the helmet appeared on one of the screens. Black studied it intently. "Lighten it a bit," he said to the graphics tech who was with the group. "Make the color normal. . . . Now take the gray out of the hair."

"How do you want it?"

"Dark . . . No, say, maybe more brown." Mr. Black watched the transformation. The result was still a little on the old side, but he no longer had any doubts. "That's him!" he pronounced. "It's the guy who was at the Zodiac Bank with his twin brother." He pointed at Sarda, who was standing with Balmer. "The one who said he was the lawyer."

Sarda stepped forward for a closer look. "He's right. That's who stopped me on the street when I was on my way there. He's the guy with the dog!"

"I saw him at the Oasis," Black told everyone. "I *knew* I'd seen him somewhere."

"He met Leppo there," Mullen said. "Dressed up like a genie. Looks like he came back into town for the wedding party."

Balmer looked at the two arrivals from Phobos. They were both tanned, unsmiling, athletically built, and expensively dressed in dark suits with white shirts. The syndicate upper hierarchy was picky about appearances conforming to position. Only the topmost levels sported lighter shades, some individuality in adornment and style, and an allowance of color. "Well, that's over with now," he said. "They'll be going back to Tharsis. *That's* where Elaine and the other Sarda will be too . . . *and* the key to finding your quarter-billion dollars."

The two expediters conferred briefly, then spoke to the leader of the backup force. "Board your men and let's get out there," the one who was in charge said.

Meanwhile, in the upper atmosphere, the vessel from Asgard began its braking maneuver to descend from orbit. It was of a fast, robust design capable of landing on the Martian surface, making it unnecessary to transfer to a shuttle at Phobos. Aboard, in the forward lounge, Hamilton and Achilles Gilder, Thornton Velte, Mervyn Quinn, and Slessor Lomax stared woodenly with greening, blotchy countenances at the wall screen showing a view of the surface. Marissa sat anxiously with the others who had accompanied them. There would be no fooling around with the doctors at Lowell, who had accomplished nothing. The only person to show any understanding of the affliction and demonstrate a successful cure had been the Khal, but the Khal had since vanished. But there was another who had tried to warn them: the eccentric but seemingly equally capable Keziah Turle, with Professor Hashikar's scientific group at Tharsis. Very well, Hamilton had decided. Then they would descend directly to Tharsis.

# ⋙ 24 ⋘

At Cherbourg, Kieran and Mahom disembarked from the APC with Leppo and Casey just inside the lock. While the APC shunted across to the outbound lane to gain immediate exit with the next lock cycle, they took an elevator down a level and hurried to where the *Guardian Angel* was parked. Within minutes, Leppo and Casey had the *Angel* up to flight readiness. They taxied back up, left after a short wait, and were soon climbing into the strange, pink-blushed Martian sky with the Cherbourg plateau and its spaceport, and below it, Lowell nestled in the folds of the Valles Marineris canyons, shrinking amid an expanding vista of wilderness.

"Sure handles smooth and easy," Mahom complimented, giving Leppo an approving nod. "Solid on the drive, too. Seems like maybe you did pick up a few useful things after all."

"These are gonna be big one day," Leppo promised him. "You sound like maybe you're angling for a share of the action."

"I'll take whatever's going," Mahom said unabashedly with a shrug.

It seemed that Leppo had decided he was back in the security business again.

A call from Trevany confirmed that Everit and his force had arrived and were preparing positions around the expedition's camp. Chas Ryan's crew was digging slit trenches away from the vehicles as a precaution. So far there had been no hostile appearance. Trevany had barely finished saying this, however, when Harry Quong interrupted to say that three blips had appeared on the Juggernaut's radar, heading their way—one leading, and two close together following a few miles behind. Moments later,

Everit's pilot reported the same contact from the APC. Everit ordered the APC off the ground, to take up a low-level circling pattern behind the mountains bordering the valley on the far side from the plateau.

But it soon became apparent that the approaching craft were heading not for the expedition's camp but for the Troy site, where the Mule transporter that had brought Banks and his group, along with the eviction squad's Venning troop carrier and scout car, were still standing by the two original Zorken shacks. Until a medical team arrived to begin checking through the vehicles, the site was deserted; but presumably the incoming force, who had to be the syndicate's heavy team from Stony Flats, didn't know that. This seemed confirmed when the leading blip swooped down in a dive following the plateau edge toward the shelf.

"Rudi's got it via Gottfried," Trevany reported. "It looks like they're attacking."

"Patch it through," Kieran told him.

The cavorting, intermittent view from the robot high on the cliff showed a dark arrowhead that could only be the gunship they'd seen in the satellite image coming in on a low-level run. It released two missiles, followed up with a burst of heavy cannon fire, and broke off to go into a climbing turn above the valley. The missiles struck above the shelf, causing a minor avalanche of rock and debris to tumble down around the shacks and the vehicles. The cannon shells traced a line of smaller explosions along a line below, across the zigzagging approach road. It was a warning, demonstrating the firepower available. If anyone down there wanted to play games this time, the message said, the next ones won't miss. There was no responding fire. In fact, there was no response at all.

"No return fire," the gunship c-com/weapons operator reported to the command flyer holding fifteen miles back behind the two troop carriers. "Nobody's coming out. Looks like they're staying holed up."

"It means we've got them rattled." The strike commander, Colonel Sedger, came in from the lead troop carrier. "It's the right psychological moment. They weren't expecting anything like this. It's a steal. If we go down now, we'll be able to walk right in."

In the command flyer, Mullen looked at the two expediters from the Firm, their impeccable dark suits now overlain by light-duty EV suits. In the seats behind, Sarda and Balmer waited tensely.

"Do it," the senior of the two ordered.

Then the gunship CWO came in again. "Alert all. Unidentified contact on bearing one-one-zero—coming in from direction of Lowell."

"How far out?" the strike commander asked over the circuit.

"ETA seven minutes."

"Cover us while we go in. When we're on the ground and secured, break off and investigate the intruder."

"Roger," the gunship pilot acknowledged.

"Radar interrogation signature," Casey announced, eyes on his console screens. "They've picked us up."

"It had to happen," Kieran said neutrally. Then, to the screen showing Trevany at the expedition's camp, "What's happening at Troy?"

"We're not sure. Gottfried isn't behaving. Its vision's out, and it seems to have started wandering. Rudi's having trouble trying to control it. He thinks one of those missiles might have damaged something."

Just what they needed, Kieran thought. Suddenly, no eyes at the center of where everything seemed to be happening.

"From radar, the two blips that were together are going down," Harry Quong said. "Losing them . . . they're going under my horizon. Looks like they're landing."

"Confirmed," Casey said, in the *Angel,* in front of Kieran and Mahom.

"What's that gunship doing?" Kieran asked tensely.

"Climbing, turning . . . oh shit. Coming this way, chief. They're checking us out."

Kieran bit his lip, thinking frantically. "Head east," he told Leppo. "Lead them away from Hamil's camp. They don't need to know about that."

The *Angel* veered away, but the gunship rose, accelerating onto an interception course. Leppo turned away again. The gunship pursued.

"They're closing," Leppo said, consulting a readout.

"*Weapon designator scanning!*" Casey shouted. "Christ, they're not fooling!"

"Use your ECM," Mahom called from behind.

Casey flipped switches feverishly. "Already am . . . Lock on! Pod ejected. *Break! Break!*" Leppo threw the *Angel* into a sickening downward turn; an instant later, a plasma bolt flashed by, hissing pink and violet streamers. The *Angel* climbed; the gunship twisted ten miles back to follow. "They're lining up for a missile launch," Casey said.

"You have rear-firing missiles, right?" Kieran said. He had hoped it wouldn't come to this, but the opposition weren't giving much choice.

"Arming and activating now," Casey said. "Target acquisition . . . Steady up, baby. That's it. . . ."

The two craft dipped to go into a high-speed, hide-and-seek chase among the peaks and ravines of the Martian landscape. It was a game of nerves not unlike an old-time pistol duel. Cracking first and missing would let the other close for a virtually clean shot. Kieran had no measure of how skilled Leppo and Casey were. Against a professional military crew, he didn't care to guess the chances. He felt his throat going dry but said nothing. There was little he could contribute now.

Then Casey threw out another decoy pod, gambling on the momentary confusion it would cause, and announced, "Firing!"

But nothing happened. Instead, a tattoo of malfunction lights appeared on the c-com and flight engineer panels; at the same instant, Kieran felt the limpness in the craft's responses that came with flight systems losing power. Desperately, Leppo pancaked into a flat, lifeless glide, summoning enough thrust at the last moment to just clear a line of low crags ahead.

"*It's that voltage compensator!*" Casey yelled at Leppo. "*I told you the boost suppressor needed more smoothing.*"

"*And I'm telling you it tested out ok—*"

Mahom cut in, "Would you two please talk about that later? We're sitting ducks."

Which was true. Mustering maybe half power, the *Angel* clawed its way upward into clear sky. Behind it, the gunship closed for an easy kill. A warning of target designator transmission locking on sounded from Casey's console. Throttling back to little above stall speed, Leppo ejected a crimson distress flare and flipped his mike to the universal emergency band. "Mayday, mayday. Okay, you've got us cold. Our power and weapons are out. We're dead in the water here. Will follow instructions."

A gloating voice replied. "Well, that's too bad. I guess it just ain't your day. You should have stayed home."

Casey's face was dripping perspiration. Leppo looked back at Kieran in a wordless appeal for help. Kieran did the only thing he could. Tilting the cockpit video pickup to point at himself, he looked into it squarely. "Maybe you should check with your bosses before you do anything hasty," he said. "Yes, recognize me? I'm the person you want. You've probably found out already that there's nobody down there at the camp. I'm all you've got. Lose us, and you'll never know where the money went."

The circuit went quiet. Leppo eased into a gentle turn to avoid highlands ahead. The gunship moved up to position itself a few hundred yards astern and to one side. After several agonizing minutes, the voice came back on again. There was a distinct note of disappointment in it. "Okay. Continue the turn onto a course of two-seven-three degrees back to the site. There are two desert-camouflaged troop carriers on the ground there, next to some other flyers and shacks. Put down in front of the carriers. We have a missile homed on you. One sudden move and we fire."

"Understood," Leppo replied.

The view on the wall screen in the forward lounge of the incoming craft from Asgard showed the shelf high on the plateau side, where the Zorken survey camp had been sited. The Mule transporter that had borne Justin Banks and his team was there, along with the two vessels left by the military support unit. But now there were two more carriers as well, painted in brown and pink blotches. "I don't know who they are," the flight commander's voice said over a speaker from the front cabin. "It was supposed to be empty there. The thermal signatures on the ground say they've only just shown up." The original intention had been to land at the archeological expedition's camp, which from high altitude had been spotted a few miles away across the valley floor. Radio contact with the leader there, the Professor Hashikar who had tried unsuccessfully to plead his case with Banks, had revealed, however, that Keziah Turle was not present at the camp. Nobody there knew where he was. And so, as the vessel continued its descent, attention had shifted to the Zorken site not far away.

Achilles stared at a hand mirror that he'd had with him all through the trip. "It's getting worse!" he lamented. "We've got to find him. I can't stay looking like this."

"It isn't *your* livelihood," Mervyn Quinn reminded him. Throughout, the flight had been a contest between them of whose vanity was the most injured.

"Oh stop, both of you," Marissa said wearily.

"Turle might have gone back there for some reason," Thornton Velte said. "At least there are obviously people there who might know something. That's more than can be said for any of those scientists."

Gilder gave orders to the flight commander to redirect descent to the Zorken site on the plateau side. The flight commander responded that he had just received a radio contact from there, demanding identification. Gilder told him to connect the channel through and requested a repeat.

"My name is Colonel Sedger, acting ground commander," a none-too-friendly voice informed them. "Identify yourselves and state your purpose."

"This is Hamilton Gilder, chief executive and president of Zorken Consolidated. We *own* that entire area, Colonel. I don't have to justify myself or my purpose to you for anything."

There was a short pause. Then, "Land at your convenience."

As the ship lined up tail-first to make its approach, two more craft appeared from the east, coming in slow. The first was an unusual looking blue-and-white flymobile that seemed to be in trouble and went straight in for a landing, drawing up along-side the two desert-camouflaged transporters. The other, a gun-ship that appeared to have been escorting it, made a slow circle around the area while the vessel from Asgard landed. As the engines died, Gilder's flight commander reported another inbound radar contact.

"What in Hell's going on?" Gilder asked the others bemusedly. "Half of Mars seems to be coming out here."

"At least, someone in all this should know where Turle is," Slessor Lomax muttered.

But further interest in Keziah Turle quickly evaporated. They didn't need him anymore. The screen showed four figures getting out of the blue-and-white flymobile and being surrounded by troops with leveled weapons. Two were white, one large and black, and the fourth, in a red EV suit, a shade of brown. An instinct made Gilder have the flight commander zero in on him with a zoom view of the head inside the helmet. It was as something had told Gilder it would be: the figure in red was the Khal of Tadzhikstan!

"Incoming vessel identified," the flight commander's voice reported. "Military pattern command car."

So, the Khal's disappearance from the Oasis was explained, if not yet the reason for it, Gilder told himself. But why were he and the three people with him being detained by soldiers . . . ?

Kieran turned to look back at the ship that had descended to the shelf while the *Guardian Angel* was making its run in. It was a light transfer vessel, suitable for fast travel around the vicinity of Mars and capable of surface landings in thin atmospheres. It also carried the logo and markings of Zorken Consolidated. Somebody sent to check up on Banks and his crew, who were no longer here, was the only guess Kieran could hazard.

"Don't make any fast moves. Keep your hands away from belts and weapons," a voice said over the local channel. Mahom and the others looked at Kieran questioningly. Kieran could only shake his head and return a shrug—which probably wasn't visible outside his suit. A figure with officer's insignia, obviously the speaker, stepped forward from among the troopers.

"And to whom do we owe the pleasure?" Kieran inquired.

"I am Colonel Sedger, acting ground commander."

"And by what authority do you command anything here?"

"I just follow orders. You can ask them in a few minutes." Sedger gestured with an arm to indicate the direction to Kieran's rear; at the same moment, Kieran became aware of the swelling sound of engines. He turned and saw that yet another craft was coming in to land. He identified it as a scout/reconnaissance type, painted desert camouflage to match the two carriers that had brought Sedger and his force. Typical, Kieran thought to himself. Now that the action was over and the area secured, the management in charge from Stony Flats was showing itself at last. Brown and Black would no doubt be there, itching to meet him again; possibly some high representation from the syndicate, too.

He wondered if Sarda-One and Balmer had come out of hiding also to crow at the last act. The craft came down near the far end of the clear section of the shelf and began rolling toward them. Kieran raised both arms high and wide as he stood facing toward it. It was partly a reaction to the soldiers behind, showing that he and his companions were unarmed; partly, it simply acknowledged his acceptance of the situation. But to Gilder and the others watching from the ship that had just landed, it looked as if the Khal, facing his enemies serene and unperturbed, was invoking the intercession of Higher Powers.

Far above, Gottfried, responding erratically to Rudi's attempts to reestablish control, gyrated in a wobbly circle and then toppled over a lip of rock to land on an unexploded charge left from the pilot borings made during the Zorken survey. Although small, the resulting explosion was enough to dislodge one of the lesser rocks wedged under the Citadel and preserving its balance on the plateau's edge. The huge rock tilted, slid, tearing loose more rocks and debris, and then tumbled noisily and terribly, collecting sand and rubble to become a minor avalanche bearing down upon the shelf. It hit the command car broadside, engulfing it, and swept it over the edge to spill across the valley floor far below amid a pall of red-brown dust.

# ≷ 25 ≶

"And that was enough for Hamilton—and the rest of them, as far as I can gather. I mean, they *saw* it! All of the ringleaders and prime movers of those who threatened armed violence against the Khal, wiped out before their eyes. The obvious lesson was that the ones who had initiated violation of the ancient site would be next. Hamilton dictated a directive renouncing all claims on the area right there and then. Couldn't sign it fast enough. It's all Hamil's now. He sounds as if he's planning on setting up an archeological city there."

It felt good to be back at June's. She sat in her favorite pose, draped along the couch with a glass of vodka tonic. Guinness, by now over his excitement at having his master back again, was sprawled contentedly in the kitchen doorway with Teddy actually curled up close alongside, enjoying the warmth.

"Well, it's a macabre solution to the problem, but I suppose it does settle the question of having two Sardas around," June said.

"By his own rules he shouldn't have been there," Kieran reminded her. He swilled his own drink and conceded that it was a rather macabre subject to dwell on. "We agreed before. The whole technology is too problematical to let loose on the public for a long time yet. Look what happened through one controlled experiment. Leo and Elaine are far gone, and with luck things will stay that way until you and I are past caring about it."

"You think they'll be okay?" June said. "After the effort the syndicate put into trying to find you, it won't all catch up with Leo and Elaine eventually?"

"I don't think it can," Kieran replied. "The only people who had any leads on Kennilworth Troon and his dog have all just been buried again after being dug out of a pile of rocks and rubble at Tharsis. The book's closed. The syndicate is just going to have to write it off in the uncollectible debts column."

He eased back in the recliner and contemplated the mural panel, which was showing a window view looking out over Ecuadorian jungle.

"You know, maybe I should go into the mystic business seriously," he said after a silence. "I thought that line I put together for Marissa sounded pretty good. She certainly did. Hamilton wants to commission a book on it, if he can only track down the Khal again. Maybe I should go back to being the Khal permanently. How about a retainer as Zorken Consolidated's official mystic, guru, and caller-down of Higher Powers? What do you think it might pay?" June was giving him a curious look. Kieran took it that she was turning the proposition over. "Millions?" he prompted. Then he realized that she was allowing him time, as if waiting for him to say something. For once, he had no idea what. "What?" he invited.

"You mean this story you concocted about the ancient builders being able to manipulate physical probabilities in ways that favored desirable outcomes?" she said.

"Yes. I thought the idea of tying it in with quantum reality was pretty neat too. Maybe I should write a book . . ." Kieran saw that the enigmatic look, as if inviting him to think some more about what he was saying, hadn't left June's face. "What?" he asked again.

"You told Marissa that to anyone who didn't know what was going on, it would look like chains of improbabilities and strange coincidences," June said. "Inexplicable accidents . . ." She waited again. Kieran's jaw dropped as the message finally percolated through. June concluded anyway, "But, Kieran, think about all the things that *did* happen!"

He stared at her. "Oh, my God," was all he could manage.

"Makes you think, doesn't it?" June said.

They stared at each other in silence for a long time. Guinness sensed the raptness between them and signaled his participation by thumping his tail against the floor. There wasn't a lot that either of them could add. The speculation was valid. No amount of debating would resolve it. One day, maybe, they might learn more that would enable them to say more about it.

But for now, there was nothing to be done. Kieran straightened up and finished his drink. "In the meantime life must go on, and people must eat," he declared. "After all I've seen of deserts in the past weeks, tonight we hit the town. Anything you care to name, with a couple of bottles of the best wine in the place. Pick a spot."

"I'd better make it an exclusive one," June said. "It isn't every night that a lady gets a chance to dine with the Khal of Tadzhikstan. Should we make it Native or Terran?"

Kieran raised a hand to his face. He'd forgotten about that. The dye that he'd used was the wrong kind and would take several more days to get off.

"I think not," he said. "The syndicate mightn't have anybody left in Lowell looking for him, but there's still a chance that Hamilton's scouts might be out and about. Maybe we ought to go Arabian. Somebody should be able to fix me up with a robe and a burnouse. How would you like dinner with an oil sheik tonight?"

"Does that mean I have to go in a hood and a veil?"

"No. You can just be the white slave girl—you know, a couple of dimes and a watch chain."

June looked at him reproachfully. "Oh that you should be so lucky."

"Not a bit of it." Kieran winked at her saucily. "Luck doesn't come into it. Remember, I manipulate the probabilities of space and time to order. How about that glass place up in the roof at the Trapezium? Hamil tells me the home-reared duck there is delicious. Even Rudi couldn't fault it. Walter said he saw him there with Katrina. Now what do you think might be going on between those two . . . ?"